THE SHEPHERD'S HEART - BOOK 1

THE SHEPHERD'S HEART - BOOK 1

ROCKY MOUNTAIN Oasis

Lynnette
BONNER

Pacific Lights

Rocky Mountain Oasis
THE SHEPHERD'S HEART SERIES, Book 1

Published by Pacific Lights Publishing
Copyright © 2009, 2012, 2015 by Lynnette Bonner. All rights reserved.

Cover design by Lynnette Bonner of Indie Cover Design, images ©
www.bigstock.com, File: # 50282366
www.bigstock.com, File:# 2223441

Author photo © Emily Hinderman, EMH Photography.

Scripture taken from the New King James Version®. Copyright © 1982 by
Thomas Nelson, Inc. Used by permission. All rights reserved.

ISBN: 978-1-942982-01-2

Printed in the U.S.A.

TO MARTY

Words are not enough to express my love and respect for you. You encourage me at every turn and remind me to focus on the One who continually blesses us. I love you!

AND TO CASTLE, CALEB, TYRELL, AND SKYE

I thank God for each of you. You are such a blessing to me! I pray that you will grow to love the Lord God with all your heart and with all your soul and with all your mind, and that you will learn to love your neighbor as yourself. I look forward to many more years of watching each of you develop and mature into all that God has planned for you. I love you!

ACKNOWLEDGEMENTS

This book would not be what it is today without the invaluable editing of my mom. She spent hours poring over the manuscript until I teased her that I'd have to buy stock in the red pen market. Thank you, Mama, for all you do!

The historical details for this story came from two main sources: A little book called *And Five Were Hanged: And Other Historical Short Stories of Pierce and the Oro Fino Mining District* by Layne Gellner Spencer and the University of Idaho's historical archives. If any historic facts are muddled, the fault is entirely mine.

Psalm 23
A PSALM OF DAVID

The Lord is my shepherd; I shall not want.
He makes me to lie down in green pastures;
He leads me beside the still waters.
He restores my soul;
He leads me in the paths of righteousness For His name's sake.
Yea, though I walk through the valley of the shadow of death,
I will fear no evil;
For You are with me;
Your rod and Your staff, they comfort me.
You prepare a table before me in the presence of my enemies;
You anoint my head with oil; My cup runs over.
Surely goodness and mercy shall follow me
All the days of my life;
And I will dwell in the house of the Lord Forever.

★
Chapter One

Lewiston, Idaho Territory
August 1885

Brooke Marie Baker pressed a hand to her thumping heart and forced herself to breathe normally as she walked into town beside the last wagon of the caravan. Whether she wanted to be here or not, they had arrived. Six months of grueling travel across rugged prairies and mountain passes. Aching back. Aching feet. Oppressive heat and little to eat. Yet she'd be willing to travel on forever if it meant she didn't have to be here. Didn't have to give up her freedom.

This morning, Harry had said they would arrive in Lewiston today, but she had hoped something would delay the inevitable.

The weathered facades of the clapboard houses she walked past and the monotonous creak of the wagon wheels turning over the graveled street proved her hope had been futile.

Along both sides of the road, as they turned onto the main street, people stopped to stare. Brooke didn't meet their gazes but kept her perusal focused on the buildings. Real buildings with boardwalks, stairs, and windows. The last time she'd seen boardwalks had been three months ago at Fort Laramie.

Ahead, someone let out a loud whoop of joy.

She looked down the line of bonnet-topped Conestogas.

The first wagons had come to a stop, and apparently the gathered crowd had been anxiously awaiting their arrival. Toward the front of the throng, a cluster of men stood, studying the caravan expectantly.

Almost all of them had long, tobacco-stained beards. Not one looked like he was under fifty-five, and several had no compunctions about scratching themselves in public. One man, thick black suspenders holding up his baggy pants, ogled Brooke from head to toe. Then, still scrutinizing her, he leaned to one side and spat a stream of tobacco.

She felt a familiar quiver of fear and glanced away, offering the man no challenge.

"Let's get on with the marryin'," a deep voice toward the back shouted. "I got plenty o' work waitin' for me back ta home." A loud grumble of agreement followed.

An older man scratched at his beard and complained, "You all was supposed to be here two days ago."

"Gentlemen! Gentlemen!" Harry's spurs jangled as he jumped to the ground from his position in the lead wagon. He was using his let's-stay-calm tone—the same one he'd used when Emily Donaldson had discovered the much-too-friendly beaver in the bathing hole back on the Platte and every last woman had rushed screaming from the water. "Give me a moment to gather your brides, and then we can proceed."

The grumblings ceased, and apparently satisfied the men had gotten his message, Harry turned and strode Brooke's way, thumbs hooked into his large silver belt-buckle. "Come on, ladies. Everybody circle up. We're here." His familiar *rap-rap* as he knocked on the side of the first wagon resounded down the street.

Her stomach threatened to empty right there in front of God and everyone. She stepped back behind the tailgate, drew in a long breath, held it, and eased it out between pursed lips. Pushing aside memories of days gone by, she forced her shoulders to relax. While she dared not hope that things would be different this time, neither did she want her nervousness to be apparent.

Rap-rap. He'd reached the second wagon. Only four more to go.

She took another breath and released it on a low whisper. "You can do this. Calm down."

A moment later, he peered around the end of the wagon. "Brooke? I need everyone to meet up front, please. The men have a minister here already."

"I know." The words emerged on a squeak, and she pressed moist palms together, rubbing them in circles.

Harry gave her a sympathetic look. "You don't have anything

to worry about. I'm real careful to make sure all the men are honest, upstanding citizens."

Emily Donaldson rounded the wagon, her red-painted lips puckered in aggravation and one dark eyebrow arched. "Comforting, I'm sure, Harry, for a young girl like her." She pierced the wagon-master with a glare.

If only Emily knew. But she didn't. None of them knew anything about her or the real reason she was here.

Harry snorted and stalked off, grousing, "Just be up front in five minutes. And best you follow instructions this time, Emily Donaldson!"

Emily huffed. "What do men know?" She put an arm around Brooke and rested one cheek on the top of her head. "Come on, now." She gave Brooke a gentle squeeze. "No use us trying to postpone the inevitable."

"I suppose you're right." Brooke trailed after her past the row of wagons, feeling sweat trickle down her back.

All the women gathered on one side of the street under the overhang in front of the bank. The men clustered across the way, looking them over like meat on a market table.

She swallowed down the burn pressing at the back of her throat. Of course she hadn't expected anything better. She pressed the sleeve of her dress to the beads of moisture dotting her forehead. If it wasn't so hot, this might be easier to face.

The minister in the dusty street between the two groups raised his arms for silence. "All right, listen up now. To make this as efficient as possible, I will call forward each man. He will present me with his documents, and then I will call forward one of you women, and we'll have a ceremony for that couple, then move on to the next one. My wife and Mr. Preston here—" he glanced over his shoulder at a plump woman and a frowning man standing off to one side, "have agreed to be witnesses, and the hotel down the street has prepared a special meal for the occasion."

A chorus of appreciation rose from the men. The women remained silent. Only one or two even shuffled their feet.

"Oh and one more thing." The minister again gestured for

everyone's attention. "Is there a Miss, ah—" he patted several pockets, then finally pulled a paper from the one in his shirt and consulted it "—Brooke Baker, here?"

Brooke blinked in surprise. Could this be a reprieve? Maybe the man Uncle Jackson had pledged her to had died or changed his mind. She stepped forward.

But Harry spoke before she could find her voice. "Yeah, she's here. What do you need with her?"

The minister peered at her over the top of his spectacles. "Miss Baker?"

Mouth dry, she nodded.

"Your intended has asked that I escort you by stage to a town about half a day's ride from here called Greer's Ferry. So you won't meet him until tomorrow."

Brooke's knees nearly gave out in relief, but by some miracle she stayed on her feet. "Oh, thank you, sir." Heat rose up from her collar and into her face. She'd sounded a trifle too gleeful.

Easing to the back of the crowd, she relaxed against the building's warm brick and tucked her trembling hands behind her. Her eyes dropped closed, and she tilted her face to the sun.

One more day. One more day of freedom.

Pierce City, Idaho Territory
August 1885

Evening shadows stretched long as Sky Jordan placed the last of the supplies onto his pack mule. The leather of the packs creaked as he settled them into place, cinched them down, and made sure everything was in proper order. He stood in front of Fraser's Mercantile, scratching the mule behind its long gray ears, surveying Main Street.

A lone pine tree grew in the middle of the dusty street at the south end of town, its shadow falling due east. Summer crickets chirped lustily from the bushes nearby, and he could hear the occasional *tink* of bottle on shot glass emanating from Roo's Saloon across the street.

From an upper-story window in the Joss house, a Chinese woman emptied a pail of water onto the street, splattering mud on Gaffney's Pioneer Hotel next door and leaving a small muddy patch in the alley between the buildings.

"Sky! You comin' in here? Food's gonna be cold 'fore you ever set down to table!"

A rough, gravelly voice interrupted his perusal of the town. He glanced up at the friendly, round face of Jed Swanson, who leaned over the rail in front of his boarding house.

"Food ain't gonna be fit for hogs if'n you don't get in here," Jed complained, rubbing a plump hand down the front of his greasy, apron-clad belly.

A smile stretched Sky's face. Jed's food always fell somewhere between burlap and leather, but Jed invariably claimed that was because it had been left sitting too long.

"Your food? Fit for Hogs?" Sky taunted, unable to pass up the opportunity to tease his old friend.

"Hmmph!" Jed shook his wooden spoon at Sky. "Mind your manners, or you won't be gettin' any o' my fine fixins." He turned away, slamming the door as he went inside.

Sky gave the mule a friendly slap on the neck, left it tied to the rail, then trooped wearily up the steps to Jed's boarding house, the building next door to Fraser's Mercantile.

The rough wooden door opened on squeaking hinges as he entered. He hooked his black Stetson on a peg in the wall and scanned the room.

The only light in the gloomy confines of the rugged log building emanated from a small oil lamp set in the middle of the dining table and a brightly burning fire in the fireplace on the back wall. The stone and mortar hearth, stacked high with logs on one side, held the wrought-iron hook by which the coffee pot could be swung into the heat of the fire. Off to the left, on the back wall, he could see the dark shadow of the doorway that led to the rooms Jed rented out.

Sky turned to his right. Several men were already seated around the coarse plank table, shoveling food into their mouths as though it might disappear before their eyes, their forks clanking loudly against tin plates. His interest piqued as he noticed his cousin, Jason, sitting in the dim light at the end of the table, his back to the wall. A hefty man with unwashed blond curls covering his head, Jason looked as surly as ever. His large belly, the result of his love of beer, protruded over his huge silver belt buckle, bumping the table.

Sky sauntered casually to an empty chair, sat down with his back to the room, and began to serve his plate, listening to the conversation around him.

Fraser was speaking. "This boy is a lunatic, I tell you, and he wants to court my Alice. She's only fifteen, and I sent her down to Lewiston to get an education, not to court boys. So I told him straight out, when I was down to Lewiston last, that he had better stay away from her. Now, with her being over seventy-five miles from here, that in itself wouldn't give me a whole lot of comfort, since I wouldn't trust that boy as far as I could throw him. But I also told Judge Rand that the boy was not to come around anymore, and if anyone will make sure he don't, it'll be the judge."

Sky's mind wandered to his little sister back home as he added a spoonful of greens to his plate. *Wonder if boys are coming to call on Sharyah already?* She was about the same age as Alice Fraser. He smiled to himself. Knowing Sharyah and her blond curls and beautiful sunny smile, the boys were lined up for a mile outside of the little white farmhouse back in Shiloh. *Dad's probably going through the same thing as Fraser.*

Jed slurped his coffee noisily. "Judge Rand be a good man. Speakin' o' which, I hear tell Lee Chang is up to his ol' tricks again. Nigh on got hisself killed by a trader that came through the other day, way I hear it. 'Cept Chang's goons came to his rescue and ran the feller out of town. He tried to pay the man with some o' that bogus gold he's gettin' a reputation fer usin'." Jed shook his head. "Someone ought to take Chang to court. The judge would see to him, sure 'nuff."

Sky's curiosity lifted his brow. "Bogus gold? What's that all about?"

"You ain't heard that story, yet?" Jed motioned at Fraser with the point of his knife. "Tell 'im, Fraser."

Fraser twisted his mug in a circle. "Louise came to see me a couple months back. Right after the last time you came through for supplies."

"Louise? The Nez Perce woman who brings garden produce to town to sell?"

"That's the one." Fraser nodded.

Sky sawed at his meat, waiting for Fraser to continue.

"Well, she brought me the gold that Chang had paid them the last time they sold to him. He'd taken small pebbles and dipped them in gold. They were only worth a fraction of their promised value. She, Jane, and Running Fawn nearly got arrested last time they were down to Lewiston when someone there discovered the deception, but they managed to convince the authorities that they themselves had been duped. Anyhow, Louise came to me. Wanted me to go and confront Chang about it." He stabbed a piece of rawhide-meat and stuffed it into his cheek irritably.

Sky leaned back in his chair, amazed at Chang's gall.

He knew Lee Chang. His character was questionable at best and downright despicable at worst. He dealt in opium and women and offered no mercy when it came time to pay up for either. But this was the first he'd heard of the man being a cheat.

Max, a miner seated next to Jason, grunted. "Don't see why she didn't confront him herself."

Fraser looked up. "You know Chang—he's got his thumb on just about every individual in the county. The women are afraid that if Chang gives the say-so, all the other Chinese in the area will boycott their business. They would certainly be out of business if he did that to them."

"Hmmph," Jed growled, "that there Chinese is one man this here town could do 'thout. He shorly is a cussed buzzard, that'n."

Fraser huffed his agreement. "And do you know," he leaned forward and pierced Sky with a look, "when I confronted him, the man had the nerve to admit to the whole thing!"

"Does he plan to make it right?"

Fraser wiped his mouth with the back of his hand, chewing the food for a moment before he spoke. "Nope. He said he paid them and they accepted payment and that he hoped they would be a bit smarter next time." He glanced around the table, knife and fork held vertically by his plate in suspended animation, then shrugged. "The man showed no remorse whatsoever. I don't know what else I can do." He stared back at his plate and continued to hack at the black slab that passed as a piece of meat.

"Leastwise you tried. Best you watch your back, though," Jed added. "That Chang, he don't cotton to no one gettin' all up in his business."

Jason gave a low snort from the other side of the table, and Sky looked down to the shadows at the end. His cousin shoveled another mouthful of food, then belched. Seeming to notice that everyone's eyes were on him, he spoke. "This town would be better off if we got rid of all the Chinks. I tell you, I've never met a respectable Celestial. Not one. Always sneakin' and spyin'. Lazy cusses, too." He swiped his greasy mouth on his shoulder, the stain there proof that he did so often.

Max made no sound but nodded emphatically as he shoved a huge forkful of potatoes into his mouth.

"This town wouldn't exist if it wasn't for the Chinese, Jason." Sky kept his voice nonchalant. He picked up his glass and took a drink of water, his eyes fixed on his burly cousin over the rim.

Jason snorted again. "You always were too partial to them Celestials, Sky. If you had any sense, you'd realize the type of scum they really are."

Sky changed the subject. "How have you been, Jason? Haven't seen you for awhile." His tone was friendly, but Jason glared at him.

"You been pinin' away for information on your beloved cousin?" he asked, expression caustic.

Sky, accustomed to his cousin's recent foul moods, shrugged and turned back to his food, praying silently that one day his relationship with Jason would be restored.

Jed's gaze bounced between them as he squirmed in his seat.

After a minute, he fixed Sky with a pointed look. "That news about Chang…well, that ain't the only news you missed hearin' about. You need to get to town more often."

The venomous glare Jason sent Jed piqued Sky's interest. "Oh yeah?" He cautiously tried a bite of potatoes. Not too bad this time. Maybe he could smother the meat with them.

Jed's twinkling eyes remained fixed on Jason, and a smile twitched the corner of his mouth as silence filled the room.

Sky looked to his cantankerous cousin, one eyebrow raised in question. Several of the men shifted uneasily. Everyone seemed to know what Jed was referring to except him.

Jason waved away his unspoken question with a flip of his hand.

"Aw! Ain't you gonna tell ol' Sky here about yer plans?"

Jason ignored Jed and scooped another bite into his mouth.

Sky turned his questioning eyes on Jed, continuing to eat calmly.

Jed spoke around a mouthful of meat. "Your cousin is soon gonna be married. Or so he's been tellin' it."

Sky's fork stopped halfway up from his plate and he blinked in surprise. *What woman in her right mind would marry Jason?*

Jason growled, throwing his fork onto his plate with a clatter. "Jed, you wouldn't know a secret if it bit you!" He turned belligerent eyes on Sky. "That's right. I've got a mail-order bride coming in on tomorrow's stage to Greer's Ferry. I'm going to have me a pretty little wife to cook for me…and keep me warm at night." He jabbed his elbow into Max's ribs, a dissolute leer spreading on his face.

Sky set his fork down quietly. Pushing away from the table, he stood and walked over to the blackened coffee pot near the fire. Pouring himself a cup, his movements deliberate and casual, he contemplated the situation. His heart went out to the poor girl. He couldn't remember the last time he'd been so surprised.

"You got a picture of this woman?" He hooked a thumb through his belt loop, watching Jason through the steam drifting up from his mug as he took a sip of coffee.

Jason gave his habitual snort. "Like I'd show it to you. Pretty little thing, though. And young, too. I'm really looking forward to tomorrow night." The lewd grin was back before he stuffed a large piece of meat into his cheek.

"Well, let me be the first to offer you my congratulations." Sky lifted his coffee mug in a toast. "To the happy groom." No one in the room responded; he hadn't expected them to. Turning back he gazed into the fire. A log dropped, shooting a cascade of orange sparks upwards. The silence in the room hovered palpably; only the crackling of the fire and the clatter of silverware disturbed the stillness.

Lord, what should I do? I wouldn't give a dog I liked to Jason. You know I care for him, but... Sky tried to think of a solution. Nothing came to mind.

Weariness weighted his eyes and, remembering he still had to travel home tonight, he set his cup down.

Turning to Jed, he placed a hand on his stomach and grinned. "Best hog swill I've had in a long time, Jed."

Jed grunted, waving his fork in dismissal.

To Fraser, he said, "Been a pleasure, Fraser. See you again soon."

Fraser regarded him with a friendly smile as he wiped the corners of his mouth with long, slender fingers. "Sky, always good doing business with you." Sky nodded and Fraser's eyes held Sky's for a moment, questioning what he was going to do about Jason's situation, before he turned back to his food.

"Good night, gentlemen," Sky said to the rest of the men at the table. The leather of his hat felt smooth against his fingers as he removed it from the peg by the door and pushed it back onto his head, exiting onto the now-darkened street.

The muffled sound his boots made in the soft dust of the roadbed didn't carry far into the cricket-serenaded night. At the rail in front of Fraser's Mercantile, he untied his mule. Leading it further down the street toward the livery, he studied the starry sky. *Jason getting married.* Unshakable heaviness settled on his shoulders.

"Get a grip, Jordan," he grumbled and forced himself to focus on the road ahead as he resettled his hat. There was nothing he could do for the poor woman. And maybe she'd be good for Jason.

With renewed determination to let the matter go, he retrieved his stallion, mounted up, and cantered out of town, leading the mule behind.

★

Chapter Two

Lewiston, Idaho Territory
August 1885

I
n the shadow cast by the telegraph office, a man stood with
his head bent low over a telegram. He leaned one shoulder
into the building as a sardonic smile twisted his lips, and he
read the message again.

> It's in the back room STOP Come at your convenience
> STOP Have men in place STOP
> L C
> Pierce City

He rubbed his hand across his chin, still staring at the paper
before him. His first two fingers paused on his chin, and he
tapped it slowly twice as he thought. The news was good, but so
many plans still had to be made. He peered both up and down the
street. Although it teemed with traffic, no one looked his way, so
he slipped back around the corner and into the telegraph office.

The operator was just heading out the door. Startled, he pulled
his round spectacles to his eyes by the rim. "Oh, hello again—"
one side of the paunchy little man's mouth tilted up nervously,
his eyes darting across the room to a board with several wanted
posters pinned to it "—did you forget something?"

"I need to reply to this message." He made sure his tone and
face emanated calm.

The operator quickly returned to his side of the counter and
took up a pen. With a shaking hand, he dipped it into the inkwell
before him and waited expectantly.

The man dictated, "Coming by stage to Pierce City. STOP.
Wait for my arrival." He glanced at his watch. *11:59 a.m.* As the
operator reached to send the message, the man leaned across the

counter and gripped his shoulder. Jumping, the operator turned toward him with a frightened expression, but he only said, "Wait," and paced across the room to peruse the wanted posters.

Slowly the second hand ticked around until the time read *12:05 p.m.* He nodded at the operator, who was now sweating profusely. "I will wait until you have sent the message."

With shaking fingers, the operator tapped out the message to Pierce City. Once the message had been sent, he allowed his face to soften. He even thanked the operator politely for his help and patience.

Mopping his sweat-covered brow with a white handkerchief, the operator smiled his relief and nodded, face calming.

The man turned toward the door and took two long strides. Then, suddenly changing his course of direction and not bothering to use the gate, he placed his hand on the counter and, in one smooth motion, leaped across it to the side where the now gaping, slack-jawed operator sat. Grabbing the trembling telegrapher by his collar, he dragged him into a small room he could see at the back of the office, pressed the trembling man against the wall, forearm to his throat, and pulled a knife from his sheath under his jacket.

He turned the blade, watching as the light glanced off it and made pleasant patterns on the operator's plump face. "Be a shame if somethin' were to happen to your missus," he murmured.

The little man clutched at the arm pressed to his neck and nodded vigorously.

"Funny thing about those wanted posters. They seem to pop up all over the place. A man can't get any peace."

This time the telegrapher shook his head. "I have never seen you, I swear."

Chuckling, he pressed the tip of his blade to the soft skin under his captive's eye. The man scrunched his eyes tight.

He grinned. *As though that will protect them from my blade.*

"P-Please. I won't say a w-word."

He let the knife point bite the flesh just enough to draw blood. "See that you don't. I've seen your missus, and it would sure be a shame if somethin' were to happen to such a pretty little thing, if you catch my meanin'." With one last surge of pressure, he pushed away from the shuddering man. "And take the poster down. It's an awful likeness. Makes me look as though I'm some unkempt hooligan."

The operator nodded and, as the man turned to leave, he heard him slide down to the floor. He smirked and sheathed his blade.

Moments later he stepped out onto the boardwalk. Smoothing the front of his coat and squinting into the sunshine, he walked up the street toward the stage that waited for boarding passengers. Tipping his hat, he smiled at a woman with a young child in tow.

Pierce City
12:03 p.m.

Lee Chang lumbered up the street toward the telegraph office. Opening the door, he eased himself into the small, dusty room. The office had been shut down several years ago, when the population had dwindled to the point that there were no longer enough people in town to warrant its use, though the telegraph was still operational. An occasional message came through, though, and if someone who could read Morse code happened to be passing by on the street to hear it, sometimes it even got to the person for whom it was meant.

On this day, however, Lee knew a message would be coming through and didn't want to chance someone walking by on the street and hearing the clatter of the code. Especially not David Fraser, who understood Morse code.

Leaning out the door, he scanned the street to be sure no one was near. Finally satisfied he was alone, he eased the door shut. He had just turned toward the desk in the darkened corner of the room when the telegraph began to click and tap out its message. He scrambled for a pencil and paper.

Lewiston
12:15 p.m.

Brooke placed both hands beside her on the seat to help keep her balance as the stage careened around corners and over bumps, heading toward Greer's Ferry. She tried to ignore the chatter coming from the man opposite her. Brushing a stray curl of hair out of her eyes and tucking it behind her ear, she peered out the window at the passing scenery and tried to swallow the lump of nervousness in her throat.

Wondering what the man she was to marry would be like, she wished again that Uncle Jackson had not sent her away. *I could have gone to work and helped support him.* Even living with Uncle Jackson was preferable to being married to a man like the ones she'd seen yesterday.

But his cutting words still rang in her ears. *You good-for-nothing little tramp. I should have sent you off the moment I became your guardian.* His laugh had been cruel as he continued, *At least I'm getting fifty dollars for the trouble you've been! Congratulations on your upcoming marriage, my dear.* She shuddered, giving herself a little shake to dispel his face from her memory, and forced her mind back to the present.

Besides the minister, who traveled with her to perform the marriage ceremony at the trail's end, two other passengers had gotten on the stage. One, a burly mountain man who resembled how she'd always imagined a mountain man would look—with a long, tangled gray beard. It evidenced the fact that often when he spit tobacco juice, he didn't really spit at all but merely let the juice dribble out the corner of his mouth...a most disgusting phenomenon Brooke had witnessed more than once on the trip. When he'd hauled his considerable girth onto the stage, he'd grunted a greeting, let his eyes rove over her form, and then slouched in his seat with his muddied boots stretched out as far in front of him as they would go. Giving Brooke another appreciative look, he'd rested his head against the side of the coach and fallen fast asleep. His snores would have been enough to harry a hen laying eggs, but any hens in the vicinity had probably already been disturbed by the second personality who'd joined them on the stage.

This man had not been quiet for more than five consecutive seconds since his foot first touched the floor of the stage. His blond, frizzy hair poked from his head in unruly abandon, giving him a rather wild look. He wore a pair of round spectacles that invariably slipped down his nose, and he constantly pushed them back up. He would cease to expound on one topic, and Brooke would sigh in relief, thinking there couldn't possibly be anything more to say on the subject, when he would begin anew. As annoying as she found the talkative man across from her, Brooke did find that she learned a lot about the area that they drove through.

"There are really some fascinatin' rock formations in this area." He gestured out the window with fingers so heavily laden with gaudy gold rings that Brooke wondered how his slender hand supported the weight. "Take that one down there across the river…do you see it?" Even before Brooke nodded, he continued, "The Ant and the Yellow Jacket."

Brooke regarded him quizzically.

He pushed his round spectacles up on his nose with a bony forefinger. "Yep, the Nez Perce say that the ants and the yellow jackets lived peaceably together until one day, their chiefs got into an argument. The yellow jacket—of course the Indians just call them 'Ant' and 'Yellow Jacket,' like that was their names or somethin'." He chuckled. "Anyway, the yellow jacket chief, he had found this piece of dried salmon and was eating it on a rock. The ant chief comes along, and he is hungry, see? So he gets jealous of the yellow jacket and starts hollerin' at him that he should have asked permission to eat on that rock. The yellow jacket responds, 'I don't have to ask your permission for anythin',' and they raise up on their back legs and start fightin'. Well, the old coyote, who the Nez Perce believe is very wise, comes along. He sees the piece of salmon and those two a-whalin' on each other. He's across the river, so he hollers at them, 'Hey, you two, quit your fightin'!' but they pay no attention. So the magic coyote turned them into those rocks you see over there just like that—" He snapped his fingers. "The coyote crossed the river and ate the salmon, and to this day, the ants and the yellow jackets are feudin' among themselves.

"Yep, sure is some interesting country you have come to Miss... Hey, I haven't introduced myself. I am Percival Hunter." He bowed from the waist, as good a bow as one can give from a sitting position, removing his bowler hat. "And you are?"

Brooke smiled; she was beginning to like this talkative man before her. "Brooke Baker. It's a pleasure to meet you." She extended a hand, which he took and raised to his lips.

"The pleasure is all mine, I assure you."

Brooke pulled her hand away and focused on her lap, not wanting to give him the wrong impression. She was, after all, on the way to her wedding.

Percival cleared his throat. "Well, as I was sayin', this sure is interesting country you've chosen to come visit, Miss Baker." He continued without pause, or Brooke would have informed him that she was not here by her own choice. "Take the ferry we'll use to cross the Clearwater. Did you know that the Greer Ferry, as it is called, was constructed in 1861 by two enterprisin' souls who saw a sure-fire way to make some money off of the gold strike up in Pierce?"

Brooke shook her head, resigned to listening to his prattle for the rest of the trip.

"They built the ferry to aid the miners in crossin' the river on their way to Pierce City, where gold had been found. As I see it, their venture was a lot more profitable than goin' on up the mountain to dig for gold. There are even sleepin' quarters where we'll stay tonight."

The minister, resting his forearms on his knees, added, "The first ferry and sleeping quarters were burnt to the ground a few years ago in the Indian War of 1877 when the Nez Perce used it to cross the river and get away from the army chasing them. They crossed the river on the ferry, then torched it and the cabin so the army would have a harder time following them."

Percival nodded. "That's right. After the war, though, a new ferry and cabin were built. Those are the ones we'll see this evenin'."

"I'm amazed at how much you know about this country, Mr. Hunter," Brooke said.

He grinned and shrugged, indicating it was no big deal. Then, after only a short silence, he went on to tell how the Nez Perce Indians made their camp on the Camas Prairie each fall in order to collect the Camas bulbs that grew there in wild abandon. "All the bands of the Nez Perce come together and place their teepees in six camps over a two-mile radius. It's quite a sight."

He told of many men who, in the winter of 1861, while making their way to the gold camps, were blinded by the brilliant, glistening snow and were never found until the spring thaw. Brooke shivered, but if Percival noticed, it only inspired him.

On and on the stories went, and when suddenly, the stage came to a jerking halt, Brooke was amazed to find that the day had ebbed away. They had come to the place where they would cross the river. But as she looked out the window, she was surprised to see that the river still lay below them a good 1500 feet.

"Now comes the fun part," Percival said.

Brooke felt dizzy as she stared down the precipitous pitch to the water. "What are we doing now?"

Her answer came in the form of the stage driver, who poked his head in the door. "Ya'll can get out and stretch a mite if ya want to. We'll be here a few minutes while we hitch up the tree drag."

Brooke wondered at the term *tree drag*, but as she stepped down from the stage, she saw it was just what it sounded like. The stage driver and the man who had been riding shotgun were hitching a large tree trunk to the back of the stage. Her gaze returned to the river, and her stomach pitched. "We are going to drive down *that*?"

"Yep," Percival answered. A little too gleefully, if she were the judge.

"Well, if I die, at least I won't have to get married," she mumbled under her breath as she gazed at the steep track before her.

Soon they all climbed back into the stage except for the mountain man, who had never gotten off. He was awake now, though, and took the opportunity to stuff another wad of chewing tobacco in his cheek. He considered Brooke wolfishly. "Best hold on tight," he told her, winking boldly.

With a shouted "Gidd'up!" the driver cracked his whip in the air, and the horses lurched into the descent. Brooke gripped the edge of her seat and wondered whether she wanted to look out the window or close her eyes as tight as she could. Deciding that if she was going to die, she wanted to see it coming, she peered out and watched the scenery fly by.

Even Percival held his silence. *Thank goodness!*

It was soon apparent that the log hooked to the back of the stage was what saved them at each corner from launching over the edge of the trail into open space. The horses dug their heels in until they almost sat. Still, the stage careened down the steep incline.

Dust boiled up, whirling into the coach in a suffocating cloud. Choking and coughing, Brooke closed her eyes against the grit. Waving a hand in front of her face did nothing but stir the thick, roiling cloud. Feeling something pressed against her face, she realized that the minister was offering her his handkerchief. Gratefully, she grasped it, tears streaming from her eyes as she tried to see what was happening outside.

Then, as quickly as it had begun, the death-defying ride was over. She slumped back in relief. The river meandered placidly beyond the coach's window. They had made it down, and she was still alive.

It couldn't have taken more than a handful of minutes to plunge down the side of the mountain, but to Brooke it had seemed like an eternity. The coachman pulled the snorting horses to a stop and stepped down to unhitch the tree drag.

Brooke glanced down. Her dark blue dress was literally

brown with dust. She touched a hand to her face and patted her hair. *I must look a mess!*

The ferry waited for them on the near side of the blue-green river, a smiling, kind-looking man standing on the landing. Brooke eyed the little raft tied to the bank dubiously. *Ferry* was really too grand a term for the wooden contraption floating on the water. *Will that even float with the stage on it?*

The horses walked onto the wooden platform with the loud clatter of hooves, and they pushed off into the river. She glanced out the window, looking back at the path of their descent in utter disbelief. *Well, the descent from that ridge didn't kill me; maybe I'll drown crossing the river.*

Her stomach felt like it was tied in knots. The man she was to marry would be waiting for her across the river at the landing. *My dress! I can't get married looking like I've been wallowing in a mound of dirt! Oh, what will the man think when he first lays eyes on me? So much for first impressions.*

She did her best to beat some of the dust from her skirt but saw that it was no use. He would have to take her the way she was. It was his own fault, after all, for not wanting to come to Lewiston to meet her. She'd learned he had paid the minister an extra five dollars to escort her to Greer's Ferry and perform the ceremony there.

The swaying of the ferry stopped. Her hands, fisted in her lap, were white-knuckled, but she lifted her chin. *You can deal with this!* Hadn't she survived Uncle Jackson all these years? If she could survive his beatings, then she could survive the abuses of any man. Hadn't she proved that with Hank? Moving out of Uncle Jackson's house to move in with Hank had been like jumping from the frying pan into the fire. She still had nightmares about Hank, but she was alive. She would be fine. But she must be strong.

Yet she could taste fear at the back of her mouth.

These past months, traveling west, she had not been beaten or abused once. Could she truly put herself back into such an environment? There was no doubt that life here would be the same as back in St. Louis. All men were the same: *Father, Uncle*

Jackson, Hank. She shut her mind off from that line of thinking. She would not dwell on the past; she needed all of her strength to face the future.

She took the hand that the minister offered and stepped out into the bright sunlight, raising one hand to shade her eyes from the glare.

Sky watched the ferry cross the river, wishing he wasn't here, yet knowing he couldn't be anywhere else. Holding a single, yellow, dark-centered daisy in one hand, he reached with the other to flick an invisible speck of dust from the sleeve of his black suit coat. Black, perfectly creased pants encased his legs, tapering down to his highly polished black boots. His black Stetson protected his eyes from the glaring sun as he looked out over the river considering his present situation.

Would there really be a woman on board who had come this far to marry Jason? *Of course, she doesn't know what Jason is like, or she'd never have agreed to marry him.* Then again, maybe she would have. What did he know of the woman coming across the river? Perhaps she would be a bawdy, boisterous madam, just Jason's type. But then he remembered Jason's description of her. "Young and pretty" had been his words. No, he didn't think the woman would be risqué, but he found himself wondering what she *would* be like. *It doesn't matter—no woman deserves to be left to Jason.*

She won't be beautiful, though. She wouldn't be coming west to find a husband if she had any hope of finding one back home. With this thought in mind, he cleared his vision of the beautiful Victoria Snyder, his childhood sweetheart who lived back home in Shiloh, and prepared himself for the task at hand. Reaching up, he straightened the string tie at his throat and banished all concern about Jason. The Lord knew about his future, and this gave Sky the peace he needed to face the decision he had made.

The stage pulled off the ferry with squeaking wheels and the minister descended. "It's now or never, old boy," Sky mumbled to himself as he sauntered toward the coach, twirling the daisy between his fingers.

He stopped several yards off as a small, dusty hand grasped the minister's, and a woman stepped down to the ground. She reached one hand up to shade her eyes from the glare of the sun and Sky saw her apprehensive fear. He knew at that moment he'd done the right thing in coming. All his doubts fled. Jason would have thoroughly ravished the enchanting creature before him, destroying her serene spirit.

She was beautiful. *Very beautiful.* Her hair, though covered in dust, was a curly reddish-blond. Large blue eyes peered out from a tanned face accentuated by high cheekbones and a full, soft mouth. A vulnerable expression tightened her features, and his heart constricted in his chest. Her uncertainty gave her magnetic charm. He took a step closer. She bit her lower lip, drawing his attention to her mouth momentarily before it snapped back to her eyes. Blinking in the sunlight, she slowly focused on his face, her lips pinched together. *She's scared to death!*

Sky saw the surprise in her eyes as they adjusted to the glare of the sun and came to rest on him. He stepped forward, smiled lightly, and, lifting his hat, nodded in her direction. "Ma'am, it's a pleasure to make your acquaintance." He held out the daisy like a peace offering, watching her carefully, his eyes never leaving her face.

She looked down at the flower but did not move for several seconds. Then she took it with one slender hand and glanced back up into his face.

Lifting the daisy slightly, her generous mouth serious, she said, "Thank you." The words held the note of a question, and her voice was moderated so low that he almost couldn't hear what she said.

Sky felt his heart go out to her as he again realized how apprehensive she must be. He wanted to smooth the fearful frown off her brow, but he simply nodded, and they stood looking at one another. He wondered what she was thinking.

She was the first to avert her gaze, bringing her hands

together in front of her. Her next words captivated Sky: "If you don't mind..." All color in her face disappeared and something flashed in her eyes. Was it fear? She quickly schooled her features and brought her eyes back to his.

When she spoke again, her words sounded strained. "I would like to clean up before the ceremony." A slight lift of her chin and a glint of determination in her eyes dared him to tell her no, yet her chin trembled slightly.

He carefully kept his curiosity from showing on his face and attempted to put her at ease. "It's a dusty ride down the grade." He gestured across the river to the trail she and her fellow passengers had descended and smiled. "I've made that trip on several occasions myself." Holding his hand out toward the log cabin that functioned as the sleeping quarters at Greer's Ferry, he added, "I don't mind waiting." It was the truth. He was still having a hard time believing that he was here, considering marriage. *And to a woman I've only just met.* He wanted a few more minutes to think things through.

A look of gratitude crossed her face. Nodding serenely, she turned, picked up her small carpet bag, and headed toward the building.

Brooke sighed in relief, clutching the handle on her bag with both hands as she entered the little log cabin. It had two rooms. The front room contained several bunks, a wood stove, and a long table constructed out of logs sawn in half and laid side by side with the flat sides up. Various utensils hung from pegs above the black stove where a pot of coffee perked cheerfully. The smell of venison stew wafted through the cabin.

The heels of her boots echoed on the rough plank floor as Jack Greer led her to the second room in the cabin.

"You can clean up in here," he informed her kindly. He glanced down at her hands, and his face softened.

She realized her double-fisted, white-knuckled grip revealed more than she wanted others to know.

"If you need anything, don't hesitate to ask."

She nodded mutely, wishing she could think of something to say. As he left, closing the door, she collapsed onto the edge of the bed, her quaking legs unable to hold her upright any longer. She stared at the wall for several minutes before her thoughts began to register coherently.

She glanced around. This room held a double bed and a chest of drawers.

A small wash basin sat next to the door, fresh water filling the blue pitcher on the table near it. Light flooded the room from the window in the back wall, illuminating a table and two chairs that sat against the wall across from her.

Her thoughts wandered to the man who'd met her when she stepped off the stage. He was very attractive. But that didn't stop the shaking of her limbs as she pulled her dress off over her head. She was thankful that…what was his name? Jordan…? Jason…? She bit her lip. *That's just great. I can't even remember his name. Well, at least he doesn't look anything like those dour old men did yesterday.* Still, she had found Hank attractive too. A man's looks had nothing to do with the way he acted.

Thoughts of the evening ahead assailed her and she glanced at the room's one window. What would her chances of survival be if she made a run for it? She walked over to it, but the window had no latch and couldn't be opened. Sighing, she returned to her bag. *Your only option is to go through with this. You have nowhere else to go.*

Pulling her hand mirror out of her bag, she examined her reflection, wrinkling her nose in disgust at the dirt she saw on her face. Pouring some water into the basin, she washed her face and arms as best she could and then, seeing no towel, dried them on her petticoat, which mercifully had missed most of the dust. Pulling the pins from her hair she brushed it out, plaited a braid, and coiled it at the back of her neck. Wispy curls fell out and framed her ashen face, but she did not take time to tuck them back in.

Removing her only other dress from her bag, a dark green

full-skirted frock that had once belonged to her mother, she gave it a brisk snap to dispel any dust that might be on it and settled it over her head. It was her nicest dress, and she felt thankful that she had decided against wearing it on the trip. The fitted bodice had a V of cream lace that came down to just above the nipped-in waist. The full skirt and puffed sleeves of the dress accentuated her slender curves, and the dark green material made her eyes look like emeralds instead of sapphires.

After shaking out her dark blue dress, she folded it up and placed it neatly into her bag with the brush on top. She smoothed the front of her skirt with nervous hands. *I've already taken far longer than necessary. I can do this!*

She opened the door and peeked into the outer room. None of the men were inside. As she started to cross the room, she remembered the daisy. No man had ever given her flowers before. It had been a touching gesture. A spark of hope had sprung to life in her heart when he handed her the daisy, but she had quickly smothered it lest the pain of the inevitable abuse be too much to bear.

Turning back, she retrieved the flower and then made her way outside into the golden sunshine.

Conversation ceased as she stepped out and all eyes turned toward her. The admiration on their faces only added to the turmoil in her soul. She had seen firsthand what admiration could do. It was Hank's admiration of her beauty that had first drawn him to her.

But this was her wedding day, and she determined to ignore the looks. A gust of wind blew a strand of hair into her eyes. Reaching up with one hand, she tucked the curl behind her ear, her eyes coming to rest on the face of the man she was to marry. Somehow his look was different from all the rest. He was not smiling, but she saw something in his face. What? Concern? Was he worried about her, or was he having second thoughts about marrying her? She fleetingly hoped he might reject her. She would be fine with that. But it wasn't rejection she glimpsed. What then? It wasn't an expression she'd seen on any man's face before.

The minister was the first to break the silence. Gesturing to the hard-packed dirt in front of the cabin, he asked quietly, "Shall we commence?"

Her soon-to-be husband stepped forward and offered her his arm. She stepped up beside him, facing the minister, the yellow daisy clutched in her hand like a lifeline.

Skipping the "dearly beloved" speech she'd heard at so many weddings back home, the black-coated minister launched immediately into the vows. "Do you, Brooke Baker, take this man to be your husband? Do you promise to love him, honor him, and obey him until death do you part?"

Brooke hesitated only a moment before she said quietly, "I do."

"And do you, Jason Jordan—" The minister's words were cut off as the man beside her raised a finger.

"Skyler. Skyler Jordan."

Brooke looked up at him, surprised, and the minister, taken aback, glanced down at the names before him, as though to be sure he had read correctly. He paused only a moment, though, then continued, "Do you, *Skyler* Jordan, take this woman to be your wife? To love her, honor, cherish, and keep her until death do you part?"

"I do." Skyler's voice was firm.

Skyler! Why couldn't I remember that?

"Then by the power invested in me, I now pronounce you Husband and Wife." The minister stepped back, his expression saying he was pleased with a job well done. Clasping his hands in front of him, he looked back and forth between them expectantly, his eyes twinkling.

Brooke's heart sank. They were supposed to kiss.

At first Skyler stood still and unmoving. Then he faced her.

Brooke called on every ounce of self-control in her body to prevent herself from running for the safety of the cabin. She looked up as her new husband ran a hand back through his curly blond hair and resettled his hat, a pained expression in his deep brown eyes.

After a moment more, the minister cleared his throat and frowned. "You may kiss the bride."

Skyler stepped closer, his movements deliberate and casual. Her heartbeat thundered in her ears.

He placed his hands gently on her upper arms and gazed down at her. She wondered what he could be thinking. Then, his dark eyes holding hers, he lowered his head, his lips brushing hers for the briefest of seconds.

Her tense shoulders relaxed as thankfulness coursed through her. He had not kissed her possessively as she had seen so many of the men do the day before. Maybe he really was the gentleman he appeared to be.

But her quick cynicism returned, reminding her it couldn't be true. *So! He's the type that likes to appear the gentleman in public.*

A spattering of applause greeted them as he stepped back from her, and Jack Greer called out, "Congratulations!" Then, turning to the small group of men, he gestured toward the cabin and called, "Grubs on! Come and get it."

Brooke rubbed the stem of the daisy nervously between her palms, its head twirling crazily in a yellow blur, as the men began to turn toward the cabin, leaving her alone with Skyler.

Percival was the only one who approached her. Holding out his hand, he said, "My congratulations, ma'am. This gentleman here," he nodded toward Skyler, "is one lucky fellow."

She smiled at him, allowing him to bow over her hand and offering a murmured thank you, then watched his back as headed toward dinner.

When Skyler did not move for some time, she looked toward him, suddenly aware of the rushing river only paces away. Long fingers draped casually over the front of his pockets, he stood, hands resting on slim hips, his black suit jacket pushed open. He watched her intently. *What's he thinking?* His deep brown eyes were disconcerting, and she turned her gaze to the twisting golden daisy, trying to calm the deluge of butterflies in her stomach.

But he never looked away in the long silence that followed. Finally, out of pure curiosity, she peered back up at him.

"Are you hungry?" he asked gently.

She shook her head, not trusting her voice.

"You should try and eat something; you've had a long day."

When she still did not answer, he took her elbow and turned her toward the house. "How was your trip, other than the last stretch?" He grinned down at her, even white teeth contrasting with his deeply tanned face. His smile was meant to ease her tension, she was sure, but it only added to it.

"It was fine," she managed, before her throat closed completely. This was the time she had been dreading since before the wagon train had left St. Louis. She had told herself she was strong enough to handle the abuse any man meted out to her, but memories of past anguish caused her heart to rebel against her mind's logic. She did not want to go through this again. She berated herself for allowing his apparent kindness and good looks to soften her estimation of him even in a small measure. It would only make the inevitable all the harder to bear.

As they entered the dimly lit cabin, all her fears were confirmed. Jack turned toward them with a knowing smile. "You two newlyweds will have my room for the night. There's food on the table in your room." He paused, a twinkle in his eye as he looked at Skyler, and said conspiratorially, "I didn't know if you would want to eat now or later."

Brooke suddenly wondered why she'd thought this man was so kind earlier.

Skyler nodded in his direction, touching the brim of his hat, but there was no amusement in his eyes as he placed his hand in the middle of her back and gently guided her toward the room she had used earlier.

Visions of Uncle Jackson's whip and Hank's fists danced through her mind. She didn't know what to expect from this man, but she knew that if he were anything like the men she had known, it would not be pleasant. Her heart clawed at her throat as she walked woodenly into the room, and Skyler turned and shut the door behind them. She jumped as the latch clicked and knew by the soft clearing of his throat that he had noticed.

He walked slowly to where she stood, twirling the now limp daisy between her palms, and rested his hands lightly on her upper arms. She tensed noticeably, hating herself for her weakness as tears pooled in her eyes and her legs quivered. Past experience had taught her that things only got worse if you tried to resist, so she waited helplessly.

She was surprised when he led her not to the bed but to one of the chairs at the table, easing her down into it. Taking the daisy from her, he laid it next to her plate. Squatting down on the balls of his feet, he pushed his hat back and looked into her face. She glanced at him momentarily but then turned to stare stubbornly at a knot on the pine-wood wall, not wanting to meet his dark, penetrating eyes. As he placed one hand gently on her cheek, she stiffened. With gentle pressure he turned her face toward him. She looked at him for a brief second, glanced away, and then looked back, studying him intently.

"I will not hurt you." His voice was low and tender. "I promise not to touch you until you say it's okay."

She searched his face, hoping to find truth there, yet unable to believe she would.

His face was placid as she studied him. His fingers trailed down her cheek as his hand dropped back into his lap and he reaffirmed, "I promise. You have nothing to fear from me."

Placing her hands over her face, she couldn't stop the sobs wracking her body as relief washed over her. After only a few seconds, ashamed she had shown such weakness, she stopped as suddenly as she had begun. Pulling herself together, she smoothed her tears away with the flats of her fingers, got up slowly, and walked to the bed. Removing one pillow and the top blanket, she held them out toward him. His eyes never leaving her face, he came closer to accept her offering.

He was turning away. *I have to say something!* When she touched his arm, his warmth seared her fingers and she quickly pulled back, afraid he might somehow misinterpret her intentions. She rubbed her palms nervously in a circular motion, staring at the blue water pitcher on the table by the door, trying to force the words from her throat. When she finally glanced his way and saw his questioning gaze. she was able to find her voice. "Thank you, Skyler," she whispered. She wanted to say more, but no words would come.

He nodded. "Sky. Just call me Sky."

She turned and lay down on the bed fully clothed, too emotionally exhausted to do anything else. Closing her eyes, she let sweet, peaceful sleep wash over her, somehow knowing that, if only for this one night, she could trust her new husband.

★

Chapter Three

The sky was inky black when Brooke awoke and sat up in bed. *I can't do this.* Fear coursed through her with the remembrance of the wedding ceremony. *I married a stranger!*

Slipping silently out of bed, she glanced furtively around the room as she made her way to the window, feeling along the inside of the frame for some sort of latch. *Ahhh!* There was a latch. She had missed it earlier. Carefully, so as not to make a sound, she eased open the window and crawled out. The ground was blessedly cool as her bare feet hit the grass. She had forgotten her shoes, but she couldn't go back for them now. She began to walk away from the cabin. She didn't know where she would go, but it didn't matter really. Anywhere was better than here.

Suddenly she heard a noise from behind her and an echoing voice yelled, "Hey! *Hey...hey...hey.*" Picking up her skirts, she tried to run, but the grass tangling her feet impeded her progress. It wrapped around her ankles so that every step required a huge effort. She could hear the man's pounding footsteps now.

"Come back here, you wench! Run from me, will you? I'll show you what happens to little girls that run away!"

Her dress slipped out of her hands. She tripped on the hem and fell headlong. Her palms oozed blood from the deep scratches left by the rocks, but she felt no pain. Only terror. *I must get away! Must escape! Anywhere! RUN!*

But she knew it was too late. She could hear the breathing of her pursuer now. She turned on her back, raising her forearms to protect her face. The menacing form of Uncle Jackson, with whip raised above his head, stood over her. She watched as the whip descended toward her face....

Brooke sat up with a gasp. She was still in the cabin—not

laying on the cold ground outside with Uncle Jackson standing over her. Heavy, frantic breathing filled the room, and it took her a moment to realize it was her own. She took a deliberate calming breath and forced her clenched fists to unfold. Pulling her knees up to her chest, she wrapped her arms around them and rested her forehead there. A shudder ran through her body, and she wept. Wept for the innocence she had lost so young. Wept because she was afraid of what tomorrow might bring. Wept because she couldn't banish the memories of the past that paraded through her mind one by awful one. Wept because she didn't know what else to do. Finally, after she had no more tears, she lay down on her side, curled herself into a ball, and closed her eyes to sleep.

Golden sunshine streamed into the room the next morning. She stretched and, sitting up groggily, batted her mass of tangled curls out of her face, wondering momentarily where she was. Pushing the covers back, she swung her bare feet over the edge of the bed, glancing around the room. Reality slammed home as her eyes collided with the brown gaze of Sky. A gasp escaped as memory flooded in. He looked as if he'd been up for hours.

He sat at the table, leaning nonchalantly against the wall, the front legs of his chair not touching the ground. One hand was wrapped around a mug of steaming coffee. The suit from the day before had been replaced with buckskin. His fringed, buff-colored shirt hung on his frame loosely, revealing the contour of well-defined muscles underneath and drawing her attention to his masculinity. Her eyes came to rest on the soft blond curls revealed at his opened collar, then darted away as she moved on to study his face.

He was not wearing his hat, and she found that she liked the transformation. His deep brown eyes contrasted nicely with his curly, clean-cut, blond hair, adding to the attractiveness of his angular face.

He tasted the coffee, his eyes on her over the rim of his mug, and when he set it back down on the table, an amused smile played on his lips.

I'm staring. She glanced down, a blush shading her cheeks.

Suddenly she recognized that she had been *under* the covers. Her hand went to the back of her head and her eyes widened in astonishment. Her hair pins had been removed! And her shoes! Quickly she tucked her bare feet up under her skirt and began to gather her hair at the back of her neck. *What must he think of me?* She had been too tired the night before to worry about such things. She wondered at his kind treatment of her. Never before had a man treated her with such thoughtfulness.

"Sleep well? I put your hairpins on the dressing table." He sipped his coffee casually as though nothing were out of the ordinary.

She looked away toward the window. Fear was added to her embarrassment as she noticed the late hour. "You should have woken me."

He grinned. "I tried." The legs of his chair rapped on the floor as he stood in one fluid motion, setting his coffee cup on the table, his face suddenly turning serious.

She felt the blood drain toward her toes in a sickening swirl. She had seen this same calm look on Uncle Jackson's face a thousand times right before he exploded. This man had shown her more kindness than any man she had ever known, but now it had come to a swift end.

Brooke bolted up off the bed, her whole body trembling violently. "I'm sorry!" Her voice shook. "I won't sleep so late again!"

He had begun to walk across the room, but as Brooke jumped out of bed, she saw him stop. He was only a foot from her. She tried to stand still but couldn't seem to stop shaking.

Bringing hands to his hips, he contemplated her with a strange expression. Shoulders hunched, rubbing her palms together, she watched him warily, noticing as his eyebrow winged its way upward. He stood still for a moment; then his hand moved.

She flinched, bringing her arms up and turning her head toward the wall.

"Brooke?" He stopped once more, his voice gentle.

Out of the corner of her eye she saw him slowly raise his hands, palms outward, to shoulder height.

"I'm not going to hurt you. Brooke—" he spoke her name a second time—"look at me." His movements awkwardly deliberate, he lowered his hands to his sides.

She kept her head toward the wall, feeling foolish…realizing that if he was going to strike her, he'd have done so by now. Then she turned away from the wall, her shoulders relaxing, but could not bring her eyes any higher than the blond curls at the neck of his shirt.

"Brooke." He waited, tilting his head down to gaze into her face.

She reluctantly raised her eyes. His look was tender, and a strange emotion pulsated in her heart. But she dared not hope this man's gentleness was for real.

"Brooke, I was going out." He nodded at the door, just to her left. "I would never…" His voice trailed off, as if unable to say the words. There was a slight pause; then he spoke before he moved. "I am going outside to get things ready to go. I will come back in a few minutes to check on you, okay?"

She nodded mutely, and after a moment he moved easily toward the door, leaving her alone.

Stepping out of the room, Sky leaned against the closed door, tipped his head back and closed his eyes. She had thought he was going to…hit her? For *oversleeping?* The thought was agonizing. What had she endured in the past?

He knew she'd had a nightmare in the night. He had been awake when she sat up with a start and began to cry. He had done the only thing he knew to do that would not frighten her. He had lain still in his bed on the floor and prayed for her.

Uncertainty assailed him as he realized he didn't know one thing about her background. Yet, without a doubt, he had done the right thing in marrying her. If Jason were married to the beautiful young woman in the room behind him, her future might be the same as her past must have been. But Sky determined to give her better. He would protect her.

The thought of Jason moved him to action, and he headed outside to saddle up. When he got home, Jason would either be blind with rage, dangerously calm, *or maybe he will have seen the truth of the words I spoke to him.* That was the dangerous side of Jason Jordan these days. One never knew how he'd react in any given situation; he might be explosive and volatile one time, yet composed and lethally quiet the next. But always under the surface, in the last several years, ran a cruel, vengeful current of maliciousness.

He prayed Jason would listen to the truth as he let his thoughts wander back to the night he had learned of his cousin's plan....

After arriving at home that night, he'd spent a good deal of time in prayer. Heaven knew he hadn't wanted to get involved. He'd argued with himself that it really was not his problem and, deciding he'd better just leave well enough alone, had gone to bed to try to sleep.

He had been on the verge of drifting off when the face of Victoria Snyder entered his mind. He opened his eyes, staring up into the darkness overhead.

What if it were Victoria? He sat bolt upright, his heart pounding in his chest. Victoria, his childhood sweetheart, had a caring and sweet spirit. What if this girl was like Victoria? The very thought of a girl like Victoria in Jason's control was unthinkable. He would never be able to live with himself if he didn't try to do something.

Getting up, he quickly penned two identical notes, then saddled his stallion and headed back to town. Jason, a permanent resident at Jed's place, would probably be passed out in his bed by this time of night.

Praying for wisdom as he pulled up in front of the darkened edifice, Sky swung down and headed for the door. He banged loudly, then leaned his hands, fingers tapping, against the doorjamb, waiting for Jed to answer. Feeling impatient and wanting to complete the unpleasant task at hand, he pounded on the door again after only a moment.

"Comin', Comin'! Hold your britches on!" Jed hollered from inside. When he opened the door and saw Sky, he frowned. "Shoulda taken care o' business 'fore you left in such an all-fired hurry, 'stead o' disturbin' people in the middle o' the night. I knew you'd be back." Stepping back, he nodded toward the door that led to the sleeping quarters and grumbled, "Go on. Jason's in his room same as always. Conked out with his bottle o' whiskey."

Sky stepped past Jed, the sound of his cowboy boots loud in the stillness of the room. He did not bother to knock on Jason's door. He probably wouldn't wake up anyway. Opening the door, he stepped inside. Jason lay sprawled on the bed in the corner, snoring loudly, his usual bottle of booze grasped in one hand, his still-booted feet crossed at the ankle and hanging over the end.

"Jason, wake up." Sky's voice was firm. There was no response, so he grasped the toe of Jason's bottom foot and threw his feet off of the bed. They landed on the floor with a thud, but all Jason did was mumble something unintelligible, smack his lips, and turn his face to the wall.

Seeing that a more drastic measure was needed, Sky scanned the room.

Picking up the full pitcher of water that sat by the wash basin, he threw its contents in his cousin's face. Bolting upright, sputtering and choking, Jason looked wildly around the room, water dripping from his double chin as the bottle of whiskey clattered to the floor. "What the blazes!" He started to reach for his gun belt slung carelessly over the head of the bed, but Sky got there first, pulling it out of his reach.

Recognition dawned on Jason's face as he regarded Sky through glassy eyes. "Shhkyy." The word was slurred as he blinked hard, no emotion in his voice. "What are you doin' here?" He ran a hand over his wet face in an apparent attempt to clear his vision.

"We need to talk."

Jason started to lie down, waving a careless hand in his direction. "Come back insha mornin'."

"No, we will talk now." Sky had him by the lapels of his grimy red shirt, pulling him to his feet. Jason stood there, swaying, then stumbled after Sky as he turned and left the room.

Back in the main room, Jed, who had stoked up the fire, waited for them.

"Coffee's on," he said with a meaningful look in Sky's direction, nodding to the fireplace.

Sky pulled out a chair, motioning for Jason to sit. Walking to the fire, he poured a steaming mug of thick, black coffee and set it on the table in front of his inebriated cousin. Then, pouring himself a cup, he sat down next to him, turning his chair so he could look into Jason's face.

He let Jason sip his coffee for several minutes before he said anything. "I'll buy her from you." The words were spoken bluntly. Money was the only thing that might sway Jason's mind.

Across the room Jed, who had been leaning one arm on the mantle, stood erect in surprise.

"Wha…? Who?" asked Jason, his befuddled mind apparently only beginning to clear.

"The girl you are supposed to marry tomorrow. How much did you pay for her?"

Jason rubbed the heels of his hands against his bleary eyes, leaning his elbows on the table. Then, looking at Sky, remembrance flooded his face. "I'm getting married tomorrow." The words emerged as if this were news to him.

Sky, one hand wrapped around his mug, sipped quietly, waiting for what he had said to sink in. He did not have long to wait.

"You want to buy her?" Jason rubbed a hand over his face, the stubble on his cheeks rasping as his hand passed over it. He picked up his coffee, took a large swig of the scalding brew, and grimaced.

"How much did you pay for her?" Sky asked again.

"Seventy-five bucks. Fifty to her uncle and twenty-five to the wagon master who fetched her out here. Plus an extra five to the minister, so he'd do the ceremony at Greer's Ferry."

Sky swirled his coffee, staring into it. He still had his seed money. He had put a lot of work into the south field, hoping to plant it in wheat come spring. He set his cup down on the table. "I'll pay you two hundred for her."

Jason snorted. "Not likely. Five hundred maybe."

Without hesitation Sky extended his hand. "It's a deal." It was all the money he had.

Somewhat befuddled, Jason shook his hand, sealing the deal.

Taking two pieces of paper from his shirt pocket, Sky placed them on the table. "You got pen and ink, Jed?"

Jed was gone only briefly, returning with a blue ink bottle and a turkey-feather pen. Carefully dipping the pen into the ink, Sky filled in something and then handed Jason the pen, shoving the papers toward him. "Sign them."

Jason grinned at him. "Where's my money?"

Pulling the money out of his shirt pocket, Sky laid it on top of the papers. A light danced in Jason's eyes as he picked up the money and fingered it.

Then, taking up the pen, he scrawled his signature across both the papers.

Motioning to Jed to come to the table, Sky handed him the pen and he signed his name underneath Jason's.

A weight lifted off Sky's shoulders. He had freed the girl, and he had a signed paper to prove it. Carefully folding one paper and placing it back in his chest pocket, he walked over toward the fire.

Jed busied himself with stoking the blaze but paused as Jason stood from the table.

Scratching his belly, he yawned loudly and shuffled across the floor, heading back to his room.

Pouring himself a cup of the black brew on the fire, Jed looked at Sky. "Well, ya done it now. Whatcha gonna do with her?"

"Do with the girl? Send her home, of course. I don't want her," Sky spoke as he handed the other paper to Jed.

"Hmmph," Jed snorted, "I can see you ain't thought things through very good. Ain't no wagon trains gonna be headin' east till spring. What you gonna do with her inbetwixt time?"

Sky brought one hand up to rub the back of his neck, staring into the fire in thought. "Send her to Lewiston maybe. She could stay there."

"Hmmph. 'Thout a chaperone? Know what's gonna happen to a poor girl left to fend fer herself midst a pack of wolves, don't you? She be et up, I tell ya. Taken advantage of, sure as shootin'. Hmmph, Lewiston he says!" The last sentence was aimed at the fireplace mantel, with a gesture of his hand in Sky's direction.

Again the face of Victoria Snyder jarred him to action. The very thought of Victoria all alone in a strange town and left to fend for herself made his mouth dry. "I could bring her up here, I guess. She could stay out at my place till spring."

Jed rolled his eyes in derision and smacked his forehead twice in succession with his palm. "An' who'd have the girl after he be findin' out that she lived in a cabin in the woods with a fellow for six months? You got to think o' the girl's reputation! You're just gonna have to marry that girl. Ain't no two ways about it."

"What's the difference? Whether I marry her or not, she's still going back east come spring."

"I ain't never said nothin' about sendin' the girl back. That be all your idea. You get married, you do it for keeps. Love'll come. Mark my words, love'll come." With that, Jed threw the dregs of his coffee into the fire and stalked out of the room, signifying the end of the discussion.

Sky stared into the fire for a long time. Finally, he began to pray for the strength to do what needed to be done and exited quietly to ride for home.

Sky slept late the next morning and had just gotten up when he heard the irate curses of his cousin as he stormed into the yard. When Sky stepped out onto the small porch of his cabin, he could see that Jason's horse was lathered and heaving, proof he'd ridden him hard the whole way from town.

Jason jumped from the saddle even before the steed came to a stop. Stumbling across the yard, he glared at Sky. "You thieving low-life scum!" He swore. "You can't have her! I don't care what I said. I don't care how much you paid for her. You can't have her; she's mine!" His chest heaved, and his balled-up fists shook at his sides as he glowered at Sky.

Sky merely raised one eyebrow and smiled. "Good morning, Jason. Not having a bad day, I hope?" He'd been expecting something like this. "Can I get you a cup of coffee?"

"You're a cheating scoundrel!" Jason's tone was disgruntled as he started toward Sky again, but some of his anger seemed to have dissipated.

Raising one hand palm outward, Sky spoke as his cousin stopped. "Maybe I should read you something." He pulled one of the notes penned the night before out of his pocket. Unfolding it carefully, he began to read,

"I, Jason Jordan, do solemnly swear that the following statement is true and correct. On the night of August the 2nd, 1885, I sold to my cousin, Skyler Jordan, all rights to do as he sees fit with my betrothed, a mail-order bride due to arrive at Greer's Ferry on August the 3rd, 1885. The sum thereof being the amount of $500."

Sky folded the letter, tucking it back into his pocket. "It's signed by you and witnessed by Jed. There is nothing you can do about it. And," he added meaningfully, "Jed has a copy in his safe." His tone softened at the dejected slump of Jason's shoulders. "Sorry, Jace. I couldn't let you marry her."

Jason stared off into the trees. "You've always been better than me, haven't you, Sky?"

"Jason." Sky sighed. "I just believe that what we were taught when we were growing up is true. Somewhere down in your heart you have to know that the way you are living is wrong. I can't believe you could throw all Grandma Jordan's teaching to the wind."

Jason stared at the ground, rubbing the back of his neck. All the fight seemed to have drained out of him.

"I know you're miserable, Jace. I can see it in your eyes,

especially at times like this. You can't go on living like you are. You know too much of the Word."

Jason scuffed an arc in the dust with the toe of his boot. Then he huffed, "Gram. She always made us memorize the Word."

Sky grinned and leaned his shoulder into a post. "You always knew the verses better than me and got the first warm cookie from the oven."

An imperceptible smile softened Jason's lips. "You heard from her lately?"

Sky nodded, knowing how much Jason loved Grandma Jordan. She had raised him after his parents died.

Jason had always been one of Grandma Jordan's favorites growing up. It had hurt her to no end when Jason had turned his back on God. Though it pained her not to write him, she had decided that would be best. She wrote to Sky every month but had asked him not to share with her about Jason unless it was good news.

"Gram is doing fine. She writes that she prays for you constantly. And that Marquis is doing well, although she misses you." Sky watched him carefully. Were those tears in his eyes?

Jason quickly turned away. "I won't fight you about the girl. She's probably gonna be more trouble than she's worth anyway." He started to turn toward his lathered horse.

"Jason?"

Jason paused and looked back over his shoulder.

"Want some coffee?"

Turning, Jason considered him for a beat, as if judging whether the offer was genuine. Then he shrugged. "Sure."

Sky had ridden away an hour later, leaving Jason sitting at his table reading all of his letters from Grandma Jordan.

Now as he finished saddling his stallion, he prayed this would be a turning point in the life of Jason Jordan. Adding a prayer for his new wife, he headed back toward the cabin to see if she was ready.

Chapter Four

B rooke, Jack Greer, Percival, and the minister sat around the table chatting easily. The burly mountain man had gone on the night before, and the stage driver and the man who rode shotgun were outside hitching the horses to the stage in preparation for the ride back to Lewiston.

Brooke, her back to the door, tasted her tea. What she wouldn't give for a nice cup of strong coffee. Uncle Jackson was strictly a coffee person, but he had insisted she drink tea "like a lady." On the wagon train west, she'd refused to drink anything but coffee and had developed a taste for it.

"Tell me a little about your trip out west," said Percival. "You said you came out the old-fashioned way, by wagon, right?"

"Yes."

"Why? The train would have been much faster."

"Our wagon master brings lots of mail-order brides out west. Sometimes he comes by train. This time, wagons were cheaper because there were so many of us."

"I always wanted to join a wagon train just to find out what they're like."

Brooke's eyes twinkled. "There's something you don't know about, Percival?"

He laughed good-naturedly. "My mother always tells me that I talk too much. So, what was the most interesting thing about your trip?"

Brooke smiled. "Actually, I learned a lot about this area from you yesterday. It might come in handy someday' you never know." She took a sip of tea. "Miss Emily Donaldson was the most interesting thing on the trip, I guess."

The men looked at her questioningly.

"She was an older woman who was rather—" Brooke searched

for kind words for the woman who'd been the most like a mother to her on the trip— "accustomed to having her way."

The men smiled knowingly.

"The wagon master often had to help her out of situations she got into because she never listened to what he said." She stared at the wall. "I miss her."

Sky entered the cabin through the outer door, which had been left standing ajar to allow the cool morning air in.

"So, what was the funniest thing that happened to her?" asked Percival. Brooke, her back to Sky, chuckled softly, and Sky stilled, knowing he was seeing her relaxed for the first time. "Miss Donaldson drove our wagon. There was supposed to be a man to drive it, but he didn't show up at the last minute, and she said she would do it. We had come to some river—the Platte, I think. Anyway, she didn't think that the place where we were crossing was the best place to cross. She thought another place just downriver would be smoother. But Harry—he was the wagon master—said it wasn't a good place to ford. Emily couldn't pass it up, though. She always thought she knew best. I made her let me down, and I rode the ferry across. But she pulled out of line when Harry wasn't looking and started across the river. She wasn't five feet out when our horses' feet went out from under them, and the wagon started to float downriver."

Brooke chuckled again. "I shouldn't laugh. She could have really been hurt, and I was so scared for her at the time, but I'll never be able to think of Emily Donaldson without seeing her dancing on the seat of our floating wagon, her skirt up around her waist, her bloomers showing for all the world to see. She was screaming, 'Harry! You were right! Save me! Harry! You were right! Save me!'" Brooke mimicked her screams in falsetto.

Laughter filled the room.

At that instant Brooke saw movement out of the corner of her eye. Turning, she found Sky's gaze fixed on her. His eyes darted to Percival for a moment, slight suspicion there, but quickly came back to hers. He didn't laugh, but merriment danced in the depth of his eyes, a light smile playing on his mouth. Brooke quickly pulled her eyes from his. *Is he going to think I was flirting?* Memory of Hank and a similar situation assailed her, and her heart beat faster.

"Jack," Sky said to the ferryman when the chuckles had died down, "thanks for everything. We should be heading home now." The men shook hands, then he turned to Brooke. "Ready?"

"Yes. Just let me get my bag."

She started for the bedroom, but Sky preceded her. Her small bag rested on the bed. He picked it up and asked, "Anything else?"

"No." She shook her head.

They went back into the main room, and Brooke bade everyone farewell. Percival lingered in a slow bow over her hand.

Sky shuffled his feet and took her elbow but offered, "Come visit us sometime," with a tip of his hat toward Percival.

Percival stepped back and smiled, his eyes never leaving her face. "I think I just might."

Sky glanced down, a momentary frown creasing his forehead. But just as quickly as it appeared it was gone, and he pressed a hand to her back, guiding her to the door.

The sunlight shone golden bright, glinting off the surface of the rushing river as they stepped outside. Brooke noted with some unease that only one horse stood in sight, and Sky was tying her bag to the pommel of the saddle.

Sky swung up and settled easily just behind the saddle. "Do you ride?" he asked, looking down at her.

She swallowed and nodded.

And before she knew what was happening Jack Greer had her by the waist and had handed her up to Sky. She hooked one leg around the saddle horn naturally, although she preferred to ride astride. Uncle Jackson had caught her twice, and both times she had received a beating for behaving in such an unladylike fashion.

Sky scooted up close behind the cantle and reached around her to take the reins. The hardness of his chest and the brush of his muscled arms as he held the reins sent her heart into an erratic flutter. She did not like these muddled feelings. One moment, she felt terrified, and the next, she was hopelessly attracted. And caring for a man was something she had promised herself she would never do again. The repercussions of it on one's emotions were too painful after the inevitable betrayal. She took a deep breath and tried to still the beating of her heart, but he began to talk, and she found that the deep resonance of his voice did funny things to her as well.

"I should tell you that I am not Jason, the man you agreed to marry when you came west."

She had suspected as much yesterday at the ceremony but had been too overwhelmed to question him.

There was a long silence and finally she said, "I never agreed to marry anyone. My uncle made the agreement, and I don't suppose he'll much care as long as he got his money."

"I see," he said.

She wondered at his strange tone. It didn't help that she couldn't see his face.

"Well, just so you know a little about me, my full name is Skyler Tyrell Jordan. I was born and raised on a ranch in the Willamette Valley of Oregon. My parents are Rachel and Sean, and I have one brother named Rocky and one sister named Sharyah. All of my family still lives in Oregon, so you won't meet them for some time."

Brooke was relieved to hear this.

Sky continued, "Other than that, there's not much to tell about me. I own a small farm on up the hill a ways and have lived in this area for about five years."

She wanted to ask who Jason was but kept quiet and began to take in the scenery around her.

The trail wound its way up the opposite side of the gorge that the stage had plunged into yesterday. It was narrow and dusty. Tall evergreen trees shaded it in most areas, but some of the hillsides grew nothing but huge expanses of yellow daisies and an occasional patch of scrub brush. The droning of bees could be heard amid the stillness of the day, and birds twittered happily, darting in and out amongst the trees as they chased one another. After yesterday's long trying day, the warmth of the sun, the creaking of saddle leather, and the sounds of nature combined to make her very tired.

Her head nodded, and she jerked it up, hoping Sky had not noticed. What would he think of her? She had slept in this morning, only to be falling asleep not an hour down the road! She wanted to sing to keep herself awake but was too embarrassed, so she had to content herself with pinching her arm every few seconds. But the pinching didn't work very well, and her head nodded for a second time.

Sky slipped one arm around her, pulling her back against his chest and pressing her head back onto his shoulder. "Rest."

Everything in her urged resistance, but it felt so good to lean back and relax that she gave up the fight.

"That's better," He whispered in her ear, "Go to sleep. You've had a long couple of days."

Brooke didn't awaken until they splashed across a creek. She opened her eyes, perplexed for a moment, then realized how heavily she was leaning on Sky and jolted upright. Hoping she had not caused him undue discomfort, she sat forward and looked around, realizing they had leveled out at the top of the ridge. A long gently rolling plain stretched before her, golden heads of grain nodding in the breeze. Interspersed here and there amongst the grain, clusters of yellow pine stood in stark contrast to the brilliant blue of the sky beyond. A single white cloud traced its way through the blue, drawing Brooke's eyes upward.

"It's beautiful," she murmured.

"Welcome home." Sky's words were soft. "The house is just beyond that knoll." He pointed up ahead.

Brooke wondered at the word *home*. Would this place ever really feel like a home to her? How long would she be here? Would this man who had married her find she wasn't satisfactory and send her back to Uncle Jackson, demanding his money back? Or, worse yet, would he simply abandon her, leaving her to her own fate? That's what Uncle Jackson would do. She pondered these questions until they topped the knoll that Sky had indicated, and he reined the horse to a stop.

She could see a small log cabin nestled amongst some trees setting back against the rise of a hill. Off to the left stood another structure that she assumed to be the barn, a corral extending off the side. Several chickens pecked and scratched in the grass, looking for choice morsels, and a cow lowed from the barn.

Sky had started down the hill now, and she turned her attention back to the house. It had at least two windows, one on the front to the left of the door and one around the left side of the house. The house faced south, she noted with satisfaction, so there would be plenty of sunlight during the day. The covered porch had a split-log rail along the front and sides with a break in the middle where the stairs led up to the door. A pile of wood was stacked on the porch to the right of the door. At the back of the house, she could make out the top of a rock chimney.

Everything in sight looked neat and clean, from the evenly trimmed shrubs at the corners of the house and the carefully swept yard, to the cedar shakes on the roof that were free of moss and other lichens.

She sighed, now knowing she would have the strength to endure this man. She had hoped the man she was pledged to marry would be clean and hard working. She had even dared, on a few occasions, to hope he would not be cruel. But no matter what came her way, this house was enough. It would be her refuge. She loved it already. She would take time to find joy in this one little thing. A nice home. It was enough to bolster her belief in her own strength and ability to persevere.

She was only just now in her relief and thankfulness beginning to see what a toll the stress from this situation had taken on her. She had not been herself since Uncle Jackson had come to her and told her she would be traveling west in two weeks' time to be married to a man she had never met. She had reasoned it would be doubly humiliating to be beaten and bruised by a total stranger. But at least the pain of having loved him would not be there, she tried to comfort herself.

Sky pulled the black stallion to a stop in the yard in front of the house. Sliding agilely off the back of the horse, he came to her side and offered her a hand. She slid to the ground but immediately realized that her leg, which had been wrapped around the saddle horn, had fallen asleep. Knowing she would fall on her face if she tried to move, she tried to look casual as she stood unmoving on her good leg glancing around the yard, but Sky eyed her questioningly as he untied her bag from the saddle.

Turning to her, he took her elbow and stepped toward the house. When she didn't move, he stopped and raised an eyebrow.

"My leg—" she gestured helplessly—"fell asleep. I'll be able to move in a second."

Without hesitation he set her bag on the ground and swept her up into his arms. Her heart lurched as her arms reflexively clasped about his neck.

Carrying her up the steps and across the threshold of the house, he grinned down at her. "I guess this is the way newlyweds should enter their home anyway."

To cover her fear and confusion, she scanned the interior of the little cabin. The single room functioned as kitchen, dining room, living room, and bedroom all in one. To the right of the doorway against the front wall of the house, was a small square table with two straight-back chairs at opposite sides, and a window just behind it on the side wall. A cupboard sat on the floor at the rear right corner, its back to the side wall. Above it hung a shelf stacked with several pots and pans, some dishes, and a pile of poorly-folded white towels. Pegs drilled into the wall below the shelf held an assortment of utensils and a metal wash basin. On top of the cupboard sat two crocks.

In the middle of the back wall, stood a rotund wood stove, a copper kettle on its polished black surface. Behind it, and on the floor underneath, a rock facade of white quartz stones mortared together formed a fire shield. The mantle had been constructed of flat rocks set into the wall horizontally. *It's beautiful*, she thought as her eyes continued to scan the room.

To the left of the stove was the room's only bed. A colorful quilt smoothly spread over it, and there was a window just above it. To the left of the door were a cane chair and a loveseat that looked to have been made from stripped ash. The color of the wood was exquisite, but the chairs didn't look very comfortable since they had no cushions. The room's third window graced the wall by the cane chairs, casting a brilliant pool of light on the plank floor.

She finished her perusal of the interior as Sky set her into one of the chairs at the dining table. He sat across from her and began to stack a scattered group of letters. "I want you to make yourself at home here." He gestured to the cupboard. "There is food in the cupboard as well as in the cellar out back. I will give you a tour of the place as soon as I take care of the stock. If you find that there is anything you need, please don't hesitate to ask. Pierce City is not too far away, and we can get some things there, but it may be that I will have to make a trip to Lewiston." He shrugged, glancing around the room. "It's not much, I suppose, but I hope you will be comfortable."

She tried to smile reassuringly. "I'll be fine, thank you."

With that he stood, set the bundled stack of letters on the mantle, and went outside. Returning a few moments later, he set her bag inside the door along with another small satchel she had not noticed before. When he went back out to take care of the stock, Brooke realized she hadn't moved since he had placed her in her chair. Her leg was no longer asleep, so she had no excuse, but she felt dazed. She still couldn't believe this man had not mistreated her in any way…had not even spoken roughly. Shrugging, she tried to push away these thoughts.

Getting up, she crossed to the cupboard, remembering it was past noon and Sky would probably be hungry; she knew hunger pangs gnawed at her. Finding some bread, butter, and a chunk of dried meat, she made some sandwiches, placing them on two of the speckled, black tin plates.

She was tempted to go ahead and eat without him but decided it would be better to wait. He came in a little while later and eyed the fare hungrily. "Would you like some milk?" he asked.

"Yes, that would be nice. I thought of going to look for the cellar but didn't know where to start."

"I'll be right back. We can eat, and then I will show you around the place. Sound good?"

She nodded, setting two of the tin cups on the table by their plates.

When he had returned with the milk, he sat down and glanced across the table, holding out his hand to her. She eyed his hand, and he said, "When I was growing up, we always held hands around the table as we said grace. Do you mind?" His tone was not condescending, merely questioning.

She placed her small hand in his palm and bowed her head, but as he began to pray, she studied him with surprise.

His prayer was not a memorized text but a true communion of the heart with God, giving Him thanks for the food, for Brooke's safety as she had traveled, and for their future together as husband and wife. He prayed that God would lead them, guiding them closer to Him, and then closed in Jesus' name.

He picked up his sandwich and had it halfway to his mouth when he evidently noted her surprise.

She wanted to hide her emotion but something held her in check. "Do you really believe God cares?"

"Yes, I do. The Bible says He does." His brown eyes showed genuine interest in her question.

"And so if the Bible says it, that makes it so?" Her tone held more than a little sarcasm.

Sky set his sandwich back on his plate. "Yes." It was a simple statement of faith. "Brooke, I want to talk to you about this morning."

She had not expected this so soon. Picking up her sandwich, she took a bite. Her past and how it related to her reaction this morning was the last thing she wanted to talk about. Trying to keep her face free of emotion, she chewed slowly.

Sky raked a hand through his hair. "I don't know what you've been through in the past, but I could tell by your reaction to me this morning that it probably hasn't been pleasant." He watched her intently.

She took another bite of sandwich, trying to ignore the pain squeezing her heart.

"I just want to tell you again that I would never," he paused, "*will* never hit or abuse you in any way. I meant what I said to you last night; I will not touch you until you say it's okay." He placed his hands on the table. "I will not touch you in *any* way. Understand?"

Brooke hated the tears that pooled in her eyes. She nodded mutely, but her skepticism rose to the fore. *The probability of his keeping his word is about as good as finding an oasis in the middle of a desert.*

He sat back, apparently satisfied, but still eyed her as though unable to tell what she was thinking.

She blinked the tears away and turned back to her food, as did he. Finishing his sandwich in five bites, he got up and made himself two more. Brooke, somewhat wide-eyed, made a note to make him several sandwiches in the future and hoped he wouldn't be too irritated that she had not done so this time.

Sky watched Brooke as she took in the cellar he'd just shown to her. Cut back into the side of the hill behind the house, it had large, heavy doors that kept the room cool on the hottest of summer days and provided enough insulation so that even on very cold winter days the milk did not freeze.

As he stood waiting for her, he contemplated their earlier conversation. "Do you really believe God cares?" she had asked. *Lord, I don't know what this woman has been through in the past, but it's obviously been painful for her. Help me to be able to show her Your love. Bring her to know You, Lord. And help me to be thankful. Help me to see the good side of things—not just the inconvenient, uncomfortable side. There are things to be thankful for; please open my mind to them. Help me to be sensitive to this woman. To be kind, thoughtful, and caring. Help me to see Your blessings, Lord. Bring us through this difficult time.*

He stared off at the surrounding countryside. Things to be thankful for...*at least I like her.* She could have been loud, pushy, and boisterous, or demure, coy, and deceitful, but none of these qualities evidenced themselves. From the moment he'd laid eyes on her, a protective spirit had risen in him. She was somehow like a wounded animal he needed to nurture back to health. Her blue-green eyes wore a hunted, fearful look that he wanted to soothe.

His thoughts turned to Jason. *I wonder where he is?* Thankfulness that he had had the opportunity to talk to his cousin about the Lord welled up in his heart. Jason could have reacted in any number of different ways, but God had worked it out so that Sky could remind him of his past relationship with Jesus. *Yes, God is good.*

He brought his attention back to the present, his dark eyes resting on Brooke. She tucked a wind-blown curl behind her ear with one small hand, contentment on her face. *I can be thankful that...* But he would not let himself finish the thought. The fact he found Brooke enticingly beautiful was an issue he didn't yet feel ready to deal with.

She turned to him with a smile, gesturing to the cellar and the surrounding buildings. "It's all very lovely. You've worked hard to build such a nice place."

Another thing to be thankful for. She understands that it takes a lot of hard work to make a place like this. He glanced around. "Yes, I have, but it has been enjoyable." He didn't add that it might be more enjoyable now that there was someone else with whom to share his accomplishments. "Would you like to see the barn?"

She nodded.

"When I first started this place, I lived in the barn until I had enough logs cut to build the house. I have since converted the room that I stayed in into a tack room." He walked toward the barn, her soft footsteps following him.

The earthy smell of cut hay, manure, and animal sweat

assailed them as they stepped into the dim interior. Sky had always loved the smells of a barn. The aroma brought back many happy memories of days gone by. He chatted easily as he showed her around.

"This is old Bess. She had a calf this last spring. He's out in the pasture right now. She'd be there herself except she has a sore leg." The cow peered at them over her back with cinnamon eyes, lowing mournfully, bits of straw hanging out of the corners of her mouth. Sky slapped her on the rump as he passed, continuing his tour. "I keep a couple of steers for plowing and those kinds of things, and a pack mule, but they are all out to pasture. I have a small herd of cattle that I'm slowly building up. I hope to one day quit farming and turn to ranching." He gestured to the stallion they had ridden up the hill that morning. "Geyser there is the only horse I've got. I also hope to be able to get another horse next spring." His mind went momentarily to the money he had paid to Jason. It had been all of his savings, and he wondered how they would make it through the winter, much less buy a horse come spring, but he said nothing to her, knowing she would feel somehow responsible.

"Geyser?"

Her question brought him back.

He chuckled. "The first time I saw that horse, I was down in Lewiston. I was at a roundup, and his owner made a bet with all the men standing around that if anyone could ride him, they could have him. If you fell off, you owed five dollars. A couple of them tried it. When that first man hit the saddle and they took the blinders off his eyes, he shot straight up into the air just like a geyser I saw over in Montana one time. That first fellow didn't last more than two seconds in the saddle, and the second one didn't do much better. I let a couple more guys go before I gave him a try. I figured he'd be a little tired out by then." He grinned. "He wasn't, but I won, and his owner got twenty dollars out of the deal. I can't think of a name that would fit him better. He's just like a geyser. You never know when he's going to erupt." He grimaced. "He's thrown me more times than I care to admit. He's getting a little older now, though, and doesn't feel his oats so often."

During this recital, Geyser had come to the door of the stall and put his head out. Brooke stood petting his muzzle, one hand resting lightly on his neck. She crooned nonsensical words to the horse, and Sky's heart contracted at the sight. What was this feeling? He knew he didn't love this woman. Not yet. But the way his blood pounded through his veins, he knew that if he allowed himself, he *could* love her. Very easily. At times like this, when he saw her at ease, he realized just how tense she usually was. She always had her guard up, as though on the alert against hurt of any kind. What did her past hold? He only knew that the desire to comfort and protect her grew stronger the more he observed her true spirit.

She glanced around the barn, then up to the loft. A smile played on her lips. "My sister and I used to play in the loft of our barn for hours." She turned back to the horse, but her eyes had a faraway look, and Sky knew she was seeing into the past. "We would dig tunnels in the hay, making passageways and rooms. One time, we took Mother's best silver tea service up there and had a genuine tea party." Her smile broadened as she turned back to Sky. "We got in trouble for losing the sugar bowl. We never did find it. The last time I remember playing with Jessica, we looked for it again." A sadness washed over her face. "Well," she made an attempt to brighten her countenance, "is there more to the barn? Maybe I should go in and start dinner." Her guard rose back into place.

"Not much more. Just let me show you the chicken coop, and then you can head in if you want." He led her to a small door that opened on the side wall of the barn. As they came out on the southern side of the barn, the sun shone brightly, reflecting off the water in the trough a few feet away. A lean-to stood against the side of the barn with a wooden ramp leading up to the opening where the chickens went in and out. "Since I don't have too many chickens, I made the coop small." He lifted the hinged roof of the structure.

A hen, surprised by the burst of sunlight, launched through the opening, cackling, flapping, and sending feathers flying through the air.

Brooke jumped with a sharp intake of breath, her hand going to her heart.

Sky smiled. "Sorry. You okay?" When she nodded with a chuckle, he continued, "I made the roof hinged so it would be easy to collect the eggs. All the roosts are on top, so all you have to do is reach down in and gather them." She came closer and peered inside the coop, then looked up at him.

"Thank you for showing me around. I think I'll head in and fix dinner now."

"That's fine. I have a couple of chores to finish, and then I'll be right in."

As Brooke gathered dinner ingredients, she couldn't seem to keep her mind off the double bed in the corner. He had said he wouldn't touch her, but there was only one bed. Fear crept back into her soul. He had been kind and courteous all the time she'd known him, but experience had taught her that men were explosive, choosing to do whatever they wanted, often on the spur of the moment's whim.

Nervousness made her fidgety, and she jumped when the door clicked open. If Sky noticed, he did not let on but went straight to the wash basin and cleaned up as she placed dinner on the table. Thankfully, Darcy, Uncle Jackson's cook, had taught her to prepare several different dishes. Tonight she had relied on an easy favorite—beef stew with potatoes and carrots. Hot biscuits with butter and honey also graced the table.

"Do…do you prefer coffee with your dinner or m-milk or… water?" Brooke stammered.

He dried his hands on the towel, watching her as though he knew something was bothering her. "Coffee is fine." He nodded at the pot and took his chair, his back to the main part of the room.

She moved to the stove, picked up the coffee pot, and let out a yelp of pain. Reflexively, she let go of the searing handle, spilling the contents all over the stove and floor.

Sky was at her side in an instant. "Here, let me see that."

He took her hand into his, examining her palm and adding to the turmoil already churning in her heart. Her pulse began to race at the tender touch of his hand. Averting her eyes from his expression of concern, she focused on the droplets of coffee that sizzled and danced across the stovetop, sending steam wafting through the air. On the stone firebreak. On the patchwork quilt covering the bed. On anything to get her mind off the way his touch curled her stomach and increased her breathing. A floorboard creaked under their feet, and somewhere outside an owl sent a lonely call into the night.

Only a split second had passed, but she couldn't stand his closeness any longer. Snatching her hand away, she rubbed it down the side of her skirt. "I'm okay, really. I'll clean up this mess," she gestured to the spilled coffee, "and put on another pot. You go ahead and eat while the food is hot."

He shook his head, leading her to her chair and gently pushing her into it. "Don't move," he commanded as he headed out the door. "I'm going to get a bucket of cold water."

Brooke felt a surge of irritation. *Who is he to tell me what to do?* She got up the instant he was out of sight and, crossing the few steps to the stove, began to clean up the mess. Mopping up the coffee, she wrung it out into a bowl, her burnt hand stinging unmercifully every time the warm coffee soaked through the towel and touched the seared flesh. But she kept on, willing herself to forget the sensations his touch had sent coursing through her.

Only when she heard Sky come back in the door did she pause to consider what her impetuous actions might cost her. She had just cleaned up the last of the mess and was down on her hands and knees wiping up the floor when Sky spoke from behind her.

"I told you not to move."

She tensed, half expecting a blow, but then realized that his voice had been gentle.

He took her elbow to lead her back to her chair.

Embarrassment at her own carelessness and anger with herself for allowing the feelings this man evoked sparked her temper. She jerked her elbow from his grasp. "Someone had to clean this up—" she gestured emphatically to the stove and floor, "—before it soaked into everything and made stains that wouldn't come out!"

When the surprise on his face registered, she felt chagrined. She walked back to her seat and sat down.

Coming over beside her, he set a small bucket on the table. She obediently put her stinging hand in the cool water, watching as he set about making a second pot of coffee. When he sat back down, she said, "I'm sorry, I shouldn't have lost my temper."

A twinkle lit his eyes. "Think nothing of it, Mrs. Jordan. I'm sure there will be plenty of times in the future when I will need to be put in my place. That temper of yours might come in handy."

Plenty of times in the future? Suddenly, the morrow seemed to stretch out for eternity. Could she live with this emotional stress for the rest of her life?

He ladled stew into both of their bowls, and they ate in silence, the only sounds in the room the metallic *tink* of silverware on tin bowls and the perking of the coffee. When she finished eating, she removed her burnt hand from the water, finding that it felt much better.

Still, the closer it got to the time to turn in for the night the more nervous she became. She was attracted to this man like she'd been to Hank at first, and the thought that he might turn out to be like Hank scared her more than she would admit, even to herself.

As she washed dishes at the sideboard, Sky read an old paper in the cane chair by the door. But when she dropped the second dish with a metallic clatter, she heard him get up, his stealthy footsteps coming nearer. He spoke from directly behind her. "Brooke?"

She stilled, not daring to look at him.

"Brooke, look at me please."

Slowly she turned and fixed her eyes on his intense face, her wet, soapy hands held over the wash basin.

He stood casually with his hands behind his back. "Do I look like a liar to you?"

She was caught off guard by the question and could only shake her head.

"I made you a promise. Last night and again this morning. I always keep my promises, Brooke. You have nothing to fear from me." He slid one hand over his head, his eyes intent on hers. "I have made myself a bed in the barn. I hope you will be comfortable in here. Feel free to look around if you need anything. If it's here, you are welcome to use it."

With that he bade her good night and, picking up his bag by the door, went out into the night.

Brooke finished the dishes and crossed to the bed, tears of thankfulness coursing down her cheeks. *I don't deserve a man like this. Are there really men in the world who are the same in the privacy of their homes as they appear to be in public? Maybe it has something to do with his religion?*

She quickly dismissed this idea. Uncle Jackson had been faithful to attend church every Sunday. Wasn't it at a church social that she had met Hank? And once her inebriated father had beaten her when he found out she'd forgotten to say her prayers before bed. With a sigh, she blew out the lamp and dressed for bed. Sleep didn't come for quite some time as she pondered the mysterious man she had married.

Chapter Five

A t dawn the next morning, the crowing of the rooster penetrated her consciousness. Brooke rolled over with a groan, not yet ready to wake up. But the memory of how late she had slept the day before propelled her out of bed.

She had the bed made and was in the middle of making coffee when she heard men's voices outside. She recognized Sky's voice, but the other was unfamiliar. She went to the front window and peered out into the yard. Sky stood talking with a huge burly man. Greasy blond curls hung limply about the man's head and a sweat-stained red shirt stretched across his broad chest.

She saw Sky turn, heading for the house, and went back to preparing the coffee pot. When the door opened, she turned with a questioning smile. "Good morning."

"Morning," he returned, a strange light in his eye. "We have company."

"Yes, I saw. Should I set an extra place at the table?"

He ignored her question. "He is my cousin. His name is Jason." Giving the name time to sink in, he finished, "Jason Jordan."

Her hands stilled, and she turned to him. "Jason Jordan? *The* Jason Jordan? The one I was to marry?"

He nodded, his eyes intense.

"So? What? Is he angry? If we have him in for breakfast, is he going to pull a gun and shoot us both?" She tried to inject a light tone, but nervousness tinged her words.

He stared at the wall for a moment before he addressed her. "He isn't angry now, but he may be when he sees you."

"Why?" she voiced incredulously. "What do you mean by that?"

He shrugged. "You're very beautiful. It won't prove to be a very pleasant meal, I'm afraid."

She gave an unladylike snort, but a tingle of pleasure traversed her spine. *He thinks I'm beautiful?* Without a word she crossed to the table and set three plates on it. But as he headed for the door, she stopped him. "Sky?"

He turned.

"How is it that I came to marry you instead of him?"

His eyes softened. "God's intervention."

Brooke decided that if Sky could eat as much as she had seen him eat yesterday, his beefy cousin could probably eat twice as much. She warmed up the biscuits, left over from the night before, and set them out with some strawberry preserves from the cellar. A plate heaped with scrambled eggs steamed in the middle of the table, and cool milk sat at each place. Sky and Jason entered minutes later, as she was giving the last stir to a large pot of oatmeal.

Although she didn't understand the whole situation, Jason was, after all, Sky's cousin and therefore family. She didn't want him to feel that he was not welcome in their home, so she smiled what she hoped would be a warm welcome, extending her hand. "Hello. Sky tells me you are his cousin, Jason. I am pleased to meet you."

A light of approval gleamed in Sky's brown eyes before he seated himself at the table.

Jason nodded, his gaze raking over her form. He shook her hand and leered. "So, did Sky also tell you how he swindled me? Convinced me to sell you to him so he could have a pretty little wife around the place seeing to his needs?"

She blanched, cleared her throat, and had to forcefully pull her hand from his grasp. She didn't know what to do now. Jason's expression was scathing. Brooke knew in an instant that this was the type of man she understood.

Sky saved her. "Jason, have a seat." His tone held an edge of steel. Jason reluctantly sat down at the table.

Then Jason's words registered in Brooke's mind. *Sky bought me?* Disappointment coursed through her. Sky had been so kind to her that she had not considered the fact that he had purchased her. Of course he had. She was a mail-order bride—someone a man bought because he needed a woman around the place to help with the work, and because they wanted a physical companion by their side. She had been so hopeful at Sky's kind treatment, so surprised, that she had neglected to remember the circumstances that led her to this situation.

A spark had begun to burn in her heart. A spark of hope that one day Sky might become attracted to her, maybe even fall in love with her.

But with Jason's cruel words, reality crashed in like a flood, extinguishing the spark before it could grow to a flame. Sky would never love her! She was a mail-order bride. Purchased for convenience…not for love. Brooke walked rigidly to the stove, picking up the coffee pot with the pot holder. She poured first Sky's cup, then Jason's, then sat in the cane chair Sky had pulled over to the table. *It's not going to kill you, Brooke. No one but Mama and Sis have ever loved you before. Why should things change now?*

She was surprised beyond words when Jason bowed his head for the prayer without so much as a thought. When grace had been said, she looked up to find Jason's angry eyes fastened on Sky. With a measured look, Sky returned the stare, only his face showed no emotion.

Brooke rubbed her palms together in front of her, hoping they were not going to break out into a fist fight over the breakfast table. "Do you want some cream for your coffee, Mr. Jordan?" she addressed Jason.

Instead of answering, Jason sneered at Sky. "Got yourself a real polite one, didn't you? Does she do *everything* as well as she welcomes guests to your home?" He gave a meaningful look to the bed in the corner.

Brooke looked down into her lap, mortified.

"Brooke." Sky spoke to her quietly, but his snapping eyes never left Jason's face. "Did you gather the eggs yet this morning?"

She took the hint. He knew she hadn't even been outside yet

today. "No, I'll go and do that right now." She rose and fled the house to the relative safety of the barnyard.

As soon as Brooke left the house, Sky stood. Walking deliberately around the table, he grabbed Jason by the collar of his dirty shirt and jerked him to his feet, propelling him toward the door. His tone deadly calm, he said, "Get out of my house and don't come back until you can show some respect for my wife."

Jason was already sorry, but he didn't let it show. Reaching up, he knocked Sky's hands from the front of his shirt with a slap. He had always been the bigger of the two, but Sky was invariably quicker. He debated taking a swing at Sky but decided against it. He knew he'd acted childishly; still, it galled him that Sky always seemed to make the right decisions when he chose to make the wrong ones.

He wanted to fight in the worst way; wanted to be right. But he knew he was wrong. He had been rude to a woman he didn't even know because he was jealous of his cousin and didn't have enough self-control to check his emotions.

As he glared into Sky's eyes, his thoughts turned to his grandmother Jordan, but he carefully kept any emotion hidden.

Gram had loved him like her own son as he grew.

His parents had been some of the first settlers when gold was discovered in Pierce City back in the 1860s. His father's luck had come to the fore, and he hit it rich. But he had a consuming gambling addiction. He had gotten into a fight in a saloon one night when Jason was only five. He was beaten to death.

Jason's mother had kept only sporadic contact with her late husband's family, but he could remember that a letter arrived faithfully every week from Grandma Jordan.

His earliest memories were anything but happy. His mother, in her grief, had begun to smoke opium to "calm her nerves," she had said. Lee Chang had been happy to supply her with the vile drug, but he required cash. So she had turned to a life of prostitution to support her growing habit. Jason could remember more than one occasion when he and his sister, Marquis, had been forced to hide under the bed while his mother entertained a customer.

Two weeks before his eighth birthday, his mother had overdosed, and Jason had been the one to find her. He and Marquis had been sent to live with Grandma Jordan, and she had raised them as her own.

Sky and his family lived near her, and every Sunday after church, everyone gathered at Gram's house for lunch. Gram invested every minute she had teaching her grandchildren about Jesus and His love, often making them sit at her kitchen table to memorize Scriptures. She had shed many tears over Jason in his lifetime, and he knew she'd have shed more today if she had seen how he'd treated Brooke.

He was ashamed of himself but refused to admit it.

He and Sky were still glaring at one another. Jason dropped his gaze and turned on his heel without saying a word. He stalked across the yard to his horse waiting at the hitching post by the barn, mounted, and spurred the animal away from the house, trying to run from his conscience.

Once out of sight of the house, he slowed his horse to a walk. *What did I hope to gain by going there today?* He had wanted to thank Sky for letting him read Gram's letters. He had wanted to ask Sky to pray for him. He wanted to change. However, when he had walked into the house and seen the beautiful woman who might have been his, jealousy had overcome him. Why was it that no matter what Sky did, he always seemed to come out on top? His jealousy had turned to bitterness. Bitterness came easily these days.

He reined his horse to a stop. Sliding to the ground, he rubbed the back of his neck, staring up at the covering canopy of evergreen needles above him. He was chagrined to feel tears pricking the back of his eyes. He blinked hard. "How did I come to be here, Lord?" The words surprised him—he couldn't remember the last time he had prayed.

As soon as Jason galloped out of the yard, Sky went looking for Brooke. He found her standing on an overturned bucket, gathering eggs from the chicken coop. "Here, let me do that." He tried to take the bowl in her hands from her. "I didn't really mean for you to come gather the eggs. I was just giving you a reason to leave the house."

She did not relinquish the bucket but kept on gathering eggs, her face set in stone.

Thinking her silence was due to Jason's earlier behavior, he said, "Jason is gone. I told him not to come back until he could be polite."

"You think that's what this is about?" she snapped, turning blazing eyes on him.

He couldn't have been more surprised if she had thrown the bowl of eggs at him. *She's mad at me?* He was bewildered. "What *is* it about?"

"You *bought* me, didn't you? And for what? So you could have someone around the place to do your cooking and the chores and—" She rolled her hand through the air, her cheeks flaming in embarrassment at the next thought that apparently swept through her mind. She stuttered for a moment before she finally said, "Well, *cooking* and *chores* I can do! So here I am!" She turned back to searching for eggs.

"It wasn't like that."

"Oh really? What was it like, then?"

He stared at the barn wall, unwilling to malign Jason's name even with the truth. "It was just something I felt I should do."

"Oh, I see!" Her tone held more than a little sarcasm. "Do you get these urges often? To go out and buy women, I mean? Here I have been thinking that you were the kindest man I'd ever met, but now I see the truth. You're just like all the rest of the men I've ever known."

"Brooke!" This woman was maddening. One minute she was so nervous she could hardly function, and the next minute she was hotter than a mother bear protecting her cubs. His anger sparked. "You were a *mail-order* bride, in case you have forgotten! That's what mail-order brides are, women *purchased* by men!" He regretted the words the minute they left his mouth. All his anger drained away.

Hurt flashed across her face. "Yes, I've remembered that now, thank you. You don't need to worry about the chores and things; they will get done. It just came as a surprising reminder, that's all. You're very good at deception, making me think you were the perfect gentleman. I would expect that from a man as uncivil as your cousin, but not from—" Heat washed her features. Jumping down off the bucket, she brushed past him.

Wondering what she had been about to say, he wanted very badly to reach out and stop her. But he remembered his promise not to touch her in any way. Instead, he calmly kept pace with her as she stormed toward the house. She took three steps for every one of his. It was not hard to keep up with her.

She slammed into the house, marched over to the counter, and set the bucket of eggs down with a loud thump.

Sky pulled the cane chair from where it sat by the table over in front of the door. Pouring himself a cup of coffee, he sat down and leaned coolly back against the door, the front two legs of his chair not touching the ground.

He watched, amused, as she violently scrubbed the eggs in a pan of water, wondering how many she would break.

Brooke finished the job and turned with the pan of dirty water to cross the room, but stopped, noting for the first time that he sat directly in front of the door. Her eyes took in each of the room's three windows. None of them opened. There was no other way out of the house.

He looked at her over the rim of his cup, amusement dancing in his dark eyes as he sipped the brew casually.

"Don't you have chores to do?" she asked, chin in the air.

He nodded but did not move.

She stepped back and set the pan of water heavily on the

counter. Turning toward the table to clear it of the breakfast dishes, she stilled. Sky had come soundlessly to stand behind her, and her face was only inches from his chest. She took a step back but felt the counter pressing into her lower back. She brought her palms together in front of her, fear coursing through her veins. Why hadn't she kept her mouth shut?

All amusement now gone from his face, he stepped toward her.

She slid down the counter toward the wall until she could go no farther. Advancing steadily, he kept his eyes on her face. She wanted to look away but found she couldn't pull her eyes away from his dark, serious gaze. She held her breath as he placed one hand on the back wall of the house and one on the side wall. He had her effectively cornered.

He leaned down so his face was directly on her level. "Would you rather be married to Jason?" he asked, his voice deep and resonant.

Her eyes widened as she let out her breath. This thought had not occurred to her. She shook her head.

He sighed, leaning heavily on his imprisoning arms. "Jason is…wild. He knows the way he is living is wrong, but he doesn't seem to want to change. When I heard Jason was getting married, I didn't want to get involved. But I believe God led me to the decision I made, so here we are. The only reason I *bought* you, as you put it, was because I could see no other way to convince Jason to relinquish his rights to you." Standing upright, he folded his arms across his broad chest, looking down at her. "I'm sorry I made that remark about you being a mail-order bride. I didn't mean to make you feel…"

"Purchased?"

He shrugged. "Yeah. I only wanted to save you from Jason. You don't have to do any chores you don't want to do. And I don't expect anything else from you either. I've told you that."

She looked down. "I just—" She fluttered her hands helplessly. "It's been a crazy year. I don't expect you to understand. I'm sorry for saying those things. It came as quite a shock when I realized what he had said and…" Tears misted her eyes. "I don't know what to believe. You have been so kind to me. I keep telling myself this can't be real, that things are going to crash down around me any minute." She stared at the wood stove, willing herself to remain in control.

Her voice choked with emotion when she finally spoke again. "I just feel like I have been living in the desert all my life, and suddenly I've come upon this oasis. I don't know whether it's going to turn out to be a mirage or not." She looked at him to see if he understood. The tender comprehension she saw in his eyes made her heart do an erratic flip.

Her mind groped for a change of subject. "I've got to wash the dishes."

She moved toward the table, obviously not remembering that no one had eaten. She was brushing past him for the second time that morning, but this time he let her go, knowing she needed some time alone. He grabbed four biscuits and headed outside to do his own chores. As he walked, he said a prayer that one day she would come to know Jesus and understand what made him different than the other men she had known.

★

CHAPTER SIX

Shiloh, Oregon, in the Willamette Valley

Rachel Jordan put one hand to the base of her throat and sat heavily on the couch, which, thankfully, was directly behind her. She was suddenly grateful that Sharyah had stepped out to get some supper ingredients at the Mercantile. This was something she and Sean should discuss before they informed Rocky and Sharyah.

The telegram in her hand trembled for a moment and then sagged, limply dangling from the corner by which she held it. "Sean?" The word stuck in her throat and came out somewhere between a frayed whisper and a whine. She cleared her throat and laid the paper on the coffee table in front of her as she called his name once more. "Sean?"

"Yes dear? Coming." She heard her husband's voice from the kitchen where he was putting the finishing touches on her new screen door.

As she waited for him, she eyed the telegram warily, hands clasped tightly in her lap. She had read it twice. She knew what it said, but surely this was all a cruel joke. But Sky wouldn't do that to them. Jason, on the other hand…

She closed her eyes and pinched the bridge of her nose. Too much of the story made sense. This was just the sort of thing Jason would pull. And Sky was the sort to gallantly come to the lady's rescue. She and Sean had taught him that. For one brief moment, she regretted it but shook her head to ward off the thought. She looked up in time to see her husband walk into the living room, wiping his dirty hands on one of her dishtowels. When he saw her, his face immediately registered concern, and he sat by her, taking her hand.

"Rachel? Are you all right?"

She looked deep into the blue of his eyes, needing to pull strength from him right now. At length, she spoke. "I'm fine, but we've had a message from Sky." She indicated the paper on the table.

"Is he all right?" Sean blurted out. "What about Jason? What has he done now?" All these were asked even as he reached for the telegram on the table.

Rachel sighed as she smoothed the skirt of her yellow dress. "Just read it, dear." She kept pushing at the imaginative wrinkle while she waited for Sean to finish the telegram, glancing at his face every once in a while to see what he was thinking.

Sean read the short message. She already had it memorized and knew exactly what it said.

Am married STOP Jason's mail-order bride STOP She needs Jesus STOP Wounded soul please pray STOP.
Sky
Pierce City

Sean came to the end of the telegram but still sat staring at the page. He was just as surprised as she had been, but she only knew that because she had been married to him for twenty-five years. Sean was a master at concealing his features. He had to be—he was a lawman. But she knew his face.

Suddenly he blinked and looked over at her.

She smiled slightly. "We have a new daughter-in-law."

He glanced back at the page in awe. "Yes, I guess we do."

Suddenly tears sprang to her dark eyes, and she reached up to pat her graying hair into place. "I only wish it was under better circumstances." She pulled an ever-present hankie from the wrist of her sleeve and dabbed at the corners of her eyes. "I've prayed for so many years for the perfect girl for Sky and now..." She waved her hand at the message in his hand, unable to go on.

Sean patted her shoulder. "Remember, dear, God works all things for the good of those who love Him. And Sky definitely loves the Lord."

She nodded, trying to staunch the tears flowing down her

cheeks, and spoke in a choked voice, "We have to pray for them. They are going to need our prayers."

"Yes, they are. Let's do that now."

They bowed their heads and lifted up their son and new daughter to the Lord. Asking Him to watch over them and protect them. To help them form a relationship as strong and lasting as could be. But mostly, they prayed for Brooke's eyes to be opened to her need of a Savior, and that God would help her overcome the wounds that scarred her past.

Brooke was running, running hard. Her breath came in great gasps as she leaped through the field grasses, her lungs burning. She had been holding her skirts up as she ran, but now exhaustion overcame her. So tired! Letting one side of her skirt go, she brought her hand to her chest as though she could help herself breathe easier.

She turned to look back. He was there. Looming just behind her with a wicked sneer, his amused eyes fastened on her. He was walking, not exerting any effort. Strolling even, one hand placed casually in his pants pocket, the other swinging easily by his side, and still keeping up with her frantic flight.

She turned back around, determined to keep going. To get away. But as she turned, she saw, too late, the log on the ground in front of her. Unable to avoid it, she tried to jump over it, but as her feet left the ground, Hank reached out and grabbed the skirt of her dress, pulling her feet out from under her. Falling on her back with a thud, she fixed her frightened eyes on the leering face of the handsome man who stood over her. Slowly he withdrew his hand from his pocket, and she saw the handle of Uncle Jackson's quirt.

"You've done it now, Brooke, my dear." His voice came from far away, sounding as if he was talking into an empty rain barrel. The man's face morphed—one moment it was Hank's, and the next it blurred into the visage of Uncle Jackson. "There was no dinner on the table when I came home tonight. You know what happens when there is no dinner on the table, don't you?" The monster's head tipped back in an open-mouthed laugh that sent chills of fear down Brooke's spine. She did the only thing she knew to do— curled into a ball and put her arms over her head.

With the first blow of the quirt her body jerked and her eyes flew open. The room lay in semi-darkness. Peering out from between her arms at the side of the cold black stove only a foot away, she shuddered, trying to calm her breathing. Her body was soaked in sweat. Uncurling her arms from around her head, she sat up quickly, pushing her mass of curly hair away from her sweaty face. Her eyes jerked around the room, going from one shadow to the next, making sure she truly was alone in the cabin. Still in a hazy stupor, her befuddled mind slowly realized she was safe inside Sky's house. Tears of relief burst forth. She sucked in air, trying to calm herself, but couldn't stop the wracking sobs. She lay back down, burying her face in her pillow, her shoulders shaking with the cadence of agonizing anguish.

How long she cried, she didn't know, but when she could cry no more, she lay silently on her pillow, one hand by her face, staring at the side of the stove, seeing nothing. Nothing but the tormenting memories that paraded through her mind, one by painful one.

Smoothing the last of the tears from her cheeks with the flats of her fingers, she turned on her back to stare at the ceiling, her hair fanning out on the pillow. The rooster crowed, but she didn't move. She hated days like this.

She had had them before. Many times. She wouldn't be able to forget about the dream all day long. And the dream would bring back many memories, actual ones, that she had no desire to remember.

The only thing that propelled her out of bed was the memory that Sky would be in soon—and expecting breakfast to be on the table.

As it was, Sky came in sooner than she had expected, and the meal wasn't ready. Bacon still sizzled in the pan, the eggs hadn't been cooked, and the coffee was just coming to a boil.

Sky paused, taking in her red, swollen eyes.

"I'm—" she gestured helplessly at the stove—"I'm sorry. It will be a few minutes still." She spun around nervously, tapping her foot as if that could make the bacon cook faster. Finding nothing for her hands to do but poke and prod the bacon, she set the fork down and put her hands to use rolling up her sleeves.

Sky studied her intently. "Brooke, are you all right?"

"Yes." She answered too quickly, trying to give a reassuring smile. "I'm fine."

Her hands shook as she removed the bacon strips a moment later and began to crack eggs into the pan. She gave the eggs a stir and then turned to where he sat at the table. "I'll run out and get the milk. The eggs should be done when I get back; then we can eat."

His eyes held hers for a moment in question, but he said, "That's fine."

As Brooke went out the door to get the milk, Sky shoved a hand through his hair in vexation. Something was wrong. Very wrong, he could see that. It was so frustrating trying to understand this woman when he knew nothing about her. The only thing he knew was what he'd assumed from watching her react in different situations. Something was troubling her, but he had no idea what.

Suddenly, he wished he was a little boy again and could call on his father to help him figure things out. But as the thought crossed his mind, he chuckled. "You got yourself into this, Sky, so you're going to have to figure things out on your own."

Getting up, he absentmindedly stirred the eggs, trying to figure out a way to let her know that he cared. That he wanted to help her. Would she ever come to trust him? She had obviously been mistreated by someone in the past.

How could he make her understand that he would never do such things to her, or anyone else for that matter?

He heard her come in the door behind him, picked up the pan of eggs, and began to move toward the table. But when he saw her expression, he stopped. She looked nervously from his face to the pan in his hand and back again. Quickly she set the can of milk on the table and gestured at the pan. "I can do that."

He smiled. "I don't mind." In the minutes before she walked in the door, he had decided that the best thing he could do for her was to be himself. It would take time, but she would eventually see that he meant her no harm. He moved past her and scooped some eggs onto her plate. "Enough?" he asked.

She nodded, moving to get the plate of bacon. He noted that her hands shook as she set the plate on the table and took her seat. Pouring them each a glass of milk, he set the can on the floor and bowed his head to say grace. When he looked up from the prayer, he found her nervous eyes on him. He smiled easily. "Smells wonderful." Stabbing a forkful of eggs, he asked, "How did you sleep last night?"

"Fine," she lied. Her eyes were on him as she reached for the bacon, and she knocked over her glass of milk.

Sky's reaction was lightning swift. He stood, his chair scraping against the floor as his knees pushed it back, and reached over her head to grab a towel off the shelf behind her. But at her reaction to his movement he froze, stunned, the milk forgotten.

Brooke, ducking down, her face almost touching the table, had curled her arms over her head, as if to protect herself from a blow. Sky sucked in a slow breath. On her forearms, revealed by her rolled-up sleeves, were criss-cross scars that looked as if they had been left there by a whip of some sort.

He couldn't remember the last time he had felt like crying, but tears stung his eyes now. He wanted so badly to pull her into a comforting embrace, but he had to keep his distance if she was ever going to know that he could be trusted. Instead, he squatted down by her, one hand on the table and one hand on the back of her chair. He whispered, "Brooke?"

She didn't move at first. The silence in the room was broken only by the steady drip of milk hitting the floor.

"Brooke." His voice cracked with frayed emotion.

She moved this time. Uncurling herself, but not looking at him, she stared across the room at the wall.

Sky dropped his head toward the floor. He didn't know what to say. When he felt her move, he looked up to find her teary eyes on his face. He shook his head slightly. "I was reaching for a towel. Not…" He shook his head again, his shoulders slumping. "When I think of what you must have been through in the past, Brooke, I get so…so…angry. I can't even imagine hitting you, but someone used to hit you, didn't they?" He gazed into her face.

She looked away, but nodded slightly.

Tears welled in his eyes. "I will tell you this. It's not going to happen to you anymore. As long as I am alive, I am your husband, and I will do everything in my power to protect you, not harm you. You have nothing to fear from me, Brooke. I know those are just words, but I mean them from the bottom of my heart. I wish I could make you believe them, but I can't, so I will have to show you." He paused. "Brooke?"

She turned her eyes back to his.

"I'm sorry for your past, the way you have been treated, but it's not going to happen in our house." He shook his head slowly to emphasize his point. "You said something the other day, when you mentioned feeling like you've been living in the desert, that reminded me of a passage in the Bible. I'd like to read it to you now. Would that be all right?"

She nodded.

Getting his Bible, he opened it to the 23rd Psalm and began to read. "The Lord is my Shepherd; I shall not want. He makes me to lie down in green pastures; He leads me beside the still waters. He restores my soul; He leads me in paths of righteousness for his name's sake."

He thought on what to say. "That's not the whole Psalm. I'll mark it so you can read the rest later if you want." He set the Bible down on the table. When he spoke again, it was with tenderness. "Brooke, without Jesus life *is* like living in the desert. Dry and parched. But there is an oasis. You've had a hard life, and I'm sure there will be hard times in the future as well, but you don't have to go through the hard times alone. I want you to remember that. I want you to allow God to lead you to those green pastures and to restore your soul. Jesus wants to bring you to a place of rest and peace. Cool green pastures with fresh water nearby.

"This is not a mirage, Brooke. What you see in me is real. It's not going to fade away before your eyes, because what you see in me is Jesus. My love for Him won't allow me to mistreat others, because I know how much He cares for them. He cares for *you*." He looked deep into her eyes. "I can't force you to turn to Him, but I want you to think about what I am saying. Will you do that for me?"

He saw tears rise in her sea-green eyes and spill over, trailing down her cheeks. She nodded. And he was surprised beyond words when she reached out her hand and let her thumb trace over his cheek bone, brushing away a tear. He hadn't realized that his own tears had brimmed over until that moment. She let her hand fall back into her lap and turned to survey the milk-sodden table.

Sky knew no more needed to be said right now. He got up slowly and began to wipe up the spill.

CHAPTER SEVEN

Sharyah Jordan placed the bowl of fluffy, steaming mashed potatoes on the table and straightened the silverware for the umpteenth time.

Mama, coming in from the kitchen, smiled at her nervous actions and patted her shoulder. "The table looks fine, dear. You can't make that knife any straighter than straight."

True, but she wanted this meal with her brother's best friend, Cascade Bennett, to be perfect. Sharyah grinned over her shoulder at her mother.

"There is straight, and then there is straightest."

Rachel threw back her head and laughed even as they heard the knock on the front door.

Sharyah smoothed the front of her dress and patted her blond curls into place as best she could. Her curly hair usually had a mind of its own. "Do I look all right, Mama?" Her dark brown eyes, so much like Skyler's, shone with anticipation.

Sean entered the dining room on his way to answer the front door. "You look wonderful dear. Any man would have to be blind not to notice how beautiful you are tonight."

Sharyah sighed, some of the tension leaving her shoulders, and Rachel smiled. Had she ever been this distressed over having a young man come to dinner? Then she remembered the first night she had gone to dinner at Sean's house. She had practically run in circles that night trying to make sure she looked just perfect. *Still, I was a couple of years older than sixteen then. I can't stand to see her growing up so fast. My last baby…*

Rachel's thoughts were cut off as Sean ushered Cade Bennett into the dining room, and Rocky entered the kitchen from the back door, having finished the nightly chores out at the barn.

"Cade, how're you doing?" Rocky called from the kitchen sink where he had paused to wash up.

Cade, Rocky, Sky, and Jason had all been the greatest of friends—and the worst of enemies—during their maturing years. Fishing, hunting, and sports had brought them together, and it was usually a girl that drove them apart. But the bonds of friendship had been greater than the throes of infatuation, and as they grew and matured, they had become very close.

Since Jason and Sky had moved away, Rocky and Cade spent every moment they could spare from their busy schedules together. *I imagine that's how Sharyah fell for Cade. He's been at our house so much in the last several years.* With the young man's charm and good looks, how could a girl keep from noticing him?

Rachel was afraid, however, that Cade only saw Sharyah as a younger sister and hoped and prayed Sharyah's heart would not be broken too badly.

Cade removed his hat and tossed it on the hat rack in the corner. An easy gesture that said he felt at home. "Hey, Rock! Just fine. Looking forward to some of your mother's and Sharyah's fine cooking. I don't get fed like this out at the ranch, you know." His dark hair and face, deeply tanned from all the hours spent in the sun on his father's ranch, contrasted with his twinkling, ocean-blue eyes as he glanced around at the people in the room.

Rachel laughed. Cade's mother, Brenda, her best friend, was one of the finest cooks in the whole county. "You are a flatterer, Cade Bennett. I will admit I enjoy compliments about my cooking, but wait until I tell your mother what you said."

A pained look crossed his face. "Ma'am, if we could keep that little comment between you, me, and the doorpost, I would greatly appreciate it." He gave a mock shudder. "I might live a whole lot longer, too." Rachel, Sean, and Sharyah burst out in laughter at his exaggerated, pained contrition.

When the laughter had died down and Rocky had sauntered into the room, Sean spoke up. "Have a seat, Cade." He indicated the seat immediately to his left. To Cade's left sat Rocky. Rachel was at the head of the table closest to the kitchen, and Sharyah sat across the table from Rocky and Cade.

They all held hands for grace and then the meal commenced with the clatter of utensils on bowls and plates and easy conversation. Rachel noticed that Sharyah hardly ever took her eyes off Cade, but he seemed oblivious.

Halfway through the meal, he grinned across the table at her. "Sharyah, you are looking especially nice this evening. Do you have an admirer coming over later?" He winked at her with a teasing glint.

Sharyah blushed and shook her head.

"What's the matter with those boys in town, Rocky? Don't they have eyes in their heads? Why, when we were kids—" Rachel and Sean caught each other's eyes and lifted napkins to their mouths to hide their smiles. At twenty Cade was hardly more than a kid himself—"we would have gotten into our biggest fight ever if there had been a girl as beautiful as Sharyah in our class."

Rachel pierced Rocky with a stare. She did not want him to embarrass his sister further.

He gave her a discreet nod and made no mention of the number of boys who had indeed shown interest in Sharyah, only to be turned down. Instead, he met his sister's warm brown eyes across the table and smiled reassuringly.

"Yeah, I guess we would have." Then he turned the conversation away from Sharyah. "Remember the fight we all got into the day that Victoria came to town?"

"Remember? I still have the scar along my jaw where you cracked me with that uppercut! Sky and Jason—"

"I can't believe you boys!" Rachel tossed her serviette on the table in disgust. "Still laughing and reminiscing about that day! Brenda and I were so disappointed in you, and all Sean and Smith could do was laugh after we finally got you all apart. Oh," she threw her hands up in disgust, "that was one of the worst days of my life, seeing you boys brawling like that and over a *girl*, and here you sit laughing about it like it was one of the most exciting things you ever did. I will never understand the male species! Never!"

She marched into the kitchen to get the coffee pot, but not before she glared daggers at her husband, who was busy trying to hide his smile as he stared into the bottom of his empty coffee cup.

Sharyah watched the whole exchange with a quizzical look. Rachel knew she hardly remembered the day of the fight. She'd been drawing at the kitchen table when Rachel and Brenda, Cade's mother, had come into the kitchen crying, but she had been too young to really understand what it was all about. The boys had been ten, Jason and Sky a little older, and she had only been six at the time.

A long awkward silence enshrouded the room as Rachel refilled each coffee cup, returned the pot to the stove, and took her seat once more.

Rocky was the first to break the silence. "We got a telegram from Sky the other day, Cade. He got married." Rocky left out all the details. He would probably fill Cade in later.

Rachel sighed. Her firstborn son had gotten married to a woman the family had never met, and no one from the family had been at the wedding. No one had even known about it until afterward. To top it off, Sky's new wife apparently wasn't even a Christian—that was the hardest of all.

Before Cade could respond to this surprising statement, Sean broke in, "Your mother and I have been meaning to talk to you and Sharyah about this, Son. Since Cade is practically family, we can discuss it now. We feel like we should go and meet Brooke, so we want to take a couple of weeks and go out there to visit. Do you think you could handle the Sheriff's office for a couple of weeks?" The question wasn't necessary. Rachel and Sean both knew that their son was perfectly capable of handling any situation that might arise in his absence.

Rocky shrugged. "Sure, Dad. If anything big happens, we will leave any decisions until you get back."

Sean nodded and then turned to Sharyah. "With school about to start, I don't think you should make the trip with us. Do you think you could handle the household chores while your mother and I are gone?"

Sharyah began to nod when Cade spoke up. "My parents would be happy to have Rock and Sharyah stay out at our place for a couple of weeks. It would mean a little longer ride in the morning for both of you to get to town, but you're more than welcome."

"That would be such a relief," Rachel said. "I worried about Sharyah trying to do her school work and the cooking and cleaning, too. That would set my mind at ease some about leaving."

Sharyah wondered how she was going to stand staying in the same house as Cade when he didn't even seem to notice that she existed as a woman. He treated her like a little sister! She held the threatening tears at bay and escaped to the kitchen on the pretense of filling the sugar bowl.

Sighing inwardly, she *thunked* the sugar bowl onto the counter and leaned heavily on locked elbows. She stood still for a long time, staring down with unfocused eyes. Timothy Jorgenson had come calling again yesterday. Maybe she ought to accept his invitation to Friday night's dance. She gave herself a shake and reached for the sugar canister.

Someday, Cade Bennett, you will see I'm a woman. I just hope I'm not old and gray by then.

It had been two weeks since the morning of her last nightmare about Hank. Brooke was very thankful for the reprieve in her nighttime torment. The days began to fall into a pattern. Waking up with the call of the cock, she would get up, make the bed, start the coffee, then head for the hen house to collect the eggs, always finding an empty bucket on which to stand.

By the time Sky finished the morning chores and came into the house to wash up, she had a sumptuous breakfast on the table. This day wasn't any different than the others. Watching as he heaped hot cakes onto his plate, Brooke smiled. It never ceased to amaze her how much he could eat.

She was beginning to feel more and more relaxed in his presence. She still didn't understand why, but this man had not mistreated her in any way, and somehow, after having known and watched him for the last two weeks, she couldn't envision him doing any such thing. He was always gentle and thoughtful. What made him different, she wasn't sure. He said it was Jesus in his life, but whatever the reason, she was very thankful for his kindness.

Her mind wandered to what he'd said, about letting Jesus bring her to a place of rest and peace. Was that even possible? Sky didn't know about her past improprieties. Maybe God sent all the hard things in her life to punish her for the way she'd lived. Maybe God wanted her to suffer. *If I weren't so bad, maybe my baby...*

"How is Old Bess's leg this morning?" she asked, refusing to allow herself to continue the thought.

Sky frowned as he swallowed a mouthful. "Not good, I'm afraid. I have tried every trick I know to get the swelling in that leg down, but nothing seems to be working." He shook his head. "I might have to take her down to Orofino and have Doctor James look at her."

Brooke nodded. She wanted to ask if he would mind if she looked at the cow's leg but didn't know what he would think of a woman working over an animal. Uncle Jackson would have punished her just for asking.

When he finally pushed his plate back and leaned into his chair, she said, "What? Only twenty pancakes?" She deliberately exaggerated. "There are still five on the platter. Won't you have some more?"

He groaned and put one hand to his stomach. "Woman, you are going to be the death of me." Then he winked at her. "You better quit cooking so well, or you are going to have the fattest husband this side of the Mississippi."

She eyed his trim form as he got up to pour himself a cup of coffee and gave a snort of derision. "I can see. You've really put on weight since I got here."

He froze, quickly looking down at his stomach. Then he

laughed, shaking a finger at her. "You had me there for a second." He took a sip of coffee, his eyes smiling at her over the top of the mug.

She gave him a cheeky grin, and his gaze suddenly turned thoughtful but did not leave her face.

At his serious, thoughtful look Brooke's smile faded. *I have become far too comfortable with him.* Staring down at her plate, she moved a piece of pancake back and forth with her fork. She couldn't look into those deep brown eyes and keep her thoughts straight. She vowed, yet again, not to let her guard down so easily.

Setting his cup on the table he reached for the door. She could feel his dark eyes still on her face when he said, "I'll see you later."

He was almost out the door when she blurted, "Do you mind if I look at her?"

"What?" He turned back.

"Would you mind if I looked at Bess's leg?"

He shrugged. "Sure, I don't mind. Do you want to come out right now?"

"No. I'll come out as soon as I've finished with the dishes."

"That's fine. I'm going to be working in the south field today, so I won't be around, but if you think you need my help, just ring the triangle hanging on the porch."

"Thank you." She was pleased he was willing to let her look at the animal and hoped there would be something she could do for the lame cow.

She rushed through the dishes, looking forward to getting out of the house for a while. The days during the past weeks had begun to be a bit monotonous. Once she had thoroughly cleaned the cabin, she had to search for things to fill her long days, so the prospect of caring for the cow was a welcome distraction.

Setting the last of the dishes on the shelf above the counter, she removed her apron and headed out to the barn with a song in her heart. The sun felt pleasantly warm as it beat down on her shoulders. A large bee rumbled by on its quest for flowers, and a fat squirrel, stocking up for winter, busily dug a hole in the ground a few yards away.

She pushed the squeaky barn door open and stepped into the dim interior. Old Bess lowed a welcome. Brooke loved taking care of animals. Uncle Jackson had owned a ranch, and she had always wanted to be out in the barn, but he had deemed it an "unladylike" place and had forbidden her from ever stepping foot there. Often, when he had gone away on business trips, she had ventured there, though, and Solomon, the old black stable hand, had welcomed her. He had shown her many different cures for sick animals, and she now hoped one of them would come in handy.

Stooping, she ran her hand softly over Bess's injured leg. "Hey, girl," she crooned, "do you have a sore leg? Let's take a look at that and see if we can't fix it."

Her soothing words set the cow at ease as she checked over the leg. She began to sing as she examined the leg, probing here and there, trying to see exactly what the problem might be. Deciding on a warm poultice, she headed back to the house to mix it.

Within ten minutes, she had the poultice mixed and plastered on the animal's leg, and found that she was once again left with trying to find something to fill the rest of the day.

He lay on his belly in a thicket of brush, binoculars pressed to his eyes. As Brooke crossed the barnyard, he followed her with the glasses. "Mmm…Mhhh!" His gaze roved up and down her slender form. "She looks better today than she did last time. Mmm…Mhhh!" he exclaimed again. "That is quite the little tart. Maybe I have time for a bit of a diversion today."

Turning the glasses, he scanned the surrounding fields. There was no one in sight.

Satisfaction curled through his belly. "Yes, I think I do have time for a little diversion today," he said cheerfully. He started to move toward the house but saw Brooke pick up a pail and head into the forest.

Moving quietly, he followed.

★

Chapter Eight

Deciding that the day was too beautiful to waste indoors, Brooke picked up a pail and went in search of a berry patch. She really had no faith that she would find one, so was quite pleased when, a short way from the house, she came upon a large patch of blackberries at their peak of ripeness. Humming to herself, she happily plopped the juicy purple berries into her bucket.

When she heard a horse approaching a moment later, apprehension crept across her spine. Should she have come out here on her own without telling Sky where she was going? What if she met Jason out here by herself? What would she do if he chose to get nasty again—with Sky nowhere around to come to her rescue?

Suddenly, she noted how still the forest had become. There were none of the natural sounds that one normally heard in the woods, except for the wind rustling the tree tops.

Somewhere, a twig snapped, and Brooke's heart lodged in her throat. Her pulse raced, and she dropped into a crouch.

She looked around frantically for a place to hide but saw nothing. She was turning to flee when she noticed a Chinese woman riding her way. Brooke stopped, her heart rate slowly returning to normal.

The woman had jet black hair that was pulled away rather severely from her round face, accentuating the slant of her eyes. Her full, plump figure stretched a bright red dress adorned with gold, fire-breathing dragons at the hem and cuffs. Some Chinese characters were also embroidered down the front of the dress.

When the woman saw Brooke, she reined in her horse. As she swung down from the saddle, she eyed the brush behind Brooke as if to make sure she was alone. Her dark eyes then turned back to Brooke, and she smiled pleasantly, her face lighting up. "Hello."

Her voice, low and melodic, held a heavy Chinese accent. "You come heeya by yourself?"

Brooke nodded.

"You no should come out by yourself in these woods. Many bad men." Brooke felt a chill run up her spine but wasn't about to admit that she had been thinking that exact same thing.

Instead she noted practically, "You are out by yourself." Her tone was not defensive, merely observing.

Again the woman smiled. "Men know my husband. He kill them if they touch me." With a meaningful pat to the butt of a rifle in the scabbard of her saddle, she continued, "I haf protection." She paused meaningfully. "And I not beautiful, like you." Her eyes took in Brooke's hair and form in one sweeping gaze, but Brooke saw no animosity there.

Holding out her hand, Brooke smiled. "I am Brooke Ba—, Jordan."

Taking her hand the plump woman replied, "I Jenny Chang."

"Did you come to pick berries?"

She nodded. "I bake pies. Sell in town." She grinned. "Men not say no to blackberry pie."

Brooke giggled, imagining the profits this woman could make from selling pies to a bunch of bachelor miners.

They chatted freely as they continued to pick, and Brooke realized for the first time how much she had missed female company in the last couple of weeks. She shared how she had come to be in the area, about her marriage to Sky, and some about her past.

She found Jenny's story fascinating. She and her husband had emigrated from China many years before and made their way west. When gold was found in Pierce City in the early 1860s, she and Lee, her husband, had moved here. The gold had not lasted long, but they liked the area and so had stayed, opening a Mercantile in town.

Brooke saw a sad light come into Jenny's eyes as she said, "Lee, he hard man. But—" she shrugged "—he know how to make money. So we do good."

"Do you like living in America?"

Jenny shrugged again. "I stay with husband."

By this time both women had filled their buckets, so they seated themselves in the warm August sunshine on a fallen log as they talked. Brooke completely forgot about the time until she heard another horse approaching through the brush. When she looked up and saw Sky riding toward her, she flew to her feet and looked up through the trees, trying to see where the sun was. *How late is it?*

Hiding in the bushes close enough to the women to hear their conversation, he cursed his bad luck. First, Chang's wife had come on the scene and now this. He clenched his fist in frustration and eased back through the trees toward his waiting horse.

"There will be another day," he promised himself. "Another wonderful day—with no interruptions."

Sky reined to a stop a few paces away and slid to the ground.

"Sky, I am so sorry. We got to talking, and I lost track of the time."

He nodded his acceptance of her apology even as he smiled at her companion. "Hello, Jenny. How are you today?"

"Fine." She gave him a charming curtsy. "I thank you for letting Brooke keep company with me. She has made my birthday very enjoyable."

"Well! Happy Birthday!"

Jenny nodded. "Thank you."

Sky's eyes twinkled as they turned in Brooke's direction. "I am sure Brooke enjoyed the visit as much as you did."

Brooke pulled Jenny into a quick hug. "It was very nice to meet you. Do you think you could come by for a visit sometime?"

Jenny looked down. "Lee, he—" she shrugged, looking back into Brooke's face "—he no like me to visit white people."

"Oh." Disappointment was thick in Brooke's voice, but she

managed a smile. "Well, the next time I come to town, I will be sure to stop by and say hello. Would that be all right?"

Jenny looked uncertain, but said, "I like that much." With a smile, she mounted her horse and rode away toward town.

Sky's face turned serious. "I wish you had told me where you were going. I found some strange footprints in the yard. I'm glad you're all right." He scanned the brush around them with a troubled expression.

Brooke lifted her chin. The last thing she wanted on a wonderful day like today was to be lectured. "I planned to be home before lunch. Are you hungry again already?"

His face did not break into a smile as she had hoped it would. "These woods are no place for a woman to be wandering around alone. Anything could have happened to you."

She shrugged off his concern. "I am fine, aren't I? You found me, and I am all in one piece. Can we go home now?" She turned toward the horse.

"Brooke!" The steel in his tone froze her movements. "Look at me."

She turned slowly until their eyes locked. Seeing his deep concern caused her conscience to prick, and she began to realize just how serious he was.

He took a step nearer. "The next time you need to get out of the house, or away from the farm, let me know. That's fine. I want to be able to accompany you and make sure you are safe. There are men around here who would…" He let his voice trail off but she understood what he meant and looked away, crimson tingeing her cheeks.

"All right. I'm sorry. I never thought about it not being safe until I was already here. Next time I will tell you." She knew there wouldn't be a next time, though. How could she justify keeping him from his work so he could accompany her berry picking? She would stay home rather than bother him with such paltry matters.

He led the horse closer and then turned, looked at her questioningly, and gestured toward the saddle, asking for permission to help her onto the horse. With sudden surprise, she reflected over the past two weeks. He had not touched her even once during all that time. He didn't even hold her hand during grace anymore; had not since the night she had been so nervous and he had been forced to repeat his promise not to mistreat her. Of course, she had known that he meant he would not touch her intimately or abusively, but apparently he was refraining from *any* contact in order to prove his pledge sincere.

Her mind raced back to that night two weeks ago when she had spilled the coffee and burned her hand. When Sky had cared for her so tenderly that her emotions had run away with her. She glanced at his outstretched hand, willing her heartbeat to stay steady. Even for all of Sky's kindness she did not want to become too emotionally attached to him. She had never known a man like him and still felt he was a little too good to be true. Riding home with him would involve sitting, once more, within the circle of his arms.

She pressed her lips together.

He still waited patiently, concern on his face. She realized it was too late to keep her heart rate steady. Steady? It hammered in time with the staccato beat of the woodpecker she could hear a few trees away!

Swallowing her apprehension, she gave an almost imperceptible nod, bending to pick up her bucket of berries. His large strong hands encircled her small waist and lifted her into the saddle with ease. He swung smoothly up, and she tried to still the trembling of her hands, balancing the wooden bucket carefully as he settled just behind the cantle.

Sky leaned in and whispered, "Remember, I always keep my promises." Tingling warmth raced down her spine as his breath tickled her ear. She tightened her grip on the handle of the berry bucket.

Reaching out, he tapped the back of one of her white-knuckled hands with his forefinger and continued in the same soft voice, "You have nothing to fear from me, Mrs. Jordan."

Brooke closed her eyes. For the first time she felt a little disappointed hearing that promise. But she quickly checked the emotions, reminding herself that she could not afford to fall for *any* man—no matter how kind he appeared to be or how much desire she felt.

Thick shadows deepened the gloom of the forest. He stamped his feet, trying to return the warmth of circulation to them, the pine needles underfoot muting the sound. Bringing his gloved hands to his mouth, he blew on them in an attempt to warm his stiffening fingers. Pulling a gold pocket watch from the front pocket of his vest, he tried to read the time in a weak shaft of moonlight filtering through the swaying tree tops but had to give up in frustration. The temptation to light a match was strong, but no one must know about this meeting, so the risk of a light, even as small as a match, could not be taken. Irritably shoving the watch back into his vest, he rubbed his hands together, breathing on them again.

The timber overhead creaked eerily, and a night owl called. Somewhere a twig snapped, and he stilled, drawing himself back against a tree trunk, trying to blend with the shadows, his eyes alert. He could make out footsteps now. Pulling a derringer from its sheath in the sleeve of his coat, he waited.

A soft chuckle sounded right behind him, making him jump and spin around, the small gun held at arm's length, coming up to chest level. This only caused the new man to laugh harder. "You are not a true woodsman."

As recognition dawned, he lowered the gun with a frustrated sigh. "Shut-up, Chang," he snapped. "Is everything set?"

Chang nodded and placed the stem of his ever-present pipe in the corner of his mouth, reaching for his pack of matches.

"Light that, and I will shoot you." His voice was deadly calm.

Chang put the matches back in his pocket.

"Now listen," he continued, "I want the town to be loud and noisy on that night. Give your people something to celebrate and make it happen big. Do you understand?"

Chang nodded, his dark eyes dancing in merriment. "It will be done." He paused, as though judging the risk he took with his next question. "I know why I am willing to do what you have asked—Fraser put his nose into my business once too often. But what did he do to you to make you hate him so much?"

He stared off into the darkness. "He thought I wasn't good enough for his daughter."

This brought another chuckle to Chang's throat, but it expired quickly when he glowered at him with deadly maliciousness.

"Everything will be done as you have ordered." Chang bowed from the waist and disappeared quietly into the forest.

He sighed in contentment as he holstered his gun and rubbed his hands together in front of his chest. He was about to reap the rewards of revenge, and he was enjoying every moment.

Brooke fluffed the cushions she had just finished making and rearranged them on the couch, eyeing them critically. They were not perfect, but they would have to do, she decided with a sigh.

Sky had given her a bag of scraps his mother had sent with him when he moved to use in patching and repairing different items. The scraps had not been very pretty, but she had done the best she could with the dull colors, and now the couch at least looked comfortable.

The front door opened, and she turned toward the sound, wondering if something was wrong. It was not yet lunch time, and Sky didn't usually come in until then.

She blinked in surprise.

Sky held out a small stool. A bouquet of yellow daisies, interspersed with golden stalks of wheat, and tied with twine, was lying on top. He smiled at her. "I was scouting at the edge of the wheat field and saw these daisies. They made me think of you, so I picked you some. The stool is something I've been working on, so you won't have to stand on a bucket at the chicken coop anymore."

Brooke didn't know what to say. She took the offering and smiled shyly. "Thank you."

He nodded. Then, gesturing toward the cushions, he said, "The couch looks nice. What did you stuff the pillows with?"

"Hay."

"Later in the spring I'll hunt some geese, and then we can fill them with something a little softer."

"That would be nice," Brooke replied as she placed the bouquet into an empty canning jar and added some water.

Sky was quiet a minute, then cleared his throat. "Well, I'll head back out now. See you at lunch."

Brooke nodded and watched him go. As she raised the bouquet to sniff the woodsy scent of the daisies, her heart hammered in her chest.

As Brooke looked out the cabin window a week later, she realized September had seeped into the surrounding countryside. Red-gold maple leaves fell in thick blankets and the Tamarack trees added yellow splashes of color to the darkly timbered hills around the cabin. The days had begun to grow shorter and frost whitened the ground on the occasional morning now.

With Brooke's careful attention and ministration, old Bess's leg was getting better. She made trips to the barn morning and evening to change the poultice and clean the infected leg carefully.

Brooke really enjoyed her new life. Sky was always tender and gentle, ever thoughtful of her needs. She could not deny that he seemed to have a peace she didn't have. There was something different about Sky Jordan, but she hadn't figured out what yet. He was still proving to be different than any man she had ever known.

She considered their marriage. *Could I learn to love him?*

Her attraction to him gave her pause. Her pulse raced even at the memory of the few times he had touched her. And as her thoughts turned to his careful attention of the past few weeks, she realized, *It would not be hard. I will have to watch myself.* Although she truly liked Sky, she didn't want to fall in love with him. She'd had enough of love and its effects for one lifetime.

As she fixed breakfast, she began to sing a mellow tune Solomon, her uncle's stable hand, had taught her.

Sky entered quietly and leaned one shoulder against the door frame, his arms folded across his chest. He loved the sound of her voice. On many occasions lately, as he approached the house, he had heard her singing, but she always stopped when she heard the door open.

Today she must not have noticed as he entered. Her back to him, she kept on. She was singing a hymn—a Negro spiritual. He closed his eyes and listened to her deep alto.

"Kum by yah, my Lord. Kum by yah.

Kum by yah, my Lord. Kum by yah.

Kum by yah, my Lord.

Kum by yah. Oh Lord, Kum by yah."

The last time he had heard the song had been in his mother's kitchen back home. He could see her with her hands submerged in dirty dish water, singing her heart's cry to her Maker. He wondered if Brooke truly understood its meaning. "Come by here, my Lord." His thoughts turned to prayer. *Lord, make that her cry. Help her want Your presence in her life. Show her how much she needs You.*

He opened his eyes. This woman was beginning to mean more to him than he had ever imagined she would. She brightened his day in so many little ways. If circumstances had been different, he never would have married her. She did not share his faith. Yet she touched his heart in a way no one ever had. *Not even Victoria.* But could he allow himself to love this woman? What if she chose to leave him because of his belief? He would have to let her go. Would he be able to do that if he allowed himself to love her?

Brooke turned from the stove, still singing. She started and squealed in alarm, dropping the spoon she held, one hand going to her mouth.

Just as suddenly as fright had filled her, anger sparked in her eyes. She stomped one foot on the floorboards. "Sky Jordan! How dare you stand there and frighten me like that!"

Sky, still leaning against the frame, glanced down at the spoon on the floor and then back into her sparking blue-green eyes. One eyebrow arched its way upward and a smile spread before he could think better of it. "A man is not allowed to stand in his own house?"

She turned her back on him with a flounce, and Sky's chest tightened. He suddenly wanted, more than anything, to gather her into his arms. It was with great difficulty that he forced himself to calmly pick up the spoon, set it on the counter, and turn toward his chair and sit down at the table. "You sing beautifully. My mother used to sing that song."

She still made no reply, but he noticed that her hands quivered as she set the pot of porridge down. He had to force his hands into his lap to keep from taking her hands in his. Not touching her in any way had become increasingly difficult, especially since he had picked her up in the woods that day. He loved the feel of her in the circle of his arms, her body nestled securely next to his chest, the smell of her soft skin filling his senses.

He smiled. What had he just been asking himself? *Could I love her? I think it's already too late.*

She seated herself across from him. He began to bow his head for prayer, but she said, "Sky?"

He looked into her eyes.

"You startled me. I'm sorry for flying off the handle like that. I keep telling myself that one day I am going to get a hold of that temper of mine." She smiled sheepishly.

"I'm sorry I startled you. But," he grinned impishly, "your eyes are very beautiful when you are angry."

"Skyler Jordan!" She feigned shock, but pleasure blushed her cheeks.

He laughed and, without thinking, held his hand out across the table, preparing to say the blessing.

Brooke looked at Sky's hand, surprised because he had not

done this since the first day they had arrived.

I'm staring. She reached out just as Sky, probably realizing what he had done, pulled his hand back. Her fingers grazed the tips of his, and her heart lurched. She blushed again, looking toward the back wall of the cabin, and pulled her hand quickly into her lap.

"Brooke, I…" Sky pushed both hands through his hair in frustration. "I didn't mean to reach across the table like that. Ever since I was a kid we prayed holding hands before meals, and it's become a habit, I guess. I would love for it to become a tradition in our home someday, but I don't want you to feel like I am pushing you in any way."

"Sky—" her eyes focused on his face—"I don't feel that way."

He cleared his throat. "Do you mind our holding hands during grace?" She forced her eyes to stay on his face as she shook her head no.

A soft smile lit his eyes as he held his hand out across the table once more.

Brooke hoped he wouldn't feel her trembling as she placed her hand in his large, work-roughened one and bowed her head.

"Our Father, we thank You for this food, only one of Your many blessings. Guide us, Lord, as we go throughout this day, and draw us closer to You. And Lord, I take time to remember Jason. Remove the bitterness from his heart and help him to find his way back to You. Open his eyes to all that he is missing, Lord. In Jesus' name, amen."

Brooke started to pull her hand from his as the prayer ended but felt his hand tighten on hers for just a moment. Her gaze flew to his face. He grinned at her, then released her hand, helping himself to a huge bowl of porridge.

"Do you really believe that Jesus can change people's lives?"

"Yes I do." His eyes were sincere.

"Why?"

"Why do *I* believe that? Or, why does Jesus change people's lives?"

She shrugged thoughtfully. "Both, I guess."

"Well, *I* believe that Jesus changes people's lives because of the changes I have seen in myself and others who have given their lives to the Lord. As for the second question…Jesus changes people's lives because He cares for them.

"Sin brings only sorrow and death into our lives, and Jesus wants better for us. The Bible says that man used to have one-on-one communication with God, but then man sinned and sin separates us from God. Jesus came to earth and died for all of us so that we could once again have communion one-on-one with God. Once we give our lives to Him, when God looks at us He no longer sees our sins. He sees the blood of Jesus. Jesus was the perfect sacrifice, covering all people for all time. It might sound complicated, but what it really boils down to is the fact that while we have sin in our lives, God can't have fellowship with us. We have to accept the fact that we are sinners and need the blood of Jesus to cleanse our lives. Then He takes our sins away, and we can have fellowship with God. That's how it was meant to be from the beginning."

"So you're one of those people who believe that unless you ask Jesus into your heart, you can't go to heaven?"

"Yes, that's true. Heaven is where God is, and we can't enter there if we have sin in our lives. Once we accept the fact that we are sinners, and we give our lives to Christ, it is as if our sins are gone. We still have to live with the consequences of our sins, but God no longer holds them to our account because of the sacrifice His Son made on our behalf. The Bible says, 'There is therefore now no condemnation for those who are in Christ Jesus.'"

Brooke thought silently. *Would I go to hell if I died right now? If what Sky says is true, then I would.* Her heart constricted in her chest as her thoughts turned to Hank. God would never forgive her for all the wicked things she had done.

The silence in the room grew heavy until Sky broke it by saying, "I thought we might go into town tomorrow."

The words brought her head up with a snap, her eyes brightening. Maybe this was what she needed to help her forget for a while. Forget the past, forget the hurt, forget what Sky had just told her.

Sky chuckled at her excitement. "If you look around and make a list of what you need or might want, we will see what we can do about it. Pierce City doesn't have a lot, but it might be able to supply some of the things you need."

Brooke couldn't remember the last time she had been so excited, but at the back of her mind, she kept replaying her conversation with Sky.

The rest of the day was spent going through the cupboard and cellar and making a list of things she thought they could use. At the end of the day she was rather appalled at the length of the list, but Sky didn't say a word when she handed it to him, just tucked it in his shirt pocket and bid her good night.

They rode into town the next morning around 11 o'clock. Brooke's first glimpse of Pierce City was fascinating. The town sat in one of the most beautiful locations she had ever seen. It nestled in a small valley encircled by gently rolling, forested hills. Several creeks surrounded the little town, the largest of which was called Orofino Creek, Sky told her.

The length of Main Street stretched out before them as they rode in from the south. A tall tree grew directly in the middle of it on the near end of town, its branches shading them momentarily as they rode underneath.

To the left, as they rode up the street, Brooke saw what appeared to be some kind of Chinese temple. A sign on the front of the building was lettered in Chinese characters. She made a mental note to ask Sky what it said later. Next door to the temple was the Pioneer Hotel. Across the street and up a little ways was a store dubbed Fraser's Mercantile.

Sky pulled to a stop in front of this building, his hands coming gently around her waist as he helped her to the ground.

Inside the dimly lit store, shelves of canned goods, bolts of cloth, and a table of tin dishes took up the main of the room. Barrels of mining equipment, garden tools, and seeds lined the walls. By the counter stood two large casks of coffee and molasses.

These filled the room with a heady pungent aroma and melded with the grainy scent of the cracked corn stacked in bags to one side.

A man stepped through a curtained alcove at the back of the store and paused to straighten a display of hunting knives.

"Hello, Fraser," Sky said. "How are things?"

"Sky!" Fraser's friendly face broadened into a grin. "Things are going just fine. Jed told me a lot has happened to you since we last saw each other." He punctuated this last statement with a pointed look in Brooke's direction.

"Jed's never far wrong, Fraser. I'd like you to meet my wife, Brooke. Brooke, Fraser is the owner of this run-down-bit-of-a-store," Sky concluded teasingly with a gesture around the room.

Brooke immediately knew these men were very good friends.

Fraser laughed as he extended his hand to Brooke. "Ma'am, it is a pleasure to meet you. It's about time ol' Sky here had some feminine influence on his manners, as you can see. You have your work cut out for you."

For some reason Brooke felt instantly at ease in the presence of Fraser's kindness. She chuckled, and said sweetly, "My first goal was to fatten him up a bit. Did you notice how much weight he's put on?"

A pained look crossed Sky's face, and he made an obvious effort to suck in his perfectly toned stomach and smooth the front of his shirt. But as Fraser threw back his head with a belly laugh, Sky relaxed, raising one eyebrow in Brooke's direction.

"She has got your number, Skyler Jordan. You had best watch out for this one." Fraser moved off behind the counter still chuckling to himself. "Snoop around and pick out whatever you need," he called over his shoulder. "I'll tally it all up when you're through."

As soon as Fraser moved out of earshot, Sky turned to Brooke. "You just wait." His eyes sparkled with suppressed mirth. "When you are least expecting it, you're going to pay for that one. That's the second time." He held aloft two fingers.

Brooke smiled cheekily, not really believing him. "It was

worth it. You should have seen the look on your face. Your pride is going to be your downfall someday, you know." She moved down the first aisle to start filling her list, Sky chuckling behind her.

CHAPTER NINE

A s they were leaving the Mercantile, Brooke asked Sky, "Do you think it would be all right if I went and visited with Jenny for a little while?"

"Sure. I'll head on down to the livery—" he pointed it out just across the street to the right "—and get some of these things loaded up. As soon as I'm done, I'll come pick you up at the Chang's store. It's right there." He pointed to a building two doors down to the left and across the street.

Holding her elbow, Sky escorted Brooke across the dusty street, then headed in the direction of the livery to get the saddle packs the mule would carry on the way home.

Brooke suddenly felt very excited to see Jenny again. She smoothed her hair and swiped at the front of her skirt, wishing she didn't look so dusty and trail-worn, even though Jenny would understand.

A small bell jangled over the door as Brooke stepped into the store owned by Jenny's husband. It took only a moment for Brooke's eyes to adjust to the darkened interior. Then she spotted Jenny walking toward her from the back of the room, a large smile wreathing her plump face.

"Brooke! It so good to see you! You come!"

Brooke giggled. "Of course I came. How did your pies sell?"

"Sell just fine. Just like dat." She snapped her fingers and smiled.

"Oh good. I'm so glad. Sky and I came to town to buy supplies, and I wanted to make sure I came by to say hello. I miss female company so much out at the farm that I head to the barn to have a chat with Bess, the milk cow."

Jenny's melodic laugh rang through the store. "You come. I haf tea in back. We drink?"

"That would be nice."

As they made their way toward the back of the store, though, the bell over the front door rang again and Brooke turned to see a corpulent, mustached Chinese man with beady eyes entering the store. A pipe drooped from one corner of his mouth. His assessing gaze took Brooke in from head to toe as he pulled a packet of matches out of his front shirt pocket. A scar puckered one cheek. He gave Jenny a calculating look as he struck the match and held it to the bowl of the pipe, puffing a few times.

Shaking out the match, he flicked it into the corner as he spoke to Jenny. "Who is this?" He nodded in Brooke's direction as though the room was crowded and Jenny might not know to whom he referred.

Jenny's voice held a note of tension that had not been there a moment before. "Lee, this Brooke Jordan. She marry Skyler Jordan little while ago."

Lee Chang turned his focus back on Brooke but addressed Jenny again.

"What is she doing here?"

Jenny paused and Brooke instinctively knew her answer wouldn't please Chang. She remembered the day they had met at the berry patch, when Jenny had said her husband didn't like her to visit with white folks. Before Jenny could speak up and condemn herself, Brooke broke in. "I was asking your wife, sir, if she had any fabric in the store. I would like to see it if you do."

Chang gave her a speculative look as he took a couple of pulls on his pipe.

Then he transferred his gaze back to his wife. Brooke cringed inwardly at the look she saw there. How many times had she seen that same expression in Hank's eyes?

Jenny did not say anything but stood mutely staring at the floor.

Chang spoke around the stem of his pipe. "Do we have any fabric, Jenny?"

Jenny silently shook her head.

"Well then, I guess we cannot be of service to you, Mrs.

Jordan. Have a pleasant afternoon." With that, Chang took Jenny by the elbow and led her toward the back of the store, effectively dismissing Brooke.

Brooke's heart ached. She wanted to rush into the back room and pull Jenny away from that awful man. To take her away where she would be safe and never harmed again, but what could she do? She was just a woman, and the man was Jenny's husband. With a heavy heart she made her way toward the door and out onto the street. She surmised what Jenny would face, now alone with her husband. Whatever form it took, it would not be pleasant.

So many times she'd wished that someone would step in and rescue her from Uncle Jackson and then from Hank. But now she knew how helpless those who had seen her own abuse felt. What could one do? Surely something…but for right now she didn't know what it might be. Turning, she headed toward the livery that Sky had pointed out to her earlier.

Later that evening, Fraser whistled tunelessly as he moved around the store locking up all the windows. He was very happy for Skyler Jordan. He had heard from Jed of the circumstances under which Sky had gotten married and had felt sorry for the man. But after having met Brooke and seeing the way Sky's eyes lit up when he looked at her, Fraser was sure that things were going to work out well for the couple. That pleased him, because he was very fond of Sky Jordan.

He had just slid the last window latch into place when he heard the bell above his front door ring. *A customer this late in the day?*

Four Chinamen entered, chatting easily with one another.

"Hello, gentlemen. What can I do for you this evening?"

One of them stepped forward as the other three began to browse through the store. "I looking for," the man held one hand up to his neck in a choking motion, "how you say?… Neck tie?"

"Ahhh!" Fraser's face broke into a smile. "You have a girl?"

The man nodded shyly.

"I have just the one for you, my man." Fraser clapped him on the shoulder as he led him toward a shelf at the back of the store. "I got some new ones the last time my packer, Jason, went to Lewiston."

"I take this one." The young man Fraser was helping picked up the cheapest tie.

"That's fine. A good choice." Fraser led the man to the counter. Marking the payment in his ledger book, he placed the tie in a small paper bag and handed it to the young man. "You have a nice evening now."

When all four of the men had left, Fraser chuckled to himself. "He must not have it *too* bad, or he would have bought the most expensive one."

Ping Chi, eighteen, licked his lips nervously as he left Fraser's Mercantile with the bolo tie in his hand. His eyes darted nervously up and down the street to see if anyone had seen them exiting the building, but no one was in sight.

Leaving his three companions, he made his way home to wait for the summons he expected would come later that evening. When he entered his little dark hut, he threw the paper bag into the corner.

Sitting on his cot, Ping rested his head in both hands. Terror pulsed through his veins. *What made me actually agree to be a part of this?* He raised his head and pressed both trembling hands together between his knees. *Lee Chang and his opium.*

Even now, as he held one hand out in front of him, it shook uncontrollably. His body was going to go through another fit of withdrawal; he could feel it coming on. Tears sprang to his eyes, and he clutched at his forehead in torment as his old familiar hallucination began. He writhed on his bed in agony, pushing and slapping away imaginary bugs, snakes, and scorpions, and crying out for someone to save him. No one came.

When the hallucination finally played itself out, he lay on the cot, drenched in sweat, the side of his face buried in his sweat-stained pillow, and cried. Pounding his fist on the metal frame of the bed, he wondered how his life had come to be such a mess. Every penny he earned, his body demanded that he spend for just one more smoke of the addictive drug that he could only get from Lee Chang.

And now Lee Chang had denied him any more opium until he completed this task. Tonight he had to kill a man in cold blood, or he would never see the other side of a hallucination-halting high again. His companions were in no better shape than he was.

He didn't want to do this. But what else was he to do? Every last nerve in his body cried out for the calming effect of just one more puff on a pipe filled with the opiate. And if he completed his task as ordered, Chang had promised to give him a generous supply.

As they walked from the Livery Stable to Jed's boarding house for dinner, Sky eyed the dark clouds quickly gathering above them. Brooke noticed his concern and wondered how they would get all their groceries home without a soaking. They had led the mule and Bess's calf behind them as they rode to town, and she knew that on the back of the mule, the groceries would be drenched by the time they got them home.

Brooke tried to get her mind off Jenny by focusing on the purchases they had made that day. *I've never had such nice things before.* She'd found everything on her list but canning jars, and she could live without those for a while. Sky insisted she buy several yards of a beautiful creamy peach fabric that Fraser kept behind the counter in his store, and she looked forward to sewing herself a new dress.

The thought of the material brought Jenny to mind, and she again tried to push the thought away. Yet she had seen something in Jenny and Lee's relationship that intrigued her. Jenny emitted calm and acceptance of the whole situation. Whenever Brooke had known Hank's intentions, as Jenny surely had known Lee's, she had been sullen and haughty, which, if the truth were known, had only worsened her predicament.

It had become her way of protecting her spirit when she couldn't protect her body. She remembered saying to Hank, "You may be able to bruise my body, but you will never be able to touch my soul!" That, of course, had not been true, but she had put up a good front. Jenny, on the other hand, seemed composed and almost serene about the whole situation. Brooke wondered what the difference between herself and Jenny was. *Perhaps I misjudged the look on Lee Chang's face?* She shook her head. *I don't think so.*

One other thing bothered her; she had seen Sky dickering with Bill, the Livery owner, over Bess's calf. Sky wanted to build up his herd, so why sell the calf? Yet she didn't feel it her place to dig into his financial matters.

Just as they entered Jed's boarding house, the first fat drops of rain began to fall, and the wind picked up.

★

CHAPTER TEN

Jed's face lit up when he saw Brooke and Sky enter the boarding house. He smoothed his mustache as he crossed the room to greet them. Holding his hand out to Brooke, he smiled genuinely. "Ma'am, it shorly is a great pleasure to meet you. I seen you two ride in earlier an' I done cooked up a batch o' my best fixin's. I'm Jed Swanson. An' you're Brooke. I been waitin' to meet ya." He gestured proudly toward the table. "Come on in! Have a seat! Have a seat!"

He took Brooke by the arm, leading her to the table where he pulled out a chair and seated her with great fanfare.

As Sky seated himself next to her, he smiled broadly, realizing that he had never received the royal treatment Jed lavished on Brooke. When Jed turned his back, Sky leaned toward her from his chair. "Don't expect it to taste like anything but shoe leather," he whispered in her ear, his eyes sparkling.

Brooke jabbed him in the ribs with her elbow, giving him a castigating look, to which he responded with an unrepentant grin.

Jed set two plates in front of them with a flourish, and, after prayer, Brooke, to her chagrin, discovered that Sky had not been far from wrong. She dug into the food, though, not wanting to insult their host by refusing to eat what he had worked hard to prepare for them. Fraser came in a few moments later and helped himself to some of the fare, eating with knife in one hand and fork in the other.

"Where's Jason?" asked Sky.

Fraser waved his fork in the air as he finished swallowing his bite. "He headed down to Lewiston to bring up some supplies for the store. He won't be back until late tonight."

Brooke glanced at Sky. Did she see relief in his eyes? Yes,

relief and something else. Sorrow? She turned back to her food thoughtfully, hoping that one day things would be different. Hoping that Jason would one day come to see the sorrow his actions brought into his own life and the lives of others.

What was the difference between Sky and Jason? Something drew her to this man like she had never been drawn to anyone before—not even to Hank—and that scared her. There was something special about Sky. The difference? Jason acted like all the men she had ever known—unpredictable and uncontrolled. And Sky…well, he was just the opposite.

Then there were men like Fraser and Jed. She didn't know if they believed like Sky did about God, but she couldn't imagine either one ever abusing a woman. She reflected over the last couple of months. She used to believe all men were the same—arrogant, inconsiderate, and abusive—but now, since knowing Sky, she could see the prejudice in that way of thinking. All men did not fit into her preconceived mold. Holes perforated the walls of logic built up around her heart.

The rain came down harder now, the soothing muted sound vibrating through the roof. Conversation around the table was light and congenial, and Brooke relaxed until Jed offered, "I got a room, Sky. You cain't travel home in these here cats and dogs. I'll just go an' make sure that everything is in tip shape for you an' the Missus."

Sky said, "That's fine, Jed."

Brooke rubbed her hands together in front of her. She looked around the room, trying to appear casual, but her gaze collided with Sky's and she saw that he understood the deep turmoil churning within her. He took a sip of coffee, his eyes holding hers. Over the rim of the mug, his dark eyes were soft and tender, dropping momentarily to her hands as he set the cup on the table, and then moving back to her face. He shook his head almost imperceptibly and she knew that he was reminding her of his promise.

The trouble was, she didn't know if she wanted him to keep that promise anymore.

Realizing that they were staring at one another, they both tore their eyes away at the same time, turning toward Fraser. He had stopped eating and grinned at them, his knife and fork pointed at the ceiling and unmoving by his plate. "It's nice that things worked out for you two," he said, eyes twinkling.

Brooke wondered what he meant, but before she could ask, Jed returned. "The room's all set, Sky, and don't you worry 'bout a thing. You look at this here stay as a sort o' weddin' present."

"Thank you, Jed." Sky downed the last of his coffee, stood, and pulled Brooke's chair out for her. Leading the way across the room, he held the door to the hallway open. As she passed through, he followed close behind.

The room that Jed had prepared for them was comfortably furnished, if somewhat bachelor-like in appearance. The bed, which Brooke noticed first, had its head pushed against the middle of the right-hand wall. It had no head or foot board but was supported on a frame of logs that rested directly on the floor. The quilts, though somewhat faded and ragged in appearance, looked clean. The room's only oil lamp sat on a small stone ledge inset into the log wall to the right of the bed. One small window in the far wall looked out onto the alley between Jed's boarding house and Fraser's Mercantile.

Lightning flashed, and Brooke caught a glimpse of the rain streaking down from the heavens. The following rumble of thunder caused a shiver to run down her spine, and she turned, without moving her feet, to finish her examination of the room. The only furnishing in the room, other than the bed, was a washstand next to the door, a broken piece of mirror hanging on the wall above it.

Brooke heard the latch click shut. She stood with her back to the door and waited for Sky to speak. She felt, more than saw him approach, stopping just behind her. "Brooke?"

She turned slowly after a brief pause, her eyes not rising any higher than the V at the neck of his buckskin shirt. If he asked, she would give him permission to touch her. That decision she had already made. Still, she knew she didn't feel prepared to take this next step. She now knew he would never force himself on her. She didn't fear him. No, her nervousness stemmed from the fact that this night might propel their relationship onto a whole new level. And she didn't know if she was ready for that. *I don't want to love this man—any man.* It was too risky.

Sky bent down until her eyes met his. "Do you think this room will suit your needs?"

A frown creased her forehead at the word *your*, but she turned to survey the room once more. "It's fine." She gestured to the room in general.

"Good. Then I'll see you in the morning, all right?" He stared into her face with concerned eyes, making sure she really was all right.

She looked up at him questioningly, and not until he turned toward the door did she realize that he meant to leave. "Sky?" She suddenly knew she *wanted* him to stay.

He paused, his hand on the latch, looking back at her.

"Where will you sleep?"

He shrugged.

"It's pouring rain, Sky, and you don't have any blankets."

He merely looked at her, not saying a word, just shrugging again.

Brooke stared down at her hands, but when she heard him start to open the door, she blurted, "You can sleep in here if you like." Her heart hammered in her ears.

He shut the door and leaned his shoulder into it, folding his arms and crossing his ankles casually, the toe of one boot resting on the floor. The light from the lamp cast golden highlights on his hair and he gazed at her, tenderness in his dark eyes. "You sure?"

Brooke nodded, looking down at her hands.

"Brooke?"

She glanced up.

"Thank you."

She nodded and blushed. He could have forced her to do anything he wanted, and yet he stood here thanking her for allowing him to sleep indoors on a rain-soaked night.

He walked purposefully toward the bed, removing one blanket and one pillow. Spreading them on the floor between the bed and the door, he removed his hat, boots, and the belt that sheathed his knife and stretched out, hands behind his head.

Brooke stood still, watching all of this as relief flooded her heart. Sky was so understanding.

He watched her now, a slight smile playing on his generous mouth, one eyebrow raised. "Do you sleep standing up?" he teased.

She smiled wryly, shaking her head, and moved toward the bed, blowing out the lamp as she went.

Sitting out in the main room of the boarding house, Jed smiled as he poured himself another cup of coffee. It was good to know that he still had the touch. His cat-like ears had heard the bedroom door open and then close again, and now there was no sound coming from the hallway. He had stayed up, so he could offer Sky the floor of his room when he came through to go outside, but his plan had worked better than even he had hoped.

At dinner it was obvious both of the young people were hopelessly attracted to each other, but tension hummed between them like a tight wire. Time spent together would take care of that. He'd figured maybe they needed some help—a little prodding in the right direction. The rain had been a godsend. Finishing the last of his coffee, he headed down the hallway toward his own room.

Just inside the darkened forest east of town he crouched, cursing the pouring rain. He moved closer to the trunk of the tree under which he stood, trying to find the driest place possible. "Cussed country!" he muttered in disgust.

He thought he heard something and cocked his head like a mountain lion listening for the rustle of its prey. Yes, he heard it again. Satisfaction curled through him, even as he ran his hand over his face to brush off as much of the trickling water as he could. The Chinese party had begun. He moved deeper into the trees, picking up the reins of his horse and leading it away from town. He'd give it an hour, then he'd be back.

Hearing the first volley of fire crackers, Sky sat up. The rain still beat a tattoo on the roof, and an occasional flash of lightning lit the room with a blinding glare. He glanced over to see Brooke sitting up in the bed as well, staring at the window.

"It's just a party. Sometimes they go all night. Hopefully you'll be able to get some sleep."

She did not turn toward him but kept staring at the window. "Why are they having a party? You mean the Chinese, right?"

He nodded, then realized she couldn't see him. "Yes. They have them for all sorts of reasons. Any excuse to get together and have some fun. Someone's birthday or anniversary. Or maybe someone found some gold in their mine today. Who knows?" He shrugged in the darkness. "Do you think you'll be able to sleep?"

Brooke gave a dry chuckle. "I can sleep through anything."

"Yes. I seem to remember that now." His tone was light and teasing as he remembered the first morning after their wedding.

He heard her get up softly and move to stand by the window. Lightning flashed, and he could see that she stared out the window with a faraway, frightened expression.

His heart beat erratically. He earnestly wanted to know more about this intriguing woman. He wanted to soothe away her haunting fears with a warm embrace, but to do so would only make matters worse. Instead he lay back down, face to the ceiling, and asked, "Would you tell me about your uncle? Jackson Baker, you said his name was?"

Out of the corner of his eye, Sky saw her stiffen and he wondered again how cruel this man had been to his niece. His fists clenched involuntarily behind his head at the mere thought of someone mistreating her. Was her uncle the man who had left those scars on her arms?

He turned now to look directly at her. Arms crossed, she rubbed her hands up and down the sleeves of her dress. She had not answered his question. He would never sleep as long as the fireworks were going on, so he got up, lit the lamp, and went over to where she stood. Turning his back to the wall, he slid to the floor, looking up at her and waiting. When she finally glanced down, he patted the floor by his side. She hesitated, then slid down beside him, hugging her knees to her chest.

He kept quiet, still fighting the urge to draw her into the comfort of his arms. She looked so vulnerable, so frightened and fragile. Could the mere mention of her uncle bring such terror?

Lifting her chin from her knees she leaned her head back against the wall and began to talk softly. Her fingers, resting in her lap, played with a small piece of wood she had picked up off the floor.

"When I was fifteen—" Her voice cracked. After a moment, she went on. "My mother, father, and sister were killed in an accident. Their buggy came too close to the edge of a road with a steep drop-off during a torrential rain storm, and the buggy rolled down into the canyon. It was a Sunday. I had stayed home from church that day because I didn't feel well."

Pain for what she must have gone through washing over him, Sky closed his eyes.

"I was sent to live with my uncle. Jackson Baker, yes," she said, answering his earlier question. She paused, as if trying to decide how to finish the story. "While I lived with him, I learned a lot of things about life." She stopped, but Sky had heard the bitter edge in her voice. She went on, steering the conversation away from her uncle. "Darcy, the cook, taught me all she knew, and I would often visit the barn when Uncle Jackson was away. From the stable man, Solomon, I learned a lot about treating sick animals."

"That explains why Bess's leg has healed so quickly." He peered down at her in the dim light. "Why did you only visit the barn when your uncle was away?"

She shrugged and waved away the question with a sad

expression full of painful memory. "I lived with him for three years, and then he sent me here."

Sky knew she would say no more on the subject tonight. He felt thankful for the brief insight into her past.

They sat in companionable silence for a while before she spoke again, turning her face toward him, her head still resting against the wall. "You have never told me how you came to this area. You said you grew up in Oregon?"

Sky brought his knees up, resting his forearms on them as he spoke, leaning his head back against the wall. "Yes, I did. My parents own a ranch in the Willamette Valley. My father is a lawman, and I used to be the Deputy Sheriff in my hometown but—" he shrugged "—Jason moved here. He was born in Pierce City during the gold rush days, and something brought him back. I felt like he needed some family near him, and I had nothing really keeping me at home, so I moved out here and started the farm. I've been here five years now."

Turning her head toward him, she teased, "What? No girls back home pining away for you?" However, her voice still held a note of seriousness from the earlier discussion of her own past.

Sky stared at the dark shadow of the ceiling. "There was a girl, but she is not pining away for me. Her name is Victoria Snyder. We…well, *I* had thought we might be married one day, but when Victoria found out that I wanted to be a lawman, she decided I wasn't the man for her. Her father was a sheriff. He died in the line of duty when she was just twelve, and she promised herself that she would never put her children in the same situation. So…it was never meant to be. It has taken me awhile to realize that, but I see it now. I never loved her like—" Sky's voice cut off midsentence. This was not the right time to admit his feelings to her.

Brooke didn't seem to notice his last sentence. "She left you, huh? Silly girl didn't know a good thing—"

She had started out with a teasing tone but suddenly her eyes widened, and she turned her face away from him.

Sky's heart did a flip. He quickly turned his face toward her, but all he could see was the back of her head. He leaned his head back against the wall and whispered, "Hey." She turned back partway and pressed her palms together in front of her. He tried again, his voice still soft. "Brooke?"

She turned toward him, looking him in the eye. His focus dropped to where she nervously worked her lower lip but then snapped back to her blue eyes. "I think I would like you to finish that last sentence."

When she didn't say anything, he prompted, "Silly girl didn't know a good thing...?" His eyes never left hers.

"...when she had it." Her words were whisper-soft. She took a deep breath.

One brow winged its way upward. "Those are some very enlightening words, Mrs. Jordan."

Brooke's heart hammered in her throat, and a shiver ran up her spine. He said "Mrs. Jordan" like an endearment. *I like that term just a little too much.* Shrugging, she saw a way out. "I only meant that it would have been nice for her to have a lawman around if ever there was any trouble."

His eyes sparked, and his mouth crinkled in amusement. "Did you?" His tone dripped disbelief. He lifted his head off the wall. "Did you know you can tell if someone is lying to you by their eyes? Your eyes betray you, Mrs. Jordan." He leaned toward her, all amusement suddenly gone from his face. "Would you like it if I kissed you?"

She inhaled sharply. His face remained only inches from hers, in anticipation of her answer. Her gaze involuntarily dropped to his mouth and she quickly looked back up to his eyes.

She wanted to say, "Yes," wanted to with all her heart, but the word stuck in her throat. Blood pounded in her ears, and an icy fear clenched her stomach. Memories of Hank flooded her mind, but the brown eyes before her were nothing like Hank's. These were kind eyes. Yet she knew that she must never let herself fall in love with this man. She had fallen too far in her life. She had been through too much to ever allow herself to love again. Tears began to glaze her eyes. Why hadn't she met Sky a long time ago? Her baby would be alive today if Sky had been her daddy instead of Hank.

Sky leaned back slightly. "Are you afraid of me, Brooke?"

Her eyes dropped to her lap. She shook her head.

"Come here. Will you trust me?" He held out his arms to her.

She didn't look up at him. Her courage would fail her if she did. Even against her will, she leaned toward him as tears brimmed over to course down her cheeks.

His arms, firm but gentle, wrapped around her as he pulled her against him. Her cheek resting on his chest, she let her barriers down. All the pent-up tears she'd bottled up for so long poured out onto the front of Sky's shirt.

Sky's hand smoothed her hair away from her face. Gentle rain pattered outside, a low thrum beneath the louder sounds of firecrackers and revelry. For the first time in years she allowed herself to feel the comfort another person offered. She sobbed for a long time, grieving as her mind wandered over the past few years.

Hank had approached her at a church social, but the meeting had been orchestrated by Uncle Jackson. She had not known that for a number of years.

At first, Hank had been charming and kind. He was darkly handsome, and Brooke had fooled herself into thinking that he actually cared for her. They were engaged in December with a date for the wedding set in July. Once they became engaged, Brooke gave in to his constant badgering and moved in with him. After all, they were to be married shortly; where could the harm be? Besides, it would get her away from Uncle Jackson.

Soon afterward, the abuse began. The first time he had been in a hurry to get to an important meeting. Brooke had cleaned the house that day and moved a stack of documents that he needed for the meeting. They were in plain sight, but in his rush he hadn't seen them and lashed out at her. Grabbing her by the front of her dress he lifted her off the floor and shook her. "Where are those papers? You better find them, or I'll—"

Brooke shuddered at the memory, her hand coming up to her

throat as if to rub away the memory of her dress collar cutting off her air.

The gentle massaging of Sky's fingers on her neck soothed her. "Shhh, Brooke, honey. You're all right. I'm here."

She was so immersed in the memories that she barely heard his whisper. When she became pregnant, she thought things would change. She told Hank of her condition and waited to see what would happen. He treated her well for a couple of weeks— like when they had first met. But one day, when he came home tired from work, he had found her asleep on the couch instead of in the kitchen finishing dinner. He shook her awake. "You lazy whore!" Dragging her to the kitchen by her hair, he shoved her on the floor. "Get my dinner!"

In that moment, she knew things would never change. She determined she would not let her baby suffer from his fits of anger. The next day she packed her bags and headed out the door to move back to Uncle Jackson's, but Hank had come home early to apologize for his outburst the night before. Predictable Hank. She should have expected him. After every incident, he came home, said he was *so* sorry, that it would never happen again, and would she *please* forgive him? However, on this day, when he saw her, bag in hand, he went out of his head. He beat her until she passed out. Then, seeing what he had done, he came to his senses and carried her to Uncle Jackson's. When she came to, she had already been bleeding for a long time.

Uncle Jackson sent for the doctor. "Brooke was out riding and fell off her horse," he'd told him.

Early that morning, she gave birth to a perfect, tiny, stillborn girl. Brooke could still see her ten tiny fingers and perfect little toes. Her downy little head had been full of dark hair, just like Hank's. Brooke wrapped one tiny hand around her little finger and carefully wiped away her own tears where they fell on the baby's face. *If I could only have had just one day to show this little one how much I love her.* The doctor wrapped the baby in a square of pink cloth and gently laid her by Brooke's side. The funeral had been the next day. Hank hadn't come.

Sobs shook Brooke's body now. Wracking sobs.

She had told Uncle Jackson that she would never marry Hank; he could kill her first. A week later her uncle came home and informed her she was being sent west as a mail-order bride. All that had happened less than seven months ago.

Brooke had assumed God was punishing her by allowing her baby girl to die. Yet here she was, being treated with the tenderest kindness she had known since the death of her mother and sister. Had God's hand been on her all along?

When she could stop crying, she sat up, placing one hand on Sky's chest and looking into his eyes. Giving him a watery smile, she said, "I've soaked the front of your shirt."

"I don't mind. Somehow I think you needed a good cry. Do you want to talk about it?" He tucked a stray curl of hair behind her ear.

She looked past him at the wall. Her voice was low and thoughtful. "I do, but I can't." She found she was able to be honest with him. "Someday."

He frowned slightly, still playing with the hair by her ear. "There was another man besides your uncle, wasn't there?"

She blinked. How did he know that? She wanted to tell him. To get the whole terrible confession off her chest. To ask him why God had taken her baby girl. But something held her in check. Could she ever reveal that much of herself to this man? She rubbed her hands together in a circular motion.

He moved around in front of her, sitting cross-legged with his knees touching hers. Gently, he took her hands in his own. "You do this when you are nervous." Placing his palms against hers, he interlaced their fingers, his thumbs tracing hot paths down the sides of her hands. "Why are you nervous, honey?" He bent his head down, forcing her to meet his gaze. "Will you tell me about it? Tell me about this man."

She looked into his face and wanted to tell him. Yet a thought flashed through her mind. *What will his reaction be when I tell him? What will he say when he learns that I have been with another man and borne his baby? I can't bear to see the pain in his eyes or to think what the consequences might be.* She shook her head. "I can't, Sky."

A momentary hurt crossed his face but was quickly gone. "Someday then. Someday. I'm committed to you, Brooke. Nothing you say is ever going to change that." He looked directly into her eyes. "Nothing. Do you believe me?"

She nodded slowly, but in her heart she felt sure it couldn't be true. "Brooke, look at me." She raised her eyes to his. His mouth hardened into a determined line even as his eyes softened. "I love you."

Her heart stopped and then started again with double-time rhythm.

"I didn't want to tell you like this. I wanted the time to be perfect, but somehow I think you need to hear it. I love you. You were the one meant for me from the beginning of all time. I know it now. Why God chose to bring us together the way He did, I don't know. I do know that you are the one for me. You remember that. No matter what you are feeling or what you are afraid of. Know that I love you." He brought one hand up and cupped her face, his thumb trailing over her cheekbone, his eyes never leaving hers. He leaned toward her. "Now, Mrs. Jordan, may I kiss you good night?"

How could she deny him anything, this man who had sacrificed so much for her? Brooke nodded.

His eyes sparked with pleasure, and his head lowered toward hers.

But her hands turned clammy, and, just before his mouth touched hers, she gave a little gasp and pulled away. "I can't, Sky! I'm sorry." She scrambled to her feet as if running from a fire. She stumbled to the bed, lay down with her back to him, and curled herself into a tight ball.

Sky sighed, and ran shaking hands through his hair. Lacing them behind his neck, he let his head hang between his raised knees for a moment, trying to get a hold on his ragged emotions. Then, slowly, he climbed to his feet. He made his way to the lamp and paused to look down into her face. But her eyes were closed, her expression unreadable. Blowing out the light, he lay back down. He didn't fall asleep for a long time, but it wasn't the Chinese celebration outside that kept him awake. He was praying. For himself. For his and Brooke's relationship. And for Brooke's relationship with God.

CHAPTER ELEVEN

Brooke lay silently listening to Sky's even breathing. What had happened? Lately she had been longing for his touch; hoping he would approach the subject. But when he did—asking for a kiss, nonetheless—she had run as if for her life. Her heart still had not returned to its normal pace, and she was angry. At herself. *How long am I going to keep this up? What am I afraid of?*

She knew the answer. Flipping over onto her back in exasperation, she stared at the ceiling. She wanted nothing more than to feel his lips touch hers, to allow herself the luxury of loving again. *So what stopped me?* She was no longer afraid that he would abuse her as Hank had. The fact was, that although her heart told her he cared, her mind told her it could not be true. After all, he had only married her to protect her from his cousin. She would give herself to him in a heartbeat, but he deserved someone better. Not someone with a sullied past like hers. He deserved a woman that he could cherish with all of his heart, not a mail-order bride that he felt sorry for.

This thought propelled her mind on to new channels. What would happen to her when he finally realized that his feelings for her were not love, but sympathy? What would happen when he found out what her past had really been like? Would he send her back to Uncle Jackson? At the mere thought of going back to live with her uncle, Brooke sat up, her hand going to her heart.

Getting up, she crossed to the window, staring out into the darkness.

Sky is so special. He deserves so much more than I can give him. He deserves a woman who is pure and undefiled. Someone who believes like he does. I'll never be good enough for him.

That thought hurt her more than she could have guessed. She resolved that she would not saddle Sky to her for the rest of his life. He should have better. But what could she do about it? She would figure something out.

Maybe in the spring, she would just tell him that she wanted to go back east. Then she would stop in a nice small town on the way back and maybe become a teacher or a nurse. Something respectable. Pain filled her heart at the prospect of leaving Sky, but she didn't know what else she could do to protect him.

Brooke leaned her forehead against the glass as she stood at the window staring out into the rain-washed darkness. In a bright flash of lightning, a movement in the alley below the window caught her attention. What was it? Another bright flash. She saw the alley more clearly this time.

A man stood below, and with shock, Brooke realized she recognized him. Just then, he glanced up and saw her looking down at him. A flash of surprise, and then pure venomous hatred crossed his face.

Brooke sucked in a quick breath and stepped back. *Why would anyone be out on such a dark, wet night?* Her curiosity got the best of her, and she stepped up to the window again.

With the next flash of lightning she saw that he had moved down the alley and crouched behind a wooden barrel. He peered out into the street in front of Fraser's Mercantile next door. He held a rifle under his arm, its long barrel glistening with each brilliant bolt of lightning. He was obviously hiding from something. Or was it someone?

What should I do? Should I wake up Sky? She watched for a couple more minutes, debating what to do, and was just turning to call Sky when the man stood up and moved down the alley toward the outside of town. When he got to the end of the alley, he turned, and looking up at her window, raised his gun in farewell, a leer on his face.

Her whole body trembled as she stepped back to the bed and lay down.

What's he doing sneaking around in the dark with a gun?

She did not fall asleep for a long time and even then, her sleep was fitful.

The next morning, although Brooke crawled out of bed at her normal time, she turned to see that Sky had awakened before her. His buckskin shirt and blue denim pants looked none the worse for wear even though he had slept in them, and she noted that he had already slipped on his boots and belted on his knife.

One shoulder leaning into the wall, arms and ankles crossed, he watched her. "I could get used to waking up like this." His eyes smiled, but his tone held a note of seriousness.

She blushed, sat on the edge of the bed, and looked down at the green skirt of her dress, her hands trying to smooth out some of the wrinkles. "Don't misinterpret your feelings, Sky."

He pushed himself away from the wall, but still stood with arms crossed over his broad chest. "Now what is that supposed to mean? What are you thinking in that lovely head of yours?" His deep brown eyes never wavered.

She looked away toward the window, her mind going briefly to the man she'd seen the night before. "We should go out to breakfast."

"Jed's a patient man. He can wait. I, on the other hand, would like an answer to my question."

"What question?" she asked innocently.

He lost his patience and crossed the room in two strides, sitting down at the end of the bed. He leaned toward her, his eyes intent. "What are you thinking? What feelings am I misinterpreting?"

She wanted to look away, but his eyes were magnetic. Wishing she hadn't said anything, she swallowed, her throat constricting. She didn't say a word, hoping he would give up and go away, but he did not. If anything, his gaze became more intense, and his eyes narrowed just before he spoke. "If you think I am going anywhere before you tell me what's on your mind, you are wrong. We will sit here all day if need be."

"Sky," she started, but when she brought her palms together in front of her, he reached out and grasped her hands in one of his. She tensed, her gaze flying to his face, even as she did her best to suppress the tremors quaking through her.

"You told me last night that you trusted me," he said. "Were you telling the truth?"

She nodded, her eyes on his face.

"I'm not someone from your past, Brooke. I promise not to take advantage of you."

She merely nodded again, unwilling to admit she was not afraid of him but of the emotions he evoked.

"So go ahead, Brooke. What were you going to say?"

"You just feel sorry for me." The excuse sounded lame even as she said it. Sky's golden eyebrows shot upward. "So let me get this straight. You think the only reason I'm attracted to you is because I feel sorry for you?"

She didn't nod, only looked down at the quilt, suddenly very concerned with a loose red thread.

Sky chuckled softly, and her eyes snapped back to his face.

"You are something else, you know that? I finally get up the nerve to tell you how I feel, and you don't believe a word I say." He leaned closer, his eyes merry. "You still haven't figured out that I *always* mean exactly what I say?" His dancing eyes held hers for a moment, and then his voice dropped. "It sure is going to be fun convincing you that I meant what I said last night. I know we haven't known each other for long, but you are my wife, and will be my wife until the day one of us dies, which, God willing, will be a long time from now. I will be the first to admit that when I walked into this situation I didn't think we would ever come to love each other, but God is good. So here I am, in love with my wife. Is that such a bad thing?" He answered his own question with a twinkle in his eye. "Maybe it is. I might just go crazy if you don't learn to love me back."

Brooke felt the color begin to crawl up her neck even as she shifted her gaze to the wall near the door. Sky leaned even closer. She could feel his breath on her ear when he whispered, "You are very beautiful when you blush, Mrs. Jordan."

After a long pause she turned to him. "You deserve someone better than me, Sky. There are things you don't know."

Sky shook his head, his face now very serious. "Your past may not be perfect, Brooke. Mine isn't either, but I have found peace, and you can, too. I know you've had a hard life, and I hope that one day you will be comfortable enough to tell me about it. And I hope you know that what those men did to you," he caressed her forearm, "wasn't your fault."

She dropped her gaze back to the thread, but he lifted her face again. "It wasn't. Nothing you did made you deserve any of it."

She wished she could believe him. "No one could forgive me for my past, Sky. None of it was anyone else's fault. It was always me. Something I did. Something I said. Something…" She shrugged, trying desperately to keep the tears out of her eyes.

"Brooke, listen, that's not true. What happened to you," his voice quivered, "was the consequence of men's selfish sin. No one deserves to be treated the way you were."

She nodded mutely, but all her doubts clung to her like so much refuse. Uncle Jackson always said it was her fault. She wished she could believe Sky but knew he didn't understand how terrible she really was.

As Sky and Brooke approached the table, Sky noticed the impish gleam in Jed's eyes. *The old matchmaker.*

Sky pulled a chair out for Brooke, getting her a cup of coffee, and then poured one for himself.

Jed, standing next to a wrought-iron kettle hanging over the fire, grinned, his eyes darting back and forth between the two of them. Sky noted that Brooke was blushing to the roots of her hair, avoiding Jed's gaze as best she could.

"Good morning, Jed," Sky said dryly as he came back to the fire to fill a bowl of oatmeal for Brooke.

Jed's grin broadened, if that were possible. "Mornin'." Then his voice lowered into a conspiratorial whisper as he leaned toward Sky. "How'd ya sleep?"

Brooke's bowl of oatmeal in his hand, Sky whispered back

with a grin, "I slept just fine, Jed. Your floor is a little hard, though. I recommend some hay."

Sky couldn't help laughing out loud at the bewildered surprise that crossed Jed's face. *That will teach him to meddle in other people's affairs.*

Just as Sky set the bowl of steaming porridge in front of Brooke, Jason stumbled into the room with a jaw-breaking yawn, scratching his belly. He stopped short, his bleary eyes taking in Sky and then Brooke.

The smile left Sky's face but he said politely, "Good morning, Jason."

"Good morning." Jason walked to the coffee pot and poured himself a cup. Turning toward the table, he focused his blue eyes on Brooke, who looked back at him frankly. "Ma'am, I've done a lot of thinking since I last spoke to you, and I believe I owe you an apology. I was taught better, and I feel ashamed that I treated a lady in such a manner. I am truly sorry for the way I talked to you at our last meeting, and I hope you can forgive me."

Sky shifted his gaze to Brooke, who appeared somewhat dumbfounded.

"Ah…I forgive you, Jason. Thank you for your apology."

Jason nodded, relief flooding his face, and began to take his seat. But he stopped halfway down when Jed said, "Jason, would you go an' see what's keepin' Fraser? He was supposed to be here over an hour ago. Man's breakfast is goin' all to mush. He must be sick 'cause he ain't never been late fer breakfast afore."

Sky was thoughtful as he watched Jason head out the door. *Thank You, Lord, for softening his heart. Continue to do so. Help him to give his life completely back to You. Put him in a situation where he is confronted with the man he has become, and help him not to like what he sees.*

The morning air stung bitter-cold as Jason stepped outside. The rain of the night before had turned to snow sometime during the night, and a half inch of glistening powder covered the ground.

The rising sun already warmed the day, however, and Jason knew the snow would be gone before the day was out. Grandma Jordan would have called this a day washed by God's own hand, but to Jason the beauty of the new-laid snow was only an annoyance.

He cursed the snow and cold as he trudged across to Fraser's Mercantile, but in the next second as he pushed open the door, his curses turned to prayers. "Dear God! Dear God…Dear God…" No other words came to mind.

The sight before him was so appalling that he sank to his knees in shock, but in a flash shot back to his feet. He did not want to be any closer to the revulsion than necessary. Horror pounded through him.

In the next instant, he turned and stumbled out the door. "SKYLER! JED!" He bent double, his chest heaving, trying not to retch. *Why? Why!? What if it had been me?* The next thought really shocked him. *Am I ready to go? Am I ready to meet God face to face?*

"Jason, get a hold of yourself," he mumbled. "SKYLER! JED!" He ran for the boarding house but only got halfway there before Sky and Jed burst out, heading his way.

"What in tarnation's goin' on!?"

Sky didn't say anything. He took one look at Jason's face and pushed past him, running for the Mercantile, Jed on his heels. Jason took a deep breath, bracing himself to revisit the scene as he followed them.

When Sky saw the massacred body of his good friend, the only thing he said was, "Dear Jesus…Dear Jesus, no!"

Jason couldn't help but echo the cry in his own heart.

★

Chapter Twelve

A t Jason's call for Sky and Jed, Brooke paused over the slop pail, the bowl of oatmeal she had just finished scraping still in her hand. Dread swept through her and clenched her stomach tight. She knew without even being told that something was terribly wrong.

Setting the empty bowl into the wash tub, she picked up a towel and moved out of the small back nook that served as a food preparation room for the boarding house.

She started to cross the room to go out on the porch and see what Jason had been yelling about when suddenly, someone grabbed her from behind. She opened her mouth to scream, but no sound would come, and then a strong, heavily-jeweled hand clapped over her mouth.

Her pulse hammering in her ears, she clutched at the hand, trying to pull it away and cry out for Sky. Twisting and turning, she tried to dig her elbows into the ribs of the man behind her, but she was held too tightly.

The man shook her. "Be still!" His voice grated in her ear.

Brooke paid no heed to his order. She had to escape! She thrashed her arms and kicked her legs, aiming her heel into his shins. He tightened his grip, but she fought harder.

Then something pricked her throat, and she froze, heart thudding erratically.

"That's better. Now don't scream, little lady, or it will be the last sound you ever make. One twist of your slender neck like this," he twisted her head slowly in demonstration, "and you won't be around to see tonight's sunset. Do you understand?" His voice was deadly calm.

Brooke nodded vigorously. Her breath came in ragged gasps.

"See that rifle over there?"

Her head moved in acknowledgment against his chest.

"If you call for Jordan, I will shoot him down before he is even halfway here, see?"

All hope died. She nodded again.

"Good. Now I am goin' to move my hand, and you and I will have a little talk. You do just as I say and then you won't have to be afraid for your life or the lives of your loved ones, see?" Again she nodded, and he removed his hand and went to the table.

"Bring me some coffee," he said abruptly as he pulled out a chair and sat down, his back to her.

With shaking hand, Brooke set a cup before him, wanting very badly to scream for Sky but eyeing the rifle. He would be able to get to it before Sky even made it half the distance from the Mercantile, and she had no doubt that he would shoot to kill.

Then another idea entered her head. She stepped back, trying to keep her voice steady as she asked, "What do you want with me?" She took a step toward the gun.

He took a noisy slurp of the scalding brew and laughed sardonically. "I think you know."

Brooke took another step. "No, actually..." She glanced at him. His back was still to her as he sat at the table. She licked her dry lips. *Just one more little step.* She reached for the rifle, her fingertips just grazing the action.

He spun and threw his cup at the wall, missing her head by a fraction of an inch. He bounded from the chair, knocking it over in his haste, and snatched the gun from her grasp.

Jumping back, Brooke almost screamed, but caught herself just in time. The only sound that came from her mouth was a pitiful whimper.

Grabbing her by the upper arm, he shook her, making her head snap back and forth like a rag doll. "Now you listen good," he growled. "You never saw me last night, do you understand? If you so much as breathe a word of my being in town last night to anyone, I will hunt you down. First I'll make you watch me kill that husband of yours ever so slowly, and then it will be your turn."

His grip on her upper arm tightened, and he gave her one more shake. "Get a hold of yourself and listen! Your life depends on it. Here is what you will tell him: that you saw someone in that alley, but it's not goin' to be me. You tell him you saw the Mountain Man. You remember him? The one that rode on the stage with us from Lewiston? That's who you saw in the alley. Understand? Don't doublecross me now 'cause I have ears everywhere, and I will find out about it."

They heard noises from outside in the street, and he grabbed her face with one of his hands. "I swear I will kill you if you breathe a word of this to anyone!" And with that, Percival Hunter moved down the hallway toward the back door of the boarding house.

Brooke righted the chair and collapsed into it. Smoothing her hands over her skirt, she willed away the trembling that coursed through every limb. She had to calm down, or Sky would know something was wrong the minute he saw her. She pulled in a long draw of air and released it through pursed lips. Then again.

She could do this. She had to do this. Lives depended on it.

Back inside the Mercantile, Jason once again examined the scene before him—this time with a little more calm but with no less shock. His heart thudded, heavy with dread.

Just inside the door, Fraser lay in a thick red pool of blood, his eyes wide open, lifelessly staring at the ceiling. A trail of blood led from Fraser's bedroom at the back of the store, to where he now lay. Blood splattered everything. A bloody ax lay just beyond the body, a hatchet nearer the door. The poor man's body was mutilated. He had deep cuts and hash marks all over him. The side of his neck was a gaping hole. The killing blow had come in the form of a gunshot. By the angle of the exit wound, Jason surmised that the gun had been placed in the man's mouth. Probably by that time he had been too weak to resist.

Still in disbelief, he turned to a barrel of picks next to Fraser's body.

Blood smeared some of them, as though Fraser had been trying to grab one to defend himself.

Rubbing a hand over his face he turned his eyes to the ceiling for a moment. *Unbelievable. This couldn't have happened!* Not here. Not this.

The room was deathly quiet as the men stared in shock at the scene before them. Even Jed, who was usually so talkative, was strangely silent. Looking at him, Jason was surprised to see tears streaming down the old man's face. Jed had not moved from his place by the door, just stood staring down at the body of his friend in disbelief and incredulity.

Sky was the first one to recover his presence of mind. Bending over, he laid his fingers across the staring eyes, pushing them closed. "The body's still warm," he noted out loud. "He can't have been dead for long."

Sky moved purposefully about the room, willing himself to remain calm, his eyes taking in every detail. Being careful not to step in the path of blood, where he could see bare footprints, he followed the coagulating trail back to Fraser's bedroom. Pushing aside the colorful cascade of beaded strings—the divider that separated Fraser's room from the Mercantile—he noted that the trail started on the rumpled bed, where a large dark red stain could be seen.

Turning, Sky let his eyes range over the room, taking in the door and windows, trying to figure out how the murderer had gotten into the room. He knew Fraser had always meticulously locked up his store at night. His eyes paused. The latch on one of the front windows was open. "Jason, was the door unlocked when you came in?"

"Yeah, I just walked right in."

"Jed, you had better go get Gaffney and Carle," Sky said, referring to two of the other miners in town that he knew could be trusted. "Tell Bill we are going to need three of his fastest horses.

"Jason, I know you didn't get much sleep last night. Do you

think you could ride back to Lewiston? There aren't enough of us in town to conduct a thorough investigation. We are going to need a posse."

Jed left to do Sky's bidding as Jason answered, "Yeah sure, I can do that."

"Fine, we'll put together as many of the pieces as we can and then you can ride out this afternoon. Check the ledger, will you? What was the last entry Fraser made?"

Jason walked over behind the counter and picked up Fraser's receipt book. He grimaced and swiped his fingers across his pants.

Sky's stomach clenched. There must have been blood on the cover. He still couldn't believe this was happening.

Jason ran his finger down the page. "A string-tie for seventy-five cents."

"So someone was in after Brooke and I left," Sky muttered to himself as he crossed the room to get a better look at the front window latch. When he saw that the window latch was indeed open, he stopped and scanned the room once again. Sky turned toward Jason. "Fraser always locked everything up, didn't he?"

Jason nodded.

"How long have you worked for Fraser now?"

"Six years, almost seven."

"You ever know anyone who thought he had reason to kill him?"

"There was that incident with Chang. The one he told you about." Jason shook his head. "Other than that, Fraser was just about the most-liked man in these parts. I never knew him to cheat anyone. In fact, just the opposite. He would go out of his way to make sure he treated people more than fair."

"Yeah, I was thinking the same thing about Chang. I think we should pay the man a visit."

Jason glanced down at the body on the floor. "Yeah, we should find out precisely where Lee Chang was last night."

"My thoughts exactly."

Jed returned with Gaffney and Carle, both of whom began to

swear in anger when they saw the murdered man. Bill Currey, the old livery owner, came in behind them, cursed, and then began to shake so badly that Sky helped him down onto a small wooden cask for fear his legs would go out from under him.

"Jason—" the old man reached a trembling hand in the direction of Fraser's counter—"bring me some of Fraser's special brew. I need me a drink." He rubbed his face, as if to erase the sight on the floor from his mind.

But when Jason moved to comply, Sky said, "Bill, I'm sorry, but during the course of this investigation there will be no drinking. We are all going to need clear heads in order to figure out the truth." He turned serious eyes on all of the men in the room, making sure they understood the importance of this order. His eyes were compassionate, though, as he turned back to the quavering drunk. Everyone in town knew that ol' Bill Currey was very fond of his liquor. He was always on the step of Roo's Saloon even before it opened, waiting for his first drink of the day.

Sky said, "I'll take you over to Jed's for a good strong cup of coffee in a minute, Bill." Then, turning to the other men, he began to assign tasks. "Gaffney, you go outside and check around for any footprints around the store. This fresh snow is not going to help us any, but make sure any prints are not disturbed until I can see them, if you find any. I need to go see Brooke. I don't want her walking in on this.

"Carle, I want you to take your horse and search further out. I don't know what we are looking for, so take note of *anything* that looks unusual.

"Jason, you should go around the store and see if you notice anything that's missing or out of place. I noticed there is a safe in Fraser's room, but it didn't look tampered with. Do you know if he keeps money anywhere else?"

Jason shrugged. "As far as I know, he keeps all his money in the safe." Then he amended somberly, "Kept. Kept his money in the safe."

Sorrow suddenly threatened to overwhelm Sky, and he looked at the floor for a moment to get his emotions under control. Anguish washed over him. He was too good a man to have something like this happen to him. He glanced at the body again. *No one* should have something like this happen to them.

Realizing the men were staring at him, he turned to Jason. "All right. Just see if you notice anything unusual. Jed, I'll take Bill over to your place, let Brooke know what's going on, and then you and I can move him." He nodded to Fraser.

"I'll come with you. I got an extry blanket in my room to home."

Sky led Bill over to the boarding house and pushed through the front door.

Brooke jumped and spun toward them, her hand going to her throat. He frowned. "You all right?"

She nodded, smoothing her hands over her skirt, a question in her eyes. Something didn't seem right. But he was probably misjudging the situation due to his own roiling emotions. "I have some bad news."

"Oh?" Her voice was breathy.

"David Fraser has been killed."

She closed her eyes and groped for a chair behind her, sinking into it slowly.

Sky helped Bill to a seat at the table, but his attention remained fixed on Brooke as he placed a cup of black coffee before the man.

She pressed her lips together and fiddled with her fingers, studying them intensely. This was hitting her hard.

He stopped in front of her. "Brooke? I need to get back to the Mercantile. Can you keep Bill here company for a bit?"

She glanced at Bill and nodded, her gaze returning to meet his.

"I'll be back as soon as I can." He touched her cheek, then turned toward the door.

"Sky?"

He looked back at her.

"I saw a man in the alley last night." She pinched her lips together.

He blinked. "You did? Did you recognize him?"

She nodded. Looked into her lap for a moment, then back up at him. "It was the mountain man. The one who rode the stage with me from Lewiston. You remember him?"

He searched his memory. "Vaguely. You're sure it was him?"

"Yes."

"All right. I'm glad you told me. I need to get back. Stay inside, okay?"

She nodded.

Sky stepped out onto the porch and rubbed one hand back over his head. A man in the alley the night before couldn't have been up to any good. He wished she had awakened him so he could have seen the man too. Was he involved in the murder? If so how? Had he done the killing, or had he hired someone else to do it? There were too many questions and not one answer.

An hour later, Sky decided the time had come to question Lee Chang. Jason accompanied him as he entered the Joss house. The Joss house, a two-story building on the south end of Main Street, served the Chinese as a combined saloon, gambling hall, boarding house, and temple. The bottom floor consisted of a kitchen, a living-dining room, two bedrooms, and the large gambling room. The upper portion of the building housed the Chinese temple. Sky didn't know any white man who had ever been permitted to enter the temple area.

The dingy interior of the building writhed with smoke, and debris littered every surface, evidence of the previous night's party.

Taking a moment to let his eyes adjust to the dim light, Sky composed his thoughts. The last thing he wanted to start was a racial war. There already existed enough tension between the Chinese and the white faction of the town, without letting this situation go down that road too.

One thing was clear—and it bothered him—these assailants had had a gun, so why hadn't they simply shot Fraser in the first place? He had been stabbed repeatedly before being killed, as though someone were trying to prolong the torture. Obviously, Fraser had been sleeping in bed when attacked, so why hadn't the criminals simply shot him? *A bizarre crime.* Sky had never seen another like it.

And what about the safe in the back room? Why wasn't it tampered with? Sky knew from some of his previous conversations with Fraser that he had quite a substantial sum in that safe. He had been saving to send his daughter to a finishing school back east. Maybe the killer hadn't known this fact? Still, wouldn't he have at least checked? Maybe he had been interrupted?

Accustomed to the dim interior now, Sky could see Chang sitting at his usual table in the back of the room. With a gesture of his hand, Sky instructed Jason to stay in the doorway, where he would have an excellent view of the whole room. Walking purposefully toward Chang, Sky made a mental note of the position of each of Chang's four body guards. The men sat strategically around the perimeter of the room so that if you looked directly at one, the other three remained out of sight.

"Morning, Chang," Sky said politely. "I assume you've heard about Fraser?"

Chang pulled his pipe from his mouth and nodded. Raising an overflowing tankard, he took a deep draught. Then, smacking his lips, he squinted up at Sky. "Can I help you?"

Sky cut to the chase. "Where were you last night after nine o'clock?"

With a grin Chang glanced around at his companions. "He wants to know where I was last night."

Everyone in the room chuckled but Sky and Jason.

His face turning suddenly serious, Chang answered, "I was here, Mr. Jordan." His hand swept around the untidy room. "Here, enjoying a wonderful celebration."

"What were you celebrating?"

Sky saw Chang's eyes flicker before he answered, "My wife had a birthday." He replaced the stem of his pipe in his mouth, drawing deeply.

Sky's eyes narrowed. Jenny Chang had told him it was her

birthday a couple of weeks back when she had picked berries with Brooke. So what had the celebration really been about? A noisy cover for a brutal murder? Fraser's store was just across the alley from his room at Jed's, and he hadn't heard a sound coming from the Mercantile. Surely sometime during his struggle with his assailants Fraser had yelled for help. *If the festivities—and the storm—hadn't been so loud, I would have heard him call for help.*

Sky considered his options, hands held readily at his side. *Glad I told Jason to stay by the door.* He needed to bring Chang in for questioning.

Whether he was guilty or not, it appeared he was trying to hide something.

He could come back with more men to make the arrest, but Chang might be gone by then. On the other hand, Chang had four men strategically located throughout the room—all of them armed. Sky momentarily wished he was wearing his own gun, but since he had given up law, he had quit wearing it. His only weapon was the knife strapped to his hip.

One other thing worried him. Jason. He *was* wearing a gun. His cousin made no effort to hide his dislike of anyone of Chinese descent, and Sky feared he might use this situation as an opportunity to carry out his vendetta against them. Especially Chang, whom he blamed for the death of his mother. Sky didn't want anyone innocent getting shot for moving too quickly or at the wrong time.

Suddenly deciding that the direct approach best suited the situation, Sky, his voice loud and clear, said, "Chang, you're under arrest." Just as he'd anticipated, Chang's four henchmen scrambled to their feet. But Chang held up one fleshy hand, palm out, tapping the air twice.

"For what am I under arrest, Mr. Jordan?"

"You are trying to hide something, Mr. Chang. I am not saying you are guilty of murder, but you lied to me about the reason for the celebration last night. I know it was not your wife's birthday yesterday."

Angry, Chang's eyes narrowed, his mouth hardening into

a firm line. His smoking pipe, held in a tight-fisted grip, shook perceptibly. "You are right, Mr. Jordan. But we were unable to have the celebration on her actual birthday, so we had it a little late. Better late than never. You know how the saying goes." He tried to smile casually, his voice surprisingly controlled despite the anger that radiated from his eyes.

Sky hesitated. Chang might be telling the truth; he couldn't let his dislike of the man cloud his good reasoning. "All right, I'll check into it. But don't go anywhere, Chang. You are not to leave town until your name is cleared. Do you understand?"

Chang's eyes darkened, but he nodded in affirmation.

Brooke's hands shook as she and Jenny Chang sewed Fraser's body into a large piece of black denim. They worked in the front room of Jed's boarding house. *I'll never see this room in the same light again.* She felt nauseated and light-headed, but she kept sewing. They were almost done now, but she could still see the poor man's battered body as it had been when Sky and Jed carried him in on a blanket. A shudder ran through her. *How could anyone do such a thing to another human being?* And Percival had been involved in this somehow.

She felt edgy and jumped at even the slightest noise, making Jenny look at her oddly.

Jenny Chang had been very quiet as they worked side by side. Her dark eyes, though sorrowful, did not shed a tear. She merely pressed on steadily, doing the work that needed to be done.

Brooke was the first to break the silence. "Did you know him well, Jenny?" Chagrined, she noted that her voice trembled when she spoke.

"Mistah Fraser?" A sad smile softened Jenny's face. "He good man. He always kind to me."

"How long had he lived here?"

"Long time. Lee and I, we come twenty-three years ago. He here before us."

"Does he have any family?"

"His wife die. He have a daughter. She come to visit him sometimes."

"Where does she live?"

"She staying in Lewiston with a Judge Rand. She go to school there. She fifteen, I think."

Brooke immediately felt her heart go out to this young girl. She herself had been fifteen when her parents and sister had been killed. Memories rushed in on a surge of emotion, and Brooke gasped, choking back a flood of tears. The memories added on top of this morning's terror proved too much for her.

Turning, she fled back to her room, throwing herself across the bed, sobs wracking her body. She jumped up again just as suddenly and threw the door's deadbolt into place.

Backing toward the bed, she sat down with her back to the wall and her arms wrapped around her knees. She had begun to feel safe with Sky, but she should have known better. Somehow God had it in for her, and she didn't think she would ever feel safe again.

She scrubbed angrily at the tears coursing down her face. It seemed all she did lately was cry.

Sky paused to let his eyes adjust to the bright outdoor light as he exited the Joss house. He stood for a moment, hands resting on hips, staring up and down the street, trying to decide what to do next. Sunlight glistened off the quickly melting snow as he turned to Jason. "I hate to send you down to Lewiston with no more information than we have, but if we are going to get this thing solved, we are going to need some outside assistance."

Jason's face clearly portrayed his anger. "I'll tell you how to solve this thing. We both know who is responsible. We should just take him out." He nodded back in the direction of the Joss house and Lee Chang.

His eyes never leaving Jason's face, Sky replied in a measured voice, "And if we took the law into our own hands we would be no better than him. If it *was* him that did it." He paused, one hand rubbing over his unshaven jaw. "Brooke saw a man in the alley last night." He pulled a paper from his vest pocket and handed it to Jason. "I wrote down his description. See what you can find out about him."

Jason nodded.

Another thought hit Sky, and he gave Jason a sympathetic look. "You'll have to find Fraser's daughter, Alice. She is staying with the Rand family in Lewiston. We'll bring the body down as soon as we can, probably tomorrow, maybe Saturday, but she should be told as soon as possible." Sky didn't envy Jason the terrible responsibility.

"Should we send a telegram?"

"I thought of that, but I don't know. I thought it seemed a little cold and impersonal. But…" Sky shrugged. "What do you think?"

Jason thought for only a moment. "You're right. I'll tell her when I get there." The look on his face showed that he did not look forward to the task. Sky let one hand fall to rest on his cousin's shoulder, amazement filling him once again at Jason's ability to about-face in his temperament so quickly. He had been coldly angry only moments ago and now he felt tender sympathy to the point of having to blink back tears.

Sky prayed the Lord would use this situation to reach him as they walked down the street toward Jed's boarding house. Bill Currey, leading three fresh horses, met them just in front of the boarding house. Sky noticed that his hands shook badly as he handed the reins of the lead horse over to Jason. Bill had brought extra horses so Jason could swap his saddle from one animal to the next when the horse he rode tired out. Without a rider, even though the animal had to trail behind, it soon got its wind back. In this way, a man could almost cut his traveling time in half.

Jason nodded. "Thanks, Bill."

"Sure. For ol' Fraser I'd do just 'bout—" He stopped short, rubbing shaky hands across his face. "I need me a drink."

Jason clapped him on the shoulder before he mounted the saddle. "You'll be glad you stayed away from the booze when this is over, Bill. It's going to be the trial of the century, and you'll want to be able to remember everything that happened."

Bill gave a snort and waved him off with a quavery hand.

Jason threw Sky a grin as he swung into the saddle. And Sky reminded, "You're going to have to exercise some self-control yourself these next couple of days."

The smile left Jason's face and he stared in thoughtfulness at the pommel of the saddle for a moment. Then, the leads of the two extra horses in one hand, he nodded in Sky's direction and urged his mount forward.

As Sky watched Jason ride out of town, he caught a movement out of the corner of his eye. He turned. Jed propelled an obviously terrified Chinaman down the sodden, muddy street in front of him. The young man held his hands wide at shoulder height, palms out, as Jed kept poking him in the ribs with a mean-looking 44 caliber, long-barreled pistol.

"What's going on, Jed?"

"Thought you should see this here fella fer a minute. Carle was skirtin' out at the edge o' town like you said when he come upon him trying to hide hisself behind a bush. Take a look at this here," he drawled. He pulled the man's shirt away from his body. "That's blood if ever I saw it."

Sky let his eyes drop from studying the face of the terrified young man to the large brown patch of crusted shirt that Jed held out. Anger surged through him at the sight of the blood. The thought that this could be the man who had done such a despicable thing to Fraser clenched his fists at his sides. He took a deep breath to calm himself and forced his hands to relax. Jed calmly held the gun on the trembling youth, waiting for Sky's response.

Sky turned back to the young man. "How did this blood get on your shirt?"

"I-I-I…" He stuttered to a halt shaking his head, fear radiating from his eyes.

"Were you in Fraser's Mercantile last night after it closed?"

The man shook his head. "No."

"Did you kill Fraser?"

"No." Again, the shake of the head, but Sky heard fear in the man's voice that made him wonder if he was telling the truth.

"How did this blood get on your shirt?"

"I-I-I...," he started stuttering again, but when his eyes met Sky's stare, he came to a lame halt. His hands, still at shoulder height, rose a little higher as he gave a slight shrug, turning his palms to the sky. "I kill pig two day past." He shrugged again. "Maybe happen when I kill pig. I not know how blood came to be on me."

His eyes never leaving the man's face, Sky reached down and pulled his knife from its sheath around his waist.

The Chinaman's eyes widened. "No! Please. I not know how blood got there. I speak truth."

Sky had wanted to see what the man's reaction would be, and he was not satisfied. The man was truly terrified. This didn't help him because the man's fear could be interpreted several different ways. The man might be innocent and petrified that he was about to be arrested for a crime he didn't commit. On the other hand he might have committed the murder and now was honestly frightened that he would be found out.

Sky stood for a moment, the knife held casually by his side, studying the face of the Chinaman whose terrified eyes were locked on the glinting blade.

With sudden swiftness Sky reached out and grasped the bloody part of the man's shirt. The man squeezed his eyes shut in fear, and Sky paused momentarily, realizing the man thought he was going to stab him. "I'm not going to hurt you," he said as with one smooth stroke he sliced a bloodstained piece off of the shirt to be sent in for testing. "What is your name?"

"Ping Chi."

Turning to Jed, Sky said, "Lock him up."

Jed prodded Ping in the direction of the courthouse with the barrel of his gun as he said, "Gaffney found some s'picious prints in the alley 'tween Fraser's and my place."

Sky stood, fingering the blood-encrusted piece of material for a moment before he turned toward the alley between the boarding house and the Mercantile. During the rains the night before, the ground in the alley had become soft and muddy. The snow that had covered the ground earlier that morning had melted, and Sky could clearly see the set of footprints.

He frowned. These footprints were little; barely over half the size of his own tracks and close together, indicating a person small in stature. The heel of the right boot had a crack across it.

Sky's heart lurched in his chest as he realized he'd seen these tracks before. They were the same ones he had found in the barnyard on the day Brooke had gone to pick berries.

Sky glanced up at the window of their room speculatively. He stood thinking for a long moment before he turned back to study the tracks again.

He saw where the man had squatted behind a wooden barrel, and then the tracks showed that he had turned and headed back down the alley toward the outskirts of town.

Brooke said she had seen the Mountain Man from the stage. He vaguely remembered the rugged man who had gotten off the stage that day with Brooke. His mind had been preoccupied with Brooke. But he did remember one thing. That man had been anything but small.

Brooke sat in a daze, unable to think of anything but the murder. Now another fifteen-year-old girl had no family. Terror pounded through her veins. She knew information that might help solve this crime but could not share it for fear of her life and Sky's.

She wondered what would happen to the girl now. Who would take care of her? Would she be sent to live with one of her uncles? The very thought sent a new pulse of terror through Brooke's body. Surely she owed it to the girl to help find her father's killer. Could she do any less? But then Percival Hunter's terrifying face swam before her eyes, and she heard his threats repeated over and over. *I could never do anything that would bring harm to Sky.*

Percival had seemed so kind—so harmless—on the coach coming up from Lewiston. She shivered.

At a knock on the door, she gasped, startled upright by the sound. "Who is it?" she called with a shaking voice.

"It's me, Sky."

She climbed slowly off the bed, pausing to eye herself in the mirror. She had quit crying, but her eyes were still swollen and puffy. Running fingers through her tangled hair, she moved to the door, pulled back the lock, and opened it.

"You all right?" he asked, eyeing her disheveled appearance.

She chose the safest topic of conversation. "He had a daughter, you know. She is fifteen."

"Yes, I know."

Brooke made no comment to this, only lay down on the bed. Turning on her side, her back to him, she tucked her hands under one cheek and stared at a knot on the wall.

After a long pause, Sky said, "We will be going to Lewiston early tomorrow morning. I want you to come with us."

She turned and looked at him, a question in her eyes. "I can stay out at the farm. I will be fine." But even as she said the word, she knew she wouldn't be fine. Not ever again.

Sky fingered his black Stetson. "I would feel better if you were with me, and I knew you were safe. I don't feel right about leaving you here when there could be a murderer loose somewhere."

Brooke trembled as his words drove home. Did he somehow know she was holding out on him? That she had not told him the truth about the man in the alley? She tried to read his face.

No suspicion filled his eyes. She sighed in relief before turning back to the knot on the wall. She could feel the warmth of his gaze on her back as he waited for her response. Shrugging, she nodded, indicating consent. If he wanted her to accompany him, she would. She knew she would feel much safer with him than if she stayed out at the farm by herself.

★

Chapter Thirteen

Brooke sat in the pew, quietly taking in the scene around her. *When was the last time I sat in a church? The Sunday before Mama and Daddy died, I guess.* Sky sat next to her, his hat hanging from one knee. Head bowed, he had his hands clasped between his knees, and Brooke could tell he was struggling to harness his emotions.

Little groups of people turned in their pews, talking quietly among themselves. Brooke could imagine the gist of their conversations by their facial expressions and hand signals. *"Who would do such a thing to such a fine man?"* or, *"That poor young child. What do you suppose she is going to do with herself now that her pa is gone?"*

Brooke's eyes fell on a group of surly-looking men toward the back on the other side of the church. Their conversation was punctuated with gestures that lent a sinister air to their invented dialogue. *"Justice needs to be served here. We won't stop looking for those killers until we find them! And when we do, they're going to wish that they never laid a hand on Fraser."*

Sky had shared with her last night when they arrived in Lewiston that, unfortunately, many men were already convinced this crime could not have been committed by anyone but a group of Chinese. Already, talk of vigilante "justice" circulated. Sky feared the trial in Pierce City would merely be an excuse for revenge.

Suddenly Brooke froze. Her eyes riveted to a man who sat discretely in the back corner of the church. His hat was pulled low over his forehead, but he looked like the mountain man she had met on the stage except he was dressed impeccably. He wore a black suit with a string tie resting on the front of a crisp white shirt. His hair and beard were clean and neatly combed.

No tobacco juice stained his beard. Brooke blinked, looked away, then looked back again. It was him—the mountain man cleaned up! It had to be. What was he doing here? And why had Percival insisted she say it was *him* she had seen in the alley that night?

She laid a hand on Sky's sleeve, her eyes never leaving the face of the mountain man at the back of the room. Sky turned to her, then his gaze followed hers and came to rest on the bearded man seated in the darkened corner. Before either Brooke or Sky could turn back around, he glanced their way and their eyes met. No one smiled, but the burly man dipped his head in silent acknowledgment. He recognized them. Sky repeated the gesture, eyes wary, as he and Brooke turned to face the front. Brooke did not take her hand off Sky's arm. Somehow this small point of contact gave her warm comfort.

Sky laid his hand over Brooke's and squeezed gently. His thoughts turned back to the mountain man in the corner of the room. What was he doing here? Why had he been in Pierce City that night? Had it really been him Brooke saw in the alley on that dark rainy night?

He cast a glance at Brooke. She was withholding something; he could feel it. The more he thought about the morning after the murder when he had come in to tell Brooke of Fraser's death, the more he knew something must have happened to her during the time he had been gone to the Mercantile.

He should question her but felt reluctant to push her. He wanted her to feel safe with him—protected, not threatened. Still, something troubled her. He could tell by the erratic shifting of her eyes and the repeated fidgeting of her hands. For the last two days, she had been jumpy, starting at the least little noise or jostle.

He glanced at her again. Even now, he could tell by her frown that some memory frightened her. How could he encourage her to confide in him?

A door opened at the front right of the church. A woman

wearing all black escorted Alice Fraser, also clothed in mourning, to the front bench. Brooke's eyes darted to the closed coffin sitting in front of the pulpit, and then back to the girl. Memories of a very similar scene flashed through her mind. Only in her memories there were three coffins at the front of the room instead of one.

Heart constricting, Brooke watched as the young woman cast a furtive glance at the coffin and then, face paling, collapsed onto the front pew. Her small frame shook uncontrollably as sobs wracked her body.

Brooke's free hand clenched in her lap. She shuddered, determined not to let the tears burning the back of her eyes slip down her cheeks. She knew how Alice felt. The utter incredulity of losing your entire family in one single blow. *I miss you, Mama. And Jess, oh, how I miss you.* Her sister's smiling face swam before her eyes unbidden. She shook her head to dispel the image and turned to find Sky's dark, concerned gaze on her. She tried to smile and reassure him that she was all right, but her face only contorted into a grimace as her years of suppressed mourning and the pressure of the last several days surfaced. She dropped her head and let the tears fall, pulling her hand back into her lap. She had never allowed herself to truly mourn her family. The accident had been such a shock that she had wandered around in a stupor for the two days between the time it happened and Uncle Jackson's arrival. She clearly remembered the events that took place on the night he arrived.

Brooke had been staring at the ceiling when Mrs. Brodman, the next-door neighbor, had come into her room and sat down on the bed beside her.

"Brooke, honey, your uncle is here. He just came in on the stage." She smoothed Brooke's hair away from her face as she spoke.

Brooke blinked, momentarily shutting the water stain on the ceiling from her vision.

Brooke could still picture the expression on the woman's face. One of worried concern, as though she thought Brooke might never be the same again. *I never have been.*

The kindly lady had helped her sit up. "Come on, now, come meet your uncle. He says he has never met you. He seems a very kind man. He is going to take care of you now."

Brooke sat up, staring dully at the wall. She didn't want to meet anyone. She didn't want to go anywhere. She didn't want to be taken care of. *I just want to be left alone. God, why did You do this to me?*

However, her neighbor wouldn't be put off. So, leaning heavily on Mrs. Brodman's shoulder, she shuffled one foot in front of the other until they reached the living room, where Uncle Jackson waited. He turned from the mantle where he had been eyeing a picture of the family, and his eyes scraped over her face and clothes.

Brooke knew she looked terrible. She had not bathed or changed out of her clothes, even to sleep, in the last two days. Her curly strawberry-blond hair had not been combed in the same amount of time, and hung in great knots and tangles about her shoulders. There was a hard edge to Uncle Jackson's countenance she didn't like from the moment she laid tired eyes on him.

He spoke curtly. "Go clean up...dear." The last word was thrown in almost as an afterthought as he cast a glance at Mrs. Brodman.

Brooke, mind numb, realized that, yes, she did need to clean up. The funeral was to be held in three hours. *Mama wouldn't want me looking unkempt.*

Mrs. Brodman had helped her bathe and change into clean clothes, had combed her hair, and had braided it to a thick plait down her back. The black dress was a little too small for her. She hadn't worn it since Mama had made it for her to wear to Grandpa's funeral the year before, but it would have to do.

She sat through her family's funeral, eyes dry, throat tight, still unbelieving and in shock. This could not be happening to her. She was having some horrible dream, and Mama and Jess would walk in the door from church any minute and chastise her for not having the lunch preparations done. She needed to wake up. Oh, if only she could wake up, what a relief that would be. But it was not a dream. One didn't wake up from reality.

She made it through the funeral and even through the meal provided by the church afterward, although she couldn't swallow a bite. When she and Uncle Jackson arrived home, she headed for her bedroom to curl up in a ball and never come out.

Her uncle, however, had other plans. He came in and jerked the covers off of her. "Get up and get me some dinner. I was too busy talking things over with your father's lawyer to eat at the church." He stalked out of the room. He obviously hadn't liked what the lawyer had to say.

In a daze, Brooke got up and headed for the kitchen. He sat at the table reading *The Chronicle*.

Brooke rummaged in the cupboards for some food. She didn't know what to give him. But she didn't really care, either. Placing a plate of cold chicken and potato salad in front of him, she pulled the pot of coffee that Mrs. Brodman had been kind enough to make from the back of the stove. Setting a cup down by him, she began to pour. Her mind wandered. *Was it only two days ago that I poured coffee for Papa into this very same mug?*

Hot coffee sloshed over the side of the mug onto Uncle Jackson's hand. She heard his yelp of pain, but she never saw the blow. All she knew was that suddenly she was prostrate on the floor, the front of her dress soaked with burning hot coffee. Her right ear rang and when she reached up and touched it, her hand came away red with blood. Uncle Jackson stood over her, his face scarlet with anger.

She had known then that he was not like her papa. He was much worse.

Papa had mistreated her sometimes, but never had she seen eyes like Uncle Jackson's. He enjoyed what he did. Having what he called "ultimate control" was his life's goal. Once, as he stood over her, coiling his whip, he'd said, "If you can get people to fear you, Brooke, my dear, you will have ultimate control. Then, and only then, will you be truly happy." He had paused with a smirk. "You have a long way to go to find happiness. You are nothing but a coward." He laughed, harsh and grating, as he stalked away.

From that moment, she had lived in fear. Fear that she

would do something, not do something, say something, not say something, forget something, remember something… always *something* that would set him off. She had not had time to mourn; she had lived in fear for her life. And then there had been Hank….

Now she brought her mind back to the present. It seemed that Sky had inadvertently saved her from that life. He treated her with respect, care, and gentleness—even love—in his home. And now she held an accidentally discovered piece of information that might bring him harm. Oh, how she wished she hadn't walked to the window that rainy night. Shaking her head she pushed the thoughts aside and tried to focus on the funeral.

Mourning was a part of moving past the tragedies in life and getting on with living. She was thankful to see Alice beginning the long process now. She only wished she herself had had the same freedom.

Glad for the fact that they were at a funeral—a place where tears were accepted—Brooke allowed all the wonderful memories of times with her sister and mother to float through her mind. Playing in the barn loft with Jess. Kneading bread together in the kitchen as they all talked and the girls shared their dreams with Mama. Mama had always had such sad blue eyes on those occasions. Eyes that looked back through time to similar occasions in her youth, yet with the knowledge of what had actually come of all those dreams. Eyes that knew heartache.

Brooke was not the only one who had suffered during her father's bad moods. She could remember lying awake at night, curled up in a tight ball in her bed, listening to Papa spewing drunken curses; to Mama quietly sobbing and begging; to the thud of the repeated blows. She had longed to run downstairs and pull Mother from the terror. Take her and Jess far, far away where they wouldn't have to ever be near a man again. But always, her courage had failed her, and she had just lain awake, wide-eyed with the horror of it all, unable to even cry.

Her tears now were not only for her loss of family but for all the horror they had been through. All the terrible things they had faced while living on this earth. She hoped that somehow in death they had discovered a better place.

Brooke longed to be able to have peace. To wake up each day and know that, no matter what happened, everything would be fine because someone who loved you was watching out for you, would be heaven on earth. She had tasted the possibility of it, and the thought that she might lose it terrified her. She eased a little closer to Sky.

A minister walked to the pulpit and interrupted her thoughts. She allowed herself one more reflection before she brought her mind back to the present. It felt good, really good, she realized, to be able finally to weep over her great loss.

Percival Hunter eased into the back pew of the church, taking in the scene around him. His conscience pricked him when he saw Alice's deep grief, but he quickly shoved the feeling aside. What he had done had been for her good. She was free of her father now and would be able to see how much she needed him. He would give her a few weeks to mourn while he took care of the minor inconvenience of Chang and his cohorts, and then he would go visit her. Expressing his deep condolences, he would pat her on the back, restate how much he cared for her and wanted to take care of her, and she would become putty in his hands. They would be married, and then all his dreams would come true.

Her inheritance money that he would get when they married was not a bad incentive either. He felt momentarily perturbed. If only he had had the time to break into the safe on the night of the murder, he wouldn't have to worry so much about whether Alice would accept his offer of courtship. He at least would have the money.

From the moment Fraser had told him to stay away from Alice, he had begun to make his plans. At first, he'd thought he would have to do the killing himself, but then providence had intervened, and he had learned of Fraser's confrontation with

Chang. It was then that the final details to his plan had fallen into place. Kill Fraser. Steal his money. Marry his forbidden daughter.

One down, two to go. His eyes glinted. He should have already accomplished two parts of his plan, but there had been a glitch.

Everyone knew that, although Fraser lived a very modest life, he had been saving up for years to give his daughter the best future he possibly could. The sum ought to be quite substantial, and it should have been his by now. But seeing Brooke in the window watching him had thrown him off a bit. He had feared she might call someone else and he would be caught. So he had fled town before he had a chance to break into the safe and steal the money.

He consoled himself with the fact that if all went according to plan, everything would be his in a matter of weeks. He shoved aside the fleeting thought that Alice might not look kindly on his offer of marriage. His plan would work. It had to. And then all his time-consuming, detailed planning would pay off.

After he took care of Chang and the others, he would put an end to little Mrs. Jordan and her husband, and then he would be scot-free. Percival glanced at Brooke sitting next to Skyler Jordan. He took in the cascade of curls piled high on her head, the stretch of her smooth, slender neck, her gently rounded, womanly shoulders. He smiled. Yes, he looked forward to dealing with Brooke.

He caught himself. Rubbing a hand across his face he returned it to its proper, somber, funereal expression and turned his attention to the minister's words.

When the funeral service ended, the men lent a hand clearing the sanctuary of all pews, and tables were set up and laden with food. Fraser's daughter, Alice, sat at a table pushing food around on her plate.

Brooke watched her from across the room, her heart going out to the young girl. Person after person approached Alice to give her their condolences, but Brooke knew from experience that the girl did not hear a word they said. She nodded in all the right places and even tried to give some of them a smile, but Brooke recognized the faraway, lost look in her eyes.

Brooke stiffened, and her heart began to pound in her ears as the next person approached the table. *Percival Hunter!* How dare he show his face here? She quickly looked away, not wanting to draw Sky's attention to him. Had he noticed Percival yet? She didn't think so.

"Are you afraid of something?" Sky's words warmed her ear. She jumped, gasped, and pressed one hand to her throat.

Sky eyed her speculatively as she took a moment to regain her composure. *If I don't quit jumping at the drop of a hat, he is going to know that something is wrong.* Swallowing the lump in her throat, she shook her head. "No. Why do you ask?"

"You *are* afraid of something."

The confident statement shook Brooke's resolve. And for the briefest of seconds she wanted to fall into his arms and tell him the whole story. To confess that she had lied to him and let him protect her from the fiend across the room. However, she couldn't shake the recollection of Percival's words. *"I will hunt you down. First I'll make you watch me kill that husband of yours ever so slowly, and then it will be your turn. "* Her face paled at the memory, and she picked up her water glass, taking a big gulp, her determination once again solidly in place.

Telling Sky was out of the question. It was too dangerous. She would never be able to forgive herself if something happened to him. Gathering her wits about her, she shook her head a little too emphatically. "N-no, I'm not."

With relief, she noted Percival heading out a side door in the wall behind Sky. If Sky had seen him here, she was afraid he might have put two and two together.

He leaned one elbow on the table, his dark eyes narrowing as he searched her face thoughtfully. "You are as pale as fresh snow. What's happened?"

"Nothing!" she denied angrily in a low voice. Reaching up, she began to play with her necklace nervously in a conscious effort to keep herself from rubbing her hands together in circles, a gesture he was sure to understand. "You just startled me is all. I was thinking."

He raised one eyebrow at her and leaned back in his chair, folding his arms. She could tell he didn't believe a word she said.

"Do you remember I told you the other day that you can always tell whether someone is telling the truth by their eyes?"

She ignored this comment.

Leaning forward, he took her hand in his. "Tell me what's bothering you, Brooke."

She shook her head, pulling her hand free. "I—" She took a sip of water as she thought for a minute, trying to come up with something that would put Sky's mind at ease. "I just saw someone who reminded me of a man I used to know. He looked at me kind of funny and scared me a little is all." Her tone was too light and airy, but she hoped Sky wouldn't notice.

"Where is he? Maybe I should have a talk with him and tell him you're my wife now, and under my protection."

Brooke's heart began to race. That was the last thing she wanted. "I don't see him now."

"Well, if you see him again, let me know. I don't want any man looking at you in a way that makes you afraid. I especially want you to tell me if anyone comes near you."

An icy chill raced down Brooke's spine. *Is he testing me? Does he already know?* Frowning, she studied him. If he didn't already know of her lies, why would he say such a thing? But she could tell by his expression that he simply meant what he had said. Relief washed over her and she looked away, pleased he had believed her. Sky couldn't ever find out that Percival had threatened her. Somehow she knew Sky's response would be swift, and it frightened her to think what might happen to him in the process.

Leaning back in his chair, Sky stretched his legs out before him and crossed his arms over his chest, watching Brooke reflectively.

She was lying to him, of that he was certain. But the *why* was another matter. With a good deal of surprise, he noted how much it hurt to have her lie to him. And she had done it so emphatically. People had lied to him before. It had happened often when he had been working on a case back home, but it had never bothered him this much before. *Does she care so little for me then? And why is she lying in the first place? What or who is she trying to protect by doing so?*

He raised one fist to his mouth as he thought the matter over. The room buzzed with the soft conversations of mourners. An occasional tear-choked voice rose above the rest. The *clink* of silver on china reverberated throughout the room as the guests ate, and somewhere a mother tried to hush a crying baby. But Sky tuned all that out.

He raked his scalp with his fingers. Brooke pretended to be deeply absorbed in the task of eating, as if his questions had not bothered her in the least. Raising one hand, she tucked a stray curl of strawberry-blond hair behind her ear and gave the room a casual, almost bored look as she placed a forkful of green salad in her mouth. She concentrated solely on her food and looked everywhere in the room but at him, as though nothing out of the ordinary had happened. He knew better. She had been undeniably frightened by something. *What?* And why was she trying to keep it from him? The questions were going to haunt him until he had some answers.

He was still pondering the matter when his attention was drawn elsewhere. The mountain man Brooke said she had seen in the alley on the night of the murder was just easing out the back door of the church, and Sky needed to have a talk with him.

Jason had returned from his trip to Lewiston with no more information than when he had left. No one in the Lewiston area seemed to know who the mysterious mountain man was. He had asked at a number of places, giving the man's description, and no one had any idea about the man's identity, although a couple people remembered seeing him get on the stage the day that Brooke had left Lewiston.

Excusing himself, Sky made his way out of the church after the mountain man. The man's long, gray hair blew in the breeze, and he had just mounted an appaloosa and started to move away from the church when Sky came out into the yard.

Bending quickly, he examined the prints the man had made in the dust of the church yard. He frowned. These tracks differed from the ones that had been in the alley up in Pierce City. Could Brooke be wrong about the man's identity?

Glancing again at the man, Sky noted with some surprise that he was older than he had first thought.

"Excuse me," he called, and the bearded man pulled his horse to a stop, turning to see who had hailed him. "Could I ask you a couple of questions?"

The man looked him over as if judging his trustworthiness and then, as though he had come to a sudden decision, swung down from the saddle. "What can I do you for?"

Sky stretched out his hand. "Name's Skyler Jordan. I live up Pierce City way." He watched the man to see what his reaction would be to the mention of the town.

"Howdy, I'm Trace Johnson," he said but exhibited no reaction. His face impassive, he stood quietly waiting for Sky to speak his mind.

Sky brought hands to hips. "You obviously know about the murder we had in town a couple of nights back since you are here at the funeral. Do you mind my asking, Trace, how did you know Fraser?"

He shook his head. "Didn't know him 'tall. I was here for another reason today."

"And that would be…?"

Trace Johnson looked at him blandly.

Deciding to be direct, Sky went on, "The reason I'm asking is that someone told me she saw you in the alley between Jed's boarding house and Fraser's Mercantile on the night of the murder. Can you tell me why you were there?" Sky sensed what the answer would be even before Trace answered.

"Whoever she is, she's lying to you, son."

Sky stared at the outer wall of the church. Again, his insides twisted into a tight knot at the thought of her lying to him. He felt somehow betrayed. Not wanting to let on to this fact before Trace, however, he asked, "Can you prove that, Mr. Johnson?"

"Look, son." Trace clapped a hand down on Sky's shoulder. Sky shook off his irritation with the term *son*.

"I can tell you two things. Number one, I wasn't in that alley on the night of the murder. And number two, someone else was, but I think you already knew that." Trace Johnson laughed softly. "Now, son, in my business you can't afford to go around announcing who you are and what you do, but I've read up on you."

Sky started to say something, but Trace went on without missing a beat. "You and your cousin cracked a couple of tough cases over in Shiloh, and I admire not only what you accomplished but the way you went about things.

From what I hear, there were a number of times when you two had your man dead to rights in your gun sights, and out in the west here it's sometimes tempting to just take justice into your own hands, so to speak, but I never heard tell o' you two doing that. So I am going to be straight with you." Trace ran a hand down his long beard as he asked his next question. "You ever heard of the Pinkerton Detective Agency?"

Sky nodded. "Sure. I worked with a couple of their detectives on a case over in Shiloh one time."

Trace smiled. "How did you think I knew so much about you?"

"So you're a Pinkerton?"

He nodded.

"And, let me guess, you've been hired to find someone?"

"There was this family back east." Trace seemed to change the subject. "A man and his wife and young, beautiful daughter. They had gone out for the evening, and when they returned, they found their house in the middle of being robbed. Even though he was wearing a mask and could not be recognized, and the family told him he was free to leave the premises, the burglar shot the father with no warning. When the mother and daughter tried to run, he grabbed the woman. Only the daughter escaped. The mother was found, also murdered, when the police arrived. The daughter said that the man laughed as he shot her father."

Trace stared at his hands as he spoke, slapping the ends of the reins against one palm. "The daughter ran to her grandparents' place. Her grandfather happens to be a senator back east, and he hired our agency to find the man who committed the crime. I'm following that man. We don't know what this murderer looks like—just that he is small in stature. We do have a list of the jewels that he stole from the house. Now, you don't see men out west wearing jewelry too often, do you?"

Trace looked pointedly into Sky's face. "None o' the pieces that were taken have been sold on the black market, far as we can find. But this man I've been trailing has a ring that looks an awful lot like a piece taken from the house back east. He says he bought it off a fella down California way, but I don't believe him. He's my man; I just don't have enough evidence yet. He knows I'm on his trail, though, and they always make some sort of mistake when they feel the pressure of the chase breathing down their backs."

"Can you tell me who this man is?"

"That I can't do, son. It might put your life in jeopardy."

"Do you think he might be involved in this murder up in Pierce City?"

"I wouldn't put it past him—that murder back east was similarly cold-blooded—but I'm not here to figure that out. I'm here to find my man and take him in."

"I found some footprints in the alley next to Fraser's store on the morning after the murder. They were small. Does the man you're tracking make small prints and have a short stride?"

Trace nodded.

"A crack in the heel of the right boot?"

Again a nod.

"Do you have any idea why your man might have wanted to kill Fraser?"

"No, not in the least. I can tell you he's been in the area quite a bit in the last couple of days, though. I lost his trail there for a while, right about the time of the murder, so I don't know for sure that he was in town on that night, but if I come across anything that might bring you all a conviction up in Pierce City, I will let you know."

"Thank you, and I hope you find the evidence you're looking for. If you're ever up in our area again, feel free to stop by. A hot meal and a place to sleep in out of the cold always beats roughing it." Sky stretched out his hand and the men shook.

"I'll be sure to remember that. Thank you."

Sky turned and headed back to the church as Trace mounted and rode out of the church yard.

Brooke worried as she watched Sky come back to their table. She had watched with apprehension as Sky followed the mountain man outside, knowing he was going out to question him. Surely now he knew that she had lied to him and would question her again about who she really saw in the alley that night.

But Sky didn't say a word. He merely pulled out her chair and escorted her to the door, a somber look on his face.

★

Chapter Fourteen

Brooke couldn't remember the last time she had felt so confused—so refreshed and so terrified all at once. To openly grieve had been therapeutic. First for her baby girl and then for her family at the funeral. Even so, the threats to Sky and herself constantly lingered in the back of her mind.

Were it not for that, she would feel free. Almost.

Her memories had been healing ones. Before her time with Uncle Jackson, life had not been so bad. Yes, Father had been abusive at times but usually only when he had indulged in too much drink. At least he had been predictable, although surly, when sober. Uncle Jackson, on the other hand, was never predictable.

The ride home with Sky and the other men on Monday was a solemn one. Two men from Lewiston accompanied them back to Pierce City to help with the ongoing murder investigation. Many more men had promised that they would follow on Tuesday to assist in any way they could.

They had ridden hard and arrived home late Monday night. As soon as feasible on Tuesday morning, Sky rode into town to continue the investigation and see if any new evidence came to light while he was in Lewiston.

Brooke barred the door as soon as Sky left home.

Percival could show up at any time. With every creak and natural shudder of the house, she tensed up and stared at the door in fear, expecting it to come crashing in, followed by the dangerous madman.

She knew she was being silly and that if she just stopped thinking about it so much she wouldn't be so afraid, but she couldn't keep her mind off his threats. Finally, in desperation, she picked up Sky's well-used Bible and began to read.

On Wednesday morning, Sky left just as early, and Brooke again rushed to get chores done so she could bar herself into the house and lose herself in the Bible stories.

That night, Sky came home late in the evening and dropped into his chair at the table with a sigh. He made no comment about the fact that Brooke had to get up and unbar the door for the second night in a row so he could get into the house.

Removing his black Stetson, he tossed it on the table and leaned over, elbows on his knees, resting his head in his hands. He sat this way for only a moment, then ran both hands back through his curly blond hair and raised his head. He looked toward Brooke with a tired smile.

Brooke moved to get his dinner, which she had kept warm on the back of the stove. As she set his plate in front of him with a steaming cup of black coffee she asked, "Bad day?"

Sky stared at his mashed potatoes and gravy absently. "No, not really. Just tiring, I guess. We have made eight arrests now."

Brooke could tell by his tone that something still bothered him. "That's good, isn't it?"

Sky sighed again, running a hand back through his hair. "It is good. But it could be bad, too. I'm just not sure that the men are going about the investigation the right way."

Brooke sat down across from him with a mug of coffee cupped in her hands. "How is that?"

Sky shook his head, his food still untouched. "I just..." He shook his head again and turned to stare at the percolating coffee pot, its lid gently bumping with a metallic clatter. "The only motive that they've even considered is that Lee Chang had this done to Fraser because of a disagreement he and Fraser had a couple of months back." Sky told Brooke the story of the bogus gold.

"That's awful. Poor Jenny. Did you have to arrest Lee?"

Sky nodded. "I'm afraid so."

"But you don't think he did it?" Her mind went once again to Percival slinking down the alley. Why had he been so adamant that no one know he'd been in town on the night of the murder? Was he the murderer himself?

Brooke's conscience gripped her. Eight men had been arrested. What if they were all innocent, but were convicted because she was too scared to speak up and tell the truth? Could she live with that on her conscience for the rest of her life?

What part did Percival have in this? She hadn't actually seen him commit any crime, but she knew he had been up to no good or he wouldn't care who knew he'd been in the alley that night. Her mind jerked back to what Sky was saying.

"That's just it. I think Chang had something to do with it, but there's more to the story than we are seeing at the moment. I simply can't figure out what it is. And none of the men think there is any validity in what I am saying."

"What about that man I saw in the alley? Do you think he had something to do with this?"

His penetrating eyes swung to her face, and he looked at her long and hard.

She brought her hands to her lap and began rubbing them together, then clenched them there, suddenly wishing she hadn't brought up the subject.

His eyes held a knowing look. Again, she wished she could tell him the truth. Again, she reminded herself that his safety depended on her keeping her silence. She looked away.

Finally, he shrugged. "Could be, but at this point nothing seems to fit together." Sky's gaze dropped to the table; his shoulders slumped in weariness.

He picked up a spoon and began playing with it on the table top. "I still can't believe he's gone." His voice was tight and tired.

Brooke reached across the table and rested one of her hands on the back of his. She patted his hand. "I'm sorry, Sky," was all she said, but she hoped he would be encouraged by her understanding.

If anyone knew what it meant to have lost a loved one, it was her. She wished she could think of something more to say, but instead, she got up and went across the room to finish reading the passage she had started.

When Sky finished eating, she expected him to go straight

out to the barn as he had every night recently, but he surprised her by asking, "Do you know how to handle a gun?"

"What?" Surely, she hadn't heard him right. She sat up straighter and laid the Bible on the quilt by her side, her bare feet peeking out from under the hem of her dark blue skirt. Where had that question come from?

Sky's expression softened as he crossed the room to sit on the end of the bed. "You're reading my Bible?"

She nodded, looking down at the book. Then a thought flashed through her mind. "That's all right, isn't it?"

"Of course. Have you come across anything interesting?"

"I like the stories about Jesus the best. He is a very interesting man."

"Your eyes change color." Sky said, suddenly changing the subject. "Did anyone ever tell you that?"

Brooke blinked at him. He had gone from talking about guns, to talking about the Bible, to talking about the color of her eyes. She shook her head in confusion.

"When you are wearing green, your eyes are green, and when you wear blue, your eyes turn blue. I noticed that first day when you came out of the cabin and had changed into your green dress. I had been sure your eyes were a beautiful blue, but then, there I was, looking into a pair of the prettiest green eyes I had ever seen." He winked at her.

Brooke blushed and looked away.

He eyed her appreciatively before saying, "There are going to be a whole bunch of men here tomorrow to 'help' conduct this trial. A whole lot more than we will need. I want to be able to concentrate and not be worrying about whether or not you're all right. So…do you know how to handle a gun?"

"N-no, I don't think so. I mean, I've never tried before." Brooke couldn't believe they were having this conversation. Uncle Jackson and Hank would never… Well, Sky Jordan was nothing like them.

Sky reached down and tweaked one of the bare toes poking

out from under her skirt. "Put some shoes on and meet me in the barn."

Jason Jordan lay on his bed at the boarding house in town with his ankles crossed. He couldn't believe his luck. Here he had been trying for years to figure out a way to pay Lee Chang back for the death of his mother, and now the man languished in jail, about to go on trial for murder, his life at stake.

Jason reached under his mattress, pulled out a small flask, un-corked it, and lifted it to his lips. He took only a small swig. He wanted to be alert for the proceedings that would take place tomorrow. He needed to be able to think. What if Chang was exonerated? There had to be a way he could exact his revenge without the evidence pointing back to him. Surely, in a party the size of the one that was bound to show up tomorrow for the trial, there would be a few who would be angry enough to form a lynch mob if the Chinamen were absolved. What happened to the other men who had been arrested did not concern him. He only cared what happened to one; to finally avenge his mother's death. Determination hardened his features.

Suddenly, Bible verses sprang into his mind unbidden—ones he had memorized as a boy around Grandma's kitchen table:

"My son, do not forget My teaching, but let your heart keep My commandments; for length of days and years of life and abundant welfare will they give you. Let not loyalty and faithfulness forsake you; bind them about your neck, write them on the tablet of your heart. So you will find favor and good repute in the sight of God and man. Trust in the Lord with all your heart, and do not rely on your own insight. In all your ways acknowledge Him, and He will make straight your paths. Be not wise in your own eyes; fear the Lord, and turn away from evil. It will be healing to your flesh and refreshment to your bones." Proverbs 3:1-8.

Agitated, Jason sat up and threw the flask against the wall. Why did those verses have to haunt him so? He was just about to see his desires fulfilled. Just about to see the end of the man who had caused him so much pain. Just about to be the happiest he had been in a long time. *So why do I feel so empty?*

Deep inside, he knew the answer. His desires were not right. His desires were irrefutably wrong. Life was God's to give and God's to take away. He had no right to take the life of another human being, no matter how terrible a person they might be. *Love your enemies*, the Bible said. *Do good to those who persecute you.* Where would that get him? Nowhere, that's where. That's why he had set all his childhood teaching aside and decided to do things *his* way. If God would not do anything to punish Lee Chang for all his barbarity, then Jason would take matters into his own hands and do something about it.

The issue resolved in his mind, he got up and walked over to retrieve the now empty flask. All the amber liquid had drained out onto the floor. *Probably best anyway. I might have been tempted to drink the whole thing. When this is all over, I need to get a grip on this drinking thing.*

He shoved the empty flask back under his mattress and lay back down, one hand tucked behind his head, to form a plan.

Ping paced back and forth anxiously, no longer alone in his cell. Seven other men now shared the two jail cells with him.

Rubbing his hands across his face, he tried to erase the terrible images of that murderous night from his mind. But the harder he tried not to picture what had happened, the more he seemed to think of it.

Their orders had been to go in, shoot Fraser once during a volley of fire crackers, and then leave. However, Liam, one of his accomplices that night, had started to have a hallucination just as they walked into the back room where Fraser slept and had pulled a knife, stabbing him instead.

Ping rubbed his eyes again. As long as he lived, he would never be able to escape the memory of the horrible events that had followed.

Ping glanced at his three companions from the night of the

murder. The moment that they had been brought into the jail he had known that they could all lose their lives. If the investigators had enough information to catch all four of them, surely they had enough to convict them as well.

Besides, he knew how the system worked. They were Chinamen, and the people who would conduct the trial would be white men. They didn't stand a chance.

He wracked his brain, trying to come up with a way out of this. His hallucinations had become fewer now because Chang had not made good on his promise. He grimaced at the irony. He had savagely murdered in order to obtain a few ounces of opium. Opium that he never received. Now he hadn't had any of the drug for almost two whole weeks. What a fool he had been to take Lee Chang at his word.

Then a sudden thought entered his mind, and his knees went weak as he recognized its truth. There was no way out of this thing he had done. He was going to die. Whether at the hands of a lynch mob or at the hands of a judge, he would be sentenced to death.

Fresh on the heels of the first thought came a second. Lee Chang would get away with this. Ping glanced over at the obese man who leaned against the wall of his cell, rubbing his trembling hands together. Chang himself was now inflicted with hallucinations due to his missing pipe. Why Chang had wanted Fraser dead, Ping did not know. But Fraser was dead now, and no evidence could be traced to Lee Chang. Chang had made sure of that.

Well, Lee wouldn't walk if Ping could help it. The man had manipulated him into doing a terrible thing, and Ping would use his last breath telling everyone all the details. Chang would pay if he had anything to say about it— and he would have plenty to say.

Ping called out to the man sitting at the front desk.

Snow fell softly as Brooke made her way across the yard minutes later. The barn door groaned as she opened it and stepped into the warm interior. Leaning back against the doorjamb with her hands tucked behind her, she noticed a lantern hanging from a beam in the ceiling. It cast a warm yellow glow across the room, leaving only the corners in shadow. The musty smell of hay, horse sweat, and other not-so-pleasant horsy smells greeted her, causing her nose to wrinkle momentarily. Sky's chuckle brought her eyes to one corner, where he sat on a wooden crate.

"You find the smell of my barn objectionable?" he asked as he rose and walked toward the light.

She smiled lightly. "Only at first. When I've been in here awhile I won't even notice the smell."

He did not reply, only watched her, a gentle smile playing on his lips. A straw of hay dangled from the corner of his mouth. His dark eyes never wavered as he looked at her. Only when she tore her gaze away did he come out of his reverie.

Throwing the piece of straw on the ground, he gestured toward the back of the barn where she now noticed a small, square piece of paper attached to a mound of hay. "Your target, ma'am," he said with exaggerated fanfare as he gave a deep bow from the waist, sweeping his hat from his head.

She giggled at his foolishness but raised an eyebrow in his direction. "You expect me to be able to hit *that?*"

He raised an eyebrow in return. "You doubt my instruction before it has even begun?"

She opened her eyes wide, joining in the game, and gave a deep curtsy, bowing her head to the ground. "Far be it from me, *gallant* sir, to doubt you. You came to my rescue when I was a damsel in distress. You have given my life new meaning and new hope. You have treated me more kindly than anyone ever has, and you have shown me that there is more to life than—" She broke off abruptly, as she realized that she had wandered from the silly utterances of the game into the truth, revealing her deepest feelings.

Her heart thundered like a runaway stagecoach as she stood erect. She darted a glance at his face. He no longer wore the amused expression of only moments before, but his face was serious and, oh, so tender. She wanted nothing more than for him to reach out and pull her into his strong embrace, but at the same time she feared that he would. After a split second's reflection, her fears transcended her desire and she turned to flee. Picking up her skirts, she headed toward the door.

But Sky was quicker than her. He moved around her with lightning speed so that he stood between her and her means of escape. She froze in her tracks, pressing her palms together and looking at the hay-strewn floor.

He reached out slowly and gently took her hands in his own. When she still did not look at him, he sighed in frustration. "Brooke, look at me. Please."

She lifted her head, slowly raising her eyes to his face.

"This is not a good time for a deep conversation, I know. We are newly married and under an unusual set of circumstances. That in itself is bound to bring a lot of stress into our lives. Now, on top of everything, I have this murder that is pressing in on my mind and on yours, too, I would imagine. So I know this isn't a good time, but Brooke—"

He stepped closer and she turned her face away slightly. His voice quivered as he continued. "I know you are feeling things. I know you wanted to kiss me the other night at Jed's." Her heart stumbled to a stop as his voice dropped to a husky whisper, and he fingered one of her curls. "And there are times, like now, when I know you care for me. I can see it in your eyes. Why are you fighting this?"

Deception was her only defense. Pulling her hands free from his, she looked him square in the face. "Fighting what?"

He gave an exasperated sigh, his dark eyes never leaving her face, as one hand went to his hip and the other combed back through his hair and paused at the base of his neck.

She almost caved in at the hurt that showed on his face. She wanted this, didn't she? She wanted to love him, to allow him to love her in return, but…. *I can't go down that road again.* She kept up her front, carefully concealing her emotions, knowing she could never allow herself to love him. "You don't know me, Sky. You don't have the faintest idea what kind of person I am or where I have been in the past."

"You're right. But I want to know."

"Trust me, Sky, you don't want to know."

"All right." He held his hands palms outward at shoulder height. "You don't have to tell me everything, but I am asking you to trust me. Somehow, I think you have gotten the impression that when you tell me about your past, I am going to be so horrified that I won't want to be around you anymore." Tucking a curl behind her ear, he let his fingers trail across her cheek before his hand dropped back to his side. "That's not going to happen, Brooke. I love you, honey. I don't know why God brought us together this way. This is not the beginning to the marriage I always imagined for myself. But I do know that I've fallen in love with you and that you are the woman meant for me from the beginning of time. I hope that one day, you will love me in return and will want to tell me all about yourself. But for right now, I want you to know that I am committed to you. I will never forsake you or betray you. I know I've said this before, but I am going to keep saying it until you believe me. I am committed to you, and I'm not going anywhere."

When he didn't say anything more, just stood watching her, her heart constricted within her chest. She knew what he said was true. Even if he found out the truth about her past, he wouldn't reject her. He would go on being the same wonderful Sky, and he would never have the true happiness that he deserved.

She spoke softly, "I trust you, Sky. More than you know." *I just don't deserve a man like you. And you certainly don't deserve a girl like me.*

He stepped up right in front of her and, reaching out, took one of her hands in his own. She closed her eyes momentarily against the wave of dizziness his closeness caused. Turning her hand over, he kissed her palm and then looked up into her face. "Thank you," he whispered as he let her hand fall gently back to her side. His dark brown eyes were warm and tender on her face, but his expression changed subtly.

"Will you tell me what scared you at the funeral?"

She stiffened. "I-I can't, Sky."

There was a long silence as they simply stood and looked into one another's eyes. She saw disappointment, and something else she couldn't quite put her finger on, radiating from his face. Again, she got the impression that he might know about her lying.

Brooke finally spoke into the stillness. "I-I don't really want to learn how to shoot tonight." Her hand fluttered distractedly toward the makeshift target at the back of the barn. "I'll just go inside now." She turned to leave, but he laid a firm hand on her elbow.

"Brooke, I want you to learn this. Tonight. I am not going to be here very much in the next couple of days, and there are going to be a lot of men around that may not be as gallant—" he paused slightly, and, when her eyes darted to his, he winked with a slight smile "—as me. I will feel much better knowing you can protect yourself."

It was her turn to give an exasperated sigh as she pulled away from him and turned toward the target. "Fine. Let's get on with it."

Reaching into the back of his waistband, he pulled out a small gun and held it out for her inspection. "This is a .22 caliber pistol. It is very easy to use. All you have to do is cock it like this," he demonstrated as he talked, "then point it in the right direction and pull the trigger." There was a loud crack, and the paper target jumped as a hole appeared directly in its center. Geyser nickered from his stall, eyes rolling and head swinging at the loud pop of the gun.

"Here, you try," Sky said as he handed her the gun.

Brooke tried to cock the hammer as she had seen him do, but her thumb was not strong enough. She looked at him, irked.

"That's all right. Here, just use both of your thumbs to pull it back."

When she used both hands, she found it easier to do.

"Good, now just point it at the paper and pull the trigger."

She held the gun out at arm's length and squeezed. The gun bucked in her hands, and the paper did not even vibrate. The bullet sank harmlessly into the hay, and she turned toward him with an *I-told-you-so* look.

"Good! You did great! I expected you to close your eyes when you pulled the trigger, but you didn't. That is one giant step in the right direction."

"Close my eyes?" She was incredulous. "How am I supposed to hit anything with my eyes closed?"

Sky smiled. "My point exactly. This time, try keeping a tighter grip on the butt of the pistol as you squeeze the trigger. That way it won't jump so badly."

Brooke tried this bit of advice but squeezed so tightly that the gun shook in her hands, and again, she missed the mark. She stamped one small foot in frustration and turned just in time to see Sky wiping a smile from his face.

"What kind of teacher laughs at his pupil?" she asked, more angry that she'd missed than at him.

"I'm not laughing at you exactly. You're just so…cute," he ended lamely, his eyes warm on her face.

Cheeks burning, she turned away quickly and aimed the gun once more.

"Here, let me help you."

Every muscle in her body tensed as Sky eased up behind her and put his arms around her shoulders. He took her hands and the gun gently in his and, placing her hands in the right position, held the gun steady. He was so close that she could smell the warm spicy scent he always carried. When he spoke softly into her ear, his breath brushed warmth on her neck. "I could get used to this. Couldn't you?"

Her heart thundering like a stampede of wild buffalo, she swallowed hard.

His grip tightened, and he pressed his lips against her hair. In desperation, she pulled the trigger. The paper jumped, and a hole appeared in the bottom right corner.

"I did it!" she said in disbelief. Sky stepped back slowly, and inwardly, she sighed in relief to have some space between them. She turned to him with a smile. "I hit it."

He nodded. "I knew you would be a star pupil."

"Star pupil?" She sniffed. "Just a minute ago you were laughing at me."

He gave her an unrepentant grin. "Try it by yourself this time."

She turned, took careful aim, held the gun steady, and squeezed off a shot. The paper flinched, but she could see no hole in it.

Sky stepped up to it. "You just nicked the edge. You're pulling a little to the right. Concentrate on that." He stepped toward her and asked innocently, "Maybe you'd like me to help steady the gun again?"

Brooke's heart raced but she only said, "No, I think I've got it now."

He winked. "I just thought I'd give it a try."

Despite her resolve to keep from falling for this man, his comment made her heart leap with pleasure. *Goodness! I'm blushing again!* Refusing to allow herself to think about it, she spun back toward the target, took careful aim, and fired.

Brooke enjoyed her lesson, and after several more shots, almost all of which at least nicked the target, Sky told her he thought that was good enough for one evening.

She handed him back the gun and reached a finger up to jiggle her ear. He chuckled. "Your ears ringing?"

"Let's just say I am glad you told me we were done for the night. I had begun to fear that I might not be able to hear your next set of instructions." She headed for the door. "Good night, Sky."

He opened his mouth to respond, but suddenly they heard a voice from outside. "Hello the House!"

Sky frowned and quickly reloaded the empty chambers in the gun, shoving it into the back of his waistband. He stepped out into the dark and then immediately to the right of the door pulling Brooke after him, so neither were outlined in the light cast from the lantern in the barn.

Through the falling snow, they could make out the dim outline of a horse carrying two riders.

"Sky?" came a strange voice.

"Pa?"

"Oh Sky!" cried a feminine voice as a woman slid from the saddle and rushed toward them. She flung her arms around Sky, hugging him, laughing, and crying all at the same time.

"Ma." Sky wrapped his arms around the woman in a warm embrace.

CHAPTER FIFTEEN

Brooke felt dazed. Sky's parents? What were they doing here? Would they like her? How long until they figured out that she would never be good enough for Sky, and how would they treat her when they realized it? Brooke pulled her mind back from its wanderings and focused on the conversation around her.

"We got your letter," his mother was saying, "telling us you were married, and we had to come. Your father wanted to stay the night in Greer at the ferry house and come up in the morning, but I said we had come that far, and we might as well come up tonight. So we borrowed a horse from Mr. Greer and came on up."

"Son." Sky's father approached, leading a horse, and Brooke stared, amazed at the resemblance between Sky and his father. Were they closer to the same age, they would have been mistaken for twins. The men embraced. "We heard that a merchant from Pierce City has been murdered?"

"Yes. In fact, if you had come in the morning I would have been gone to the inquisition."

Brooke shuddered at the thought that they could have come when Sky was gone. What would she have done?

Sky continued, "We are trying to determine who of the men arrested should be held over for a more extensive trial."

"Will the trial be held here?" asked his mother.

"No. They'll be taken to Murray, the county seat."

"We thought we heard shots." His father changed the subject.

"Brooke!" Sky turned, remembering her. Gesturing, he motioned for her to step from the shadows into the light cast by the open barn door. "Brooke, I want you to meet my parents, Rachel and Sean Jordan. Ma, Pa, this is my wife, Brooke."

Brooke stretched out her hand, hoping they wouldn't notice how badly she was shaking.

Rachel Jordan ignored her hand and pulled her into a gentle embrace. "I have prayed for you all of Sky's life."

Tears pooled in Brooke's eyes even as she was drawn into a fatherly hug from Sean. How disappointed these kind people would be when they learned of her past. What would they say if they knew the way she had lived her life?

"I was showing Brooke a little about handling a gun since I won't be around for the next couple of days. There's going to be more men here than we'll need, I'm afraid. I'll feel much better knowing you'll be here, Dad."

Brooke squinted up into the softly falling snow. "Sky, why don't we go into the house? I'm sure," she said to Rachel and Sean, "you are cold and tired. I have hot coffee on the stove. Does that sound good?"

"Very good!" Rachel replied.

Sky took the reins of the horse from his father. "I'll take care of the horse, then be right in. You all go ahead."

As they entered the house, a thought struck Brooke. *Where are they going to sleep?* She shoved the thought aside as she poured four mugs of steaming coffee. She made small talk with the Jordans as they waited for Sky to come in from the barn and tried not to think about the evening ahead.

Sky came in brushing snow from his sleeves. He picked up his coffee mug and took an appreciative slurp. Pulling out his chair, he asked, "How are Sharyah and Rocky?"

"Just fine. They're staying out at the Bennetts' while we're gone. Rocky will go to the house every day and take care of the animals, but this way Sharyah won't have to worry about housework and schoolwork at the same time."

"That's nice. Is Shar still determined to become a teacher?"

Brooke took a sip of her coffee. She glanced back and forth from Sky to his parents. How close their family seemed, and she'd only seen them together for minutes. She rubbed her finger around the rim of her cup as Rachel laughed, a low melodious sound.

"As determined as ever. She only has one more year, and she'll be done with her studies. Your father and I finally convinced her to slow down a little, or she'd be done already and itching to leave us."

Sean took Rachel's hand, giving it a squeeze.

"How about Cade? And Victoria? What is she up to these days?"

Brooke didn't miss the way Sky's parents glanced at one another after this last question. A tingle of jealousy marched down her spine, but she refused to acknowledge it.

Rising, she moved to refill the coffee cups and completely missed the answers Rachel gave to Sky's questions.

Sky and his parents talked late into the evening. Brooke remained fairly silent, allowing them to catch up, only speaking when she was spoken to.

Finally, Sky called the evening to a close. "I hate to end the evening so soon, but I have to be in Pierce City very early in the morning. How long can you stay?"

"As long as two weeks if that is all right with you two. We've made arrangements at home to be gone that long," Sean said.

"Great!" Sky exclaimed. "The trial should be over before then, and that will give me some time to spend with you. I hoped you weren't going to have to rush home. We have a spare room out in the barn. I built a fire in the stove out there when I was taking care of your horse, so it should be warm. The bed is small for two people, but it's comfortable."

Sean winked at his wife. "We don't mind a small bed, do we, honey?"

"Sean!" Rachel blushed but smiled lovingly in her husband's direction.

"All right, you two." Sky grinned. "Come on. I'll show you the way." Turning to Brooke he said, "I'll be right back."

She nodded but didn't look his way. She busied herself with clearing off the table and wiping it down.

Rachel and Sean lay snuggled in bed in the small room out in the barn. It was a bit chilly, but warming up fast with fragrant pine popping in the stove. Though her body was weary from a long day on the road, Rachel felt the need to talk about their new daughter-in-law before they went to sleep.

"She is very sweet and thoughtful," she said. "But I felt her trembling when I hugged her after we first arrived. I somehow think she might be afraid of us."

"I got that impression, too. I don't think she is so much afraid of us, though, as she may be afraid of what we will think of her. Do you remember how you felt around my mother when we first got together?"

"Yes, I was sure she'd know what a terrible girl her son had fallen in love with and that she'd banish me from the family for good."

"Her son was not a goody-two-shoes either, if you will recall." There was regret in Rachel's voice. "Yes, I remember."

Sean pulled her closer to him and placed a kiss on the top of her head. "It's all in the past. Let's not rehash it now. God has forgiven us, and we have forgiven each other, so we forget what is behind and press on toward our goal, right?"

"With the Lord's help."

"That's the only way, dear."

"But Sean—" Rachel turned toward her husband, trying to see his face in the dark—"do you think we should have wired ahead that we were coming? You know, given her a couple of days to get used to the idea?"

"Looking back, that probably wouldn't have been such a bad idea, but we're here now, so it's too late. We'll have to make the best of the situation."

"Maybe if I share our story with her, she will understand a little more how we feel about her? That we will love her, no matter what?"

"I think that's a good idea, honey. Why don't you bring it up tomorrow?"

There was a lull in the conversation. Then a sudden thought

struck Rachel, and she sat up in bed. "Do you think Sky has been sleeping out here?"

Sean drew his wife back down by his side. "Well, maybe, but if he has, it won't hurt for them to be pushed together a little bit. The more she's around him, the more she'll see he's not going to hurt her. I get so angry, Rachel, when I think of what that girl must have been through." She felt the tremor that pulsed through him. "Why God allows men like that to live, I'll never understand."

Rachel stared up into the darkness. "We will never understand God until we get to heaven, will we?"

Sean kissed her on the forehead. "I suppose not."

She sighed in contentment. "At least he loves her."

Sean chuckled. "Now, how do you know that? Did you and Sky have a private conversation that I missed?"

"No, dear. I can see it in his eyes."

They were quiet for a time, and then Rachel returned to their earlier discussion. "Hopefully she'll be more comfortable around us in the morning once she has had time to get used to the fact that we're here." She twirled a strand of her graying brown hair around one finger. "In all the excitement, I forgot to ask about Jason. I wonder how he's doing."

Sean sighed. "I've had him heavy on my heart for the last several days. I've really been praying that he won't forget the things Mother and I taught him as a boy. He needs to give his life back to God."

"Let's pray for him now, Sean." Rachel grasped one of Sean's hands, and they prayed together for Jason. They prayed he would remember all those things he had been taught, and that he would be convicted of the life he was now living.

"God, please bring Jason back to You. Show him all he is missing by living for himself and not trusting You with his life. Help him to return to Your loving arms. Lead him beside Your still waters. And be with Brooke. Help us to be a witness to her. She also needs Your love, Lord. Help her to understand that she will never be worthy of Your love but that it is a *free* gift, given in Christ Jesus. Bring her to feed in Your green pastures. These things we ask in the precious name of Jesus. Amen."

When Sean had ended the prayer, Rachel lay quietly in the dark, wondering just how God was going to answer their prayers.

Sky walked slowly back toward the house after showing his parents to their room. Moving up onto the porch he raised one leg onto the rail, looking up into the moon-washed sky. The snow had stopped, and now sporadic clouds scuttled lazily across its surface, alternately blocking out the light and then revealing it.

Sky folded his arms across his chest. The cold was bone-chilling, but he wanted to give Brooke plenty of time to prepare for bed before he came back into the house.

It was good to see Mother and Dad. It had been far too long since he had spent any time with a member of his immediate family. He only wished the circumstances surrounding the death of Fraser were different.

His thoughts turned toward the inquiry that would take place tomorrow. "Lord," he prayed aloud, "be in this trial. Work things out according to Your will. You know who committed this crime. Bring them to justice. And help all those who conduct these proceedings to be satisfied with the evidence. Don't let any false evidence be used just to convict *someone*. Help us to figure out who the guilty really are."

He paused in his prayer as his thoughts turned back to Brooke. "Lord, help me with Brooke. Help me to be patient with her. Give her confidence in me. Help her to know she can trust me and make me trustworthy, Lord. Show me how to be a good husband. Protect her, Lord. I don't know what she was afraid of at the funeral, but please don't let any harm come to her. Yet the most important thing I ask is that You bring her to know You. She needs You in her life, Lord. She needs to acknowledge her need of a Savior. Help her to know that nothing she has ever done is too terrible for You to forgive. Help her to find peace in You. And if You don't mind—" he smiled sheepishly at a space between two sluggish clouds "—would You make her fall in love with me, while You're at it?"

He watched the clouds for a few minutes more, enjoying the beauty of the night. Then he knocked on the cabin door.

"Come in," he heard her soft reply.

Opening the door, he moved quietly into the warmth of the house. Brooke lay in the bed with her back to the room, but the lamp was still burning on the table, so he knew she had expected him. Pulling off his boots, he blew out the lamp and then eased under the covers next to her. He felt her stiffen, but when he turned his back to her and said, "Good night, Brooke," she relaxed again. He closed his eyes, satisfied that she had accepted this next small step toward a complete relationship as husband and wife.

"Sky?"

He was surprised when she spoke. "Yes?"

"Will you please tell Jenny tomorrow that she is more than welcome to come here and stay with us for a while?"

"I hadn't thought of that. It's a good idea. I'll tell her."

"Thank you. Good night."

"Good night."

The next morning, Brooke awakened to someone shuffling through the cupboards. Momentarily startled, she sat up, wondering who it might be. Glancing toward the window, she saw it was still dark outside, but the lamp was burning low on the table. Then memory flooded her mind. "Sky?"

He stood up from where he had been bent, peering into the cupboard. "Sorry I woke you. I was trying to be quiet."

"What are you doing?"

"I'm trying to find some breakfast. You've moved things around a bit since I last looked in here."

Forgetting that she wore only her long flannel nightgown, Brooke threw the covers back and moved toward the cupboard as she said, "I'm so sorry, Sky. I didn't even think about how early you would have to be in town today. I should have thought to lay something out for you last night." She moved around, confidently getting bread out, slabs of ham into a pan, and eggs in another.

Sky stood by with a jar of preserves in hand, his mouth slack. His heart pounded like a stampede of wild mustangs as he realized what a great feat had just been accomplished in their relationship. Brooke was not nervous. Usually if something happened and she was caught off guard, like not having breakfast or dinner on the table at the right time, she would be so jumpy she was almost panicked. But today...

"Now where is that jar of jam?" Brooke interrupted his thoughts. "I know I left it right here last night."

Brooke turned toward him just as he snapped his mouth shut. "Oh, there it—" She broke off when she saw his expression. "What?" Then, looking down, she realized she was still in her nightgown. Heat suffused her face.

"It's not that, Brooke. It's just that you aren't tense this morning." She gave him a blank look.

"The last time I came in the house and breakfast wasn't quite ready, you were so nervous you almost jumped out of your skin. You even spilled your milk, remember?"

She nodded, realizing what he was saying rang true. She no longer feared Sky would turn out to be like Hank or Uncle Jackson. She had finally accepted that Sky was a man of integrity. What you saw in Sky was what you got. He didn't put on a face in public and then act differently at home. Suddenly, she wanted Sky to understand at least this one aspect of her life. She made a small gesture with her hand near her waist trying to come up with the right words to explain. "It's just that Hank...," but she found she couldn't go on. Unbidden, tears sprang to her eyes and she turned to the stove to stir the eggs.

Sky set the jar of preserves on the counter and let her stir for a moment, then gently took her hand, turning her so that she faced him. He bent down, gazing into her eyes. "I'm sorry I brought up a painful subject. But you don't know how happy it makes me to know that you are finally relaxed with me. I think that means you know I will never, ever, harm you in any way?"

She nodded.

A wide grin of relief split his face, and she couldn't help but smile in return. They looked into each other's eyes for a long moment. Then he tapped the end of her nose in a teasing gesture and asked, "How about breakfast?"

"Oh!" She turned away with a little gasp to rescue the very-well-done eggs.

CHAPTER SIXTEEN

A s Sky stood up from the table, Brooke was surprised to see him pull a box out from underneath the bed. He opened the lid, pulled a gun belt from the box, and slung it around his lean waist in one smooth motion. He then removed a mean-looking revolver, much heavier than the one they had used the night before. He spun the cylinder, checking the load, then set it firmly into the holster. As he slid the box back under the bed, he reached down to the floor and picked up something that Brooke had not seen earlier. It was the small .22 that he had taught her to use the night before. He had set it on the floor by the bed without her noticing.

"Brooke, I want you to keep this close to you at all times during the next couple of days. In fact, does your dress have a pocket?"

She nodded.

"Good. When you get dressed, I want you to put this in your pocket and take it with you everywhere. Do you understand?"

She nodded again, but said, "Sky, I don't think I can shoot anyone."

"Let's hope it won't even have to come out of your pocket, Brooke. But I will feel much better knowing you have the gun. Just carry it for my peace of mind, all right?"

She nodded a third time. Having the gun might ease her fears a little.

"All right, I'll see you tonight. I'll probably be late, so don't wait up for me. Tell my parents I said good morning, will you?"

Brooke's jaw clenched as she remembered she'd have to spend the day alone with Sky's mother and dad. How was she going to keep them busy all day long?

"Brooke, honey." Sky tilted her face up with a gentle caress.

"My parents are going to love you the way you are. Like I do. You don't have to worry about what they're going to think of you, or even how to entertain them for that matter. Just try to enjoy the day with them, okay?"

She licked her lips and gave him a weak smile. "I'll try to remember that they raised you, and anyone who taught you to be the way you are must be very special."

Sky looked thoughtful.

She swallowed, wishing she could read his thoughts. It was the closest she had come to saying she cared for him.

He chucked her under the chin. "That's the spirit. See you tonight." He stepped out, leaving a cold draft in his place.

Sky rode Geyser quickly through the brush, intent on reaching town before any of the posse from Lewiston arrived. He could see his breath in the chilly morning air, but it looked as though the sun was going to come out and warm the day up. The sprinkling of snow from the night before would be gone by the end of the day.

He pulled up in front of Jed's boarding house as the first rays of sunshine peeked over the horizon. Jed already had good, strong coffee in his pot by the fire.

"Were things quiet during the night?" Sky asked as he poured himself a cup of the brew.

"Hmmph. Quiet, you say. The night of the murder 'twas quieter 'n last night."

"What happened?"

"You ever hear tell of a fella by the name o' Lon Sears?"

"Seems like I do recall that name from somewhere. He from around here?"

Jed scratched his head, pondering this last question. "I reckon he is, sorta. He's got hisself a mine back in the hills a ways. He don't come to town very often, though. Maybe once a year. Anyhow, that don't rightly matter. What matters is that he speaks Chinese."

Sky sipped his coffee, watching Jed over the rim of his cup. "And?"

"Well, a couple o' the fellas had this here idee to sorta disguise Lon there as a drunken injun an' throw him in the jail with them jail birds to sorta see if he could make out any information, or a confession like. Only trouble was, they was all so excited about their idee that they all stayed here a chattin' an' a wond'rin' whether it was gonna work, an' I couldn't sleep for all of the ruckus they was makin'."

"So have they pulled him out yet? Do we know if he heard anything?"

"Yeah, they took 'im out this mornin', early. He didn't hear nothin' except the younger ones that been arrested plannin' to blame the whole shebang on the older ones 'cause they ain't got that long to live anyway, they said."

"Well, it was worth a try, I suppose." Sky tossed the dregs of his coffee into the fire. "I'm going to head over to the livery and stable my horse for the day."

Sky was headed out the door when Jed stopped him, "Oh, I plum forgot. One o' them there men confessed last night after you left."

"One of them confessed? A man *confessed*, and you are telling me stories about Lon Sears disguised as a drunken Indian?"

Jed had the presence of mind to look sheepish.

"If one of them confessed, why did you all go to the trouble of disguising Lon in the first place?"

"Well, the man—it was the one you an' I arrested that first morning after the murder, by the by—that one with the blood on his shirt. Anyhow, he tells us that he an' four others were involved, including Lee Chang, you should know. But none o' them other men will cop to the confession. They be stickin' to the story that they is innocent. So we wanted to see ifn we sorta caught them off guard like, if we could hear somethin'. But no such luck."

Jed turned to refill his cup but paused, looking back. "Oh yeah, an' one more thing. Carle an' Gaffney brought in another man this mornin'. So that makes nine down to the jail now."

Sky shook his head. One man had confessed and another had been arrested, but Jed had thought to tell him about Lon and his Indian disguise. A grin split his face. *Good ol' Jed.*

Suddenly, from out on the street, Sky and Jed heard horses approaching. Sky opened the door and stepped out onto the boarding house porch. Six riders cantered up the street on spent horses.

From behind Sky, Jed spoke up. "Only six o' them?"

"There will be more. Lots more."

The riders pulled to stop and looked up at Sky. A short balding man wearing a red bandanna around his neck spoke for the group. "We got the town surrounded—about seventy-five of us. John Bymaster's my name. The men have elected me to be captain of the posse. I had them form two lines of about thirty each and surround the town in case anyone saw us coming and thought about making an escape."

"Don't think that be necessary," said Jed. "We got nine in the jail now—most probably all, if not more 'n those involved."

Sky wasn't so sure, but he kept his thoughts to himself.

Bymaster looked up and down the street. "No building in town big enough to hold all of us. We'll have to set up court outside somewhere." He glanced around a little more. "Down there I think, by that tree at the end of town."

A signal was sent to the posse that surrounded the town and they made their way in, tightening their circle as they came. Soon the main street teemed with swaggering men and their horses. Bymaster directed all of them to hobble their horses and find positions at the end of the street near the tree.

As Sky led Geyser through the men to the Livery he heard more than one racial slur.

"Those Chinks are gonna get what's comin' to them now!"

"Cussed Celestials! Comin' west an' stealin' our jobs! Now they be murderin'! Best we set a good example here for others to take note of!"

Sky knew what that meant. Nothing short of a lynching

would satisfy these men. He sent up another prayer that nothing would spin out of control.

Wild Bill looked grim as he took the reins from Sky. "You think we ever gonna get to the bottom o' this thing with all them men out there wantin' to showboat their prowess?"

"We'll just have to pray, Bill. Ask God to keep things under control and orderly."

Bill gave Sky a skeptical look. "You do the praying, Sky. Me, I plan on *doin'* somethin' if things get out of hand." He pulled back the flaps of his long, ankle-length overcoat to reveal a Colt strapped to his side.

Sky eyed the gun. "Bill, don't do anything rash, okay?"

"Don't you worry about me, Sky. I don't plan on pullin' this baby out unless I have to."

Leaving the livery, Sky walked down the street. He noticed a difference about town today. Normally, there were Chinamen everywhere, but today, Sky had not seen even one. They were staying away, he assumed, to keep from being falsely accused, yet the town was far from quiet. It teemed with movement like never before. The warming sun shone brightly on the street, and everywhere he looked, groups of distraught men discussed the recent tragedy. The atmosphere in the town was tense to say the least, and Sky knew it wouldn't take much to increase that tension to the point of explosion. He prayed it wouldn't come to that.

Sky headed to Chang's store. He pushed open the front door, and the bell jangled as he stepped inside. Jenny glanced up from behind the counter. Although she looked calm, her eyes were red-rimmed as though she may have spent the night crying.

"Hello, Jenny," he murmured.

She nodded. "Sky."

"I'm sorry about Lee."

Tears sprang to her eyes. "I love my husband, Sky. He hard man, but I love him. I pray for him every day. Pray he change heart, but..." She shrugged.

"I know, Jenny. I'm sorry."

"Thank you."

"The inquiry is going to start soon, and Brooke wondered if you would come out and spend the day with her on the farm." When he saw her hesitation, he added, "My parents came yesterday, and she is a little nervous being around them, so your presence might help her relax a little."

Jenny smiled sadly. "I go for Brooke then." Yet she seemed reluctant to leave.

Sky nodded. "Good. If you get the things you'll need, I'll escort you to the edge of town and make sure you get on your way safely."

Minutes later, Sky, leading Jenny's horse behind him toward the end of the street heard a strident, nasal yell. "You there, where are you taking that woman?"

Sky and Jenny turned to see a short, enormously fat man lumbering toward them. Sky thought fleetingly that the man's high-pitched voice certainly didn't match his size.

"I am not taking her anywhere," Sky spoke calmly. "She is leaving town for the day. I will be staying here for the trial."

The man eyed Jenny coldly. "She's not going anywhere. How do we know that she didn't take part in this crime?"

Just then, Bymaster, who had heard the loud commotion, approached. "Smyth, what's goin' on?"

The obese man spoke in what could only be described as a whine. "This man, here," he dipped his head at Sky, his jowls jiggling, "is letting this Chinese woman leave town. What if she was an accomplice?"

Bymaster turned to Sky for an explanation, but Sky thought he saw a glint of irritation in the depths of the man's eyes.

"I can vouch for this woman, Bymaster. She had nothing to do with this crime. I'd wager that any man from town would vouch for her too."

"Thet's right!" hollered Jed, as by now the whole group of men had become quiet and focused their attention on the ruckus at the end of the street. "I'll vouch for her! Jenny Chang wouldn't hurt a fly."

"Me too!" yelled several of the other men in unison.

"Chang?" whined Smyth. "Isn't one of those men in there her husband?" He gestured toward the jail.

"Smyth, shut up," snapped Bymaster as he focused his attention on Sky. "Where is she going?"

Irritated by this obviously prejudicial questioning, Sky clenched his fists at his sides. He wanted to slug someone, but for the sake of peace he answered, "She is going to spend the day with my wife out at our farm."

Bymaster eyed Sky coolly, then turned to Jenny. "Ma'am—" he touched the brim of his hat—"feel free to be on your way."

Smyth looked as if he'd been denied a chance at a million dollars. "If she runs off and we find she had anything to do with this, I'm comin' after you!" Smyth jabbed his fleshy finger into Sky's chest, having to squint up a good ways to glare into Sky's face.

Calm as the eye of a storm, Sky looked down into the face of the loudmouth. His eyes narrowed. Smyth took a step back and licked his fat lips. The threat was empty. Sky knew it, and all the men standing around knew it.

When Sky continued to eye him indifferently and made no reply to his threat, Smyth stepped back further. Then, in a show of bravado, he pulled the front of his vest downward with a short jerk and swaggered off as though he had conquered the world.

Sky looked back at Jenny and she nodded her gratitude to him, turning her horse toward the woods. He watched her go, praying she would make it safely to the farm.

Swinging back around, he surveyed the men in the crowd thoughtfully, but they had already resumed their conversations. He didn't think there was any danger to Jenny, or he would have accompanied her. Knowing it was still early in the day with the trial not even started yet, he figured any potential troublemakers would still be interested enough in the goings-on to stay in town. And Jenny had her rifle in the scabbard of her saddle.

After Sky rode out of the yard, Brooke set about getting breakfast on the table. She worried about what to fix. Sky's parents would be in soon, and she didn't want them to think badly of her, so what did one fix in order to impress one's in-laws? Unable to decide, she fixed a little of everything.

Rachel and Sean knocked on the door a little while later. Brooke called for them to enter, and Rachel gasped with surprise when her gaze landed on all of the food on the table.

Brooke had made oatmeal, hot cakes, scrambled eggs, and biscuits. She had grated potatoes and fried them until they were a crispy golden brown. Thick slices of browning ham sizzled on the stove, and fragrant sausages sputtered in another pan. Two jars of preserves stood open on the table next to a loaf of bread. A glass of cold milk stood at each place, and the coffee pot bubbled on the back of the stove.

Brooke, face damp from the heat, was turning from the stove with a hot pan of muffins in her hands. "Good morning," she said, trying to sound like she meant it.

She hoped her nervousness wouldn't show too much. For Sky's sake, especially, she wanted these people to like her. She didn't want them to go back to their family and report on what an unsuitable girl Sky had been forced to marry. She had wracked her mind all morning, trying to come up with something interesting for the three of them to do today and had come up blank, but the fact that they might find her boring was the least of her worries. In the back of her mind she feared they might somehow be able to read her sins in her face, and she so wanted them to like her.

The conversation at breakfast was stilted. Brooke knew she was trying too hard. If she could relax and be herself, everything would be fine, but she couldn't force herself to calm down. The tension-filled meal culminated when Brooke, who was offering the plate of ham to Sean for the third time, knocked Rachel's cup of coffee into her lap.

"Oh! I'm so sorry, Rachel!" Brooke gasped.

Rachel's reaction was quick. She stood and pulled her skirt away from her body.

"Are you all right?"

"I'm fine." Sean and Rachel eyed each other. A silent message passed between them.

What a mess she'd made of the whole meal!

"It's all right dear, really," soothed Rachel as she wiped at the stain on the front of her dress. "I'm just going to run out to our room and change. I'll be right back."

Sean finished his meal. She could tell he was trying to make easy conversation with her, but as soon as Rachel reappeared, he said, "I saw some harnesses in the barn that need mending. I'll go out and work on that for Sky and let you two get to know each other."

Rachel chatted easily about all sorts of things as they began to clear the table. She told several stories of Sky's little-boy-shenanigans. And Brooke laughed when Rachel told of the time Sky had taken the whole cookie jar right off the kitchen counter and up to his room.

"When I walked into the kitchen and noticed it was missing, I went in search of it, of course." Brooke washed dishes as she listened, and Rachel chattered on as she wiped down the table. "I found Sky lying on his bed looking rather green. He had crumbs everywhere. All over his face, the bed, floor, everywhere! I pretended I had no idea that jar was missing and said to him, 'Son, I just filled the cookie jar with a fresh batch of cookies this morning and thought I'd come up and let you know you can have some if you like.'"

Rachel chuckled. "I didn't think it was possible, but he turned a shade greener. Well, I couldn't help it. I started laughing. He had stuffed the cookie jar under his bed, and it was empty! He had eaten every last one, and I'd filled it to the brim that morning. I didn't even punish him. I told him he would suffer enough before the night was over. He did. I don't know how many trips he made to the outhouse that night. I stopped counting after ten."

Rachel, who was now staring off into the past, chuckled again. "He was the sorriest little sinner you ever saw. The next morning at the breakfast table, I came out of the kitchen, set the refilled cookie jar on the table, and told the kids I had too much to do that day to cook breakfast, so they should just eat up. Rocky and Sharyah started to dig right in, but you should have seen the sick look on Sky's face. Poor boy, it was a long time before he ever ate another oatmeal and raisin cookie."

Rachel came to herself and waved the damp rag in her hand. "Here I've been chattering on so that I forgot we were supposed to be cleaning up, and you have it almost all done already. Here, dear, I'll dry that." She dropped the rag into the dish water and reached for the plate in Brooke's hand.

Brooke took a deep breath. Maybe this day wouldn't be so bad after all.

Chapter Seventeen

When they finished with the dishes, each woman took a cup of coffee and sat at the table. Rachel stirred cream and sugar into her cup.

"That was a lovely breakfast you fixed, dear. Really, though, I don't want you to feel like you have to go to so much trouble for Sean and me. We don't usually eat very much of a breakfast, but we appreciate all the effort you went to." Brooke looked away shyly, but Rachel went on, "I remember the first meal I ever had to fix for my mother-in-law. I didn't do nearly the wonderful job you did this morning. I felt so scared. You see, Sean and I weren't living right at the time….Well, no, I'll have you all confused if I don't start right at the beginning."

She glanced at Brooke. "You see, when I was a little girl, my mother abandoned me on the steps of the orphanage in Shiloh. I grew up not knowing anything about my past, or who my mother and father were, and that made me angry. I became very bitter toward God and decided I would have nothing to do with Him.

"But I didn't count on meeting Sean Jordan or his mama. I was thirteen when I first noticed him." A smile traced the corners of her mouth as she stared out the window. "He was the most handsome man you ever did see. He still is." She grinned at Brooke. "I had to walk right past him every day on my way from the orphanage to the school. He worked at a Mercantile as a delivery man then, and every morning, it was his job to sweep off the walk in front of the store. He was always there when I walked past. I was a lot younger than him—he is seven years older than me—so it took him a few years to notice the doe-eyed girl who wandered past him every day. But eventually he came to his senses," she chuckled, "and began to take an interest in me. Of course, by then, he was no longer working at the Mercantile. He had become one of the sheriff's deputies in town."

She paused. "Sean now, he came from a very loving home. He had just one brother, Jack—that's Jason's daddy. Their daddy had died when they were just youngsters, but their mama—her name is Eltha Jordan, and I hope you will meet her one day—loved the Lord with all her heart. She raised those boys the best she could, but in those days, it was so hard for a woman to find a good job.

She had to work very long hours in order to make enough of a living. The boys were left on their own a lot and tended to—" she stopped, as if trying to think of a nice way to phrase what she was about to say "—stray from what they had been taught."

Brooke listened with fascination to the story.

"Anyhow, Sean and I fell in love and began to get serious with one another. Our relationship was anything but godly. We went from party to party and generally lived to please ourselves. We had decided we would put off marriage, but when I found out I was pregnant—"

Rachel stopped at Brooke's gasp. But when she turned to look, Brooke was already staring down into her lap. Rachel couldn't be sure, but she thought she saw tears in the corner of her eyes. *Lord, whatever it is, draw her to You. Don't let her push You away.*

"When I found out I was pregnant, we knew we would have to get married. So we married in January, and I had Sky in July. It was right before I had Skyler that my mother-in-law came to stay with us. The first meal I fixed for her was burnt toast and soggy scrambled eggs." Rachel made a face at the memory. "I was so afraid she would pull Sean away from me. I knew we had hurt her terribly by our sin, but she never even mentioned it. And then I was afraid she would hate me and try to turn Sean and I against one another, but she never did that either. She just loved us the way we were, and I always wondered what made her different.

"Sean and I began to have trouble. We fought constantly, and it was always over something silly. Then Sean began stepping out on me. Oh, I wasn't innocent either, I probably would have cheated on him, too, but by that time, I had Sky to take care of. I remember feeling so miserable. Mother would tell us about Jesus and His love. But I felt I was too wicked a person for God to ever love. I thought I had done too many terrible things for Jesus to ever forgive me.

"I remember walking past Mother's room one day and hearing her crying. I started to go in and make sure she was all right, but then I realized that she was praying, so I paused to listen. She was praying for Sean and I, that we would come to love Jesus and serve Him with all our hearts. She prayed that God would renew our love for one another and bind us together as a family. And then I heard her pray that God would remove any bitterness that she harbored toward us from her heart. I knew then that Jesus was the One who had helped her to forgive us for all the pain we caused her. It was through her testimony, the way she loved us unconditionally, that Sean and I eventually saw how much we needed Jesus in our lives. We went to church with her one Sunday and gave our hearts to God. It took a long time for Him to get a hold of us, but we have been living for Him ever since."

Rachel stopped talking and turned toward Brooke, who was crying unashamedly now.

"Oh, honey." Rachel leaned over and rubbed one hand up and down Brooke's arm. "I wanted you to understand that I am aware of your concern—having us here and all. Maybe I am being presumptuous—if so, please forgive me. But I want you to know we're glad you're a part of our family now. We have prayed for years that Sky would be blessed with a wonderful wife, and now that we've met you, we know God has answered our prayers."

Brooke straightened and wiped at the tears on her face with her forearm. Rachel pulled a hankie from her sleeve and pressed it into Brooke's hands. She blew her nose noisily and stared out the window for a long moment. When she spoke, her voice was hesitant. "Jesus accepted you like that? You didn't have to do anything first?"

Rachel gave Brooke an understanding look and got up to refill their coffee cups. "I struggled with that concept for a long time before I finally gave in to God. I kept thinking I wasn't worthy of Jesus' love yet; that I needed to be a better person before I could give my life to Him. And that is just what the devil wanted me to think. He wanted to keep me under condemnation. But Jesus wants to convict us. There is a big difference between condemnation and conviction.

"Condemnation keeps us feeling like there is no hope. We know we are sinners and we are miserable, but we don't see a way out. We keep thinking we need to *do* something, *be* something, *have* something more before Jesus will accept us. Conviction now, conviction shows us that, even though we are sinners, there is a way of hope—and that hope is Jesus Christ."

Rachel took a sip of coffee, then went on. "Before I gave my life to Christ, I felt only condemnation. I searched to find that *something* that would make me worthy of Jesus' forgiveness. Then one day, Eltha pointed out to me that I would never be good enough. If I waited to accept Jesus until the day that I was perfect, the day would never come. You see, the whole reason Jesus had to come and die for us is that none of us is perfect. We are all sinners, and in God's eyes one sin is as bad as any other. The Bible says if we have broken the law at just one point, it's as if we have broken the whole thing."

Brooke was quiet for a time, but her next question sent silent shock through Rachel. "What about babies? If a baby dies, does it go to hell?"

Oh, Sweet Jesus, help her. Could it be this young girl had already borne and lost a child? She wanted to ask. To pull her into a loving embrace and infuse her with comfort. *What kind of pain and misery has this poor girl been through? Oh Jesus, I wish I knew more so I could help her deal with the pain.*

Rachel could barely speak around the pain in her chest. "No, I don't believe God would send an innocent baby to hell. Babies aren't able to make decisions about right and wrong. I believe when a baby dies, it goes back to heaven and finds rest in the loving arms of its Creator."

This statement brought a fresh wave of tears to Brooke's eyes. She didn't even bother to wipe them away as she turned to her mother-in-law. "Thank you for caring enough to tell me your story. You've given me a lot to think about. I think I'll—"

The clopping of a horse sounded outside.

Brooke peered out the window. The rider was Jenny Chang. She watched as Sean, his Stetson tipped back on his head, came from the barn and took her horse, gesturing her toward the house.

"It's Jenny Chang," she told Rachel. "The wife of one of the men arrested for Fraser's murder. I told Sky last night to have her come on out here. I'm so glad he remembered. It would have been awful for her to have to stay in town today."

Brooke wiped the residual tears from her face as she moved to the door. "Jenny, I'm so glad you were able to come. Come on in. I'd like for you to meet my mother-in-law, Rachel Jordan."

Jenny eyed Brooke's tear-stained face but made no comment. Instead, she bowed her head and bent both knees in Rachel's direction, her hands curled together in front of her. "It a pleasure to meet you."

Rachel smiled kindly at her. "I'm glad to meet you, too, Jenny."

"Would you like a cup of coffee? We were just having one," offered Brooke.

Jenny nodded. "Yes, thank you."

The women sat around the table making small talk for a while. Brooke found that she felt much more relaxed with Rachel now. It had helped to learn that Rachel and Sean were not the perfect people she imagined them to be.

Suddenly, she remembered a story that she had read in Sky's Bible the evening before. Some men had brought a woman to Jesus, saying that they had caught her in the very act of adultery. They asked Jesus what they should do with her. She remembered from Sunday school that it was customary in Bible days for women who committed adultery to be stoned. But Jesus gazed at the men and said, "Let him who is without sin cast the first stone." All the men walked away because every one of them knew he had sin in his own life. Jesus forgave the woman and told her to go on her way, but not to sin anymore.

Maybe there was hope for her as well. Could it really be that Jesus would forgive her for all she had done? To lay the whole burden of her sin on Him and just walk away—how wonderful that would be!

And what about Sky and his family? Would they cast stones of criticism at her when they found out about her past?

She glanced at Rachel, who was tenderly smiling at Jenny, and suddenly she knew how they would respond; they would love her as Jesus had loved the adulterous woman.

One question still remained for Brooke: Did she want to accept Christ's love? Sky's? Sean and Rachel's? Could she humble herself enough to do that?

"All right, everybody, listen up!"

As Sky listened to John Bymaster, someone came to stand beside him. It was Jason. He appeared disheveled and grim, like maybe he hadn't slept well the night before. *Wonder what kept him up? Hopefully his conscience. Lord, keep working on him.* "Hi," was all Sky said.

Jason nodded. Then both men turned to join the crowd.

"As you all know," Bymaster instructed, "last night, we appointed Hattabaugh to be the judge at this here inquiry." An older gentleman with graying hair at his temples moved through the crowd to stand by John. "Kettenbaugh is going to be the clerk," he gestured to a middle-aged man, "and I will act as the investigator. I want these procedures to be conducted with the highest regard for the law and under the presumption that those men in there," he pointed toward the jail house, "are innocent until they are proven guilty." Sky's opinion of the man elevated. "There is to be no drinking during the course of these procedures, gentlemen. Any man found consuming liquor will be thrown into the facilities along with the accused. Does everyone understand?"

A mumbled chorus of acknowledgment rose up from the crowd.

"Fine! Now let me inform you that one of the men who has been arrested has professed that he and four others were the ones who committed this crime, but—" he raised his hands for silence as the men began to murmur threateningly—"he won't give us any names except Lee Chang's. So we will proceed as though there has been no confession and see where the evidence leads."

The sun shone down brightly on the dusty street as chairs were brought out for the judge and the clerk, who also had a small table set before him on which he could write. A chair was also placed at the front of the group to serve as a witness stand. Jed produced an old dusty Bible for the swearing in, and the inquiry was put into motion.

The day was beginning to warm, and steam rose from the street as the first prisoner was brought from his cell and led to the witness stand. His hand shook as he held it out and rested it on the Bible, swearing that he would tell the truth, the whole truth, and nothing but the truth. Sky could tell as he watched that the man feared for his life, and looking at the faces of the men around him, Sky couldn't blame the man for his fear. The atmosphere was anything but friendly.

It had been decided that Ping Chi, the one who had confessed, would be brought out last so his testimony could be weighed in light of what all the other men had to say.

The questioning began. "Where were you on the night of the murder? What was the celebration that took place on the night of the murder about? Did you have any reason to want the deceased dead?" On and on the questions went. When each man had been questioned, he was seated, with his hands securely tied behind his back, in the shade of a tree not far away. Two men, with guns held ready, stood watch over them.

As Sky listened to John Bymaster question the witnesses, his opinion of the man rose swiftly. He repented of his earlier animosity toward him. Bymaster was thorough and fair with all of his questions. Never accusing but always cutting deeper, trying to get at the real truth of what happened on that fateful night.

Standing inside the covering darkness of the forest at the edge of town, Percival watched the inquiry proceedings through his binoculars. A pitiless smirk crossed his face as he watched Lee Chang being led to the witness chair. It gave him great pleasure to know that all the men Lee hired to do the killing had been arrested. It would make his next job so much easier. *Chang, you fool. Didn't you know that you couldn't pull off this job and live to tell about it?*

He had known Chang was the man for this job the minute he'd heard the story about the bogus gold. Percival smiled.

When David Fraser had denied him permission to date his daughter and had told Alice in no-uncertain-terms that she wasn't to be seen speaking to him anymore, he had gone and tried to talk her into running away with him, begged her, even. But Alice, being the good daughter she was, had complied with her father's wishes. She had refused him, said her father had opened her eyes, and now she could see he wasn't the man for her. She had wished him well, but said she wouldn't be accepting his calls anymore. In a way, this whole mess was her fault. She had been ready to marry him before her father talked her out of it. *No, not Alice's fault; she's innocent in this. It's all her father's fault!*

He had been in a saloon, brooding on a way to repay Fraser when he'd heard the men at the next table relaying the story of the Chinaman up in Pierce City that David Fraser had confronted. It was an innocent comment that had spurred his plan. "I bet that Chinaman would like to get his hands on Fraser's scrawny little neck!" guffawed one of the drunken men, laughter filling his words, as he slapped the table. "Imagine a showdown between Fraser and Chang!"

That had been the start of his plan. He had decided right then to contact Chang and put it into motion at the earliest possible moment. It wasn't like he hadn't done this sort of thing before and gotten away with it. His only qualm had been in wondering if Chang could be trusted long enough for his plan to work. After he'd met him, all his misgivings had vanished.

Now, as he stared at Chang, he smiled.

He wasn't worried about Chang spilling his name just yet. Chang was the type of man who savored his infamous reputation. The illusion that he was in control at all times was very important to him. And it would hurt his reputation to have it known that he was merely a hired killer. *Chang won't say anything about me until his very life depends on it. And by then, it will be too late.*

He lowered the binoculars and eyed the large group of men listening to the inquiry. How many men would guard the prisoners when they were sent to Murray for trial? That was his only worry.

Things had to go without a hitch. Nothing could go wrong now, and in order to insure that, he must know how many guards there would be. *Or would I?* A sudden thought hit him. He rubbed his first two fingers across the edge of his jaw as he thought the idea over.

His eyes narrowed as he stared down at the pine-needle-covered ground. The trace of a relieved smile parted his lips as he realized his newly formed plan would work to perfection.

Several plump hens scratched in the mud, searching for bugs. The rooster sat on his lofty fencepost and cocked his head in their direction. Fluffing his feathers in the warm afternoon sun, he settled down and closed his eyes to have a little siesta.

Brooke stepped up onto her stool and began to gather the eggs.

"You cry before I come?" Jenny asked.

Brooke turned in mild surprise and smiled sadly, trying to decide how best to describe what had brought the tears on. "I am not a good person, Jenny. I have done lots of very bad things in my life, and when Rachel and Sean showed up yesterday, I was so afraid of what they would think of me if they ever found out about my past. Sky is such a good man. I have never known onyone like him."

She shooed away a roosting hen and began putting the eggs into her bowl. "I thought his parents would be disappointed in me…that they wouldn't like me or accept me. I know I'm not good enough for Sky. But this morning Rachel told me a story about herself when she was young. She and Sean were not good people either, but Rachel says that Jesus accepted them and forgave them anyway. He changed their lives."

Jenny was so easy to talk to. Perhaps it was her easy-going spirit or the peace that constantly shone from her eyes. Brooke opened up to her like she hadn't done to anyone else. "I wish I could be forgiven. I'm tired, so tired of…I don't even know *why* I am tired. I just feel like I need *something*, Jenny. Maybe I need Jesus' love and forgiveness. But I'm afraid that what I've done is too terrible to forgive."

Brooke gave up gathering the eggs and sat on her stool. Jenny pulled a log from a pile against the barn wall and followed suit. The sun was warm and gentle. A companionable silence engulfed them as they watched the pecking hens. It was a long time before Brooke spoke again.

"I have watched you, Jenny. I saw the way Lee treated you the day I was in your store. I used to know some men who treated me that same way, but I did not respond to them the same way you did to your husband. You were calm and strong and even seemed to have a peace about you. Where do you find your strength and peace?"

Jenny thought a moment before she answered. "You think maybe I haf something else that help me be strong? Something not Jesus?"

"Do you?"

Jenny smiled in understanding at her friend. "No." She shook her head. "Jesus, He the One give me strength. He help me love Lee even when he bad to me. Even help me forgive Lee."

Brooke looked surprised. "You could forgive a man who treated you that way?"

Again she shook her head. "Not me only. I haf to haf Jesus' help."

"I don't want to forgive them."

Jenny nodded. "First thing first. You want to find peace? You need Jesus. You not find long peace any place else." Jenny gestured toward the house. "You haf Bible?"

Brooke nodded.

"Come. I show you Jesus' heart." Jenny headed toward the house. Brooke followed, carefully carrying the half-filled bowl of fresh eggs.

CHAPTER EIGHTEEN

Late in the afternoon, when all the Chinamen but the last had been questioned, still not one of them had come clean. The posse brought out Ping. He admitted that he and three others had gone into Fraser's store on the night of the murder, and while he made a small purchase to distract the merchant, one of the others had lifted the lock on the front window. Then later that night, after the town had become sufficiently noisy to hide the sounds of a struggle, they had gone into the store through the unlocked window and killed Fraser.

A threatening murmur rose from the crowd, but John Bymaster held up his hand for silence and continued with the questioning. "And what was this purchase you made?" he asked, pacing in front of the witness, his fingers steepled.

"A string tie." He pointed toward his neck with a rather unsteady hand.

John pulled a string tie from a bag handed to him by Jed. "And, is this that tie?"

"Yes."

"Let the court know that I, myself, went to this man's shanty this morning and found this—" He held the bolo aloft as he spoke. Turning back to the witness, he said, "What was the celebration about on the night of the murder? From all appearances, it would seem that every Chinaman who participated in that affair on the night of September the ninth is guilty of being a co-conspirator to a murder."

"No." Ping shook his head. "People were told that celebration was in honor of Mrs. Chang. A late birthday gathering. Only ones who knew about Mr. Fraser were us who kill him."

John paced in front of the witness for a minute, rubbing his upper lip. Relief rippled through the crowd when they heard that only a few men had known about the real reason for the celebration that night.

"Now, I must ask you, why did you commit this crime?" John moved on to a new line of questioning.

The Chinaman fidgeted with his hands in his lap. "We get pay."

"Someone paid you to commit this crime?"

Ping nodded.

"And who did that?"

He spoke without hesitation. "Lee Chang." His voice was sure and steady, and Sky sensed he was telling the truth.

All eyes in the group turned to the cluster of men seated under the tree.

Lee Chang, hands tied behind him, stared back at them, his red, opium-deprived eyes cold and calculating. Sky saw no remorse there. Could the man really be that hard?

Sky wondered what the man who had been in the alley that night might have to do with this. Who was he? Certainly not Trace Johnson. What was he doing there?

Lee Chang was recalled to the stand. He sat, leaning forward uncomfortably to keep his bound hands from pressing painfully into the back of the wooden chair.

"Did you pay these men to murder Fraser?" asked John.

Chang did not answer. His stare locked on Bymaster, never wavering. There was a long pause as the two men eyed one another. After several more questions to which Chang only responded with a blank stare, it became apparent he was not going to say anything, and the judge called for a short recess.

The crowd had not had a break since lunch. They stood to stretch and take turns with the dipper at a barrel of drinking water.

Sky approached Bymaster. "Would you mind if I asked Chang a couple of questions?" he asked quietly.

Bymaster ran a tired hand over his face. "Fine with me. What do you know about this situation?"

Sky told him everything he knew from the story of the bogus gold to his friendship with Fraser. He told about Brooke seeing another man in the alley between Jed's boarding house and the Mercantile on the night of the murder.

"I'm sure Ping is telling the truth now," Sky said. "When we first arrested him, he denied any involvement, but he had blood all over his shirt. I had some tests run on it, but they couldn't say for sure whether it was human or not—only that it belonged to a mammal. So that doesn't help us much. Ping's description of the attack would explain how the blood got there."

Sky suppressed a shudder as he imagined what Fraser must have gone through. "Still," Sky rubbed his chin, "I don't think Ping is giving us the whole story. He probably doesn't know the whole story. Somehow I think that there is someone else in the mix. Someone who knows Chang."

"Well, he won't talk to me, so you might as well try."

Once Chang was back on the stand, Sky didn't waste any time getting to the point. "Chang, did someone pay you to hire men to kill Fraser?"

Chang blinked and looked away. It was the first breach that the crowd had seen in his armor all day long.

Sky repeated the question, but Chang was back to his routine blank stare.

Undaunted, Sky went on, "On the night of the murder, my wife and I stayed in the boarding house next door to Fraser's Mercantile. My wife happened to look out on the alley between the two buildings and saw a man who is not from around here. Do you know anything about that?"

Chang blinked again but still said nothing.

"Long, graying hair. Full, long beard. Do you know the man?" He threw out the description of Trace Johnson to see what kind of reaction he might get.

This brought another blink from Chang, and Sky thought he saw a puzzled look cross Chang's face. Still, he refused to answer.

"How about a small man wearing lots of jewelry? Did you ever know a man who looked like that?" Sky described the man Trace Johnson was tracking as well as he could with the little information he had.

Chang's face tightened and he paled, but no answer was forthcoming.

Sky tried another tactic. "Tell me why the safe in the back room of the store wasn't even touched. Were you leaving it there for someone else to break into after Fraser was taken care of?"

Chang licked his lips, then spat on the ground at Sky's feet in contempt.

He was not going to answer any questions.

The sun sank low on the horizon. None of the posse nor the prisoners had eaten, so the court was called to a close until an hour after sunrise the next day. The prisoners were taken back to the jail, and the tired posse began to make dinner preparations and sleeping arrangements.

Sky bid Jed and Jason a good night and started to head for home, but a sudden thought occurred to him, and he turned back to Jason.

"Jason, how are you doing with all this?"

He shrugged. "I'll be fine as long as that man gets what he deserves."

Sky didn't have to ask to whom he was referring. "And what does he deserve, Jason?"

"He deserves to die!" The words sounded harsh, and Sky saw Jason flinch even as the sentiment left his mouth.

"So do we all, Jason. So do we all. But I know you know that. Good night." Turning, Sky rode off into the dusky evening.

When Jenny and Brooke got back to the house, Rachel was not there. Brooke set the bowl of eggs on the table and retrieved Sky's Bible from next to the bed.

As they sat at the table, Jenny opened the book and turned the pages. She paused to stare at the ceiling. "Give me minute. I think how to say in English." She tapped her temple in demonstration.

Brooke folded her hands and waited.

Finally Jenny spoke. "There many stories in Bible about bad men and women who find salvation in Jesus, but I not show you all them now. You say you afraid that you are too bad a person for Jesus to forgive, but I not think that your big problem. I think you love darkness."

Brooke blinked at her.

"I read, you listen." She went on. "And as Moses lifted up the serpent in the wilderness, even so must the Son of man be lifted up, That whoever believes in Him should not perish, but have eternal life." Jenny's finger moved from word to word. "For God so loved the world, that He gave His only begotten Son, that whoever believes in Him should not perish but have everlasting life. For God did not send His Son into the world to condemn the world, but that the world through Him might be saved. He who believes in Him is not condemned; but he who does not believe is condemned already, because he has not believed in the name of the only begotten Son of God. And this is the condemnation, that the light has come into the world, and men loved darkness rather than light, because their deeds were evil. For everyone practicing evil hates the light, and does not come to the light, lest his deeds should be exposed. But he who does the truth comes to the light, that his deeds may be clearly seen, that they have been done in God. —John 3:14-21."

Jenny stopped reading. Tears streamed down Brooke's cheeks.

"Come to light, Brooke. Come to light. You do bad things, so haf all people. The Bible say *whoever* believe. That mean anyone, no matter how bad. Jesus forgive you, but you let go of the darkness. Let God shine His light in your heart and clean out all the sin. You afraid of condemnation, yet you condemn yourself every day. Yes, God show us our sin, and that not feel good, but it so much better than darkness. Come, Brooke, you pray with me?"

She was ready. The darkness around her felt heavy and thick, and she was ready to let go. To step out into the glorious light of God's forgiveness. To accept the fact that, yes, she was a terrible person. She didn't understand yet how it all worked, but she had finally come to the place where she didn't need to understand, she would simply trust.

Nodding, she clasped Jenny's hands.

"Just pray. Tell Jesus what is in heart."

Brooke bowed her head. "Lord Jesus, I have sinned a great deal in my life, and I know I have hurt You by those sins. I believe that You died in my place and that You rose again so I can have life. It seems like I should have to do more, Lord. But the Bible says all I have to do is believe in Jesus, and I do. Please forgive me for all the wrong I have ever done and have mercy on me. I want to change, Lord. I want to serve You and to learn to do what is right. I want to live in the light, Lord. Help me to live in the light. Amen."

Suddenly, a great burden lifted from Brooke's shoulders. She couldn't have explained what felt different; she just knew without a doubt that something had changed. She felt light and carefree, and a great joy welled in her heart.

She lifted her head to find Jenny smiling at her from her side of the table. As one, the women stood and embraced one another.

Just then, they heard footsteps on the porch, and Rachel and Sean entered the house. Brooke turned from Jenny and enfolded her startled mother-in-law in her arms. "Oh, thank you for telling me how Jesus saved you. For letting me see that you weren't already perfect when you gave your life to Him. I needed to hear that."

When Rachel pulled back slightly and looked at her, not quite comprehending what was going on, Brooke's smile nearly split her face. "Jenny has just helped me to give my life to Jesus."

"Oh, Brooke!" Rachel gasped as she pulled the girl back into the hug. "We prayed that you would understand how much you needed God. But we didn't know how soon our prayers would be answered. Praise God!"

Over Rachel's shoulder Brooke could see Sean's smile but was surprised to also see tears running down his cheeks. Pulling away from Rachel, she turned to him, "What's wrong?"

"Not a thing, young lady." He drew her into his own embrace. "Not a blessed thing in all the world."

Jason lay on the bed in his room at the boarding house staring up at the ceiling, his hands laced behind his head. It wasn't like him to stay to himself. In fact, several men had invited him to "share coffee and swap stories" with them around their fire, but he didn't feel like company tonight. His mind was on the words he had spoken to Sky about Chang.

He deserves to die...die...die.... The words echoed over and over in his mind. *He deserves to die...die...die....*

And then Sky's answer would follow. *So do we all, Jason. But then I know you know that...I know you know that....*

Grandma Jordan's face swam before his eyes. He recalled her talking to him about this very thing when he was a young boy, not too long after he and Marquis had come to live with her. She had come to tuck him in for the night and found him with his mother's picture in one hand and the other fist clenched so tight that it shook.

Sitting on the edge of the bed, she laid one small hand over his fist. "Jason, revenge is a terrible thing. It eats a man up on the inside. All the plottin' and plannin' and schemin'—they tend to push the rest of life aside, and pretty soon the man bent on revenge finds he has no friends and no kindness left in his heart."

She reached out a cool hand and brushed his blond curls off his forehead. "I don't want that kind of life for you, my angel. Let Jesus worry about the man who caused your mama such pain. Jesus knows. Everything will be made right one day. Let Jesus take care of it. Can you do that for Gram?"

He had nodded that he would, but somewhere along the road, he had forgotten about that conversation.

He swung his feet over the side of the bed and sat up, surprised by the tears trickling down his face. He lived the exact life she had described: no friends to speak of and definitely no kindness in his heart.

He rubbed his eyes with the heels of both hands. "God, I can't do this." It was a prayer. Suddenly, he was grateful that he hadn't talked to any of the men that day about forming a lynch mob. He would let God deal with Chang. He only hoped God knew what He was doing.

When Sky pulled into the yard later that evening, he was pleased when he glanced toward the house and saw that his parents, Brooke, and Jenny were all assembled around the table eating.

He paused in the blackness to enjoy the scene. Everything was dark outside, with only a chirping cricket and the occasional creak of saddle leather to disturb the stillness. The warm, cheery house cast a welcome golden glow out of each one of its windows. Through the front window, he watched the group. He could see that Brooke was at ease and enjoying herself. Pleasant conversation drifted over to him, and he distinctly heard Brooke's melodic laughter as her head tipped back and her mouth opened wide. Sighing in contentment, he turned Geyser toward the barn.

When he entered the house a few minutes later, the smell of beef stew and cornbread made him realize just how hungry he was. He had not taken the time to eat anything since the breakfast Brooke had fixed him that morning.

"Mmm…smells good," he said as he moved toward a basin on the counter to wash up.

"How did the trial go today, Son?" Sean asked from his seat at the table. Sky looked at Jenny as he dried his hands. His heart went out to her. He could see the barely concealed pain in her eyes.

"We haven't come to any conclusions yet. We'll convene again tomorrow."

At the hope that flashed across Jenny's face, though, he knew he couldn't leave it at that. It would be cruel to allow her to hope that Lee might be released. If anything, he and Ping might be the only two who were held over for a more extensive trial in Murray. He hung the towel on its hook and walked toward her, squatting down in front of her on the balls of his feet. "Jenny, I'm sorry. A man told the court today that Lee hired him and several others to kill Fraser. I don't think he is going to be released."

She nodded and looked into her lap. There was a long pause, then she said, "I go home now."

"Jenny, I can't let you ride home alone in the dark. Do you want me to ride with you into town? Or we could make you a bed here on the floor."

She shook her head, glancing around the small room. "No, I not sleep here. Maybe you haf some blankets? I sleep in barn. I need be alone. To pray." Sky nodded, and Rachel, who had risen to stand behind Jenny's chair, laid her slender hand on the woman's shoulder, as Brooke moved to take the blanket off of the bed in the corner.

Sky moved across the room, laying a hand on Brooke's arm and stilling her movements. "There is an extra blanket under the bed," he said. Bending down, he reached under the bed and pulled out a thick, heavy quilt.

As soon as Jenny had left for the barn, Sean and Rachel stood. "We will head on out and make sure Jenny is comfortable, Son. Don't worry about her; we'll make sure she's warm enough."

"I think I saw an extra blanket in our room too, right, Sky?" asked Rachel.

"Yes, but maybe we should all take the time to pray for her before you go out. She is going to need all the strength she can get in the next couple of days."

The group took hands, and Sean led in prayer for Jenny, asking God to strengthen her and sustain her in the days to come.

Brooke set a heaping bowl of stew on the table for Sky, next to a plate of cornbread, as his parents hugged him good night. Then she gave them hugs of her own.

"Tell him all about it, dear," Rachel whispered in her ear as they embraced. "He will be so glad to know."

Brooke nodded and shut the door behind them, turning to find Sky's warm eyes on her face. She held his gaze for a moment, his searching look sending shivers of pleasure down her spine. He dropped the lid of one eye in a quick wink. She blushed and glanced away but then peered back into his face. Filled with a sudden excitement, she longed to run and throw her arms about him and tell him of the wonderful thing she had done...but she stayed where she was.

Sky pulled out his chair to seat himself. He bowed his head quietly in a quick prayer of thanks for the food and began to eat. Brooke poured herself a cup of coffee and joined him at the table.

"I'm happy to see you getting along so well with Mother and Dad," he said as he spread butter on a thick slab of yellow cornbread.

Brooke's mind flashed to the tension that had filled the room at breakfast, but she only said, "Your parents are wonderful people, Sky."

"How did you think I turned out to be such a wonderful guy?" he asked with another wink.

"Hmm...I guess I hadn't noticed."

He attempted to look crestfallen but didn't quite succeed.

Brooke debated how to broach the subject of her new relationship with Jesus. She rose from the table and began to clear the dishes. Sky ate in silence, then finally got up and poured himself a second cup of coffee, just as Brooke sat back down at the table.

"Sky, there's something I want to talk to you about." Her heart pounded, excitement thundering in her ears.

His movements stilled and he sat back down slowly, all of his attention focused on her. He raised his cup to his mouth but never took his eyes off her.

"I made a decision today that I hope you will be happy about." What was she saying? She knew he was going to be happy. He would be ecstatic.

Sky still said nothing. His expression revealed he had no idea what was on her mind.

"I had a long talk with your mother today and then with Jenny after that. I want you to know that I..." She paused. Was she going about this the right way?

One blond eyebrow raised in her direction.

She could tell the suspense was killing him as he waited for her to go on. Finally she exclaimed in a rush, "I gave my heart to the Lord today." She bit her lower lip, waiting.

He sat stock still for a split second, then was around the table and down on one knee next to her chair. He took her hands in his, his heart shining in his eyes, and gazed into her face. "You don't know how happy that makes me. I have waited for this day since the moment I met you." He cupped her face with one hand. Tears brimmed in his eyes. "God is so good, Brooke, honey. So very good."

"I know. I feel so free and happy. I know what you meant now about the peaceful green pastures and still waters. You wouldn't believe how wonderful I felt right after I prayed."

"Oh, I think I know, honey. I know just how you felt." Standing, he pulled her to her feet and into a warm embrace. Resting his head on top of hers, he prayed, "Lord, thank You so much for opening Brooke's eyes to You. Help her to grow in knowledge and understanding of how much You love her, and make her desire to serve You grow stronger as the days go by. In Jesus' name I pray, amen."

He stepped back and smiled down into her eyes, overwhelmed by the goodness of God. First He had brought this wonderful, gentle woman into his life, and now He had saved her. What more could a man ask for?

But as he traced her cheekbone with one hand and took in the contours of her face, he knew there was more that he wanted. *God, give me patience.*

He gathered her back into a tight embrace, then reluctantly let her go, moving to the couch with his coffee cup.

Even an hour later, as Brooke moved about in the one-room cabin, elation surged through him. *Thank You, Lord*, he prayed again. He hadn't stopped praying it since the moment she had told him.

Sipping his coffee, he leaned his head back against the couch, resting his cup beside him. He closed his eyes. As tired as he was, he couldn't keep his mind off of the proceedings in town for long. Something about Chang bothered him. The man knew something that he wasn't saying. And the fact that the safe in the back room of the store hadn't been tampered with still weighed heavily on Sky's mind. Why would anyone have killed Fraser? Ping said he and his companions did it because they were paid by Chang, but why had Chang hired them? Did the unopened safe in the back room have anything to do with it?

He was convinced the man Trace was tracking had something to do with this murder, but he couldn't see how he fit into the puzzle.

Reaching up, Sky rubbed a tired hand across his face. He was missing something. His mind wandered back to the day of the funeral. Something drew his mind to the story that Trace had told him. There had been a father, mother, and a *beautiful* daughter, Trace had made the point of saying. They had come home to find their house being robbed and even though they had told the perpetrator he was free to leave, he had shot the father, laughing as he did it. That suggested a personal vendetta....

Sky's mind flashed to the pretty Alice Fraser. He sat up with a start, nearly spilling his coffee.

Brooke eyed him from the table across the room where she had seated herself to read his Bible. "What?"

He shook his head, still thinking. "Nothing. I just had a thought." He stared at the floor for a minute more, then back at Brooke. She was already intent on the book before her. He wanted to question her about the funeral. To have her confide in him the reason for her sudden fear that day. But as he watched her absorbing the Bible page by page he couldn't bring himself to ask the questions. She deserved to have this one special day of all days to enjoy.

Besides, he suddenly knew the answers. The pieces had all been there. He simply hadn't been able to see how they all fit together. Her sudden fear on the day of the funeral and her lying about it and about the man in the alley were all connected. However, he wanted her to tell him about it on her own. He didn't want to have to pry the information from her. He wanted her to trust him enough to share her fears with him. He made a mental note to find Trace Johnson tomorrow and let him know what he was thinking. They would have to be prepared.

Brooke watched Sky from where she sat at the table, his Bible open before her. Conviction weighed heavy on her heart. She knew she should speak up and tell him the truth, but every time she started to say something, she would remember Percival's threats and couldn't bring herself to continue.

He had given her so much. What would she do if something happened to him? No, she couldn't tell Sky.

But for the first time in her life, she found she did have someone to talk to. As she prayed, some of her worry lifted off her shoulders.

She couldn't shake the conviction to tell Sky the truth, however, and took a deep breath, finally ready to tell him.

He stood. "I think I'll turn in. I have an early morning tomorrow."

Brooke sighed. Her confession would have to wait a little longer.

CHAPTER NINETEEN

The next morning, Brooke awoke with a heavy heart. Sky had already gone, and she wondered how he had gotten out of the house without waking her. Once again, she chastised herself for not getting up in time to get him some breakfast. She hoped he had taken time to eat something.

Heaviest of all was the thought that the lives of eight—no, nine now—men were in her hands. She might have information that could exonerate them all, but she had said nothing. What was she going to do? Some words Rachel had spoken to her only the day before came to mind.

"Honey, if ever you don't know what to do, turn to the Word. You will always find an answer there."

She sat up in bed, leaned against the wall, and pulled Sky's Bible into her lap. She had finished reading in the book of John last night.

Now, she wondered, *where do I start next?* Where would she find the answers she needed? Opening the Bible, she found herself at the book of James and decided it was just as good a place as any to start. Many of the verses spoke directly to her, and she made a mental note to read the book through a second time. But it wasn't until she got to chapter 5, verse 16, that she gasped at the impact the words had on her soul: *"Confess your trespasses to one another, and pray for one another, that you may be healed."*

The rest of the chapter forgotten, Brooke rested her head against the wall and closed her eyes, thanking God for the answer. It was time she told Sky her whole life's story. She swallowed the lump that formed in her throat at the mere thought of that daunting task and prayed for strength.

"Oh God," she prayed aloud, "Your Word says I should do this, so I know that You can give me the strength and the words

I will need. Please help me. And if Sky rejects me, I pray that You will give me the strength to go on."

She sat up straight. She'd go to town and find him right now. She could tell him all about Hank and Uncle Jackson later, but right now she had to tell him she had lied. That it wasn't the mountain man she had seen in the alley that night. The lives of nine men who might be innocent hung in the balance.

"Percival will be angry," she whispered to herself. With a shake of her head, she pushed the thought aside, knowing she had to do what was right, no matter what.

Trusting God to be their protection if he followed through on his threats against them, Brooke headed for the barn to tell Rachel, Sean, and Jenny that she was headed into town. But as she stepped out the door into the breaking dawn, she realized how early it still was. Turning back to the house, she decided to leave them a note instead.

Back out in the barn, she silently led the horse that Sean and Rachel had brought up from Greer into the yard and saddled it. Mounting, she moved in the direction of town. And as she walked the horse quietly out of the yard, she prayed that Percival would be convicted for his part in this murder—whatever it might be—and brought to justice.

Jenny had been awake and waiting in the yard for Sky when he had come out to saddle Geyser.

"I go to town today?" She saw his hesitation. "I need see Lee."

With reluctance he had agreed, and now, she rode in her saddle beside him as he headed toward Pierce City.

As they passed under the tree that stood in the middle of the street on the south end of town, something caught his attention. He jerked Geyser to an abrupt stop. The black neighed and swung his head, snorting in irritation. He was not used to being handled so roughly.

Sky grimaced and looked again at what had caused him to stop so quickly.

Jenny gasped.

Pressing his mouth into a hard line, he said, "Go to your store and don't come out for any reason. Lock your doors and stay in the back room."

Jenny didn't hesitate to comply, fear on her face.

Sky watched her go, making sure she made it safely into her store, before he turned his eyes back to the foreboding sight of the tree. He muttered, "Not if I have anything to say about it" and spurred the horse in the direction of Jed's boarding house.

Throwing the reins around the hitching post, he took the steps up to the door in one stride and burst into the room.

Startled, Jed swung quickly around from where he had just finished pouring himself a cup of coffee and sloshed the hot liquid all over his hand. "Sky! What in tarnation's gotten into you, boy? Mmmhhh!" he ended. His face screwed into an expression of pain as he gingerly held the hot, wet cup in one hand and shook the boiling coffee off his other hand onto the floor.

"Sorry, Jed. Have you seen Bymaster this morning?"

"Sure have. He 'n' a couple other fellas is down to the court house." He wiped the back of his burnt hand across his pant leg.

Without another word Sky strode out the door.

He burst into the court house with no less fanfare than he had entered Jed's, and the three men sitting around the desk jumped to their feet in surprise.

"Jordan!" they all chorused in unison.

"What do you think you are going to do?" Sky directed his question to John Bymaster.

John held up his hands. "Now calm down. It's not what it looks like."

Glancing at the two other men in the room, Sky paused, then addressed John again. "Can I talk to you outside for a minute?"

John stepped outside in answer.

"Tell me how that hangman's noose dangling from the limb of that tree is not what it looks like." Sky tossed a gesture of frustration at the lone tree on the south edge of town.

"Jordan, I know you don't know me too well, but let me be

the first to assure you that I'm not about to let any of these men take the law into their own hands."

Sky looked Bymaster pointedly in the face. "Have you forgotten that there are eighty men in town? All of them wanting justice—no, *justice* is not the right word. All of them want revenge! And you have a noose dangling from a tree! Explain to me how that is not taking the law into your own hands!" Sky folded his arms across his chest, knowing he was speaking too loudly, but his anger had gotten the best of him for the moment.

Bymaster held up his hands, palms out, in a gesture meant to calm as he looked around at the gathering crowd who had heard Sky's tirade and come to see what it was all about.

The crowd only irritated Sky all the more. "What are you planning?" He ground out the words, having finally regained control of his raging anger, although not having lost the anger in the least.

"Some of the guys had this idea that if we made it *look* like we'd hung Lee Chang and then brought the other prisoners out one at a time, that maybe they'd be a little more likely to talk. See?"

Sky was beginning to see, and he saw the folly in the idea. Anytime a noose was dangled in front of a posse bent on revenge there was bound to be trouble. He said nothing, though, only glared at John.

"What we're planning," Bymaster continued, "is to bring out Lee Chang first this morning. We make him lie down on the ground and make it look like he's dead. When we bring the next guy out we tell him that he's gonna suffer the same fate if he doesn't speak up. If he *doesn't* speak up, we force him to play dead and bring out the next guy and so on until we get a confession."

"I don't like it. The evidence of Ping's confession alone is enough to hold him and Chang. We just need to talk to Ping and find out who the other three are. We don't need more confessions."

John cleared his throat. "He told me last night who they are."

Sky blinked. "So why are you pulling this charade?"

"They won't admit to it. They still deny that they were even in town on that night! Except for Chang, of course, who says he was at his wife's birthday party. We thought if we could get them to admit to some involvement, it would go a long ways toward a conviction at the trial."

Sky pointed down the street in the direction of the noose. "That's forcing a man to confess under duress. What if one of them gets so scared that he confesses when he really had nothing to do with it?"

"Well, that's a point, but do you have a better idea? Some of these men are getting real antsy. They want to head back home to their wives and children. I heard a group of them saying last night that we should just hang the whole lot and be done with it. I'm afraid if we don't find something more soon, we might have a lynch mob on our hands." He shrugged. "I've wracked my brain trying to come up with a better idea for getting a confession out of someone besides Ping Chi, but I haven't come up with one."

"I just told you we don't need any more confessions to hold these men for trial."

By this time both the men who had been in the court house had come outside to hear what Sky would say, and the other men who had come over to see what Sky's outburst was about were no longer pretending they had no interest in the conversation.

"We ain't about to send these men in for trial with such a flimsy lot of evidence agin 'em. They'd be let go for sure!" shouted one.

"I like the idea about hanging the whole lot!" hollered another in a pinched, high voice.

Sky turned to face him and recognized Smyth, the obese man who had confronted him and Jenny the day before.

Smyth continued, "Too many Chinese up in these hills anyway. We could sure stand to cull a few of them out." He pulled a yellow-stained handkerchief from his coat pocket and mopped his brow, which was sweating profusely even in the cool of the morning, as he challenged Sky with his beady eyes.

Sky didn't say anything, just leveled the man with a cold stare, wondering how men could become so prejudiced. He knew the answer, though. It all came from not believing that God was the Creator of all life. When the miracle of life became a mere accident, men could be deceived into believing anything.

"Never did cotton to so many Celestials roaming the hills hereabouts. I say we do somethin' about it!"

Sky recognized this ranter as a small-time miner from far back in the hills.

John raised his voice to the growing group of men gathering on the street. "Now, gentlemen, we are not here to do anything but determine whether these men should be held over for trial in Murray. We are neither judge nor jury. We are simply here to aid the process of justice."

Sky could hear a tinge of nervousness in his voice.

Smyth grinned. "Then I say we aid them in savin' some money, too. We dispatch with them criminals right here, and there won't be any costs for housing or food. Not to mention the expense of keeping them heavily guarded all the way from here to Murray, if we hold some of them over."

The group of men continued raucously laughing and talking.

John laid a hand on Sky's arm, drawing his attention away from the talk, and spoke quietly in his ear. "You see what I am up against? I have to get some sort of a confession out of the guilty and try to diffuse this situation a bit.

"With the confessions, we'll be able to convince the men that the accused will never get off at a trial. Most of these men are worried that no one is going to pay for this terrible crime. They just want to do something, and in their minds, like you said, it doesn't matter to whom. So long as they can go home and say they convicted *someone*."

Sky saw the error in John's logic. What was to stop a lynch mob from forming after some confessions? Wouldn't they feel even more justified in meting out their own form of justice if the prisoners confessed? Suddenly, the fact that John was going to *pretend* to hang the men didn't seem to be what he should be concentrating on. He hadn't realized that the spirit in the camp had become so cutthroat. He wondered where Jason was. They might need to utilize their guns to protect the prisoners before this investigation was over. "I still don't like it," he said to John as he turned on his heel and went in search of Jason.

★

Chapter Twenty

As Sky headed back in the direction of Jed's boarding house in the early morning light, he contemplated what his best course of action might be. There had been a day when he would never have questioned whether asking his cousin for help was the right thing to do or not. There had been a number of times, when they were younger, that Sean had needed help to track down criminals, and Sky, Rocky, Cade, and Jason had always been included in that number. He and Jason had worked well as a team. In fact, on several occasions it had been due to their team work—and the fact that they had each known what the other was going to do before he did it—that the outlaw they had been tracking was caught.

But recently, Jason had been a loose cannon. He had let his desire for revenge on Chang consume his whole being to the point where he had even pushed God out of his life. So could he count on Jason to be willing to use his gun to *protect* Chang?

Sky sighed in frustration. He couldn't risk it. If Jason was part of the plan that he was forming even as he walked, he would have to be out of Sky's line of vision and Sky knew that would not be a wise move if he truly wanted to protect the prisoners. If he asked Jason for help and something did go wrong, he might use the confusion of the moment as an opportunity to exact his revenge on Chang, and Sky would never be able to forgive himself. No, Jason would have to be excluded from this one.

As Sky entered the front room at Jed's, he saw Jason looking like he had just crawled out of bed. His blond, curly, too-long hair was in wild disarray. He sat, his boots wrapped around the front two legs of a chair as it leaned back against the log wall. He nursed a cup of coffee. Sky eyed him. *Well, he looks a little better than he did yesterday.*

"Good morning, Jason."

"Morning."

"Have you seen Jed?"

He nodded. "He headed down to the livery for a minute. Said he'd be right back."

"Thanks, I'll go talk to him there." He turned toward the door, hating the strain that stretched tight between them. They had been so close once.

"Sky."

Sky stopped and faced his cousin.

"I was wrong in what I said about Chang last night. I know I need to forgive him. You pray for me about that, would you?"

Sky blinked in surprise. "You better believe I will. I have been." He turned back toward the door, but his movements stilled once more as he contemplated. Should he include Jason in his contingency plan after all? The contrition he had just seen on his cousin's face was no bluff, and he praised God for softening Jason's heart. But should he put him through what might become such a great temptation so soon after his newfound resolve?

He decided to compromise; he would ask for Jason's help but make sure he was within eyesight at all times. "Jason, some of the men are talking about forming a lynch mob. We might have a little trouble on our hands today. Can I count on you to back me up if I need your help?"

There was a catch in Jason's voice as he said, "Just like old times, huh?" He cleared his throat.

Sky smiled. "Something pretty close anyway. Usually it was *me* backing *you* up, remember? You were the hothead who always rushed headlong into a situation without thinking first, and it's only because of my lightning-quick reaction time that you are alive today."

There was a full-fledged grin on Jason's face now. "I seem to remember things a little differently. You remember that time Tiny Jack had wedged himself into that hollow log out in the desert and told us we would have to shoot him if we wanted to get him out?"

"Now just a min—" Sky began to protest, but Jason cut him off.

"What did you do but pick up that mean-lookin' snake that was slithering past and proceed to toss it into one end of that log? Only when you picked it up, it bit you on the calf. Remember that? Tiny Jack came out of the other end of that log like a race horse at the starting line. After I tied him up, I killed the snake, sliced your leg with my hunting knife, and proceeded to suck the venom out of your leg, remember? Now *who* was backing up *who* on that day?"

By this time Sky was laughing so hard, remembering, that he held his stomach. "And when we got the snake home, Dad looked at it and told us it was nothing more than a harmless garden variety snake that could do no one any harm."

Jason gave a snort. "And I sucked your blood," he said in disgust.

Sky guffawed again. "All the way home that day I was sure I was going to die." He studied the amusement dancing in Jason's eyes and realized how much he'd missed the times like this together.

"Well, I hope I don't have to suck any more of your blood," Jason said. "But no matter what, you can count on me today if you need help." His face abruptly turned serious as though he wanted to make sure Sky knew he really meant what he said.

"I'll count on that." Sky opened the door and went in search of Jed, hoping to catch him and Wild Bill Currey together.

Just as he stepped out the door, though, he saw Trace Johnson coming down the street.

"Mornin'," Trace called.

Sky nodded. "Listen, I wanted to talk to you about something. I don't have a lot of time, but I have this hunch, and if it pans out, I think you'll be glad we followed it. If it doesn't, we won't have lost anything, either."

"What kind of a hunch?"

"Did you ever say what color of hair that girl had? The one whose parents were murdered back east?"

Trace frowned. "I don't recall saying, but blond."

"Alice Fraser has blond hair. Did you notice her at the funeral?"

"Sure."

"Maybe I'm stretching a bit," Sky continued, "but do you think this man you're looking for might have a penchant for blonds?"

"Could be, but I don't quite see the connection."

"What if he had an interest in the blond girl back east? He took her out a couple of times, but then when he wanted to get serious, her father put an end to it? Maybe the robbery was a cover-up for his real intention—murder?"

Trace ran a hand down his long beard in thought.

Sky went on. "A couple of months ago, Fraser mentioned in passing that this *lunatic*—that was his exact word—was interested in his daughter. He told her suitor in no uncertain terms that he was not to call on Alice again. You following me now?"

Trace nodded, understanding lighting his eyes.

"I need to know the man's name. His tracks are all over here, and Lee Chang recognized his description. I think he had something to do with this."

Trace thought for only a moment. "Percival Hunter."

Sky frowned. His heart rate quickened as all the pieces suddenly began to fall into place. "He rode the stage up from Lewiston with you and my wife, Brooke, didn't he?"

"Yeah." Trace nodded.

"Well, my wife wasn't afraid of Percival then. She was very comfortable around him, in fact." Sky was thinking out loud. "But on the night of the murder she saw a man, which she claimed was you, in the alley by Fraser's store. Now, you told me you weren't here that night, and all of a sudden at the funeral that day, my wife turned pale as death itself over something. Was Percival Hunter at Fraser's funeral?"

Trace nodded.

Sky rubbed the back of his neck. "Maybe Brooke saw him and it was *him* she was afraid of. Now what does that tell you?"

"That something happened to make her afraid of Hunter

between the time she first met him and the day of the funeral."

"Exactly. I think *he* was the man in the alley. Maybe he saw her and somehow got to her and threatened her into silence."

Sky's body trembled as he spoke. He snatched his hat from his head and raked a hand back through his hair in agitation. To actually say these things out loud and realize that they made sense caused his blood to run cold with fear for Brooke. That someone had been near her, threatening her and causing her terror, was unforgivable.

He straightened at the next thought. He had seen Percival's tracks in the barnyard even before the night of the murder. Hunter had been following Brooke for a while.

Rage coursed through every vein in his body. He pictured Brooke's strawberry-blond curls and forced himself to say the next words even as his heart hammered with dread at the thought. "I think he will be paying our farm a visit, and maybe I can help you get the information you need to arrest him and get a conviction. Probably not for this crime, because Lee Chang doesn't seem to want to talk, but hopefully for that other one."

Trace Johnson eyed Sky as he turned his hat around by the rim. "Are you too close to this one to think clearly?"

Sky chuckled nervously. "Probably, but I'm all the hope you've got."

Trace nodded. "I'll head out to your place right now if it will make you feel any better."

"Yeah, I think it would, thanks. My mother and dad are out there. Dad's a lawman, but he's not expecting any trouble, so you might want to give him the heads-up. I'll be back as soon as I can." Sky pushed his hat back onto his head.

Trace moved off silently in the direction of his horse.

Sky prayed like he never had before that the Lord would protect Brooke until he could get home again.

Brooke moved the horse confidently through the brush now, not bothering to keep quiet. Pierce City was just over the next little rise. She ducked under a large branch that stretched across the trail and moved ahead, intent on her goal.

When she had first left the house, all of Sky's warnings about the men of the posse, not to mention thoughts about Percival Hunter, had come to mind. However, the heavy feel of the .22 in her dress pocket reassured her. If anyone accosted her, she would simply pull it out and point it in their direction, and they would have to let her pass.

She pressed on, wishing she had told Sky the truth earlier. Then this little morning jaunt would not be necessary. But she knew innocent men might be convicted if she didn't arrive and tell all she had really seen. Which, when she stopped to think about it, wasn't much, but she must have seen something important…otherwise why would Percival have threatened her the way he did?

What had she actually seen that night? She fiddled with the loose ends of the reins as she tried to think of anything incriminating she might have seen and just not recognized.

The snapping of branches caught her attention. She lifted her head and pulled her mount to a stop, listening. Another horse was coming through the brush to her right!

Sweat broke out all over, and she jerked on the reins, but the horse was confused by the sudden jolt and only backed up a few steps.

Percival Hunter rode his horse into the trail in front of her.

She gasped, her heart pounding in her ears. Too late! She froze, unable to think of a thing to do. All the threats this man had made against her came rushing to mind and she swayed in the saddle. *Jesus, help me!*

"Well," Percival chuckled sardonically, "if it isn't little Mrs. Jordan! Simply out for an early morning ride, I suppose?" He eyed her coldly. "You wouldn't be on your way into town to confess your little lies, would you?"

Brooke's mouth was so dry she couldn't have spoken if she had wanted to, but suddenly, her mind cleared. She had to get away from this man. Now! Spinning her horse around, she spurred it back down the trail toward home.

Hunter gave an angry roar and galloped after her.

Her breaths came in short gasps, and she tried not to think about how closely this situation resembled some of her recurring nightmares. Hooves pounded on the trail directly behind her. Looking back over her shoulder, she could see that Percival was gaining on her. Panic clawed at her heart.

She kicked her heels into the horse's side and yelled, "Come on, mov—!" As she faced forward, the thick branch that stretched across the trail caught her directly across the forehead. Pain sizzled through her in jagged shards as she jolted backwards in a head-over-heels roll off the galloping horse. She groaned once. Smashed into the ground. Then blessed blackness engulfed her.

Sky leaned one shoulder into the side of a building on the south end of town, making sure he had a clear view of all the proceedings. With his arms folded, ankles crossed, and black hat set low on his head, he affected a casual stance, but in reality, his every nerve was on edge. He took note of the positions that Jed and Currey had taken up and was pleased to see they were well spread out, as he had asked them to be.

Chang was brought out first, asked one more time if he had anything to say, and when the answer was negative, he was forced to lie down with his face against the cold ground.

"You can see 'im breathin'," called a man from the group.

"And there are no drag marks from the noose to the body," noted another. "We should at least make it look real."

Sky shook his head at the unreality of it all as these little details were taken care of. Chang was moved further away from the noose so that the other prisoners wouldn't be able to see him breathing. Another man dug the heels of his boots deep into the ground and allowed one of his friends to grab him under the arms and drag him from where the noose hung to the location of Chang's "corpse."

A sharpshooter stood close enough to Chang to remind him that if he made a move, it would be his last, but far enough away that the prisoners wouldn't wonder why a gunman was standing guard over a dead body.

Then the next prisoner was brought from the jail and questioned. He was told his fate would be the same as Chang's if he didn't tell the truth.

The man stammered out the same story he'd been telling all along. "I-I not h-here that night. I innocent!"

Bymaster slipped the noose over his head, and two other men pulled on the rope, applying pressure. The man's body lifted until his toes scrabbled for purchase on the cold ground.

Sky swallowed and looked down.

Finally, they eased the pressure, and the prisoner gasped for air. However, when he could speak again, he still adamantly clung to his innocence.

Bymaster sighed and forced him to lie face down on the ground next to Chang. "Don't move. Do you understand? Lay still!"

Sky noted Jason's grim face across the crowd and wondered if he felt the same way he did. Having once been a lawman, Sky found he didn't have enough fingers to count the number of laws broken in order to coerce some sort of confession from the accused. To even be present during such a breach of constitutional proprieties felt traitorous. Yet looking around at the angry, mob Sky knew nothing he could say would make them see it his way.

One by one each prisoner clung to his claim of innocence until the last one, other than Ping Chi, was brought out. As the noose settled around Ping's neck, Sky felt his heart go out to the young man. He couldn't be more than eighteen, but he was one of those whom Ping had indicated had been a part of the murder. His eyes were wide and his breathing spasmodic as he looked first at the "dead" men on the ground and then at the angry crowd of white people before him.

"It not me!" he shouted in response to John's questions. "It old men. They not like Fraser. They kill him! Not me!"

The moment turned to chaos. One of the elderly men lying

on the ground jumped up, ignoring the threat of the guard, and started to yell at the young man in Chinese. The guard was so surprised he didn't even raise his gun. He stood staring, slack-mouthed, at the shouting-match going on between the two prisoners.

The posse, who had been lounging on the ground, surged to their feet as one and began to argue and mill about in confusion. Above the hubbub, Sky heard one distinctively nasal voice that he recognized.

"Let's hang 'em all!" Smyth shouted.

Sky moved into action. Out of the corner of his eye, he saw Jason move, pointing Jed and Bill in the directions they should go and then slipping off in another direction himself.

Moving purposefully toward the front of the mob, Sky helped the young Chinaman down and stepped up onto the chair that sat under the dangling rope. He pulled his gun from its holster and fired two shots into the air.

A loud cry ascended as every man momentarily thought he'd been shot. Then, as each one realized he was unharmed, they began to hit the ground. All of the prisoners and most of the posse lay flat with hands over their heads, and thick silence immediately descended.

Somewhere, Sky heard a squirrel chattering in the trees and found it odd that he would notice such a thing at a time like this.

Bringing his gun down and calmly emptying the two spent chambers, Sky eyed the group of men as he reloaded. "Now, I suggest we all calm down and think rationally before we find ourselves a part of something we will all later regret."

"What's one man going to do to us, boys?" Smyth yelled from the middle of the crowd. "We can take him easy! Then we'll show these Chinks what we do to those who harm our own!"

Smyth rose to his feet and moved toward Sky. The mob surged to their feet and followed him. Sky stood calmly on the chair, not even bothering to raise his gun again.

"No!" John Bymaster stood in front of the crowd, spreading his arms wide as though he could hold the mob back. He was swept into the current of moving bodies, like a dandelion seed blown by the wind.

Suddenly, another shot rang out! A second! A third! With each successive gun blast the throng spun to see first Jason on the roof of the Joss house, then Jed on the porch of the boarding house, and then Bill hanging out the window of Gaffney's Pioneer Hotel.

"I'll put a bullet in the first man that moves," Jason said into the stillness that followed the echoing reports. He spoke in a low relaxed tone, but his deep voice carried to every ear from his elevated position.

"Gaffney, Carle, take those men back to the jail." Sky gestured in the direction of the fear-paralyzed Chinamen. Then turning back to the suddenly very orderly men before him, he continued, "I think Bymaster has something to say to all of us, and I suggest we all listen."

John Bymaster, who had finally gained his feet, stepped to the front of the unruly bunch. His voice was loud but a little shaky. "Now listen, men." He pulled at his collar and straightened his bandanna nervously. "The purpose of this inquiry was to come to some conclusions about who the potentially guilty parties were, and then to send them on to Murray to stand trial in a court of law. You all knew that. It is not our place to carry out judgment, much less punishment."

A grumbled muttering rose through the crowd, but John stood his ground and gained confidence as he spoke. "I believe our work here is done, men. We will hold over Lee Chang, Ping Chi, and the other three men that Ping indicated were involved in the crime."

He held a hand aloft as the murmuring took on a frenzied pitch. "They will be sent to Murray, where they will stand trial, and we will leave their fate in the hands of the judge and God Almighty. Now I want you all to head out of town. And Smyth! You had better be the first one gone!"

The crowd that had begun to disperse stilled its movement at this last barked word.

"If I so much as see your face within twenty miles of this place after the next ten minutes I will throw you in jail yourself and haul you off to stand trial for attempting to incite a riot!"

"We'll just see about that!" Smyth threw the parting shot over his shoulder as he turned to head for his horse.

But Sky had seen real fear in the man's eyes. He knew the type. Smyth wouldn't be back. The man had bold words, but no courage whatsoever.

Percival Hunter watched the town through his binoculars, unable to keep the grin off his face. "'Twas all for naught, Mr. Jordan," he leered. "I don't plan on letting them get more than two miles out of town." He chuckled as he lowered the binoculars and scrutinized the town. "And are you ever going to have a big surprise when you get home."

One heavily jeweled hand picked up a large bulky bag that rested at his feet, and he made his way deeper into the forest to put his plan into motion.

After this was taken care of, he had just a couple more little details to see to, and then he would head back to Lewiston and his fair Alice.

★

Chapter Twenty One

Relief flooded Sky. The inquiry was over, and no one had gotten hurt in the process! Most of the men from Lewiston had immediately headed for home, no doubt itching to spread the news of the last couple days' events. Six trustworthy men were left to guard the prisoners on the way to Murray.

John had asked Sky if he would consider being one of the guards, but he had refused. He wanted to be near Brooke, especially with Percival Hunter in the region. There was no way he would leave her right now. Not when he wondered if a madman might be coming after her. Also, his parents were here, and he wanted to spend some more time with them.

He went to Chang's Mercantile to tell Jenny everything should be safe now and to ease her fears about her husband. "You could even go visit him at the jail if you want."

"I do that," she said sadly. "You tell Brooke, I so proud of her. Happy she know Jesus now."

"I'll tell her. Thank you for leading her to the Lord." He smiled at her.

Jenny shrugged. "Some plant, some water, but God, He make it grow, yes?"

Sky nodded. He contemplated that verse of Scripture as he mounted Geyser and made his way toward home at a fast clip.

He pushed his Stetson back and felt a measure of relief as he rode into the yard. It was good to be home. And he certainly had plenty to catch up on, now that he wouldn't be needed in town anymore. He glanced toward the house.

Ma stood on the porch, wringing her hands as she watched him approach.

A cold dread started in the pit of his stomach and worked

its way upward. He spurred his horse the last several yards and didn't even bother to dismount. "What's the matter?"

"Did you see Brooke in town today?"

"No." He frowned in question. Fear constricted his chest and blocked his ability to breathe.

"Brooke left us a note this morning saying she had ridden into town to talk with you about something. Your father went after her on foot. He found the horse we rode up from Greer. It was grazing by the trail, but Brooke was nowhere in sight. There was no evidence of a struggle, but as soon as he came back to let me know he'd found the horse, he rode it back up the trail to see if he could find any clues. Didn't you see him on your way here?"

Sky's heart sank further with every added word. He shook his head. "Did a man named Trace Johnson come by here today?"

"No. I wonder how you missed Dad?"

"I took a shortcut. It's pretty steep, so I don't usually go that way, but it cuts off about ten minutes of travel time between here and town. I probably missed him somewhere in there. I'll go after him." He turned back down the trail, trying to calm his pounding heart. What could have happened?

"Sky?" Rachel shouted after him.

He pulled on the reins and turned toward her. Every muscle tightened with dread at the trepidation in her tone.

"I'm sorry, Son, but there was blood all over the saddle and the back of the horse."

His heart dropped in his chest, and he clenched his eyes shut. He felt sick. Someone might have hurt Brooke. Absolute frustration quickly followed in the face of his own helplessness. He had no idea where she was.

He suddenly remembered his innocent words to Percival Hunter on the morning after their wedding. "Come visit us sometime." Percival had smiled and replied, "I think I just might."

Rage pulsed through Sky's veins. He spun Geyser toward the trail and cantered out of the yard, his eyes fastened to the ground, searching for any clue that might lead him to her. He would do his best to find her. He only prayed he would before it was too late. It would be dark soon, and the chances of finding her after dark…

Carrying a basket of sandwiches, Jenny made her way toward the jail. The town felt ghost-like in its silence. Absolute stillness cloaked it, and were it not for the tell-tale evidence of smoking campfires and the churned-up mud on the street, one would never know that nearly eighty men had been in town only that morning.

She prayed as she walked. Hoped that this might be the day Lee would listen to her. She couldn't count the number of times she had told him of his need for a Savior, and his consequent rejections.

She eased open the door to the jail and stepped inside.

Jenny nodded. "I bring food." She lifted the basket.

"That's fine." He suddenly looked embarrassed. "Uh, it's not that I don't trust you but…well, I'm gonna have to take a look in that there basket."

"Oh." Jenny nodded in understanding, holding out the basket in his direction.

After satisfying himself that there were no hidden weapons or files in the basket, Gaffney gestured her past the desk toward the cells only a few feet away.

Jenny's heart constricted at the vulnerability that crossed Lee's face as he met her gaze. She had not seen him look that way for a very long time. Not since they were kids back in China, before he became a respected, hardened man of power.

He quickly schooled his features, though. Stepping to the bars, he rested his forearms there as he watched her approach.

"I can give you ten minutes, Mrs. Chang, that's all," Gaffney spoke as he sat back down at his desk.

Nodding, she held out the basket to Lee. "I brought you some sandwiches. I thought you might be hungry." She spoke in their native Mandarin.

He smiled his gratitude as he reached for the basket, an

unfamiliar expression for him. For the first time in years, Jenny saw that he still cared for her, at least in some measure.

Stripped of his pipe, he reminded her of the young man she had fallen in love with. A little heavier, balder, and grayer, with much harder eyes, but the same man nonetheless. She felt a tenderness for him that she had not experienced in quite some time. She laid a hand on his unshaven cheek, even as he chewed hungrily on the food she'd brought.

"I could use my pipe," he said around a mouthful. "Do you think you could get it for me?"

She sighed, pulling her hand away. Sadness welled in her heart. "I thought about it, but I just can't, Lee. Maybe this time will be good for you. Help you see that you don't need to depend on that drug to get you through the day. There is something else to depend on. Some*one* else. One who is a much greater help than any drug will ever be."

Lee rolled his eyes in exasperation. "I have told you a thousand times that I don't need some man who lived two thousand years ago to help me with anything. I have done very well for myself. Look at all we have." He gestured with his sandwich in the general direction of their store.

"Yes, and look where it has taken you." She gestured around the jail.

He eyed her. "I have been thinking about that." He lowered his voice even though Gaffney couldn't understand Chinese. "Listen, you could help us get out of here. Remember that little gun I keep under the counter at the store?"

Tears misted Jenny's eyes, and she shook her head.

He went on. "You could bring it to me…smuggle it in under some food or something, and then we could all get out of here. You and I could go back to China and see our families again. What do you say?"

The tears spilled down Jenny's cheeks. "No, Lee. I will not help you out of this one. Too many times I have turned my back on your evil, and I won't do it again. You had a man *killed!* And for what? What did you get for this job? A little money? How long will it last you? Or have you spent it already? This life is but a vapor, Lee." She snapped her fingers. "We're here for a moment and then gone tomorrow. The day is coming when you will have to stand before your Maker and give an account for your life. What are you going to say?"

She swiped angrily at the tears on her cheeks. "I have prayed, Lee. Prayed that you will get out of here. But I must be honest with you. I don't think that is going to happen—and I know what happens to murderers. Especially Chinese murderers." Her face crumpled. "Hard as life has been with you, I hate the thought of having to live without you."

He averted his eyes and folded his hands. Shrugging, he looked back at her. "Just my pipe then?"

Her heart sank. He hadn't heard a word she'd said. She backed toward the door, her eyes never leaving his face. "I love you, Lee. Even now, after all you have put me through, I still love you. But I will not help you escape. Not physically, and not mentally. I want you to be able to think clearly about all I have ever told you about Jesus and His love."

She gulped back her tears, wondering if this might not be the last chance she would get to talk with him. What else could she say? "Good-bye, Lee." She swung around and moved toward the door.

"Jenny!" he called out to her.

She stopped, turning to face him.

"I will think about what you've said."

Thankfulness washed over her, and she nodded. "That is all I can ask." With that, she made a hasty exit and headed home. There she threw herself across the bed and sobbed herself into an exhausted sleep.

The long night passed in nightmarish fashion for Sky. He had caught up with Pa on the trail to town, but they had found no clues to Brooke's whereabouts. Just before darkness descended in full force, they found the place where she had apparently been knocked from her horse by an overhead branch, but she had been riding away from town, not toward it. At the sight of the dark stain of blood on the patch of pine needles where Brooke had fallen, Sky felt the blood drain from his face. He hated being so helpless in the face of her danger.

Whipping around, he started for his horse, ready to head toward town and keep searching, but Pa laid a restraining hand on his arm. "It won't do any good to keep looking in the dark, Son."

Sky wanted to keep on searching all night until he found her, but knew even without the insistence of his father, that traipsing around in the dark would not only end in failure but might destroy any tracks that could lead them to her in the morning. He sighed in resignation, hating the fact that he could do nothing.

He spent a restless night, pacing back and forth in their little cabin, and praying as best he could, hoping above all hope that they would find her alive someplace, first thing in the morning— that nothing terrible would happen to her between now and then.

Jason lay in his usual position on the boarding-house bed, hands clasped behind his head. He had gotten little sleep because of the thoughts that plagued his mind. Yesterday morning, when he and Sky talked, he had felt a measure of their old camaraderie return. It had felt good. He didn't want to walk away from that friendship again, but he knew there was a more important decision he needed to make.

The first verses of Psalm 23 kept coming to mind: The Lord is my shepherd; I shall not want, He makes me to lie down in green pastures; He leads me beside the still waters. He restores my soul; He leads me in paths of righteousness for His name's sake.

Jason had once walked by those still waters. He knew what it was like to have peace in his life, and for the last several years, he had had no peace.

He thought back over the time he had lived in Pierce City. He had come here bent on revenge, seeking to drown his bitterness in the bottom of a bottle. But God had thwarted his plans at every turn.

There had been no opportunity for him to carry out his vendetta against Lee Chang. He had sought every opening to exact his revenge, but there'd never been a time when he felt he could do so without getting caught, so he had never followed through on his many murderous desires.

As for his drinking, what had that ever gotten him? It certainly hadn't removed his bitterness. If anything, it had sharpened it, making it more intense. And it was often, when he was in the throes of a hangover, that Scriptures he'd committed to memory as a boy would come back to haunt him.

When he had sought to bring a young woman into his home for his own selfish indulgence, God had stepped in then, as well, sending Sky to intervene on her behalf and ultimately forcing Jason to look clearly at his own life and see it for what it was. Empty and dry.

Wherever he turned, peace and pleasure eluded him. Even now, when Lee Chang, the man he had hated for so long, would probably hang for murder, he didn't feel the happiness he'd imagined, nor the peace he'd hoped for.

He suddenly came face to face with the truth. He longed for the peace he had once known. He yearned to be led by still waters, to feel the cool refreshing richness that comes only when one's life is right with God. He wanted God to restore his soul.

He had made a step in the right direction when he'd decided that revenge was a poor choice and that he would let the Lord decide what happened to Chang, but he knew he needed to do more than that. He needed to surrender his soul to Jesus.

"Oh Lord, I have fought You for so long. I know You've been here convicting me, trying to show me how much harm I was doing to myself, because I have never felt right about the things I was doing. I need Your help now, Lord. I give my life back to You. Do with me as You will. Forgive me for my selfishness, for only wanting things done my way. Help me in the future, even when I don't understand why You are doing the things You do, to trust

You. Help me to always remember that You are just, and never again want to take that justice into my own hands."

The healing tears began. "Restore my soul, Lord. Come back into my heart and make me clean again. Let me walk by Your still waters once more."

He hadn't moved from his place on the bed, but suddenly his heart felt right. He hadn't experienced this feeling of peace for a long time, and he knew, without a doubt, that God had heard his prayer. "Thank You, Lord," he whispered.

His prayers changed then. He began to pray for all of his family and loved ones. He prayed for Uncle Sean and Aunt Rachel. For Marquis, his sister. For Rocky, Sharyah, Cade Bennett, and Victoria Snyder. He prayed for Jed and Sky and Brooke, thanking God that he had not been allowed to ruin that young girl's life and asking that she and Sky find true happiness together. Then his prayers changed yet again, and he found himself praying for Lee Chang.

He sat up. There was something else he needed to do before Lee Chang was taken to Murray to stand trial.

Glancing out the window, he saw that the sun had climbed well above the horizon. He'd need to hurry if he wanted to talk to Chang.

Hastily pulling on his clothes, he hopped toward the door, still working at getting his foot properly settled into his second boot.

Despite his rush, the prisoners were already gone when he got to the jail.

"Just headed out about fifteen minutes ago," said Carle, who happened to be at the court house. "If you hurry, you can probably catch them."

When the party came around a corner and he saw the short, hooded man blocking the trail, Ping Chi knew his time on this earth had come to an end. The man held a sawed-off shotgun casually in the crook of one arm. Jewels glittered on his fingers. Calculating eyes peered out of the slits cut in the hood.

Ping glanced to the right. Off to the edge of the trail, a pole was slung between the forks of two trees. Five hemp-rope nooses dangled from it.

He had his hands tied behind his back, and his legs lashed to the stirrups like all the other prisoners. So Ping knew they would not stand a fighting chance against even this one small man.

"Howdy, gents," the man called casually. "If you boys who are supposed to be escorting these here prisoners to trial will just disappear, I have something I would like to discuss with them."

"Sorry. I'm afraid we can't do that," drawled one of the guards. "We've been paid to escort these men to Murray, and that's where we intend to take them."

"If you'll look around you, gentlemen, you'll see that you are surrounded, and if you value your life, it would be prudent to do as I ask."

The six guards glanced around the forest, shifting uneasily in their saddles. Ping saw there were at least five other men surrounding them. He frowned. Something was not right. All that could be seen of the other men were the nasty weapons that protruded from their hiding places behind bushes and trees.

"Well now, I think we might be willing to reconsider," one of the guards capitulated.

All six guards turned as one and rode their horses into the forest. Ping swallowed hard.

The hooded man sneered. "Fools," he muttered as the men rode off. Then he turned to Lee Chang. "Chang, you should have known I would never let you live to tell about this."

Hope quickened in Ping's heart. Maybe the man only wanted Chang. But all hope died when the man removed his mask. Never before had Ping seen such hard, hate-filled eyes. And now that he and the other prisoners had seen his face, they too would be held under the same suspicious distrust as Chang.

Hot tears pricked the back of Ping's eyes. He had wanted so much more from life. He was still young—only eighteen.

Ping glanced at Chang to see what he might do.

The big merchant eyed the pole with its dreadful ropes

dangling in gruesome prediction of the future. "You wouldn't dare double-cross me like this." Chang's gaze returned to the man in the trail.

"Just watch me, Chang." The man laughed sadistically. "You are the worst kind of a fool. I played you right from the beginning."

Chang strained at his bonds. "You won't get away with this, Hunter. The girl saw you. She talked. Her husband knows everything, and there are men out looking for you even now."

Ping knew he was bluffing, but kept silent, hoping Chang would somehow figure out a way to get them all out of this.

Another laugh. "You don't think I know about the girl? She didn't talk, not to the men in town anyway. I made sure of that. Now her husband…I haven't figured out yet whether he knows or not, she might have told him…but I'll take care of them shortly. Neither of them will be doing much talking after today."

As he spoke, Hunter led Chang's horse over and stopped it just under one of the ropes, keeping his sawed-off shotgun trained on the other four men. He must have seen the thought of escape gleaming in Ping's eye because he raised the gun in his direction. "Ah, ah, ah. I would just as soon shoot you as hang you, so don't move."

Ping's face blanched, and his throat went dry as Hunter stepped up on a box, slipped the noose over Chang's head, and cinched it down with finality.

Chang's lips were moving now, his eyes closed, and if Ping hadn't known better, he would have sworn Lee was praying.

Pulling a gleaming knife from the scabbard at his waist, their murderer made a clean slice through the bonds that kept Chang's legs tied to the saddle, first on one side and then on the other.

Ping closed his eyes as Hunter slapped Chang's horse sharply and it lunged forward. Much as he disliked Chang, he didn't want to watch him die, especially not with his own death looming so close.

★
Chapter Twenty Two

Sky was up well before dawn and riding down the trail on the way back to town. His brown buckskins blended with his surroundings, making it difficult for any potential enemy to spot him. Knowing any sound he made could be his last, he had traded in his boots for moccasins. Wearing moccasins, he could feel a twig underfoot before it snapped and readjust his step to prevent the noise. His ability to move soundlessly through the forest would be needed on this day.

He knew Brooke had not merely had an accident and gotten lost trying to find her way home. This was far more serious than that.

Darkness still cloaked the heavens. The place where they had found Brooke's blood the day before was a good four miles from his cabin. He wanted to get there early so he could renew his search at the first hint of light.

He had not awakened Pa, knowing that as soon as day dawned, he would come. Sky hoped by then, he would have some evidence to go on.

His long wait during the night had given him plenty of time to think, and he'd realized he must slow down and act rationally. He had known too many men who had let their hearts dictate their actions in tense situations and had lost their lives because of it. His ability to keep a cool head, even in the craziest of situations, had enabled him on more than one occasion to capture his foe, but his heart had never been so involved before. Because of that, on this day he would have to be even more careful than usual.

When he got to the place where Brooke had been knocked from her horse, he settled down to wait for the light. Sky wondered what had happened to Trace Johnson. Could it be that he was in on this? He didn't think so.

Everything about the man said that he was trustworthy. But where was he?

His thoughts turned to Brooke, wondering if she was all right. He refused to allow himself to think about the possibility that he might be too late to save her life. He chose instead to pray.

He must have sat for an hour talking to the Lord, before he finally allowed himself to start following the trail. The light, under the thick branches of the overhead trees was still dim, but he couldn't force himself to wait another minute.

His moccasins made not even the slightest of sounds as he squatted next to the patch of pine needles bloodied by Brooke's wound.

In the light of day, Sky noticed something they had missed in the gathering darkness the evening before. Brooke had been picked up after she had fallen from her horse, and placed on another horse.

Sky closed his eyes, his dread mounting as he read the tracks. They were the same tracks he had found in the alley the day after the murder; the same tracks he'd seen in the barn yard the day Brooke had gone berry picking.

Sky swallowed the lump in his throat. He had dreaded this, hoped he was overreacting, but now the evidence proved it. Percival Hunter, a man he suspected of cold-blooded murder, had his wife. "Oh, Jesus, be with her."

Sky berated himself. He'd been expecting the man to come to his house. He had not expected this. The first rule he had learned as a young lawman was never to underestimate his enemies. Yet he had ridden off yesterday morning, sure that Brooke would be fine until he came home. He had trusted too much in the fact that his father would be there if anything happened, never foreseeing that Brooke would take it into her head to ride into town. Now she was missing, and the evidence before him said a murderer had her in his clutches.

Percival had led the horse carrying Brooke away from the trail. Sky followed the tracks, leading Geyser behind. Moving uphill, he picked out the clear trail with ease, walking quickly but soundlessly through the brush.

Brooke came to with a groan, opening her eyes mere slits. Bone-chilling coldness permeated her body, and she shivered violently. She tried to raise her head and gasped as numbing pain shot all through her. With every beat of her heart, pulse waves of agony throbbed through her head and down into her shoulders. The pain originated from a large gash on her forehead, but it was so intense that even the back of her head felt tender to the touch. And the dim light she could see only caused the pain to worsen.

She closed her eyes and tried to remember where she was. What had happened? Moving one hand carefully along the ground, she tried to feel around herself to see if she might gain a clue as to her whereabouts. Although the ground was very cold, she laid on something semi-soft. Her hand came into contact with a hard object. Picking it up, she pulled it to her face and eased her eyes open, not daring to move her head for the pain it caused. Focusing slowly, she saw that the object in her hand was a pine cone.

She frowned. Sudden memory flooded in. Percival Hunter! She had been knocked from her horse while trying to get away. He had brought her here, and then this morning, she had come to for a moment and seen him moving off up the hill. She remembered trying to get up but must have passed out again, because she was in the same location. Where had he gone?

She forced herself to sit up. Pain shot through her head, and her stomach churned with nausea. She closed her eyes and tried to concentrate on not passing out again. A low moan escaped her lips as the throbbing pain in her head sent a wave of dizziness over her. She leaned back against a tree trunk, bringing her fingers to her temples as though she might be able to massage the pain away. She paused, her hand running over the side of her face. From her forehead to her temple and spreading back into her hair on the right side of her head there was a sticky mass of drying blood. She pulled her hand away, gazed in shock at her reddened fingers, and began to tremble.

She must get away from here. But where was she? Glancing around, she didn't recognize anything. Which direction should she go? Where was the nearest help? And where had Percival gone? How long had it been since she had seen him moving off up the hill? He couldn't be far away.

This thought propelled her into action. She must escape while she had the chance! Turning slowly, she grasped the trunk of the tree and painstakingly pulled herself to her feet. Too exhausted with the effort to think further, she simply stumbled from tree to tree in the direction that her feet were pointed.

She headed downhill. Not knowing whether that was good or bad, only caring that she was moving away from this place and heading in a different direction than she had seen Percival Hunter going.

How long ago had she fallen from her horse? Where was Sky? Had she been gone long enough for him to miss her? Was he even now out looking for her?

With sudden clarity, she realized just how much she loved him. She had denied it—to him and even to herself—but back in the recesses of her mind she had known. She must find him, tell him.

Tears pricked the back of her eyes at the thought, and she prayed that God would give her another chance to talk to him. To tell him how much he meant to her. What a balm his gentle kindness and tender care had been for her wounded soul. To thank him for modeling the love of her Heavenly Father. To tell him that she loved him with all her heart. *Please God!*

She also wanted to get to town and explain what she had seen on that terrible night. She didn't know if any of the Chinese prisoners were innocent, but she knew that if she didn't tell what she had seen, she would always feel responsible if they alone were convicted. Percival had had something to do with this.

She had not gone very far when her foot came down on a large pine cone. Although she tried, her body was too spent to right itself, and she tumbled down the hill. It was not far to the bottom, but she felt fresh blood running down her cheek as she rolled to a stop. Excruciating pain pounded in her head.

She wanted to curl into a ball and let the blessed blackness claim her. To get away from the pain and the nightmare of this whole situation. But she forced herself to go on. She pressed her palms to the ground, slowly trying to push herself up onto her knees. As she lifted her head, she looked into the cruelly amused eyes of Percival Hunter.

Her heart sank. How did he get here? He had gone the other way, *up* the hill.

Terrified as he made her feel, it wasn't until she peered past his shoulder that she gave a little moan of horror. There, only a short distance away, she could see five Chinese prisoners hanging. All of them were dead.

She was too late then. Had any of those men been innocent?

"Surprised to see me? I should have tied you up, I see. I underestimated you, but that won't happen again."

Grabbing her roughly, he swung her up over his shoulder with surprising agility. Picking up a large duffel bag at his feet, he headed past the dangling bodies and up the other side of the ravine. "Come on. Let's go set a little trap for that husband of yours. I can't have any loose ends hangin' around."

As the pain coursed through her once more, Brooke, exhausted from her effort at escape, lost the fight against the incoming blackness.

Her body slumped into the dead weight of unconsciousness.

Percival smiled and moved slowly up the hill with his burden, being sure to leave clearly evident tracks as he went. He didn't want Sky to somehow miss the trail and ruin all his carefully laid plans.

It was time to get this whole messy business over with and move on with his life. And in order for that to happen, Jordan needed to follow him.

Jason rode hard. Driven by his newly reclaimed peace with God, he wanted to be able to clear his conscience of one last thing. He wanted to tell Chang, the man who had caused his mother's death, that he forgave him. And make sure Chang understood he was able to do so only with Christ's help.

Rounding a corner in the trail he suddenly pulled rein. His horse skidded to a stop on its haunches.

Jason turned unbelieving eyes to the scene before him. The five prisoners hung from a pole suspended between two trees, their lifeless bodies swaying in the early morning breeze.

Hadn't Carle said they'd only left fifteen minutes before he did? How could this have happened so quickly? Where were the guards who were supposed to be protecting these men? Were they the ones who had done this?

A sadness overwhelmed him as he studied the face of Lee Chang. He had spent a good portion of the last years hating this man, but now, in his death, Jason could only feel sorry for him. He had gone to meet his Maker, and Jason could only hope he'd taken time to make his peace with God before he died.

The thought that it could have been him who did this to these men made Jason sick inside. Even to think that he had contemplated such an act shamed him, and he now thanked God once more for protecting him from himself.

Sorrow gripping his heart, Jason moved toward Chang. "I came out here to tell you that I forgive you for all the pain you caused my mother and our family back when I was a kid," he said to the lifeless form. Emotion clogged his throat. Blinking, he looked away. "I only wish I had gotten here a few minutes ago. Maybe I would have been able to save your life."

Then, realizing he was wasting precious minutes, Jason turned his horse back toward town, leaving the bodies as they were. "I forgive you, Chang," he said quietly.

He was not really speaking to the dead man, for he knew he

could not hear him. Jason needed to hear the words for himself, to seal them in his heart.

Sky stopped and bent down. "Dear God," he muttered. Reaching down, he touched the thick carpet of pine needles and raised his hand to examine the tips of his fingers. They were red. Brooke was bleeding again! From the evidence he could see, she had lain here for quite some time and then had attempted to rise, but had fallen. The fall must have started her wound bleeding again.

He glanced around. She had been here not too long ago. And she had headed downhill.

Frustrated by the fact that she had gone down the opposite side of the hill he had just climbed, he moved after her, following the footprints.

Brooke suppressed a groan when she again awoke. She felt light-headed and feverish. Red-hot coals of pain pulsed outward from her forehead, and her right eye was so swollen she couldn't see out of it. She lay on her side once again on the bitter-cold ground. A hard lump pressed painfully into her hip.

Rolling onto her back, she stared at the rocky ceiling above her, her one good eye taking a moment to adjust to the dim light. She lay in a cave of some sort, perhaps a tunnel. Light emanated from somewhere in the direction of her feet, and she could smell the musty fragrance of freshly turned dirt.

With a heavy heart, she realized how much she missed Sky. Had it been only two days ago that he had come home and she had told him of her salvation? *Lord, help Sky to find me before it's too late.* How she wished she had simply told him the truth in the first place.

She knew now that Percival had planned to come for her all along. He hadn't planned on letting her live, no matter what. Maybe if she had told Sky, things would have turned out differently somehow. *Well, it won't do me any good to dwell on that now.* She forced herself to think on something else.

Feeling to see what the lump she had been laying on might have been, she was puzzled to find nothing on the ground under her. Her hand moved slowly to the skirt of her dress, and she felt something there. Memory flooded in like brilliant light. The gun! Percival hadn't found it! She reached into her pocket to pull it out but heard movement and stilled.

"You've come around again, I see. I really should just kill you and be done with this whole mess, but I can't trust to the fact that you didn't mention anythin' to your dear husband. Of course, I could kill you and then go to his place and finish him off, but he has visitors out there, doesn't he?"

He stared at the rock ceiling overhead. "No. If I went out there, I wouldn't be able to trust to the fact that they had not seen me. Then I would have even more people to kill, and this business of killin' people is gettin' a little bothersome."

He dusted his jacket and straightened his sleeves, talking on as though he were merely discussing everyday politics. "The best way to deal with you two is to get you out here alone. You're the bait for my trap, see? First I'll shoot him and then—" he rubbed his hand slowly across the uninjured side of her face, his voice turning lecherous—"you and I are goin' to spend a little time together. But I'm afraid I will have to finish you off soon, my dear. Too bad. I really found you quite enchantin' that day we first met. Such a pity I can't keep you around."

Brooke, revolted by his touch, jerked her head away. She sucked in a sharp breath and closed her eyes as searing shards of fire coursed through her at the abrupt movement.

"Now dear, it's no use tryin' to get away from me. You are in no condition to be movin' about." Starting toward the entrance to their hiding place, he said, "You just lie here awhile. I have to go watch for your Mr. Jordan. But—" he looked down, an evil glint in his eyes—"don't worry, I'll be back."

Brooke knew she must act now. Her hand was still on the pistol in her pocket, and this might be the only chance she would have to use it. She didn't know where she found the strength, but she eased the .22 from her pocket and pulled back the hammer.

Percival spun, wide-eyed, at the click of the gun.

Brooke jerked the gun toward the general vicinity of his legs and squeezed the trigger. She hoped only to maim him and give herself a chance at escape.

Percival frantically dove to one side.

The bullet flew harmlessly out the opening of the cave. "Why, you dirty little—!" He lunged toward her.

★

CHAPTER TWENTY THREE

ollowing Brooke's trail down the hill, Sky came to a place where she had slipped and fallen. Her tumble down the hill had left a wide path of broken vegetation. Dread tightening his chest, he trotted down the hill, eyes fixed on a dark splotch of blood that showed where she had come to a stop. He glanced down at the ground, back up the hill, then turned forward to see where the trail led next and froze.

"Dear God, no," he muttered. The five Chinamen's bodies dangled before him in a grim row.

Futility and grief washed over him. Lifting his hat from his head, he raked his fingers back through his hair in despair. He had risked his life to save theirs—and all for naught.

Who had done this? He scanned the area. The large splotch of blood at his feet caught his eye. The answer to that question would have to come later. He could do nothing for these men now, and immediate danger threatened Brooke's life.

He shoved his hat back onto his head, bent, and examined the footprints more closely. He grimaced. Percival had, once again, picked Brooke up and carried her off. He'd been hoping she had escaped him. Sky continued on, following in the direction Brooke had been taken.

Coming to a clearing, he stopped and eyed the open hillside before him.

Up until this point Percival's tracks had been very obvious—almost as though he wanted Sky to be able to follow them with ease—but suddenly the trail seemed to vanish.

A long bare slope rose before him, its surface covered only with low, sparse foliage. If he stepped out, he would be clearly exposed to anyone who wanted to take a shot at him from above.

Keeping well back into the covering shadows of the trees, he searched the hillside for any sign of movement but saw nothing. Still he did not step out. Something didn't feel right about this, and he wasn't about to move out into the open until he knew what he was facing.

Leaning his shoulder into the trunk of a tree, he methodically began a sweeping search of the slope. And then he saw it. Three quarters of the way up the hill, a dark spot indicated there must be a small cave or tunnel of some sort there. Piled around the entrance were numerous mounds of rock and shale that at first glance had appeared to be no different from the other small rocks and boulders that littered the hillside.

The spot was a good three hundred yards from where he now stood, but he had seen enough diggings to know a mine entrance when he saw it.

Hunter must think that Brooke told me all about him being in town that night. Without a doubt, Sky knew Percival had Brooke in the mine. And this was a trap, set to lure him out into the open where he would be an easy target.

As he considered all his options, he recognized that the trap was well laid.

The mine was situated in such a way that in order to get to it, he would have to be out in the open for quite a ways. Anyone sitting in the shadows of the cave would be able to clearly see him. However, he wouldn't be able to see anything but the black opening, and he couldn't fire randomly into the entrance for fear of hitting Brooke. He scanned the top of the hill. Even if he eased around and approached from the top, he would have to move out into the open for at least ten yards before he could get to the entrance of the mine.

Squatting down, he pressed a fist to his mouth as he weighed his options.

He glanced over at his horse, ground-hitched a ways back in the trees. Ears pricked in the direction of the hill, Geyser stood still, listening, then raised his head to the breeze, nostrils flaring, but his eyes intent on the slope. If Sky had had any doubts about

Percival and Brooke being in the mine, they vanished. The horse's manner confirmed his notion.

Suddenly Sky knew what he would do. Experience had shown Sky that a man grew overconfident when he thought he knew his opponent's only options. The best way to capture such a man was to catch him off guard.

There was usually more than one way to skin a coon, no matter how outlandish it might be. Sky remembered his father's motto, "'Expect the unexpected and act accordingly.' Don't ever do what they are expecting you to do," he had told his boys on a number of occasions. "You have to put yourselves in that other man's shoes and learn to think like he does. Don't make your move until you know exactly what he thinks you're going to do. Then do something totally different." The element of surprise worked almost every time, and Sky prayed that it would work this time.

He stopped to think about Hunter. And as he eyed the terrain around the entrance to the mine, he began to see what the man expected.

Percival had convinced himself that Sky would walk out of the trees at the bottom of this hill scouting the ground for the trail he had suddenly lost and not notice anything further up the hill. He thought Sky would come traipsing right up into the sights of his gun.

But as Sky scrutinized the hillside above the entrance to the mine, he saw another option. Moving around the base of the hill, being careful to stay hidden in the shadows of the trees, Sky came to a ridge that would take him up the hill, but keep him out of sight from the mine entrance. Skirting around, he came out above the tunnel so that he now looked down on it.

From this angle he could not see the entrance, but he was within thirty feet of it and could hear voices, although he couldn't make out what they were saying.

He would have to move carefully here. Any misplaced pebble that rolled down the hill would alert Percival that someone stood above them, and would ruin his advantage of surprise.

The fact that Hunter did not expect him to come in from above would work to his advantage, but only for a moment. Sky hoped he would only need a moment.

He had one other trick up his sleeve that he prayed would buy him some time.

Removing his buckskin shirt, he silently placed it over a forked branch he had selected. He added his black hat at the neck, jamming it down onto the branches so that it would stay in place. Lashing the crude dummy to the saddle, he stepped back, eyeing his creation. It didn't look anything like a person, but he hoped it would serve to make Hunter take a second look and buy him a few more precious seconds.

Sky wrapped Geyser's hooves with some strips of cloth he kept in his saddle bags for just such a purpose, so they would make no noise as he moved across the rocky surface. Many times Sky had been alerted to the approach of someone by the soft click of a horse's hooves on a small stone, and he didn't want to give Percival that same advantage. Leading the horse so that he stood just above and to the right of the mine entrance, Sky left him there, reins wrapped around the pommel, praying he would make no sound until he himself could get into place.

Pulling his pistol from the holster he checked the rounds, then crept stealthily toward the other side of the entry.

When he was in place, he picked up a good size stone and weighed it in his hand, judging the distance between himself and Geyser. Glancing again at the path he would have to travel to get to the entrance of the mine, he memorized every twist, turn, and rock on the way.

Then suddenly, he heard the report of a small pistol from inside the mine! Spinning, he threw the rock in his hand at the haunch of the black with great force, letting out a piercing whistle.

The stone hit the exact spot he had aimed for and the horse, surprised by the loud noises and the stinging pain, lunged forward, heading down the hill at a gallop.

Sky launched into motion at the same moment, heading on swift silent feet toward the mine, praying that Brooke was alive.

Jason went first to Chang's Mercantile and entered the front door. The bell overhead clanged as the door hit it.

Jenny came out of the back room carrying an empty box, her face red and swollen from crying.

Jason cleared his throat. For the first time in years, he wished that he had stopped to wash up before paying a call. It didn't seem right, somehow, that he stood here, looking like he did in his dirty clothes and shaggy hair, about to inform a woman that her husband had been murdered.

Quickly removing his hat, he ran a hand back through his hair and then stepped forward. "Ma'am, I'm afraid I have some bad news."

Jenny set the box down on the counter in front of her. Jason could see the light of knowledge in her eyes but no fresh tears came.

"I've just come from the trail leading out of town. I'm sorry to have to tell you, but your husband and all the prisoners with him have been killed."

"How?" she questioned, flatly.

He cleared his throat. "They were hung, ma'am."

"You do it, Mistah Jordan?"

Jason blinked. He deserved that. Everyone in town knew he hated Lee Chang. Sorrowful conviction engulfed his heart. His past actions and hatred would bring the suspicion of many down on his head for this crime. "Ma'am, I have treated your husband very poorly in the past. I've held a grudge against him for something that happened to my mother many years ago, and it was wrong. I came to see that a short time ago and, although I don't expect you to believe this, I rode after him to tell him that I've forgiven him for the part he had in my mother's death. I did not..." He shook his head, unable to finish the sentence as his throat clogged with emotion. "No." He answered her question directly.

"I sorry, Mistah Jordan." She shook her head. "I should not ask like that. I know it not you."

He twisted his hat around by the rim. "Thank you, ma'am. I'm sorry for the way I felt about your husband. I want you to know that. I only wish I had gotten the chance to tell him."

She nodded. Her face crumpled as tears began to run down her cheeks. Jason stepped toward her, guiding her by the elbow to a chair. "I really need to go inform the others so we can try to figure out what happened. Will you be all right here alone?" She nodded again.

"All right. We'll let you know the minute we find out anything." He pushed his hat back onto his head and stepped outside, heading toward the jail to break the news.

The reverberation of the pistol shot still echoed off the walls of the cavern when Brooke heard the piercing whistle from outside.

Percival, who had lunged toward her, cursed and suddenly changed course. He snatched up his shotgun and lurched out the mine entrance into the bright sunlight. Turning to the right, he raised the scatter gun and fired. "Got him!" he yelled with glee.

Heart constricting, Brooke scrabbled for the .22 with shaking hands. She sat up, leaning back against the wall of the cave. *So thirsty!* She licked her dry lips. Closing her eyes for a second as a wave of exhaustion washed over her, she leaned her head back. It had to be Sky. He'd been coming to rescue her. Percival had just killed Sky. She blinked, tears coursing down her cheeks, and stretched the gun out at arm's length in the direction of the light. Waiting for Percival to come back in, she prayed that God would forgive her for what she was about to do. This time she would not be aiming for his legs!

The gun wavered, and the images in her line of vision doubled. She blinked again, trying to focus, knowing she didn't have enough strength to hold on for long.

She saw Percival lower the gun and heard him exclaim, "What the—!?" as he stared off down the hill.

Suddenly, he spun and threw up an arm as someone leaped upon him. Brooke's vision blurred. Who was out there?

Shoving the end of the shotgun aside, the newcomer slammed a large fist into Percival's face, knocking the smaller man onto his back. Percival did not move. Yanking the shotgun from his grasp, Percival's assailant carried it with him into the cave.

Brooke raised the wavering gun a little higher. Whoever he was, she wouldn't be going with him.

"Don't move, Mister, or I will shoot!" She tried to sound authoritative, but the words rasped in her throat.

He chuckled. "Well, that's some greeting for the man who just rescued you," he said in an affectionate tone.

She lifted one hand to shade her eyes, squinting against the light streaming in from behind him. It couldn't be him. Her mind must be playing tricks on her. She cocked the hammer.

"Brooke, honey, it's me." Sky stepped toward her and she tried to focus on his face. Kneeling down, he removed the gun from her shaking hands, released the hammer, and laid it on the ground. He stroked her cheek tenderly. "I didn't know what a monster I was creating when I taught you to use that gun."

Running her tongue over dried lips, Brooke pulled back, desperately trying to make out his features. Percival had just killed him, hadn't he? She swiped at the tears running down her face, trying to clear her vision.

Carefully, he eased his hands under her knees and behind her back. "Come on, Mrs. Jordan, let's get you outside."

A sob escaped Brooke's throat and she raised one hand to her mouth. It was him! It was really him! Only he could say those words in such an endearing manner. "I thought he killed you. I heard him say…he said…"

"Shhh," Sky shushed her, "it's all right, honey. I'm here now. It's all right."

Sky tried to keep all concern from his voice and the conversation light as he addressed Brooke, lifting her gently and carrying her outside into the sunlight.

She passed out almost the moment he picked her up. He

knew she had to be exhausted from her loss of blood and the stress of the last two days.

The first sight of her had sent his heart plummeting in his chest, but not until he got her into the light did he see the true extent of her injuries. His fear for her life blazed anew.

Gingerly, he laid her on the ground, easing her head down and wishing he had his shirt to pillow her head. The wound on her forehead had begun to bleed again, and he knew she couldn't stand any more blood loss.

Grabbing his knife, he sliced a long strip of material from her petticoat and used it to clean the dirt away from the nasty cut. Cutting another strip, he wound it firmly around her head, knowing that the pressure would stop the bleeding.

Standing, he turned toward the cave to see if there might be any water there. Something tugged at the muscle just below his shoulder. He frowned, looking down even as he heard the report of a derringer. He took an involuntary step backwards. A puncture wound oozed blood and briefly bewildered him, but almost instantly, he knew his mistake. Dropping to one knee he lunged to his right.

The action saved his life. He felt the whip of a second bullet flying past his head and then he crouched down and ran.

How could he have made such a critical mistake? In his hurry to make sure Brooke was all right, he had not checked Percival for any more weapons, nor bothered to restrain him, and now he was conscious and armed.

The bare hillside provided no cover. Sky sprinted in a crouched position, zigzagging to make it harder for Percival's aim to find its mark and to give himself a few seconds. Palming his Colt even as he ran, he spun toward Percival and launched himself into a back-flip. His legs framed Hunter's form for a split second, and Sky fired. He landed painfully on his shoulder blades but used his momentum to push himself over in a reverse somersault and come up on his knees, his gun extended in case he needed to fire again.

Sky's bullet knocked the derringer out of Percival's grip, and he screamed in pain, spinning around and shaking his wounded hand. Then, unexpectedly, his body jerked again and he fell over backwards, staring lifelessly at the sky.

Sky blinked, looking long and hard at the man. Though Sky had only fired once, Percival had been shot through the heart.

Suddenly, weakness washed over him, and searing shards of fire flashed through his body. Sky looked down. Blood seeped from the bullet hole in his shoulder and soaked his chest and pants. His shoulder pulsated in a spasm of pure agony, and every movement he made sliced a dagger of pain through his body.

Holstering his gun, he moved forward awkwardly on one hand and his knees, favoring the injured arm. This time he took no chances, even though he could clearly see the man was dead. Pulling the derringer away from the body, he patted Percival down, checking for any more weapons. He found none.

Sitting down, he reloaded the spent chamber in his six-shooter. He did not know who had killed Percival, but he didn't want to take any chances with the fact that he might need his gun again very soon.

The sound came sooner than he expected. Footsteps behind him. He spun, cocking the gun as he moved. Gritting his teeth against the flames in his shoulder, he leveled the gun at the chest of the approaching figure.

He paused. He knew this man, but it took him a moment to recognize him. Trace Johnson moved up the hill, using his rifle as a crutch, his face badly lacerated and swollen.

Relaxing, Sky sat back and then lay all the way down, resting his head on the ground for a moment. Trace collapsed onto the ground beside him, glancing over at Percival's body. "Did I kill him?"

Sky nodded.

"I was aiming just to injure him and give you some time to gain control of the situation, but when you shot the gun out of his hand, he spun around and it was too late. I had already pulled the trigger."

"Where you been?" questioned Sky.

"I headed for your house like we talked about. But as I was riding down the trail, someone up on the embankment stepped out from behind a tree and clubbed me in the face, leaving me for dead. It all happened so fast that I never even saw the fella, sort of like this situation." He swore. "Now I'll never know for sure whether he was the man I was looking for."

"He knew you were on to him. Maybe he thought you were getting a little too close. I'd be willing to bet that girl back east will recognize him if you show her his picture. At least she will get some of her family jewels back."

Sky's eyes closed as he spoke.

Trace grunted. "Well, this is not the way I like to close a case. But I suppose it's the best I'm gonna get this time." He glanced over at Sky and stood to his feet. "Come on. We need to get that bleedin' stopped."

★

CHAPTER TWENTY FOUR

Brooke awoke in the dark, pain washing over her as she tried to move. A low moan escaped her throat. Instantly, she heard movement, and the room flooded with light.

She blinked several times in succession, trying to keep her eyes open against the blinding glare, and looked up into the worried faces of Sky and Rachel.

Sky fingered the hair just behind the bandage that encircled her head, his eyes questioning her, seeing if she was all right. Rachel moved to the stove.

Sky smiled. "It's good to see you're awake."

"Did you arrest Percival?" she questioned in a dry, raspy voice.

"How are you feeling?" He ignored her question.

"Sky." She cleared her throat, trying to remove some of the scratchiness. "I need to tell you something."

"Shhh, dear, don't try to talk." Rachel straightened the blanket with one hand, holding a bowl in the other. "Sky, honey, I need to sit there so I can feed her some of this broth."

Sky glanced up at his mother and then back at Brooke, then rose reluctantly and stepped away from her. Their conversation would have to wait for later.

Nothing had ever tasted quite so good as the cool water and warm chicken broth that Rachel trickled into her mouth off a spoon. When she finished eating, she felt exhausted and wanted nothing more than to fall back to sleep, but she needed to make a trip to the outhouse.

She started to rise, and Sky, who hadn't taken his eyes off her for a moment since she awoke, was instantly by her side. "What do you need?"

"I need to go out."

"Brooke, you've been unconscious for a day and a half. You are not going anywhere but back to bed."

"Sky, I need to go out," she repeated, embarrassed to say more.

"And I said—"

"Sky," Rachel broke in, giving him a pointed look.

He glanced back at Brooke, still uncomprehending, and then sudden understanding lit his face. "Oh! Well, come on, I'll take you."

Brooke, mortified to feel him lift her up into his arms, tried to get down, pushing against his shoulder.

"Brooke, hold still," he commanded with a painful grimace.

"Sky, do you think you should be—" Rachel started in an anxious tone.

"I'm fine, Ma," he said, cutting her off.

Brooke glanced back and forth between them and finally gave up her struggle. Every move she made only caused Sky to hold her tighter and sent shooting pains along her temple. And even in her pain-filled state, she enjoyed the feel of his arms about her. She laid her head on his shoulder and allowed him to carry her to the outhouse. He deposited her right at the door and stood waiting for her just outside. He insisted on carrying her back to the house.

When he again set her on her feet by the bed, unmindful of the fact that Rachel sat knitting just across the room, she laid one hand gently on his stubbly unshaven cheek, letting her thumb trail over his face. "Thank you." A tender light leapt into his dark eyes at her words. "We have a lot to talk about."

He nodded, raising one finger to gently tap her nose. "Later."

"Sky, I—"

He laid a finger over her lips. "Later. Now, I want you to rest." Brooke sighed and glanced over at Rachel. "Is he always this pushy?"

Rachel chuckled, relief washing over her. Brooke would be all right. She had worried, not knowing how deep the infection from the wound on her forehead had gone. But seeing her able to joke eased her mind. With a little care and time, Brooke would get better.

Brooke fell asleep almost the instant her head hit the pillow, and Rachel gestured for Sky to sit down. She helped him remove his shirt, and saw, just as she had expected, that his bandage was soaked with bright fresh blood.

She gave him a disparaging frown. "You can't be carrying her everywhere, or this will never heal."

He grinned unrepentantly. "It was worth it." His eyes traveled involuntarily to where his wife slept, the smile still in place, and Rachel couldn't bring herself to chastise him further.

Three days later, Brooke was sitting up in bed, sipping a cup of coffee, when Sky entered the house.

The swelling had gone down in her face, and the bandage she wore no longer extended all the way around her head but just covered the cut. She felt much better and planned to be out of bed by tomorrow and back to her normal routine.

She had finally managed to get Sky to tell her what had happened up on the hill after she had passed out. He had told her Hunter had taken a shot at him, he had fired back, and Percival, in jerking away from his shot, had stepped into the line of fire from Trace's gun.

As Sky entered, she glanced up, wondering if he had learned anything more about the hanging of the five Chinamen. "Any news?"

He shook his head. "Nothing new. The guards still insist that they were surrounded by a group of masked, armed men, but the evidence doesn't point to that. We've scouted around but can't find any clues as to what happened."

"Did you tell them I saw Percival Hunter right by the bodies?"

He shrugged. "Yeah, but there's no evidence he was the one who did it. He could have just been in the area. We'll keep looking for a while, but the longer it takes to find out what exactly happened, the less likely it is that we will." He changed the subject then. "I have a visitor outside. Are you up to seeing someone?"

"Oh yes. Give me a minute to get properly dressed and then you can show them in."

"No."

She blinked at him in surprise. "What?"

"I want you to stay in bed. You're finally on the mend, and I don't want anything to happen that might change that."

"Sky!" She sighed in exasperation. In the last three days he had not let her out of bed, except to use the necessary. He insisted on walking with her every time she needed to go outside and even made her take her meals in the bed while the rest of the family ate around the table. He fussed over her like a mother hen, making sure she was warm enough, had enough of this and not too much of that, until he was driving her crazy.

"Come here." She patted the edge of the bed, and he came and sat down.

Placing his hands on either side of her and leaning in, he eyed her questioningly. "I am feeling much better, Sky. By tomorrow, I plan on being out of bed and doing the things I normally do. And," she held up a hand to stop his protests, "you are driving me crazy." She punctuated this last statement with a sharp jab to his shoulder and did a double take when he jerked and sucked in a breath of pain. "Skyler Jordan! You're hurt, aren't you?"

Gingerly, he rubbed the spot she'd just jabbed. "Uh, yeah."

"How? What happened?"

"I was shot after I found you at the cave."

For the briefest of seconds, she couldn't think of anything to say. Her mouth dropped open in shock.

He rose quickly and headed for the door. "I'll give you a minute to get dressed and then bring Jenny in."

"Sky!" she cried. She meant for him to stop.

He merely winked at her and kept going.

Seeing that he wasn't going to discuss it with her right now, she conceded and let the matter drop. This confrontation would have to wait. Still, she couldn't resist teasing him a little. "My, but you suddenly changed your mind about letting me up, didn't you?"

He gave her an impish smile as he stepped outside.

"That man!" she muttered under her breath as she tossed back the covers and rose to dress.

A few minutes later, Sky showed Jenny into the house, and Brooke's heart went out to her friend. Jenny's face appeared worn and haggard, and her usual smile was not in place.

"Jenny." Brooke held out her arms for an embrace. "I'm so sorry about Lee."

Jenny nodded against her hair, her plump arms pulling Brooke into a gentle embrace. "You okay?"

"I'm fine," Brooke said with a pointed look at Sky, who hovered just behind her as though he thought she might fall over at any moment. "Can I get you some coffee?"

Jenny nodded. But as Brooke turned toward the stove, she found Sky already refilling her own cup and pouring a fresh cup for Jenny. She smiled to herself, having to admit that she really enjoyed his attention, even if it was making her crazy.

Turning back to the table, she sat down across from Jenny. Sky eyed her critically when he set the cups on the table, as though assuring himself that she would really be all right. She set her mouth and raised her brows at him, cocking her head toward the door. He rubbed one hand across his jaw, looking her over one more time before he made his way out the door.

Jenny smiled sadly at her, taking in her features. "You look better. I see you first day. You not look so good then. I give Rachel herbs to put on cut. They help it heal."

"Thank you, Jenny. I feel much better." There was a short pause as Brooke reached across the table to take one of Jenny's hands in her own, then asked, "What are you going to do now?"

Jenny rubbed her finger around the rim of her cup. "I go back to China. See my family."

Brooke's eyes misted. "I will miss you so much. We must be sure to write each other."

"I like that." Jenny smiled.

They talked for a long time about Jenny's upcoming voyage, about all the events that had transpired in the last couple of weeks, about their friendship. They reminisced about how they had met that day at the berry patch. Brooke had begun to feel fatigued when Jenny finally rose, saying she must be going.

"Thank you so much for coming, Jenny. When do you leave for China?"

"I already packed. Jed Swanson, he buy store from me. I go tomorrow. Take stage to coast and sail from there."

At the news her friend would be leaving so soon, Brooke's heart sank. She couldn't stop the tears as she hugged her friend for one last time. "I will pray for you often."

"And I pray for you, too."

CHAPTER TWENTY FIVE

S tanding on the porch, Brooke waved to Jenny until she turned the corner and disappeared. She sighed. After Rachel left, she would have only male company again.

She was about to go in search of Sky when she saw a stranger approaching. Then she recognized him and blinked in surprise.

Jason rode into the yard. Only he didn't look the same. He had unmistakably taken a bath. His clothes were clean. The red, stained shirt had been replaced with a fresh blue one, and his hair had been cut. With surprise, Brooke noted how handsome he was; she had never noticed before.

He grinned sheepishly at her astonished face. "Is Sky around?"

Brooke snapped her gaping mouth shut. "Yes. I'll go find him."

Jason stepped his horse forward and held out one hand. "Don't bother yourself. How are you feeling these days?"

She paused, surprised by the genuine caring she heard in his voice. "I'm just fine."

Jason raised one eyebrow as though to question the truth of that statement but merely turned his horse toward the barn. "Glad you're feeling better," he called over his shoulder.

Brooke smiled softly, amazed by the change in the man.

Sky was in Geyser's stall giving him a good currying.

"Sky?" Jason called as he entered the barn.

"Yeah, Jason, I'm in here. How are things going in town?" He bent and lifted the horse's back hoof to pare and clean it.

Jason's saddle groaned as he dismounted, and his spurs jangled with each step that brought him closer. "Not good, I'm afraid. It looks like they're going to drop the investigation. There doesn't seem to be any evidence to show exactly what happened. Some are saying, though, that maybe the Nez Perce are responsible; that they hung Chang to take revenge for the times he cheated their women."

Sky snorted. "Didn't the guards say the man who spoke to them talked in clear plain English? The Nez Perce can speak English, but I never met one who didn't have an unquestionable accent when he talked. I'm not even convinced there was a *group* of vigilantes. The only tracks anywhere near those bodies were those of Percival Hunter."

"Yeah I know. I scouted around. They've sent for the federal agent in charge of Chinese affairs in this area to come look into the situation, but he won't be able to get here for a couple of months. By then you and I both know there won't be any evidence left to find. Nobody wants to believe it was Percival. Everyone who ever met the fellow seems to have genuinely liked him."

"Not me."

Geyser shifted and allowed his weight to rest on Sky's shoulder. Sky grunted and gave the horse an elbow.

Jason chuckled. "You didn't like him because the first time you met him he made you jealous."

Sky gave a quiet laugh. "Look who knows so much!" Done with the hoof, he dropped it and turned in Jason's direction. He froze and blinked in shock at the transformation. "Jason?" He raised hope-filled eyes to his cousin's face.

Jason shrugged and smiled. "I gave my life back to the Lord, Sky. I want to thank you for not giving up on me all these years."

Sky stepped out of the stall and had his cousin wrapped in a bear hug before he had even finished speaking. He tried to think of something to say, but his throat closed tight with emotion, so he contented himself with thanking his Heavenly Father for this new miracle.

Jason pulled back. "I'm going home, Sky."

Sky nodded. Suddenly, the thought of home grew very appealing. "Home sounds good. There won't be anything keeping Brooke and me here with you gone." Sky got a faraway look in his eye. "Who would have thought that I would meet and marry the most wonderful woman in the world? And all because of you?"

Jason looked askance. "Yeah…well…that reminds me of something else I wanted to talk to you about." He pulled a small pouch from his pocket and handed it to Sky.

When Sky opened it, he looked up at Jason. "I can't take this."

"Sure you can. It's the money you paid me for Brooke. I can't keep it."

"She was worth every penny."

"Sure, don't you think I know it? Go ahead and rub it in." He tried to sound angry but at Sky's quick look, he grinned. "I want you to have the money back. You have a family to look after now; you're going to need it."

Sky decided to give up the fight and compromise. "Will you at least take the eighty dollars that you paid to bring her out here?"

Jason looked momentarily embarrassed. "Maybe someday, Sky. Right now I don't want any more money in my pocket than I am going to need to make it back home." He hesitated. "I'm afraid I might be tempted to buy myself a couple of drinks along the way. I never imagined giving up something could be so hard." His shoulders slumped in despair.

Sky laid a hand in sympathy on Jason's arm. "I'll pray for you."

"Thanks. I have a feeling I'm going to need a lot of prayer in the future. You might as well practice praying for me now." A smile played across his cousin's mouth, but Sky knew he was serious.

"When do you leave?"

"I thought about going home with Uncle Sean and Aunt Rachel."

"They would like that. They've probably prayed for you as much as Gram and I have."

Jason scuffed an arc in the dust with the toe of his boot. "Do you think Gram is going to…?"

"Gram was heartbroken when you left, Jace. Nothing will make her happier than to see her prodigal son coming home."

Jason sighed. "I hope you're right."

"I know I'm right." Sky clapped him on the back.

"Do you know where your mother and dad are? I'd like to talk to them."

Sky nodded. "They took a walk over that direction. They will be so happy to hear about your decision."

He watched until Jason crested the small rise he'd indicated, then glanced at the cabin. "I have someone I need to talk to myself," he mumbled.

Grimacing, he headed for the house. Brooke wouldn't like his confession.

The longer Brooke had to think about Sky's injured shoulder the more frustrated she became. He had to have been shot when he came to rescue her! He had told her Percival shot *at* him, but not that he had actually *hit* him! He could have been killed! Why wouldn't he have told her such a thing? Here he had been waiting on her hand and foot, and he had a bullet hole in his shoulder! By the time Sky walked into the house, her frustration had bubbled over into anger.

Sky eased himself into the chair across the table from where she sat fiddling with her cup of cold coffee. She refused to look at him. Fixing her eyes on some unseen point outside the window, she pretended to be enjoying the cup of coffee she hadn't touched in the last half hour.

When they had sat in total silence for a full minute and she still hadn't met his eyes, he reached across the table and tried to take one of her hands in his own. She pulled away from his touch and turned blazing eyes in his direction.

"Here I've been feeling so bad that I didn't tell you about Percival Hunter being the one in that alley that night. And now I find that you lied to me as well! I had begun to think we might be able to make this marriage work, but—" she choked back a sob "—you don't even care enough about me to tell me when you're hurt!"

Sky blinked, taken aback. "Brooke, that's not fair, and you

know it! I didn't tell you about my injury because I didn't want you to worry about anything but getting well. This," he indicated his shoulder, "was not life-threatening like your injury was!"

"You were *shot*, weren't you?" Then her eyes widened in dismay. "I didn't shoot you, did I?"

Despite himself, Sky chuckled. "No. Although for a minute there, I thought you might."

"How can you laugh at a time like this?" She glared at him. "Did Percival shoot you?"

He nodded.

"Let me see it."

"Brooke, it's only a flesh wound. Nothing serious."

"Nothing serious? You were shot, Sky!" She stood abruptly, pushing back her chair, and suddenly her anger gave way to its root of fear. She continued in a choked voice, "Shot coming to save me, and I wouldn't have needed saving if I had been honest and told you the truth in the first place."

She folded her arms and stared out the window, tears streaming down her face. Sky stood and reached for her. She moved without hesitation into his arms, sobbing against his broad chest.

"Shhh, Brooke honey, it's all right. Everything's all right." He rubbed her back and rested his chin on top of her head.

After a moment, she pushed back, staring up at him. "What if you had been killed?"

He lifted one eyebrow and asked quietly, "Am I to understand that you would have missed me if I had died on that hill?"

"Missed you? Oh, Sky…" Her eyes dropped to his mouth and, in answer, she lifted up on her tiptoes and kissed him softly.

Sky lifted his head, both eyebrows winging upward. His eyes twinkling, he tucked her closer and whispered, "I'll take that as a yes, Mrs. Jordan."

She nodded, her eyes never leaving his face.

With a sigh of satisfaction, he lowered his mouth to hers once more, and Brooke pressed into his embrace, wrapping her arms around his neck.

He kissed her gently, but when he finally pulled away, Brooke was breathless.

She rested her cheek against his chest. "I'm sorry I didn't tell you about Percival, Sky. I was just so scared. He said he would kill you if I told, and I already loved you so much that I couldn't stand the thought. Now I know he intended to kill us both all along." She lifted her face to his.

Bending down, he rubbed the tip of his nose against hers. "Say it again."

"He intended to kill us both all along?"

He chuckled, pulling back. "The part about loving me."

She smiled innocently. "Did I say that?"

His eyes sparked with amusement. "Why, yes you did, Mrs. Jordan."

She raised one finger to trace his lips and gazed into his eyes as she said in a whisper, "I love you, Sky, but there is so much about my life that you don't know."

"We have all our lives for you to tell me about it."

Taking his hand, she led him to the couch. "I'd like to start now, if you want to listen."

Reaching up, he tucked a stray curl of hair behind her ear. "I've wanted to know more about you since the moment I first laid eyes on you."

She searched her memory. "I don't know where to begin."

"Tell me about your mother and sister. You spoke of them once. You miss them very much, don't you?"

Brooke nodded and began there. She left nothing out and didn't stop until she came to the part about God convicting her to tell him of her past. When she looked over at him, tears shimmered in his deep brown eyes.

He picked up her hand and played with her fingers. "You have been through more than I ever imagined."

"Yes. But you showed me the way out of the desert. I know that, no matter what the future holds, I will always have an oasis to turn to, because I've finally figured out that this is not a mirage."

He grinned. "I don't know. I keep thinking you're going to

disappear right out of my arms." He winked at her. "Maybe I need to kiss you again to make sure this really is real."

She smiled and leaned closer.

As Sky's lips moved across hers, heart-jolting tremors raced through her chest. She suppressed a moan of pleasure as she slid closer to him. She leaned into his solid strength, her fingers entwining themselves in his hair.

Sky had accepted her without reservation; loved her despite her past. Her fears and emotional uncertainty about their relationship, which had already been dwindling, now vanished like morning mist in the desert, and she thanked God for bringing her home. Home to her oasis.

EPILOGUE

Six Months Later
Shilohh, Oregon

Brooke stood in the middle of the kitchen and ticked off all the things she still needed to finish on the tips of her fingers. "Rolls in the oven. Butter in the ice-house. The potatoes are mashed. Sky will slice the roast. Oh—" she slapped a hand to her forehead—"I almost forgot the pies!" She started toward the pantry, but two strong hands slid around her from behind, stilling her progress.

Sky chuckled and kissed her neck as he pulled her back firmly against him. "Don't worry. I'm not likely to let you forget about those pumpkin pies."

"Sky!" Brooke spun and peeked around him toward the large open archway between the kitchen and the dining room of their home. "Your family will all be here at any minute!" She could see the front door propped open to welcome the family inside when they arrived. Sunlight from the unseasonably warm day streamed in through every window, and the red tablecloth on the polished plank table Sky had given her as a housewarming gift billowed softly.

He nuzzled her ear. "So? All they will see is a man who's smitten with his wife."

She planted her palms firmly in the middle of his chest and pushed. "Later. I want this first meal with all of us in our home to be perfect." Her push would have had about as much effect on a rock wall.

Leaning in, he gave her a quick kiss, tucking her nearer. "My family loves you just the way you are." His gaze roved over her face.

She grinned. "And I'd like to keep it that way."

"And I'd like to keep you this way." He gave her a squeeze and stepped even closer.

"Sk—"

The cajoling press of his lips stole her protest and her breath. Her resistance flew out the open door and she gave in, wrapped her arms around his neck, and stood on tiptoe to meet him kiss for kiss.

She lost all track of time until someone cleared their throat.

Brooke gasped and jerked back, spinning toward the sound. Sean, Rachel, Rocky, and Sharyah stood in the entryway, each with a grin to rival a carved pumpkin.

She felt her face heat, and she pushed Sky back, giving him the biggest don't-make-any-more-of-a-scene-than-you-already-have glare that she could muster.

"Knock-knock." Jason poked his head in the front door, then stepped inside, guiding his sister by the hand. Gram, escorted by Cade, entered right on their heels. Everyone's attention zoned in on them.

Sky stepped back with an unrepentant grin. He rubbed his thumb across his lips and turned to face his family. "Hi, everyone. Welcome. Brooke was just, uh—" he glanced around the kitchen "—finishing up in here."

Sean smirked. "I like it when your mother finishes up in the kitchen just like that."

"Dad!" It was Sharyah's turn to turn crimson as she tossed a glance toward Cade.

Brooke suddenly realized Rachel was holding a pie in each hand. "Oh, here," she brushed past Sky, "let me get—" A puff of black smoke belched from the depths of the oven. "Ah! The rolls!" She changed course, snatching up a potholder and pulling open the oven door.

Rachel bustled into the kitchen and set her pies on the counter. "Sharyah, dear, bring Mama and Marquis in here and help us. Sky, why don't you take the men to the living room. I'm sure we'll be ready to eat in just a few minutes."

Batting smoke from before her face, Brooke plunked the tray

of bread rolls onto the counter. Dismay washed over her. She'd wanted this meal to be just perfect.

Marquis, her unseeing gaze fixed on nothing in particular, sniffed. "They don't smell too bad. I bet the middle will be just fine."

Sharyah pulled a face. "They *look* pretty bad, Marquis."

"Now, all is not lost," Rachel proclaimed. "We have plenty of food. We'll just put them on, and if anyone wants one, they can have one, and if not, well then, Cade's pigs will get a nice addition to their slop this evening."

Eltha sidled up beside her and wrapped her in a one-armed hug. "Don't you worry about a thing, dearie. We won't boot you out of the family over a few burnt rolls, especially not when we all know it was that scoundrel Skyler's fault!"

Brooke blinked away tears of happiness as they all put the finishing touches on the table. And minutes later, when they were all gathered around with chatter flowing freely, she thought her heart might burst from the joy of belonging in such a wonderful family.

After the meal, as she set dessert out, Jason cleared his throat in an obvious attempt to gather everyone's attention, and slowly the room quieted. "I wanted to let you all know I've decided to take a job as the drive foreman for a cattle ranch. I'll be leaving for Texas within the week to begin negotiations for bringing a herd this way come spring."

"That's great, Jason. You'll do really well at that." Cade said.

"Yeah, but—" he twirled his fork in the top of his pie "—there are a lot of saloons between here and Texas. I'd sure appreciate all your prayers for strength."

"You got them." Sky nodded, and everyone else agreed.

"You two heard anything more from Pierce City?" Sean glanced back and forth from Jason to Sky.

Sky set his fork down and steepled his hands. "Got a letter from Jed the other day. He said the agent for Chinese affairs did come through town, but he didn't have any further light to shed on the incident. They are still supposing the lynching was done by the Nez Perce as revenge against Chang."

Jason sighed. "I don't suppose we'll ever really know for sure."

Brooke sniffed. She knew good and well who was responsible for the death of those men.

Sky looked at her solemnly, then told Jason, "Jed did say that Alice took her father's money and went back east to a finishing school like Fraser would have wanted. And Trace Johnson, had dropped by and said the young girl from back east confirmed that much of the jewelry Percival Hunter had on him belonged to her family. So Trace has put that case to rest, as it is almost certain Percival was indeed the man he was looking for."

"Well," Sean spoke around a bite, "that's at least one good thing that came from this situation. The girl can be at rest that her parents' killer is no longer on the loose." He glanced back and forth between Sky and her. "How are you two settling into your new place here?"

Polishing off his last bite of pie, Sky leaned back and rested his arm along the top of her chair. He looked at her. "Pretty good. I put the finishing touches on the broken steps on the back porch yesterday, and Brooke has just about scrubbed away the floor and windows in every room now."

Brooke smiled at that. She had put in a lot of work to get the place clean. Rachel chuckled. "Well, it wasn't in the best of shape, but I'm so glad you are just down the street from us! I say it was pure providence that the Conrads moved away when they did."

Sky reached over and slid his hand over hers, giving her a squeeze. "Lots of pure providence in my life lately."

Jason, Rocky, and Cade teased with choked coughs.

Sky's warm gaze never left her face. He pumped his eyebrows and tossed her a wink that said they simply didn't know what they were missing.

Every eye at the table was fixed on them, and heat crawled up from the depths of Brooke's collar.

Sean glowered at the boys as he laid his napkin down by his plate. "Well, this has been good." His gaze encompassed the table.

"I'm glad you thought of this, Brooke. We should have family meals like this more often."

"Yeah." Rocky picked up a roll and clunked it against his plate. "Only we need to keep Sky out of the kitchen while Brooke is cooking!"

"Rocky Jordan!" Eltha and Rachel gasped in unison.

He had the grace to look sheepish. "Sorry."

Brooke eased back into her chair, contentment washing through her. Only a few months ago, she never would have imagined the joy found in family camaraderie. And now she had the best family anyone could ask for.

She closed her eyes. *Thank You, Lord. Thank You for bringing me home.*

Dear Reader,

I hope you have enjoyed reading Rocky Mountain Oasis as much as I enjoyed writing it. But most of all, I hope that God used this book to draw you closer to Him somehow.

Tragically, the murder at the heart of this book really happened. David Fraser was indeed a merchant in Pierce, Idaho, and was murdered as brutally as I've depicted in the book.

Five Chinamen were arrested for his murder; however, even though most of the evidence pointed in their direction, it was circumstantial and never conclusively proved that they were the perpetrators. (The names I used in this book for the Chinamen are different than the names of the men actually arrested, and my characters are in no way meant to be like the actual historical men.) Unfortunately the men were assumed guilty and justice was taken out of the hands of the law before the truth could be found out.

All the events I portrayed of the trial—from the man disguised as a drunken Indian, to the use of a noose as a means of coercion—actually took place.

Percival Hunter is entirely a product of my imagination. No one ever figured out the motive behind Mr. Fraser's demise, so I produced a plausible one. Mr. Fraser did have a daughter named Alice who was living in Lewiston, Idaho, attending school at the time of his death.

To this day if you travel to the city of Pierce, Idaho, you can visit the sight of the hangings and enter the actual jail the prisoners were held in during their inquiry.

If you would like to learn more, I recommend the book And Five Were Hanged: And Other Historical Short Stories of Pierce and the Oro Fino Mining District by Layne Gellner Spencer.

I'd love to hear from you. You can find out more about me by visiting www.lynnettebonner.com.

Now Available...

THE SHEPHERD'S HEART - BOOK 2

HIGH DESERT
Haven

Is Jason Jordan really who he says he is?
Everything in Nicki's life depends on the answer.

Oregon Territory, 1887

When her husband dies in a mysterious riding accident, Nicki Trent is left with a toddler and a rundown ranch. Determined to bring her ranch back from the brink of death, Nicki hires handsome Jason Jordan to help. But when William, her neighbor, starts pressing for her hand in marriage, the bank calls in a loan she didn't even know about, bullets start flying, and a burlap dummy with a knife in its chest shows up on her doorstep, Nicki wonders if this ranch is worth all the trouble.

To make matters worse, terrible things keep happening to her neighbors. When her friend's homestead is burned to the ground and William lays the blame at Jason's feet, Nicki wonders how well she knows her new hand...and her own heart.

A desperate need. Malicious adversaries. Enticing love.
Step into a day when outlaws ran free, the land was wild, and guns blazed at the drop of a hat.

High Desert Haven

PROLOGUE

California
July 1883

As Dominique Noel Vasquez methodically scrubbed clothes in the tub of soapy water, she listened to the quiet, strained tones of her parents who sat against the shady side of the house.

Scorching afternoon sun shone on the hard-packed, earth yard of the small adobe hut. Heat waves, radiating from every sun-baked surface, turned the landscape into a shimmering sepia blur. Dead brown land lay in every direction; the only hint of green life was the small scraggly plot of corn that would hopefully feed the family for the year to come. Even the wheat struggling to grow added to the dull brown vista. A solitary chicken, scratching for a meager meal, sent small puffs of dust filtering across the yard and a lonely cow, the children's only source of milk, rested her head on top of her split-rail fence and let out a low bellow.

In this heat everyone should have been down for a *siesta,* but on this day only the smallest children of the household were resting. Tension rode the heat waves.

Dominique plunged harder and glared at the clothes. The creditors had come again this morning. Last year Papa had been forced to borrow money for seed, and now for the second season in a row the rains had failed them. There were no crops; they were down to their last chicken; the one cow's milk was needed by the children; and the creditors were howling for their money like a pack of hungry wolves hot on the scent of lame prey.

Nicki tossed an angry glance at the sky. "Lord, where are You when we need You?" Sweat trickled down her temple and she rubbed it roughly across one shoulder as she shook out a little skirt with more vigor than necessary and tossed it across the line. Gentle conviction washed over her. She was throwing a bigger temper tantrum than two-year-old Coreena did when Papa told her "No."

Nicki's anger eased. "Forgive me, Lord. You alone know and care about our plight. But if there were anything I could do to help Mama and Papa, You know I would do it." She paused in her prayer, thinking, then continued, "What is there to do, Lord? Show me what I can do to help."

Mama called across the yard, interrupting her prayer. "Nicki, you work too hard. Sit! Rest! We will finish the washing when it is cooler."

"Almost done, Mama. Then I will rest."

"That girl!" Mama turned to Papa but the rest of her words were drowned in a dry, hot breeze.

Nicki smiled. Mama often castigated her for working too hard, but with twelve children, nine of whom were still at home to feed and clothe, Mama needed and appreciated all the help she could get.

Silence reigned for a time. The only sounds filling the afternoon air were the soft swish, plunge, and gurgle of Nicki's washing and the giggling of her two younger sisters splashing each other with cool water by the well. Nicki gave the last small shirt a snap and deftly flipped it onto the line where the laundry was drying. Dumping the soapy water in front of the door, which helped keep the dust down, Nicki hung the wooden bucket on its nail and moved to carefully empty the contents of the rinse bucket on the one small rosebush at the corner of the hut.

"Girls, please!" Juanita Vasquez called from the shadow of the house to Rosa and Juna, who were getting a little wild and loud with their splashing game. "I have just gotten Manuel to sleep. Quiet!"

This sent the girls into another gale of giggles. Their mother's voice had been twice as loud as theirs. But when Papa tipped his sombrero back and glared at his two wayward offspring, the giggles ceased immediately.

Nicki shook her head fondly at her sisters' wayward ways and sank to the ground next to Mama, suppressing a groan of satisfaction as she leaned back against the cool adobe wall. She was tired. All morning she had helped Papa haul water from the well to carefully water their acre of wheat and corn. A large enough plot to hopefully get them through another year. Later they would repeat the process, because watering with buckets did not soak the ground like a good rain would, and the crops needed plenty of water if they were to produce well.

Nicki closed her eyes, trying to ignore Mama and Papa's furtive conversation.

"The chicken, Carlos?"

"Mama, the chicken will not bring in enough to get us through one day, much less pay the money we owe."

"Yes. You are right, of course, and it has stopped laying, so we don't even have the eggs from it anymore." Mama sighed. "Ahhh, maybe we should have chicken tonight, *sí?*"

Papa sighed at Mama's little joke. "We could sell the cow."

"Papa, she is the only milk for the children. I would like to keep her if we could."

Hot tears pressed the back of Nicki's eyes, and she leaned back against the wall. What were they to do? Papa would be taken to jail if he didn't come up with the money by next week, and then they would all die for sure. The creditors would take their meager crops to recoup as much of their money as they could. They wouldn't care that they'd be leaving a woman and her nine children to starve to death. Where was Juan when they needed him? Were he here, he'd think of some way to make the money they so desperately needed.

A slight breeze rustled the dried grasses, and Nicki pulled her skirt up around her knees, not caring that Mama would chastise her for such an unladylike action. The small breath of fresh air was worth it. Reaching up, she brushed at the long wisps of black hair that had escaped her braid and rubbed the perspiration from her upper lip. She wanted a drink of water but felt almost too tired to get up and get it. Eventually the thought of the cold water won out. She shifted forward. Mama and Papa could surely use a drink as well. "Child, you don't sit still for even a minute! What are you heading to do now?"

"A drink, Mama," Nicki said lovingly. "Would you like one as well?" She pushed herself up from the wall.

Mama's voice turned tender. "What would I do without you, child?"

Nicki chuckled. She was hardly the child her mother kept insisting she was. At seventeen she more than carried her weight, but Mama didn't like to see her children grow up. Nicki remembered Mama calling Roberto "my little man" on the day of his wedding! Those had been happier times, Nicki thought as she walked to the well. The rains had been good in those years, and debt had not hung over the little adobe hut and its occupants.

As Nicki cranked the lever that would pull the bucket up from the depths of the well, she scanned the horizon and stiffened. "Papa." Her tone held a soft warning. Someone was coming on the trail.

Papa rose and stood by her side. Nicki pulled the bucket toward her, filling the dipper with cool water. If the creditors had come to take her papa away, he would go having just drunk his fill from the chilled water of his own well. She handed the dipper to her father. He drank, never taking his eyes off the rider heading their way, then handed the dipper back. Nicki filled it and moved toward her mother, who still sat in the shade, tears filling her eyes.

"They said not until next week." Mama's words stabbed a knife of pain through Nicki's heart. Whatever happened, Nicki knew Mama would die a slow death once Papa was taken. Not from starvation, but because the love of her life would be gone.

Fierce determination filled Nicki as she marched with the empty dipper back toward the well. Tossing back a gulp of water, she wiped the droplets from her chin and pivoted to glare at the man coming into the yard.

She froze. He was not the man who worked for the bank.

"Howdy." The man tipped back his dusty, black hat and smiled down at Carlos. The smile didn't quite reach his eyes. His gaze flicked past Papa and came to rest on Nicki. Considerable interest flamed in their depths. He nodded to her, the smile now reaching his eyes, and touched the brim of his hat in a one-fingered salute. "Ma'am." He ignored Papa and spoke directly to her. "I was thinking how nice a cool drink of water would be. I'd sure be appreciating it if I could light a spell."

Carlos stepped between Nicki and the newcomer, effectively blocking his view. "Draw fresh water, Dominique." He stretched his hand toward the man, indicating he could dismount. "Welcome."

But Nicki could hear an edge in his voice. This man could mean trouble.

"Obliged." He nodded and swung from his saddle. The man was tall, had graying hair, steely blue eyes, and a wad of chewing tobacco stuffed in his cheek. He stretched his hand toward Carlos as Nicki pulled up a fresh bucket. "Name's John Trent."

Papa took his hand. "Carlos Vasquez."

Mr. Trent studied her over the dipper as he drank his fill. Nicki averted her eyes but held the bucket for his next dipperful. She had received more than her share of such looks and knew what he was thinking. For although this man would say nothing to her in front of her father, the men down at the cantina showed no such qualms whenever Mama found it necessary to send her there. The thought of their suggestive remarks burned a blush across her cheeks. John Trent lifted the dipper again and raised his eyebrows in amusement.

Papa made small talk about the long hot spell as Nicki pulled buckets of water from the well for the man's horse, but Nicki didn't miss the looks John Trent kept throwing her way.

When he mounted up to ride out, Mama, still seated in the shade, gave an audible sigh. Nicki couldn't deny she felt plenty relieved as well.

Just as he arrived at the crest of the trail, the man paused, and Nicki stiffened. John Trent rubbed a hand across his face and said something to himself, then swung his horse once again toward their adobe. His eyes raked her more boldly this time as he pulled to a stop in their sun-baked yard.

Leaning his arms casually on the horn of his saddle, he spat a stream of tobacco into the dust, turned toward Papa, and brazenly asked, "How much for the girl?"

Nicki and Mama gasped in unison.

The bucket in Nicki's hands crashed to the ground, splashing water over her feet. Quickly she bent and picked it up. She spun on her heel and marched toward the well to return the bucket to its hook. *The audacity!*

Papa spoke with authority. "The *señorita* is *not* for sale."

John Trent's eyes scanned the small house and the scraggly field beyond, then traveled pointedly to seven of Nicki's brothers and sisters who had gathered in a little clump to watch the goings-on. Then he stared into Papa's face before spitting another stream of brown sludge. "I think everything's for sale as long as the price is right."

"My daughter is *not* for sale, *Señor*. I have to ask you to leave us now."

Ignoring him, Trent reached into the pocket of his vest and pulled out a coin. He tossed it to the ground near Papa's feet.

A twenty dollar gold piece! Nicki had not seen Mama move, but the audible click of a cocking shotgun cracked into the afternoon stillness. All eyes turned toward the door of the house to see her there, the gun aimed squarely at John Trent's chest.

Nicki's eyes dropped to the money on the ground. That little piece of gold could save Papa's life. It would get him out of debt and even give them enough to start over somewhere. Remembering her earlier prayer, she started to step forward.

But Papa beat her to it. Picking up the offensive gold, he

threw it toward John Trent as if it were too hot to touch. "She is not for sale!"

Trent deftly caught the coin, pulled two more pieces just like it from his pocket, and tossed all three on the ground. "I want that girl. Now I am trying to go about this in a civilized manner, but if I have to, I will take her by force." He sat up straight and casually rested a hand on his thigh near his gun.

Nicki felt dizzy from the sheer shock of this proposition. Her eyes flashed from Mama, bravely holding an unloaded gun on the man insulting her daughter, to Papa, stooping to pick up the offensive coins, to the hand of John Trent inching toward his holster. She surprised even herself by what happened next.

"Papa, wait!" She stepped forward. *Sixty dollars!* "I will go with him." Her hands trembled as she smoothed the material of her skirt.

"Nicki, NO!" Mama screamed.

"Mama, *por favor!* The money! You will be free from all this trouble! I will be all right. God, He will go with me, *sí?*"

"Dominique, don't do this." Papa's words were thick with restrained emotion. "We will work something out with the bank. You take too much on yourself for one so young."

"Papa." Nicki wrapped her arms around his neck. "You are the one who taught me to be strong, *sí?* Take care of Mama and make Rosa help her now." Nicki pulled back, gazing deeply into his dark eyes, so much like her own, and rested a hand on his stubbly cheek. "She would have died without you, Papa."

She spun toward her mother, throwing herself into her arms, before the threatening tears could overflow. "Mama, *te amo!*" The choked words were all she could squeeze past her constricting throat. Would she ever see her beloved mama again?

Nicki hugged her brothers and sisters in turn, giving them each a piece of advice on how to be helpful to Mama and Papa, drying their tears with her skirt and promising she would see them again someday. Going into the house, she ran her fingers across the baby-soft cheek of little Manuel, the only member of the household still sleeping through all the commotion.

And then, head held high, she walked out into the searing sun and allowed herself to be pulled up onto the horse behind John Trent's saddle.

"Wait!" Mama ran toward her, carrying the family Bible. She pressed it into Nicki's hands, making the sign of the cross and blessing her daughter one more time, as she had done every day since her birth.

Nicki didn't let her family see her cry, but as she rode away from the only home she had ever known, part of her felt like it died. She allowed herself the small luxury of quiet tears.

They rode north for several days. Nicki was thankful that John Trent seemed to be a kind man. A justice of the peace married them in his dusty office in a small, one-street town that Nicki didn't even know the name of. By evening, they were moving north again.

They had been traveling for more than two weeks, making mostly dry camps at night, when Nicki heard her husband utter an oath of awe. It was mid-afternoon and Nicki, her forehead pressed into John's back, was almost asleep when she heard his exclamation. Lifting her head, she blinked into the sunlight, almost unable to believe the sight before her.

A lush valley stretched before them. A small creek meandered through its center, merging with the Deschutes River at one end. The Deschutes was normally inaccessible due to its steep canyon walls, but here the descent to the river was simply a long, smooth slope. Here and there a cluster of evergreen trees could be seen, but the verdant meadow was what had drawn John's eye.

It was like a vivid oasis dropped in the middle of the high-desert sagebrush they had been traveling through for the last week. The swaying grass was belly high to a good-sized horse.

At that moment, Nicki knew she was looking at her new home. The valley was a rancher's paradise, and John had talked of nothing else since their journey began. He wanted to become a rancher. A rich rancher. And this was where he would make his start.

They made camp early, and Nicki sighed in satisfaction as she waded into the creek for her first bath in a week. She rolled her head from side to side, rubbing her neck, working out the kinks of knotted muscle.

John waded in as well, and she stiffened as he slid his arms around her waist from behind, pressing a kiss to her neck.

Apparently sensing her tension, he sighed. "I'm gonna make you a good husband. You'll see, Dominique. We're gonna have one fine spread across this valley. One day you'll wake up and realize what a good life we've had, and you'll no longer regret the day you first met me."

Nicki bit her lower lip, hoping he was right. She didn't think she'd be able to live with this dreadful despair all her life. She closed her eyes, missing Mama and the family. Willing herself not to cry, she stepped out of his arms and turned to give him a tentative smile, but her heart did not lighten.

They found the soddy later that evening. There was also a run-down barn, a partially erected bunkhouse, and a corral all clustered on the lee side of a knoll just tall enough for the soddy. But the spread had long since been abandoned. The windowless house was dark, and when they lit John's lantern, Nicki saw the spiders scurrying to escape the light. She shivered and went in search of some brush to use as a broom. Soon the room was cobweb-free, and they made a bed on the floor for the night.

It was still dark the next morning when she heard John saddling the horse. She roused herself and set about making coffee. He only took the time for one cup before he rode out with a terse, "I'll be back soon as I can."

He was gone for two weeks. When he came back, he informed her they would be staying.

★
CHAPTER ONE

Shiloh, Oregon, in the Willamette Valley
January 1887

The tepid January sun struggled to warm the day, but this winter had been one of the Northwest's worst in a number of years. The temperatures barely reached the teens.

At the knock on the door, Brooke Jordan rose from scrubbing the kitchen floor and dried her hands on a towel. Pressing a hand to her aching lower back and resting one hand protectively on her rounded belly, she moved to see who it was.

"Who do you suppose would be knocking on our door at this time of day?" she asked the unborn child.

It had become her practice to talk to the baby during the day to ease the loneliness of Sky's absence. Since they had moved back to Sky's childhood home from the Idaho territory where they had met, Sky had gone to work as a deputy sheriff for his father and was gone most of the day. She missed him terribly but couldn't bring herself to tell him, knowing how much he loved his new job, even though it kept him away from home for hours at a time.

Swinging the door wide, Brooke gasped. "Jason!" She pulled the blond man, almost the spitting image of her husband, into her cumbersome embrace. "Come in! Sky and I were just talking about you last night, wondering where you might have gotten to."

Jason smiled as his eyes dropped to her midsection. "I see I've missed some news of my own while I've been gone."

Brooke's grin broadened. "This isn't the only news you've missed. Just let me send the neighbor boy to call Sky, and I'll be right in. Make yourself at home."

Brooke waved him inside and headed for the house next door.

Jason entered the little house, noting the bucket on the kitchen floor and the line delineating the clean side from the dirty. Hanging his black Stetson on the back of a chair, he bent down and took over where Brooke had left off.

"Oh, Jason," Brooke said as she came back into the house, "get up off that floor and sit down!"

He grinned at her. "Not on your life. You just plant yourself in that chair right there," he pointed toward the dining table, "and start filling me in on all the news I've missed."

Brooke sank into the indicated chair. "First I want to know all about what you've been doing. My, you've lost a lot of weight."

Jason hated the heat he felt wash his face. "Most of my weight was due to the fact I drank too much. Now that I've given that up, I can't seem to keep the pounds on."

Brooke smiled tenderly. "We are so proud of you, Jason."

He nodded but did not look up. His life had changed because of his relationship with the Lord, not because he was so great a person. There was no reason for Brooke to be proud of him, but knowing she hadn't really meant the words exactly as they sounded, he kept this thought to himself.

"So tell me what you've been up to," she prodded.

"Oh, not much. I've punched a few cows here and there, but I thought it was time I came home to see how all the family was doing. I've really missed Marquis," he said of his sister. "I would have stopped by there first, but your house was on the way, so I wanted to stop and say hello."

"Well, we're all doing fine. As you can see—"

The front door opened. "Jason!" Sky strode in. "Where've you been? Brooke and I were talking about you last night."

Jason and Brooke exchanged amused glances.

"Sky." Jason extended his wet, soapy hand, but Sky pulled him into a manly embrace. Then the cousins stepped back and eyed one another.

"How are things?" Sky asked.

"Fine." Jason grinned. It was good to be home.

"I mean with your relationship with the Lord," said Sky.

Jason grinned at Brooke again. "He sure knows how to get to the point, doesn't he?"

Brooke smiled in response, but her eyes held the same question.

Jason swallowed and fiddled with the scrub brush. "I'm doing good, Sky. I've had my struggles, especially giving up the bottle, but I haven't given in so far. God has given me the strength I needed every time."

"Praise God! We haven't given up praying for you even for a minute."

"Thanks." The one word could never express his deep gratitude. He tapped the scrub brush against his palm. "Brooke told me I've missed a bunch of news."

Sky sat next to his wife and took her hand. "Have you ever."

Jason bent to continue scrubbing the floor, curiosity filling him. "Well?" he asked, waiting.

"Let's see. First, you can see Brooke is expecting. We'll have an addition to the family sometime around the end of this spring."

"Hopefully sooner than later," Brooke said, reaching one hand to her lower back.

Sky continued, "Then there is Sharyah. She's finished her schooling and plans to find a teaching position for this fall."

Jason rocked back on the balls of his feet, letting the scrub brush hang between his knees. "Sharyah. Wow, I seem to only remember her as the little pig-tailed beauty who drove all the boys at the church picnics crazy 'cause she only had eyes for Cade Bennett."

Sky smirked. "Well, she still drives all the boys crazy, but I don't know about her having eyes for Cade Bennett anymore. He's been seeing a lot of Jenny Cartwright."

"Oh, honey!" Brooke voiced exasperation. Turning back to Jason, she rolled her eyes. "Men are so blind! Of course she's still in love with Cade, but he doesn't have a brain in his head where Sharyah is concerned. If he had a thimbleful of wisdom, he would have snapped her up a long time ago!" She emphasized her point with a snap of her fingers.

Sky chuckled. "As you can see, Brooke and my family don't get along very well."

Giving a mock frown, Jason agreed, "Yes, I can see that."

Sky went on. "Rocky is still a deputy in town. He, Dad, and I keep the town running criminal-free." A twinkle leapt into his eyes. "And I guess that's about all that's new."

When Brooke spun, wide-eyed and incredulous, in Sky's direction, Jason surmised that Sky had been teasing her and the largest piece of news would be forthcoming. He swiped his cheek against his shoulder and returned his concentration to the last section of the kitchen floor. *Someday, Lord, if You're willing, I'd like to have someone to love that way.*

After giving Sky a friendly punch, Brooke said to Jason, "Your cousin is deliberately withholding information from you, but maybe we shouldn't ruin her surprise. You'd better go visit Marquis right away, though. She'd be terribly disappointed if you heard the news from anyone else."

"Is she all right?" Jason asked, tension crawling through his chest. "She's fine," Sky assured.

Jason's shoulders relaxed, but a niggling worry still clung to the back of his mind. "Maybe I'll mosey on over that way." He stood and picked up the scrub water. "Can I empty this for you somewhere, Brooke?"

"Oh, to one side out the back door is fine." Brooke waved him through the kitchen.

As he made his way back to the front of the house, Jason grabbed his hat, trying not to let his worry over his sister's news show on his face. He'd always been a little overprotective of her, since a childhood illness had robbed her of her sight. He had been gone for several years when he headed to the Idaho territory to exact revenge on a man that he blamed for their mother's death. But he'd known that, since Marquis was living with his grandmother, she was in good hands. Since his return to the Lord, finding work had forced him away from his family, but he had faithfully sent Marquis money every month. Now he wondered what news Marquis could have that she wouldn't have told him in her last letter.

"I'll head on over to Gram's, then. It's good to see you both... and congratulations."

Brooke embraced him once more. "Thank you for stopping by. On Sunday everyone is getting together at our place for lunch, so come on by and join us."

"I'll do that." Jason settled his Stetson and headed down the street to Gram's house, which sat on the edge of the snow-bound little town.

The Prineville bank was stuffy and hot. The teller had obviously forgotten to turn down the damper on the wood stove. The heat had felt nice to William Harpster for a few minutes after coming in from the single-digit temperature outside. Now, sitting across from the banker, Tom Roland, he frowned.

Behind his desk, Tom mopped his sweaty brow and tossed an occasional irritated glance at the teller.

William paid no attention to the teller. His eyes were fixed solely on the short, paunchy, balding Roland seated across from him. "I told you it would take some time."

"It's been over two years!" The words were forceful but voiced low so as not to reach the ears of the clerk. "The Association is going to be running *us* off if we don't come up on the good side of this deal. We guaranteed them we'd have the small-timers gone by next month. You said you could get the job done!"

William's eyes narrowed. "Do you think I don't know that? You're the one who said he was the perfect man for our plan! It's not my fault he's welching on his end." His voice became a little too loud and drew a look from the curious teller.

But at that moment a patron entered the building, taking the man's interest off their conversation. When it was once again safe to resume, Tom's pale blue eyes flashed. "Keep it down, would you? This is not my fault. First," the banker held up one short finger, "his wife isn't nearly as timid and withdrawn as you said.

She's made friends with over half the country, for goodness' sake! Second, he's no longer willing to go along with our plan. And now..." A third finger joined the first two. "You're telling me you think he might have a herd of horses back in those hills that could pay off his loan?"

William rubbed the back of his neck. "I don't know. Things just don't add up. He's been making his payments?"

"Right on time, every time."

William sighed. There was only one way to ensure their plan would work. "We know what the Association thinks. But how badly do you want your share of that land?"

Tom Roland dabbed at his glistening pate with a handkerchief. Then, leaning back, he lit a cigar and blew a ring of smoke in William's direction. He wanted that land. The original owner had given up on ranching and moved back to Chicago, leaving the land up for sale. Tom had been tempted to buy the land himself, but then John Trent had walked into his bank. The only reason Tom had loaned John the money was that he was almost assured the gambler wouldn't be able to come up with his payments. Then the land would revert to the bank, where Tom could discreetly snap it up at a lower price. That and the fact The Stockman's Association had needed a scapegoat for their dirty work. But then John had developed a conscience. And, on top of that, he hadn't missed one payment.

Tom ran his handkerchief across the back of his neck. Five thousand acres of the finest range land in central Oregon, and half of it was to be his. Well, maybe more than half, but he was careful to keep that thought off his face. Yes. He wanted that land very much. But a couple of things bothered him. "What about his wife?"

William smiled sardonically. "Let me worry about the little woman. Once John is out of the way, she'll give up. There's no way she'll be able to make a go of it. They've only got two hands."

"The Stockman's Association will break loose with all the fury of Hades if this doesn't pan out," Tom warned. "They were plenty upset that I let him buy that land in the first place. And if things don't work out for me, you know they certainly aren't going to work out for you, right?"

"Things couldn't be clearer. Have I ever let you down before?"

Tom blew another ring. "No, William, you haven't. But let's make sure this isn't the first."

William's gaze hardened. "Tom, this better be the last time you need my services. A man's patience can only be stretched so far."

"Just do your job, William. Do your job and let the future take care of itself."

The men glared at each other across the desk. Tom didn't want to be the first to look away. Finally William conceded the battle.

Tom looked down at his desk, pulling in a deep drag on his cigar. "Now, back to the job at hand. I think we both know there is only one way to solve this little problem."

The two men's eyes locked. A silent understanding passed between them.

William stood, straightened his cowhide vest with a tug, and placed his hat carefully on his head. He shook Tom's fleshy hand and said loud enough for the teller to hear, "Thanks. You won't regret making me this loan, Mr. Roland."

With that, he moved toward the door, stepping out into the cold. He took a cleansing breath of the refreshing air, then headed toward the livery, his boots thudding loudly on the boardwalk. He had a job to do back home. And maybe, just maybe, if he played his cards right, by the end of the year he'd be owner of some of the finest range land in Oregon, not to mention the husband of one beautiful, desirable Mrs. Dominique Trent. A smile lifted the corners of his mouth at the thought. Yes, indeed, now that was a dream worth chasing.

CHAPTER TWO

"Sawyer Carlos Trent! *¿¡Que es esto!?*" Nicki threw up her hands in distress at the mess on her kitchen floor. Flour, beans, rice, and sugar were all scattered delightfully across the earthen floor, swirled together and crawled through. Baby handprints on a mound of flour and beans showed where the budding artist had patted his creation together.

Clenching her fists at her side, Nicki went in search of her little virtuoso. It wasn't hard to find him; she just followed the flour-white footprints on the dark, hard-packed, earthen floor. He was crouched behind the chest that held their clothes. As she scooped him up and started back toward the kitchen, Nicki found herself wishing for the umpteenth time that she could put the supplies up somewhere higher, but there just wasn't anyplace else to store them. There was barely room enough to stand up straight in the low-roofed, tiny kitchen, much less add higher cupboards.

Sitting the boy down firmly in the middle of the mess Nicki gestured to the floor around him. "Look at this mess you made for Mama to clean up!" She squatted down in front of him, tucking an escaped strand of hair behind her ear, the other fist resting under her chin.

Sawyer's chin dropped to his chest and his lower lip protruded in a calculated pout.

Nicki tried not to give in to the smile that suddenly tugged at the corners of her mouth as she gazed into his sweet face. "Sawyer, Mama has told you not to get into the food. This is very naughty."

Tears pooled on his lower lids, making his huge dark eyes seem even larger. The pout was still in place. "I sowwee, Mama."

"*Está bien.* That's good. I'm glad you're sorry, but we have talked about this before. You are going to sit in the corner while I clean this up."

His rosy lower lip still pooching out, he stood to his flour-dusted feet. Dark head bent toward the floor, he crossed his arms over his chest and did not move.

"Go on, Son. I will come get you when I'm done."

Feet dragging, he made his way to the corner and sat, casting a how-could-you-do-this-to-me look over his shoulder before he slumped forward, resting chubby cheeks on chubby hands.

When Nicki was sure he wasn't looking, she allowed herself to smile. Poor boy. The winter *was* getting long. If only the weather would warm up, then they could go outside and he would have more room to play.

Looking back to the mess, she tossed her hands toward the ceiling in frustration and moved to get the broom and dust pan.

When the mess was cleaned up, Nicki walked over to get Sawyer, only find that he had fallen asleep on the floor. Stooping, she picked him up and rested his head against her breast. She grinned down at the white print of his bottom on the dark earth floor, then gazed lovingly into his sleep-flushed face. Tenderly she dropped a kiss onto his rosy cheek as tears pooled in her eyes. Blinking, she raised her face to the ceiling.

Thank You, God, for this precious little boy. He has kept me going these past couple of years. You knew just what I needed to make it through this life, didn't You? You have blessed me beyond measure.

Moving to the room's one bed, she laid Sawyer down and smoothed his dark curls. Gently covering him with his favorite patchwork blanket, she moved to add more wood to the stove. Today was exceptionally cold.

She eased herself down at the table, thankful to have a little quiet time. Reaching for her Bible, the one Mama had pressed into her hands that day that seemed like a lifetime ago, she thumbed through the pages. She settled on one of her favorite psalms and leaned back to read. But she only got to verse four.

Pausing, she stared at the page. But she wasn't seeing the words, she was hearing them.

"Yea, though I walk through the valley of the shadow of death, I will fear no evil; For you are with me; Your rod and Your staff, they comfort me."

Nicki could remember like it had happened yesterday—Father Pedro from the mission school she had attended as a child, explaining those words. *"The psalmist, he was a shepherd, no?"* The class had nodded. *"And when his sheep were in danger, what did he use to protect them, besides his sling shot?"*

"His rod and staff," the class echoed in unison.

"Good! You sometimes listen when I teach, eh?" He smiled good-naturedly. *"Yes. The rod and staff, and in the same way, when death comes knocking on our doors,"* he rapped loudly on his wooden desk for emphasis, causing several of the girls to jump and a titter of laughter to pass through the room, *"we know that our Heavenly Father, who loves us much more than a shepherd loves his sheep, will come to our aid, yes?"*

Again the class nodded.

"Good! God loves you. He is not going to abandon you to the wolves, and predators of this world. It says He will be with you! Imagine that: God with you, helping you, protecting you. Ahhh, now that is a God worth serving, yes?"

The thunder of horses' hooves in the yard brought Nicki back to the present. She frowned and stood to see who it might be. John was not supposed to be back from checking the ranch perimeter until later this evening.

Jason whipped off his hat, taking the four creaky stairs up to Gram's porch in two strides. The hinges groaned loudly as, not bothering to knock, he opened the door and entered the house where he had been raised. Excitement built inside him. Gram hadn't changed a thing about the house since he'd left. Her rocker still sat by the front window with her worn Bible and spectacles on the table beside it. The woven rag rug that he and Marquis had spent all one winter creating still graced the floor in front of the fireplace. The settee still sported one of her handknit afghans draped across the arm, and the painting he'd done of a wolf pack when he was about thirteen still hung on the wall above the mantle in all its hideousness. He grinned. He'd tried to talk her into taking that down a number of times, but she had never done it. She said it was her reminder to pray for him. Well, he wouldn't argue with that anymore. He could use all the prayers he could get.

He made his way quietly through the house, anticipating the delighted surprise that would dawn on Gram's face when she saw him.

The living room and dining room were at the front, but at the back there was also a small parlor used just for family. It was there Jason assumed Gram and Marquis to be. If they were anywhere else in the house, they would have heard him enter through the squeaky portal.

Jason stepped into the back hallway.

"Jeff, don't!" Marquis' voice drifted through the door from the parlor.

His heart seized in his chest. *Don't what?* Jason had heard that strained tone before. She meant what she was saying.

"Jeff, stop it!"

Jason paused, wondering who Jeff might be. He eased the strap off his pistol and debated whether he should enter the parlor with gun in hand. "Jeff!"

Marquis' squeal sent shivers of alarm racing through Jason's veins and, without further hesitation, he barged through the door.

A man was leaning over Marquis, seated on the settee, about to kiss her! "What in—Marquis!" Jason lunged across the room, grabbed the man by one shoulder, spun him around, and smashed one fist solidly into his mouth.

The man staggered and fell to the floor.

Marquis screamed and paled. "Jeff? What happened?" Hands outstretched, she felt swiftly for her cane.

Before the man on the floor could even blink, Jason had the barrel of his gun leveled at his head. Never taking his eyes off the man on the floor, Jason said, "Marquis are you all right?"

Marquis, one hand clutching her cane and the other on her chest, asked in a tremulous voice, "Jason?"

"Don't worry, Marquis, I'm here. This man won't be bothering you again, *ever*." The last word he directed at the man on the floor who now gingerly wiped the bloodied corner of his mouth. With a gesture of his free hand Jason directed the man to get up, but the barrel of his gun never wavered.

Suddenly Marquis recovered from her shock. "Jason! Did you just punch Jeff?" Then her voice became truly alarmed. "Jeff! Are you okay?"

"I'm all right, Marquis. Who is this madman? A jilted admirer?" Jeff was now on his feet but kept his hands carefully in sight.

"Well…this is Jason." Then, "Jason, is it really you?"

"Yeah, I came home to see you and Gram."

With more confidence this time Marquis said, "Jeff, I'd like you to meet Jason."

"Well, honey, I know you have a brother named Jason, but this tornado on wheels couldn't be him, could it?"

Marquis smiled. "I'm afraid so, dear."

Jason frowned, perplexed at Marquis' endearment. "Marquis? You know this man?"

At this Marquis giggled. "Jason, I would like you to meet my husband, Jeff Grant."

"Husband!"

Marquis nodded serenely and Jeff, hands now resting on his hips, glared passionately.

Jason glanced down at the gun in his hand and then back to Jeff. A slow smile spread. "Husband, huh?"

Jeff nodded.

Jason holstered the gun and extended his hand. "Sorry."

Marquis, hearing the whisper of metal on leather, gasped. "Jason! Jeff, was he holding a gun on you?"

Jeff wiped the corner of his mouth once more, eyeing Jason's extended hand. "Yes he was, Marquis." Then a hint of a smile showed in his eyes as he spoke to Jason, taking his hand. "I guess you must love her at least half as much as I do."

Jason grinned. "What were you hollering about anyway, Marquis? With you yelling, I just assumed he was forcing his attentions on you."

A blush shaded Marquis' cheeks. And Jeff took a step toward Marquis, resting one hand protectively on her shoulder.

"Jeff was...tickling me."

Jason rubbed a hand across his mouth to hide another smile. Jeff tossed him an unrepentant grin as he gently squeezed Marquis' shoulder.

Irritation flooded in. "Well, you could've at least given me some warning. A guy likes to know when his sister is getting married. Or *is* married."

"Oh Jason, I'm so sorry. We didn't know when you'd be able to make it home. When you didn't respond to our first telegram, we sent Rocky to the Triple J to find you, but they said you had gone to Dodge City and they didn't know exactly when you would be back. So we went ahead with the ceremony. But I sent you a telegram telling you all about it."

"To Dodge City! That was November! How long have you two been married?"

"Two months."

"Two months! Marquis, I left in October. If you've been married two months that means you got married sometime in November and *that* means you couldn't have known this man for more than three or four *weeks* before you got married."

Marquis' unseeing stare was complacent. "Jason you're starting to sound a little paranoid."

Jason opened his mouth to reply, then glanced at Jeff and snapped it shut. This man was his brother-in-law, after all. And he was already glaring at him like a mad bull about to charge.

"For your information, dear brother," there was an icy tension in Marquis' words, "Jeff and I wrote to each other for two years before we ever met."

"You wrote to each other." Jason turned to Jeff. "You know Braille?" Jeff gave a single nod.

Marquis continued, "Jeff is a professor at a school for the blind in Portland. The school had some correspondence courses, one of which I enrolled in, and that is how we met."

Jason didn't feel like talking about this anymore. "Where's Gram?"

"She went down to the mercantile to get some things," Jeff answered.

Jason spun on his heel. "I'll get you some ice for that cut," he tossed over his shoulder as he stomped toward the kitchen.

In the kitchen, Jason leaned his fists into the counter, hunching his shoulders as he stared out the window in thought. What was suddenly making him feel edgy? He trusted Marquis and knew she wouldn't have rushed into marriage hastily. In fact, now that he thought about it, he remembered her mentioning she was corresponding with a man from a school for the blind. He hadn't paid much attention at the time. But now she was married and he...

He what? He hadn't been there? He was the last to know? He wasn't needed by her anymore? Was that it?

Understanding hit him like a 2,000-pound charging bull. *I'm angry, aren't I, Lord?*

Banging through the back door, Jason headed toward the dugout, where he knew a block of ice would be. As he chipped away some of his frustration on the block resting in the dim, dank cellar, he chastised himself for being so temperamental. He should be happy for his sister; instead he felt a petty irritation over the fact that she no longer needed his support.

"Okay, Lord," he said out loud, pausing to glance out the door, "if you sent this man to Marquis, then he must be what she needed. Just help me to accept him. Open my eyes to his good qualities. And help me to know where I should go from here with my life."

Marquis had a husband. So what was he to do now? Truth-telling, there were virtually no jobs to be found in the little town of Shiloh, and he had known it would take some doing to find work. He had planned on having Marquis move back into Gram's room so he could stay in the second bedroom for a while as he searched for a job. But somehow he didn't think that Marquis and her young husband would enjoy sharing a room with Gram.

The thought brought a brief smirk, before he grew serious again.

Marquis would no longer need his financial support...but Gram would. He'd start looking for work tomorrow. The Lord would iron out the housing situation. For now he could sleep on the floor.

CHAPTER THREE

Nicki rose from the table and hurried to the low door of the soddy. She had to stoop to get out the door, and the sun glaring off the snow momentarily blinded her as she exited the dim interior of the house.

Shading her eyes, she squinted to see who rode into the yard at such breakneck speed. Looking past the neglected pole corral, she saw the dark shapes of three horses thundering toward the house. Two men were upright, but the third draped over the saddle, and as the men pulled up in a skidding halt she could see he was severely wounded.

Blood dripped from a nasty, concave gash along his hairline, and one of his arms hung at an odd angle.

Suddenly her neighbor, William, was beside her. "Nicki, don't look. Come with me."

Nicki pulled her elbow from his grasp and did not move. She stared dumbfounded at the wounded man the other rider was easing from the saddle. One hand went to her mouth and she moved forward. "John!"

The man carried John toward the soddy, but Nicki quickly took charge, lifting her skirts and heading for the bunkhouse. "No! Not in there, the baby is sleeping, and he does not need to see his Papa like this." She gestured to one of the spread's two ranch hands. "Ron, go into the house and get me a clean blanket. You," she motioned to the man carrying John, "bring him over here to the bunkhouse. Conner, run clear a place to lay him."

Before they had moved the few yards to the bunkhouse, Ron was back with a blanket and hurried in ahead of them to lay it across the first bunk that Conner, the second ranch hand, had cleared off.

Nicki spoke again as she entered the dim interior of the

freezing cold bunkhouse, "Ron, go back to the house and bring me all the hot water on the stove, then put some more on in my largest kettle. Conner, go get some wood and get a fire going in here. Then ride for the doctor."

The men moved to do her bidding, and all the while the man who had first spoken to her stayed by her side. "Tell me what happened, William." Nicki finally acknowledged her neighbor's presence as she set to work cutting John's shirt away from his broken arm.

He ran a tired hand over his stubble-roughened face and glanced around the interior of the bunkhouse before he replied. "We were out checking the stock, like we always do after a particularly hard storm. John stopped in town early this morning. I happened to be there and needed to check my stock too, so we decided to ride out together. We had just come around a corner along the Deschutes River canyon...you know, that part along the edge of your place that is so steep." William stopped, rested his hands on his hips, and shook his head. "It all happened so fast. One minute everything was fine, and the next minute his horse shied away from something and John lost his balance and went over the edge of the cliff. If I hadn't had my hand Slim there to help me, he probably would have bled to death right there in the canyon bottom."

Nicki frowned. They had been riding so close to the edge that he fell off? Ron entered with the requested hot water, and Nicki used the opportunity to cast a look at Slim, who sat hunched on one of the bunks watching the proceedings with casual interest. He was a tall man, perhaps the tallest she had ever seen, which explained why he was hunched over the way he was. He was skinny too. Skinny as a corral pole. His boots were run down at the heel, and a drooping mustache completely covered his mouth. Slim nodded, indicating his assent to William's story, solemn eyes meeting hers for only a moment.

"Go on, William," Nicki said quietly as she dipped a rag Ron had thoughtfully brought into the water and washed the deep gash on John's brow. She could see the white of bone where the flesh was missing. He groaned, but he did not come to.

"Well, there's not much else to say. We got a rope around him and pulled him back up to his horse and then rode here as fast as we could."

Nicki frowned. John was a good rider. It wasn't like him to lose his balance in the saddle.

But if Nicki had learned anything in her young life, it was that the west was a brutal place. Accidents happened often here. The year she turned fifteen her brother Juan had lost his hand when he cut it on a rusty hay fork. And just last week at church the Snows had reported that their neighbor's wife had been killed when the cow she was milking kicked her in the head. The family planned to move back east, and their land would revert to the bank. Things happened that could not be foreseen or prevented.

Nicki pushed away her niggling questions about the accident. William had been their friend and neighbor since just after they moved into the valley. She knew he would have done everything in his power to help John.

Conner brought in the wood, but Ron took over building up the fire and soon Nicki heard Conner's horse galloping out of the yard. Looking at the bone protruding from John's arm and the nasty bowl-shaped laceration on his forehead, Nicki prayed the doctor would come in time to save her husband's life.

She gently smoothed his sweat-soaked hair away from his brow and considered their relationship. Although they had been married under unusual circumstances to say the least, she had come to depend on this man. He did not love her, only lusted after her, but he had treated her better than most, she knew. No, she didn't love him, but he was the father of her son, and he had been good to her.

She shivered and felt William's warm leather jacket settle around her shoulders. She glanced up.

He smiled reassuringly and rested his hand gently on her shoulder. "I'll send for Tilly to watch the boy for you," he said before heading out the door into the late afternoon gloom.

She tended John through the night as best she could, praying that Conner would be able to find Dr. Rike in time.

But it was not to be. Nicki had just pulled the sheet up over John's face when Conner and Doctor Rike hurried through the bunkhouse door.

Conner grimaced and snatched his hat off his head in a gesture of frustration.

Without a word Nicki brushed past the two men and headed for the house. She could think of only one comfort she needed at this moment. And it wasn't until she took a sleepy Sawyer from the arms of Tilly Snow, the young girl from church who had come to sit with him, that the tears came.

As Sawyer laid his little head on her shoulder she rested her cheek against the soft hair at the back of his neck and let the tears fall. How was she going to raise this precious child alone? His papa had been the world to him, for although John had not loved her, he had doted on his son. And Sawyer was going to be lost without his papa. She rubbed his little back, listening to his deep, even breathing. So innocent and unaware of the gaping, black valley that had just opened up before them.

She allowed herself to close her eyes for a minute, then reality rushed in. Her eyes snapped open. "Tilly, I hate to ask, but do you think your mother could spare you for a couple of days?"

Tilly's tender, brown eyes glistened, and she blinked rapidly. "I'm sure that would be fine, Mrs. Trent."

"I'll send Conner over to tell her. I really appreciate it."

Setting Sawyer into his high chair, Nicki busied herself getting his breakfast. If she worked, she wouldn't have time to dwell on her loss.

"I can do that, Mrs. Trent. Why don't you sit down and rest? You've been up all night."

"Thank you, Tilly. If you will get Sawyer some breakfast, I'll head out and send Conner to your parents' place. And then I need to talk to Ron Hanson about a couple of things. Would you be all right in here with Sawyer for a while?"

Tilly nodded, and as Nicki moved out of the house, she prayed for strength.

Nicki found Ron and Conner standing together next to the jumbled heap of the run-down corral, arms folded against the cold.

Walking up quietly, Nicki tucked a curl behind her ear and fleetingly realized she had not combed her hair yet today. She was still wearing William's leather coat, the sleeves rolled up, and her back ached as though someone had taken a sledgehammer to it.

The two men turned toward her. She stared off into the distance, trying to gather her thoughts and come to grips with the fact her husband was dead.

She suddenly had so many questions and uncertainties. Yesterday when she awoke it had simply been her goal to make it through another day of entertaining a fussy toddler with cabin fever. Now…

What was she going to do?

Should she pack up and head south to California and try to find her parents? What if they had moved after she had left with John? Would she be able to find them?

She could stay here. She glanced around at the run-down ranch. John had been a good rider, and he had known cattle and horses, but it seemed he had known nothing about managing a ranch. Nicki had spoken to him several times about fixing up the buildings and the corral, but he had always said he would get to it in time. He didn't want to spend money that they didn't have.

They had lived here for two and a half years, and John had not made one improvement to the ranch buildings or central holding pens except to finish roofing the bunkhouse.

The bunkhouse was made of logs that had wide gaps between them, but John had refused to chink them when she had suggested it, saying it was an unnecessary expense.

Frosty winds gushed through the gaps, making the bunkhouse bitterly cold on most winter nights. Consequently there was only one hand who had been with them the whole two and a half years they had lived here, and that was Ron Hanson.

Ron was in his late fifties with a deeply tanned leathery face and crinkle lines around his usually smiling gray eyes. His once dark hair was now liberally sprinkled with gray, but it was invariably covered by his gray flat-topped Stetson. He'd had offers from other ranchers in the area but, for some reason, he'd chosen to stay and work for the Hanging T—John's brand. Nicki knew, however, that Ron had not stayed because the accommodations and food were so good. It was his relationship with Christ and a sense of loyalty that had kept him here when there were jobs that offered much more in the way of material comforts nearby.

Nicki's gaze moved on to the little sod shanty that served as the ranch house. Dug back into the side of a hill, all that could be seen of it from this vantage point was the chimney pipe sticking up through the snow-covered dirt, the wooden door, and the one small window that John had consented to on Nicki's behalf. It wasn't much, but it was warm, and for that, Nicki was thankful.

It was the only home Sawyer had ever known. With that thought, her stomach tightened. Could she take her son away from the only home he had ever known in search of her parents, when she had no idea where they were? What if she gave up this place and went to California, only to fail in finding her parents? What would become of them then?

She glanced around the run-down place once more and realized that her mind had been made up even before she had begun this debate with herself. She would stay. It would be so good to see Mama once more, but she couldn't risk it.

Ron interrupted her thoughts. "Ma'am, are you all right?"

Nicki came to with a start. "Oh. Yes." She cleared her throat and glanced at Conner. Her voice was low and raspy when she spoke. "Conner," she cleared her raw throat again, "I need you to ride over to the Snow place and let them know what has happened and ask them if it's okay if Tilly stays here for a couple of days. Um, tell them two, for sure, and maybe three days if we can't get the minister for the…for the…before then."

"Yes, ma'am." Conner touched the brim of his hat as he moved off to saddle up, but Nicki caught the gentle compassion in his green eyes before he turned away. A lump tightened her throat. Whatever happened, she could depend on Conner and Ron.

Conner was young and had only been with them since the summer before, but he attended Sunday services in Farewell Bend with her and Ron every Sunday. She didn't doubt that he truly loved the Lord.

This thought brought another wave of sadness, for try as she might, she had been unable to convince John to join them on Sundays. He had always had something that was more important: a sick cow, a lame horse, a trip around the ranch perimeter to make sure all the fences were intact because he couldn't afford to lose stock to a neighboring spread. There had always been something that needed tending. Something more important than church. Something more important than God.

Blinking back tears, Nicki turned her face away from Ron's fatherly inspection and folded her arms against the bitter wind that had begun to blow. "Ron, I am planning on staying. Now is not the time to discuss things, but I would appreciate it if you would stay long enough to fill me in on some of the things that I don't know about this place. Other than that, you are free to leave anytime you choose. I'm sorry I don't have the money to pay you right now, but if you stop back by someday, I will be more than happy to make it up to you."

"If it's all the same to you, ma'am, I'd like to stay. You will need a good hand and someone who knows a little o' the workin's o' the place."

"I don't know when I will be able to pay you."

"All a man needs is a place to sleep and some food in his belly."

Nicki turned tear-filled eyes on him. "You are an angel in disguise, Ron Hanson." Throwing her arms around the surprised cowhand's neck, she gave him a gentle squeeze. She felt him stiffen before he awkwardly patted her back with one hand while the other hand remained stiffly at his side.

What would I have done if he had chosen to leave? Gracias, Lord.

Holding Sawyer in her arms, Nicki stared bleakly down into the dark hole that waited to receive the body of her husband.

The voice of the minister droned in the background, but somehow she could not bring herself to focus on his words. She felt numb.

All around her friends and neighbors stood in somber silence. Some listened intently to the minister. Others watched her with strange sympathetic expressions. Women held onto the hands of their husbands more tightly. Little boys glanced at Sawyer and then up at their own fathers, stepping closer to wrap small arms around strong, steady legs.

William Harpster stood to her left and Ron Hanson to her right.

Nicki closed her eyes, leaning her forehead against the toddler's. What was she going to do without John? He had been her sole means of support. Could she really run this ranch by herself? *Lord, I don't think I can do this.*

Swiftly the verses she had read only moments before John had been brought in wounded jumped to mind. *"Yea, though I walk through the valley of the shadow of death, I will fear no evil; For You are with me; Your rod and Your staff, they comfort me."*

Lord, I'm in that valley. Help me to know that You are here with me.

Comfort me. What am I going to do without him, Lord? I never realized that I cared for him so much, but I miss him. Help me, Lord, because I will never be able to make it through this without You. And please be with Sawyer. Don't let this be too traumatic for him. He has already been asking for his papa. Help me to know how to explain to him that his papa's not going to be here anymore.

Opening her eyes, Nicki suddenly felt lightheaded. She shook her head against the dizzy spell, taking a small step backward. She adjusted Sawyer to a more comfortable position in her arms. When was the last time she had eaten? She gave her head another little shake. She couldn't remember.

Out of the corner of her eye she noted Ron studying her worriedly, and William reached out to take Sawyer from her. She smiled at Ron to reassure him, then folded her arms against the chill that seeped into her bones, thankful to be free of the baby and rest her arms.

Exhaustion weighed heavy on her shoulders, even as hunger pangs cramped her stomach. A strange, almost guilty sensation crept over her that she should be feeling anything at all when John lay so cold and still in a coffin only feet away.

Another dizzy spell hit her and she reached out, taking Ron's arm to steady herself. She needed to eat. But when the ceremony ended and Ron ushered her into the small church and set a plate before her, all she could do was pick at it.

The neighbors had rallied together in support of Nicki and an abundance of food graced a long table at the back of the church. Families caught up on news from neighbors they hadn't seen since the last community event, which had been a barn-raising for Jacob and Jenny Ashland. Nicki glanced over to see Jenny proudly showing off Jake Junior's latest accomplishment… walking. He'd been a newborn at the raising. The baby was giggling and smiling at everyone who made eye contact and even coaxed a tired smile out of Nicki herself when Jenny came to express her condolences.

"I'm so sorry, Nicki. If I can ever do anything for you, all you have to do is ask. You know I'm not too far away. I'd be happy to watch Sawyer for you if you ever need someone to."

Nicki nodded. "Thank you, Jenny."

Jenny set a package of home-baked goodies on the table and, with a gentle squeeze to Nicki's shoulder, made her way to Jacob's side.

And that was how it went. Everyone came over to express their condolences and to wish her well, and everyone left something on the table beside her.

The Coles owned a large ranch on the other side of Farewell Bend. Mrs. Cole, who had lost her first husband in much this same way, had tears in her eyes as she gave Nicki a hug and set a basket of food on the table.

Mrs. Pringle had a few choice words to say about Dr. Rike, but the Pringle baby had died the winter before when Dr. Rike hadn't been able to do anything for him, so Nicki let the comments slide and simply thanked Mrs. Pringle for the food.

The next woman to come over was the newest member of the community. Mr. and Mrs. Jeffries had just moved to a small homestead only a couple of miles from the Hanging T. Nicki knew they didn't have much, but Brenda Jeffries, with her six-year-old daughter, May, at her side, set a small bundle wrapped in brown paper on the table.

"I'm right sorry to hear 'bout yer man. I be hopin' that all goes well fer ya. God, He be knowin' all about yer pain. Ya just take it all to Him, now." She reached out and laid a work-roughened hand across the back of Nicki's, giving it a little pat. "If it be all right, I'd like to come in a couple o' days and see if there be anything I can do for ya. That be okay?"

Nicki smiled tiredly. "That would be just fine, Brenda."

"Good. I'll be seein' ya then."

Mrs. Jeffries started to move off, but May tugged on her sleeve. Nicki dropped her eyes to the little girl's pixie-sweet face. Straight blond hair framed a heart-shaped face with a pair of the biggest blue eyes Nicki had ever seen.

May stepped close and whispered, "I'm sorry your daddy died." Nicki blinked back tears and bit her lip, unable to say a word.

"I have a daddy." The little girl brushed a strand of hair behind her ear and held out a finger, pointing out her father across the room.

Nicki glanced at him and then nodded, pressing her lips together to suppress the sob that threatened to escape.

"He's real nice. Ya could borrow 'im sometime if ya need 'im."

The sob escaped and Nicki pulled May into her arms, resting her chin on the little girl's head. May wrapped her slender arms around Nicki's back, and gently patted out a comforting rhythm.

When Nicki trusted herself to speak, she pulled back, wiped the tears from her cheeks, and gazed down at May. "Thank you. That's the nicest thing anyone has done for me in a long time."

"I'm sorry I made ya cry. I didn't mean to do that."

Nicki ran a trembling hand over the child's silky blond hair. "Some days are days of crying, little one. But know that you have made me very happy on the inside. If I need your papa, you can be sure I will come calling, okay?"

May nodded, giving Nicki one more quick hug before she turned and took her mother's hand. Brenda Jeffries smiled kindly, blinking to keep her own tears at bay, and then mother and daughter made their way across the room to stand by Rolf, Brenda's husband.

Nicki was just recovering her composure when Suzanne Snow, Tilly's mother, approached and set a large basket full of canned goods on the table. Suzanne pulled Nicki into a long embrace.

Nicki squeezed her eyes shut against the tears that threatened to overflow once again as memories rushed in.

John had never told Nicki where he got the money, but after he had purchased her, he made a number of extravagant purchases—several fine horses and the ranch being a couple of them—and then the money seemed to run out.

Missing her family, Mama especially, Nicki had been very lonely those first months until she had met the Snows. Ron had brought her to church with him and Suzanne reminded her so much of her own mother that Nicki had immediately been drawn to her. Suzanne had taken Nicki under her wing just as if she had been her own daughter. And now, more than ever, Nicki was thankful for her friendship.

Neither Suzanne's nor Mrs. Jeffries' gifts had appeared out of the ordinary at first but later, when Nicki got home, she found that Mrs. Jeffries' paper-wrapped package was a beautiful lace tablecloth crocheted in the most intricate of designs. *Much too fancy for the soddy.* And in the bottom of Suzanne Snow's basket of canned carrots, tomatoes, and green beans was an unpretentious looking book. The title brought fresh tears to Nicki's eyes. *Ranching in the West: How to Make It Pay.*

Suzanne had known she would stay.

Clutching the little book tightly to her chest, Nicki heaved a shuddered sigh. She had been strong all day, refusing herself the comfort of many tears. Making sure her neighbors knew she was going to be fine. Trying to convince herself she was going to be fine. But now she was alone. Just her and Sawyer.

Tilly had ridden home with Conner after promising to come back in a day or two. William had left for his ranch, promising to check on her often. Ron had gone to the bunkhouse for the evening.

Nicki could finally let down her guard. She glanced around the room at John's few things, still as he'd left them: his rifle on its pegs above the door, his extra pair of boots, a shirt hanging above the bed, the partially carved toy truck sitting on the mantle that he'd started for Sawyer a couple weeks ago.

How was it that she could miss a man who had walked into her life out of the brazen heat of a California summer and forced her to marry him?

"Papa." Sawyer banged two blocks together and looked at her as he shoved the corner of one into his mouth.

Tears coursed down Nicki's cheeks. She sank down onto the rag rug next to the bed and pulled Sawyer onto her lap. Leaning her head against the quilt, she finally gave in to the deep sorrow. Sobs shook her body as Sawyer happily banged his blocks together.

If you would like to keep reading you can purchase *High Desert Haven* here: www.lynnettebonner.com/books/historical-fiction/the-shepherds-heart-series/.

Now Available…

THE SHEPHERD'S HEART BOOK 3

FAIR VALLEY Refuge

She's loved him for as long as she can remember.
But can she trust her heart to a man haunted by constant danger?

Shilohh, Oregon, April 1887

Victoria Snyder, adopted when she was only days old, pastes on a smile for her mama's wedding day, but inside she's all atremble. Lawman Rocky Jordan is back home. And this time he's got a bullet hole in his shoulder and enough audacity to come calling. Since tragedy seems to strike those she cares for with uncanny frequency, she wants nothing to do with a man who could be killed in the line of duty like her father.

But when an orphan-train arrives at the Salem depot, Victoria is irresistibly drawn toward the three remaining "unlovable" children…and stunned by a proposal that will change all of their lives forever.

Can she risk her heart, and her future happiness, on someone she might lose at a moment's notice?

Two stubborn hearts. A most unusual proposal. Persevering love.
Step into a day when outlaws ran free, the land was wild, and guns blazed at the drop of a hat.

THE SHEPHERD'S HEART - BOOK 4

SPRING ★ MEADOW Sanctuary

He broke her heart.
Now he's back to ask for a second chance.

Heart pounding in shock, Sharyah Jordan gapes at the outlaw staring down the barrel of his gun at her. Cascade Bennett shattered her dreams only last summer, and now he plans to kidnap her and haul her into the wilderness with a bunch of outlaws...for her own protection? She'd rather be locked in her classroom for a whole week with Brandon McBride and his arsenal of tricks, and that was saying something.

Cade Bennett's heart nearly drops to his toes when he sees Sharyah standing by the desk. Sharyah Jordan was not supposed to be here. Blast if he didn't hate complications, and Sharyah with her alluring brown eyes and silky blond hair was a walking, talking personification of complication.

Now was probably not the time to tell her he'd made a huge mistake last summer....

Two broken hearts. Dangerous Outlaws. One last chance at love.
Step into a day when outlaws ran free, the land was wild, and guns blazed at the drop of a hat.

Want a FREE Story?

If you enjoyed this book...

…sign up for Lynnette's Gazette below! Subscribers get exclusive deals, sneak peeks, and lots of other fun content.

(The gazette is only sent out about once a month or when there's a new release to announce, so you won't be getting a lot of spam messages, and your email is never shared with anyone else.)

Sign up link: https://www.lynnettebonner.com/newsletter/

ABOUT THE AUTHOR

 Born and raised in Malawi, Africa. Lynnette Bonner spent the first years of her life reveling in warm equatorial sunshine and the late evening duets of cicadas and hyenas. The year she turned eight she was off to Rift Valley Academy, a boarding school in Kenya where she spent many joy-filled years, and graduated in 1990.

That fall, she traded to a new duet—one of traffic and rain—when she moved to Kirkland, Washington to attend Northwest University. It was there that she met her husband and a few years later they moved to the small town of Pierce, Idaho.

During the time they lived in Idaho, while studying the history of their little town, Lynnette was inspired to begin the Shepherd's Heart Series with Rocky Mountain Oasis.

Marty and Lynnette have four children, and currently live in Washington where Marty pastors a church.

34092306R00200